KU-737-888

Sarah Jackman was born in Berlin and has lived variously in the UK, France and Germany. She has been awarded a writer's bursary from the Academi. She lives in south Wales.

SUMMER CIRCLES

With her unusual appearance and shy nature, Hannah Ruland leads a content, sheltered life. She lives in the heart of the Fen countryside under the protective eye of Ella, her mother, and elder brother. But Ella faces her own demons and is becoming increasingly secretive; disappearing for hours and neglecting her beloved garden. So Hannah turns to a young stranger, Toby, for company. Together, they befriend the crop circle followers encamped by a local wheatfield where mysterious patterns have appeared. Then Hannah's middle brother returns home unexpectedly, and soon Kirsten, his old girlfriend, arrives on the scene. Desperate to be accepted by the close-knit family, Kirsten stirs up conflicting emotions and resentments. In the long, hot summer days, secrets thrive — and a confrontation seems inevitable . . .

SARAH JACKMAN

SUMMER CIRCLES

Complete and Unabridged

CHARNWOOD
Leicester

First published in Great Britain in 2010 by
Pocket Books UK
an imprint of
Simon & Schuster UK Ltd.
London

First Charnwood Edition
published 2011
by arrangement with
Simon & Schuster UK Ltd.
London

British Library CIP Data

Jackman, Sarah.
    Summer circles.
    1. Albinos and albinism- -Fiction.
    2. Social isolation- -England- -Norfolk- -Fiction.
    3. Family secrets- -Fiction.
    4. Crop circles- -Fiction.
    5. Large type books.
    I. Title
    823.9'2–dc22

    ISBN 978–1–4448–0779–0

Published by
F. A. Thorpe (Publishing)
Anstey, Leicestershire
Set by Words & Graphics Ltd.
Anstey, Leicestershire
Printed and bound in Great Britain by
T. J. International Ltd., Padstow, Cornwall

This book is printed on acid-free paper

Acknowledgments

My thanks as always to the team at Simon & Schuster UK, for all their work and enthusiasm, particularly to Libby Vernon and Kate Lyall Grant. Also thanks to Teresa Chris, a valued reader, agent and above all, support.

I would like to dedicate this book to all friends and family for their valued encouragement and support. A special mention to Tim Moreton, Lee Falconer, my parents, Claire, Julian and Dean.

Hannah

1

Hannah's father always said that you can tell everything you need to know about a place if you experience it at dawn and at dusk. She thought of the red three-wheel van bumping its way around Marrakech, the glass bottles of pop chiming in the crates as it delivered them from shop to shop. She thought of the hunched, elderly Italian woman, dressed top-to-toe in black, making slow, purposeful progress across the square in Urbino as the church bells called the residents in for evensong. But it was Spindle House that remained her favourite place. It was something to do with the light here, especially in the early hours. It was soft on her eyes but yet seemed to penetrate the deepest part inside her.

She had confessed her preference to her father once and almost immediately regretted having spoken, believing that he would think badly of her. After all, her experience was limited to two towns in two countries for comparison while he had travelled to amazing places all over the world, but Edward smiled and said, 'It's a magical place to live, Hannah, we're very lucky.'

Wearing only a pair of knickers, Hannah sat on the edge of the chest of drawers with her feet up on the window sill by the open window. The night had been warm and stuffy and it was only dawn which had brought a slight dip in temperature and a mild breeze, blown across the

3

Fens to tickle her skin.

It had been nearly five years since Edward had died but Hannah could still imagine him coming home. Her father had dedicated his life to amphibians and his work took him on long trips when he'd be out of contact for days, only to reappear just as Hannah had stopped expecting him.

She had always known the moment she woke up or returned from school that he was back. His presence affected everything at Spindle House: the air would smell of his aftershave; the rooms would be dotted here and there with his clothes, equipment, books; a bottle of wine would appear on the table with every evening meal and her mother's laughter came more readily.

The garden directly below Hannah's bedroom was in shadow from the tall trees at the rear; a thread of mist obscured the bottom hedge where the cooler air in the dyke had drifted up to meet the warm morning sun. Further off, she could sense how the sun was lighting up the fields behind and the sky was opening out into blue. The birds were in full voice, sounding happy, and their happiness made shivers run right through her.

The floorboards creaked as Hannah's mother got up and began to move around her bedroom. Ella was awake earlier than usual, perhaps she hadn't been able to sleep well either. The hinges on Ella's bedroom door creaked and the wooden stairs groaned under every footstep. It wasn't until she'd reached the stone floor of the hallway, which deadened sound like sand, that the house resumed its quiet.

Any moment now, Scoot would appear in the garden. Hannah's vision wobbled momentarily like a TV with bad reception, but Hannah knew the exact angle to tilt her head to get the best picture and her focus settled just as Scoot shot out across the lawn. His tail was joyfully upright; the large, black spot — like a giant's dirty fingerprint — on the top of his head was clearly visible. He came to a standstill, turned to look behind him before running in the direction of the frog pond where he disappeared.

A few minutes later, Ella came into view, hands wrapped around a mug of coffee. This week, in deference to the heat, she had foregone her daily gardening outfit of baggy cords and an old plaid shirt and had taken to wearing a pair of khaki-coloured shorts with a yellow *broderie anglaise* sleeveless blouse and a pair of Edward's old leather sandals, several sizes too big. She was already tanned and, with her dark hair pulled back in a ponytail, she looked as fresh and pretty as Hannah had ever seen her. Whereas all three of her brothers took after Edward's side of the family, Hannah was the one who looked like her mother. They both had long, slender limbs; they had the same Cupid's bow mouth, the same thin, straight nose and high cheekbones. If only, Hannah let herself wish for one moment, other people would see past her albinism and notice it too. Hannah held up a length of her hair, then let it drift back, where it settled against her breast, white against white. My beautiful moon child,

5

Ella sometimes called her, which really wasn't too bad a compliment from the prettiest woman Hannah knew.

Ella bent down to pick up something from the patio. She inspected it and then looked up at Tyler's window; it must be a cigarette end that he'd accidentally dropped from there when he was having a late-night smoke. Her brother would be in trouble: Ella was fanatical about the poison which cigarettes leached into the soil.

Ella put her mug down on the garden table and gave a low whistle before walking across the lawn towards the hothouse. Scoot's white face emerged out of the dark, leathery leaves of the laurel bush and he tore after Ella, his ears pinned low for minimum wind resistance, his legs working furiously. Hannah jumped down from her post before he had caught up with Ella. It was time for her shower.

★ ★ ★

When Ella kissed Hannah good morning, the damp scent of the hothouse was still clinging to her as if her plants couldn't bear to let her go.

'Have you had breakfast?'

Hannah shook her head. 'I'm too warm to eat.' Hannah had spent too long in the shower and on drying her hair; dressed in her long trousers and tunic overall, she felt as if she was sealed inside a bag of hot air.

'I hardly slept a wink,' Ella said. 'Those bloody owls calling all night long didn't help.' She handed Hannah her lunch box out of the fridge.

6

'Take a banana and an apple. You can eat them on the way.'

They carried Hannah's box of cleaning materials between them and put them in the boot of the car. Scoot came haring round the corner of the house and Hannah had her usual face-off with him over who got to sit in the front passenger seat.

'In the back,' Ella ordered, which Scoot reluctantly obeyed. Hannah could sense his intense sulking behind her but it wasn't long before he crept forward and risked a lick of Ella's ear.

'Oh Scoot, for goodness sake,' she said, but he didn't take her cross words as a reprimand, more as an expression of love. With happiness and excitement to spare, he gave Hannah's hair a friendly shuffle.

'I must talk to George and Ray about the state of this track,' Ella said as they bumped along towards Lavender Cottage. 'I'm sure it's a lot worse since we had this good weather.'

Hannah was relieved to see no sign of either George or Ray as they passed the cottage. She wouldn't put it past Ella to stop and get caught up in a discussion with their neighbours on the break-up of tarmac due to the unseasonably hot weather and the best method for filling in potholes. Hannah liked to arrive for work on the dot of nine, but as she was reliant on Ella to get her there, she was at the mercy of her mother's more cavalier attitude to time-keeping and they often arrived five minutes late.

As soon as they had turned right onto the

road, Ella put her foot down. Hannah tilted her head to give her eyes a chance to accommodate to the speeding scenery. To her left was a field of oilseed rape like a splash of Gauguin yellow against the soft browns and greens of reed beds and open marshes.

At the next junction they turned left and headed straight into the sun. Hannah dropped her sunglasses down from on top of her head; they were a pair of Ella's from the Sixties — a Jackie O style — and so big and dark that they were normally sufficient to ease her discomfort. Today the glare was already so strong that even with the car visor down, she had to twist sideways in her seat to shield her eyes.

Ella glanced at her. 'OK, love?'

Hannah nodded.

'Oh, shit,' Ella muttered. 'Bloody typical.'

A few metres ahead, a tractor had swung out of a field in front of them. Dry mud spat out from its wheels in every direction as it lumbered along, a couple of lumps hit the windscreen like pellets. The machine's bulk was wider than their half of the road so Ella wound her window down and leaned out to see past it. Hannah clutched one hand on the edge of her seat as the car crossed the white line and veered back again; with the other hand, she grabbed the apple to stop it rolling off her lap. Scoot let out a couple of sharp yips. Hannah closed her eyes and hoped Ella didn't try one of her overtaking manoeuvres. Ella's impatience had led to some very near misses and Hannah was increasingly fearful of her mother's growing sense of invincibility. One of these days, Hannah was convinced they were going to end up in a ditch.

'Sorry, darling,' Ella said, 'but it looks as if you might be late.'

Luckily the tractor pulled into a lay-by to let them pass. Ella stuck her hand out of the window and waved her thanks at the driver.

'About bloody time, too,' she said under her breath as the car surged forward.

A strange phenomenon of the Fens was that because it was flat and people could see for miles around, you would expect it to be a difficult place to hide, yet dotted all around the countryside were secret, isolated houses and villages, like Spindle House and Snettersley, their own village. Lying low amongst extensive fields and marshes, obscured by the skeletal poplar trees and patches of birch carr, were people living in peaceful, uninterrupted isolation. This, Hannah thought, as they approached the top of the road leading to her client's house, was the reason why it was popular with celebrities.

As the security gates came into view, Hannah took the key-card out of Ella's purse in the glove compartment and passed it to her to wave under the sensor.

Ella revved the engine like a racing car driver while the gates slowly swung open with an electric hum, but she entered the grounds at a relaxed speed under the watchful eye of the CCTV camera. This was Hannah's least favourite of the houses that she cleaned. It was owned by a producer of TV game shows which Hannah thought ironic as there was nothing fun or light-hearted about his home. The black wood of the converted barn brooded in the sparsely planted garden; the tall, red-brick wall was starkly out of place in the subtle landscape and the razor wire top seemed excessively defensive.

Scoot had inched so close behind Hannah that she could feel his hot breath on the back of her neck. He was emitting a constant low-level whine which trembled as his body quivered with impatience to leap into her vacant seat.

She unlocked her seatbelt. 'All right, Scoot, I know when I'm not wanted.'

'See you at half three,' Ella called out as Hannah was shutting the boot.

Hannah waited until she heard the gates click closed behind Ella's car before walking around the side of the house. She put the box down to leave both hands free to unlock the back door and punch in the security code quickly before the alarm went off. This house, like the other two houses, was extra hot on security and there were only fifteen seconds to deactivate the alarm before the security company came piling in.

When Hannah had been on her training course for the job, one of the other Silver Maids had told her that you could get sacked for getting the alarm wrong, so she always felt a bit panicky at this point.

The alarm sorted, her job still safe, Hannah walked up the short flight of stairs into the spacious, ultra-shiny kitchen.

The interior of the house was nicer than the outside. It was decorated in soft creams and light browns and had an attractive, round, silver-coloured wood burner in a big stone fireplace right in the centre of the huge living room. The white sofas were as big as beds and they were so soft it felt like you were lying on pillows, floating on water. Hannah hadn't been able to resist trying them a couple of times but she'd made sure her uniform was clean and had removed her shoes. The whole house was bereft of personal items which Hannah found sad. There was a large stone pot in one corner of the living room and a framed set of blue handprints in the bedroom but there was something so staged about these items that Hannah wasn't convinced the owners had anything to do with their selection. It was clear that they rarely stayed here; even the toothbrushes in the bathroom were still in a drawer in their packaging.

Hannah finished her initial security check and phoned in to the Cambridge office to let them know everything was in order.

She hadn't imagined she'd last as long as eight months in this job. She'd only applied because once she'd finished her A-levels she knew she wasn't in a rush to leave Spindle House. The ad in the local paper for Silver Maids cleaning agency had been intriguing. The company was based in Cambridge but needed someone to work three days a week for clients in the Ely area. It was the wording at the end which had really caught Hannah's attention: 'Experience not necessary. Discretion a must. All candidates will be subject to full criminal and personal disclosures.' It sounded totally mysterious — in an Agatha Christie way — so she had rung up. After being asked a few personal details — her name, age, address and contact number — they wanted to know what she thought of 'celebrity gossip magazines' and Hannah had to admit that she'd never read any. After that, Hannah didn't expect to hear anything more about her enquiry but a couple of days later a woman with an extremely posh voice phoned and asked her to attend an interview at the Cambridge office.

It was a rainy, cold October day when Ella drove her to Cambridge. They were about to give up trying to find the address Hannah had been given when Ella spotted a narrow, smoked-glass door set between two shop doors. When Hannah ran up to it, she saw a tiny gold plaque bearing the name 'Silver Maids' on the left-hand side above an entry phone. She announced her name and was buzzed inside where she followed a larger sign up to Reception.

Hannah removed her sunglasses. The reception area was expensively decorated and immaculate with sleek grey furniture and cream walls. She was being observed by a woman behind a tall desk; she had the straightest, blackest hair Hannah had ever seen, which fell like glossy leather either side of her face.

'Did you bring your CV?' As the woman reached up to take the envelope Hannah held out, her gaze travelled over Hannah's face and her eyes widened. 'Take a seat,' she said after a moment's pause.

The reception desk was made of a clear material and from her chair Hannah had a view of the woman's perfect legs from almost the top of her thighs right down to her feet which ended in a pair of shoes with incredibly high heels. Hannah looked at her low brown shoes in despair; she fingered the rough, pink, tweedy skirt she'd found in the charity shop and listened to the rustle of her stiff white shirt against the lining of her wool jacket as she shifted her shoulders. Instead of pulling off the earnest look she'd been aiming for, she felt frumpy and unnatural. If she hadn't thought it rude, she might have walked out but she made herself keep as still as stone until the receptionist called her name.

'You can go in now,' she said, jabbing a finger in the direction of a door across the foyer.

'Hello, Hannah.' The woman waved her in as she hesitated in the doorway. 'Come and sit down.'

To Hannah's relief, this woman revealed no signs of shock or surprise at the sight of Hannah's face; instead she got straight on with telling her about the background of Silver Maids.

'It's an international company, with bases in over fifty countries. We are *the* top cleaning agency for elite clients who pay us for our discretion when we are in their homes. Their privacy is extremely important to them and we *never* abuse it.'

Now Hannah understood why her lack of knowledge about the gossip magazines hadn't mattered.

'You would be responsible for caring for three houses which are occasionally occupied. We expect you to spend at least five hours in each of them every week, more if necessary to bring the house up to standard.' The woman paused for a brief moment and smiled. 'For example, if a social event has taken place. We also expect you to phone when you get there and when you leave. We spot inspect and if there's anything not up to scratch we operate a policy of instant dismissal.' The woman smiled again and Hannah managed to give a weak one back. 'So let's talk about you. Your family is well-known, itself, around here, isn't it?'

'On my father's side. My mother's not from here.'

The woman leaned forward. 'I remember there being quite a buzz about her in the Sixties. Didn't she do a bit of modelling before they married?'

'Only for one of her friends; she didn't really like it. She was more interested in travelling. Before she met my, um, dad, Edward.'

'I didn't know that.' The woman frowned and looked at Hannah's CV. 'And why haven't you gone to university, Hannah? Your results are very good.'

'I didn't want to,' Hannah said and quickly corrected herself. 'I didn't feel ready to leave home.'

'But is this how you see your career starting? Do you see this as something you really want to do?'

Hannah knew that you didn't tell the truth at this point. You didn't say it was because you needed the money or that the ad reminded

14

you of a detective novel, neither did you mention that this was one job that you wouldn't struggle to do because of your bad eyes, nor that there were other jobs you'd applied for but didn't get because people seemed to think you were weird or stupid simply because of how you looked.

'I like cleaning. I like quiet spaces. It lets me think.'

'What is it you think about?' The woman looked at her encouragingly, searching almost.

Hannah felt flustered but obliged to tell her. 'My stories. I write stories.'

'What kind of stories?'

Hannah was embarrassed. Only her family knew about her stories and it was difficult to explain them to a stranger. 'You could call them fables, supernatural fables. Some of them.'

'For children?'

'Perhaps, but not necessarily.'

Hannah looked at the woman who looked back at her. In her lap, Hannah crossed her fingers and wished that the woman would change the subject.

'What's your favourite cleaning job, Hannah?'

It wasn't anything Hannah had considered before but when she thought of the oak parquet flooring in the front room and how it shone after she and Ella gave it an annual spruce up, she had her answer. 'Polishing wood floors.'

The woman nodded as if Hannah had made the right choice. She asked her a couple of other questions and then sat back.

'That's all then, Hannah, thank you. Stop on

15

the way out and Amanda will measure you up for a uniform.'

'Oh, you got the job, then?' Amanda said, sounding surprised when Hannah returned to Reception.

'I don't think so.'

Amanda sighed and reluctantly came out from behind the desk with a tape measure in her hand. 'They don't measure you up unless you've got the job,' she said in a clipped tone.

★ ★ ★

There was a long wall of windows overlooking the pool terrace and, with the bright sun on it, Hannah noticed a light film of dust on the inside of the glass. She fetched her glass cleaner and two cloths and set to work. The garden had been landscaped around the pool with phormium, palms, and a fatsia japonica but they failed to keep out the Fen winds even on a hot day like this one.

Silver Maids had a motto: 'See everything, notice nothing,' which she had learned in the first ten minutes of her two-day training course. She also learned about health and safety, cleaning standards, how to interact with clients, how to handle journalists and a whole host of security issues. At the very end of the second day, each of the new maids was called separately into a small room. When it was Hannah's turn, she was given three envelopes containing details of her clients. She had to read these and hand them back before signing a heap of documents.

Afterwards, she was presented with two sets of uniform: black trousers and a silver-grey, tunic-style overall with a Silver Maids logo on the left breast.

Hannah had never told anyone, except Ella, the names of her clients and in the whole time she'd been working for the company, she'd only ever once met one of them — her Thursday client. He was a polite, shy man who was something to do with the London Philharmonic Orchestra and used the house as an infrequent base when he wasn't touring. The Monday client was the only name that Hannah and Ella recognized and that was because he owned a string of golf courses including the one in Ely which had caused some local controversy when it was granted planning permission. His house was a new-build set on the perimeter of the course but he lived in London and Hannah had never seen any evidence of him having been there.

Stepping outside onto the terrace, Hannah became aware of the sun-rays blading through the sky, hitting the ground. She often assessed light from the ground up, letting her eyes travel towards the source but always very slowly so that she was able to gauge the depth and strength of it before it hit her sensitive eyes.

Today the blue water in the pool seemed to shimmer under her gaze; white light glowed from the paving and colours shifted on the glass of the windows behind her. Hannah ate her lunch sitting in the deep shade of the tall, black bamboo screen. She could hear a skylark in the fields behind, its song dipping and rising. When it stopped, the silence seemed to visibly grow around her.

The job with Silver Maids had turned out differently than she'd imagined but better. She enjoyed cleaning — it was satisfying seeing visible results of her efforts — and she liked how her stories could percolate in her head while she was working. She often felt an urgency to write the moment she got home from work so in a way, she reasoned, it was like getting paid for her thinking time.

By half past three, Hannah had packed up, phoned into the office to confirm she was leaving and was waiting at the front of the house for Ella. The sun glared off the cream paved drive which made her feel slightly nauseous; even the breeze was warm and every pore including her scalp was prickling with sweat.

'How long were you out there? Did you put sun cream on?' Ella wanted to know the moment Hannah got in the car. 'You look very hot.' She tried to put her hand on Hannah's forehead.

Hannah pulled away. 'I just need some air.' She wound down the car window. 'Can't we get going, Ella?'

'We will as soon as I've found the damn key-card I've dropped.'

While Ella fished around under her seat, Hannah closed her eyes, hidden behind her sunglasses because her head had begun to ache. She opened her eyes once they were travelling in the softer light of the hedges and the fields and a cooler breeze was blowing around the car. Scoot snuffed at the open window and she felt the briefest kiss of his wet, cold nose on her neck.

She contemplated her mother's hands on the wheel of the car. The skin was brown and dotted with darker freckles and there was earth under her nails from gardening.

Ella caught her looking and said, a little distractedly, 'Everything's coming on too quickly in this weather.'

★ ★ ★

Hannah couldn't wait to take a shower and get changed out of her clothes.

'Bring them down for washing,' Ella called after her as she headed straight upstairs. She heard Tyler coming out of his attic room and waited to say hello on the landing.

'Hi, squirt,' he said. 'It's like an oven up there this afternoon.'

He was wearing the baggy blue shorts he wore every summer and had no top on. Hair covered him: from the long, unkempt hair on his head and his rough beard down to the thick pelt on his chest and belly; from the coating on his arms and legs to the dark sprigs on his fingers and toes. With his slight paunch and sweet brown eyes, he made Hannah think of a bear, a honey-drunk kind whose tummy you could tickle.

'You should go for a swim,' she said.

'Good idea,' he said and chucked her under her chin before continuing down.

Hannah knew he wouldn't go. He was on his

way to the kitchen where he'd get something to drink or eat; he'd have a cigarette outside and then he'd stretch and head back upstairs to pore over his graphs and charts and columns of little black numbers until he either joined her and Ella for an evening meal or more likely went to the pub. The Black Swan was his home from home. Tyler was the sociable one of the family; he knew everybody who went there and was on chatting terms with most of the people in the village, too; everyone liked Tyler and he had time for everyone.

It was hot in Hannah's room even though she'd left the window open all day. After her shower, she dressed in a vest top and knickers and towelled the damp ends of her hair. She picked up her notebook and reading glasses from her desk and lay on top of her duvet. Sunlight shone onto the bed, so she positioned herself with the window behind her and began to read through the last page of the story she had written.

Her eyes were misbehaving; the words jumped around and the letters seemed to travel over the page like whirligigs on a pond. Usually Hannah didn't mind; sometimes it helped when she was trying to find the right word. She could imagine the word slowly forming under the surface so that when the whirligigs settled, they did so into a pattern of letters and she could carry on. But today they didn't settle, and what she wrote was rubbish. After a few minutes, she scribbled out the last sentence she'd written, leaving an ugly, solid black line of ink which came through, spoiling the next page and making her feel even more cross.

She rolled onto her back and closed her eyes. She tried to think of her father who had always encouraged her to write. He used to tell her that it didn't matter if it took her longer. 'It's not a race, it's a passion to savour,' he'd say whenever she got frustrated. But thinking of Edward made her miss him suddenly, so intensely that when she heard Ella and Scoot coming upstairs, she rushed out onto the landing and followed them into Ella's bedroom.

The double-fronted aspect of Ella's room meant that it was much cooler than Hannah's as air was pulled between the two open windows. Hannah leaned out of the back window. Hoverflies and bees were busy on the rose and jasmine that climbed the wall nearly up to the eaves. She caught the scent of the rose whose buds were opening early this year, seduced by the early summer sun.

She joined Scoot on the bed and watched while Ella began to put away clean clothes in the chest of drawers.

'You know that pale-blue sundress you have?' Hannah was as familiar with the contents of Ella's packed wardrobe as her own. These days Ella didn't seem very interested in clothes and Hannah had already acquired several pieces from her mother.

'What, this one?' Ella extracted a hanger from the wardrobe and held up the dress.

Hannah felt she could hardly breathe. It was even nicer than she'd remembered. It was a square-neck mini-dress in pale blue with a big yellow flower on the right-hand side above the hem.

'Try it on. I don't want it.'

Hannah slipped it over her head. She looked in the mirror. It was perfect.

2

As Hannah didn't work on Wednesdays, she and Ella went into Ely after lunch to do the weekly shop and they usually made an afternoon of it, spending time in the bookshop and sometimes looking at the new stock in the charity and second-hand clothes shops.

In the morning, Hannah decided to go swimming in the river before the sun got too hot for her to be out. She dressed in her bikini and took her time applying sun cream. She had to be very careful not to miss a spot, paying particular attention to her face, her ears and the back of her neck. The cream was thick so it took a long time to dry. She sat on a towel on her bed until she was sure it was dry enough to put on her violet seersucker maxi-dress, the one Ella said she hadn't taken off the whole time she was expecting Henry. The hem rested on the top of her feet; the sleeves, which gathered in an elastic cuff were long enough to cover Hannah's hands if necessary and she pulled closed the threaded jellaba neckline. The material was so light it felt as if it was hovering above her skin and she loved how it floated about her as she ran downstairs.

There was no sign of Ella but the back door was wide open so Hannah knew she must be somewhere in the garden. Standing up, she ate some of the fruit salad left over from last night's meal straight from the bowl and took a long drink of grapefruit juice from the carton. She put on her white canvas shoes, sunglasses and her white sun hat. She picked up a packet of crisps to take with her and felt for the tube of sun cream that was under the towel in her bag.

She crossed the lawn, and passed through the gap in the hedge which they used to get down to the dyke from the back of the house and as a short cut for walking into the village. From the top of the bank, St Leonard's, the village church, sitting on its low hill, was visible. It had been an island church before the marshes were drained and the congregation used to reach it by boat. Although her vision was too poor to see anything more than a small, dark square pressed onto a cloudless blue sky, she liked knowing that further in the distance was the tower of Ely cathedral.

She had to come up onto the road to cross the dyke by the small metal bridge but she then headed away from the village for a couple of metres to the next bridge which took her over the river. She descended the bank on the other side and walked for a short distance to where a meander had formed a small, curved beach. Here, the bank had eroded from the bottom, leaving an overhang, so that it was possible to lie on the beach and be hidden from anyone until they were pretty much on top of you. It was a popular spot with the locals for fishing and Hannah was pleased to see that no one else was there.

Hannah pulled off her dress and laid out her towel on the flattest part of the shingle. Nearer the water, the ground was usually soft mud but the sun had been so hot and dry it had dried out and was beginning to crack like old leather. When Hannah stepped onto it, she felt the crust give slightly but it stayed firm underneath her weight. The water was bath-warm at the edge, and the mud was soft. Hannah spotted the flicker of a shoal of tiny, translucent fish in the shallows which disappeared the instant her shadow fell across them.

The river was lower than usual and Hannah had almost waded out to the centre before the water reached her knees. It was much colder at this depth and she shivered despite the heat on the rest of her body. She sank down quickly, and swam a couple of quick breaststrokes while she caught her breath before slowing down.

Learning to swim was one of Hannah's first memories. She'd been five years old when Henry taught her to jump off the bank. The water had seemed so very far away but she trusted her brother to pull her up if she sank. Henry's arm underneath her stomach supported her weight and kept her afloat while she kicked out her legs like the frogs Edward had pointed out to her in the ponds. She swam happily and proudly until she discovered that Henry's arm was gone and she promptly panicked and swallowed so much water he had to lift her out. When he cajoled her into trying again, she discovered she could do it on her own.

Hannah headed in the opposite direction to the village, keeping to the middle of the river. Edward once said that Native Americans believe otters represent the feminine energy and the power of the earth and waters, so Hannah liked to imagine she was an otter woman, swimming strongly, moving with the current and spirit of the water. There used to be loads of otters around when Edward was a boy; they disappeared really quickly, he said, much quicker than you could ever get them to come back. People never knew what they had until it was gone.

As the river began to shallow out, she floated face up, her hands low in the water, enjoying the slow trickle of current across her fingers. If you act like a piece of wood, Edward had taught her, the creatures begin to disregard you and go about their business, but she couldn't stay in that position for long enough; even with her eyes closed, the sun was piercing.

Back on the beach, she lay on her front and felt the heat suck the moisture off her body in minutes. She put on her sunglasses and hat and another layer of sun cream before pulling on her dress. A coot emerged from the reeds close by and began its bobbing swim across the river; a pair of swans glided into view from the direction of the village; Hannah felt the black beads of their eyes fixed on her as they approached, hopeful for bread. They floated opposite her for a while before they gave up and continued upstream.

The brightness was beginning to make her eyes uncomfortable so she pulled on her shoes and put her belongings into her bag, except for the damp towel which she carried under her arm.

Hannah walked in a dead-straight line across

the top of the bank. Every now and then, birds would give an alarm call or fly up out of the long grass. In an hour's time, they'd be lying low to keep cool in the midday sun and the fields and marshes would be dense with silence.

As she approached the gap in the hedge, Scoot appeared to escort her back into the garden, his pink tongue dangling out of the side of his mouth. He trotted ahead, his right back leg kicking out at an angle, his tail up like an antenna testing the air. He stopped by the hothouse and didn't go any farther.

★ ★ ★

Hannah had ironed Ella's sundress, ready to wear that afternoon into Ely. After showering, she tried it on again with yellow flip-flops to match the flower on the dress and a bleached denim sun hat. She shook her hair free of its ponytail so that it hung loose around her face. She went to find Ella in the hothouse.

'It's scorching in here,' Hannah said to her mother's back where a patch of sweat was blossoming in the centre of her blouse. When Ella turned, she looked at Hannah as if she had no idea why she was there.

'Bugger,' she said once it had clicked. 'Is it that time already?' She looked down at the pot of amaryllis she was holding; an out-of-season, white trumpet flower was partly unfurled on top of the long, fleshy stem.

Hannah stepped inside. Ella was right, a lot of the plants were growing quickly: the Passion flower was showing the first signs of flowering and the Moonflower in the corner was already half-way up to the roof; almost all the vegetable and herb seedlings were looking strong. The scent of the citrus flowers reminded her that Ella wanted help carrying them out to the patio before the air in the hothouse became too damp for next year's fruit to set.

'You look nice, sweetheart,' Ella said. 'I think I'd better have a shower before we go,' she added, looking down at herself.

On the way out, Hannah touched the geranium on the staging near the door and was rewarded with the sharp, lemony scent.

Hannah waited for Ella at the garden table under the umbrella. She was grateful for the way it transformed the hot glare of the sun and cast over her a cool, green light like a spell. Scoot was sitting at the back door; his haughty demeanour suggested to Hannah that he was sulking in advance of being shut in the living room for the afternoon.

'It's your own fault,' she told him. 'If you didn't howl loud enough to gather a crowd, we could take you with us.'

★ ★ ★

Hannah loved all the old buildings in Ely but the circular, stone bookshop was one of her favourites. It was laid out on three floors; the top two were for new books, the bottom — the basement — was for second-hand and antiquities. Hannah always started in the top room. It had high, geometrical, lead lattice windows with ancient glass so rippled and pitted it was like looking at the city below through water. Ella never strayed far from the gardening section so Hannah left her and descended to the second floor down the stone staircase with the rope hand-rail attached to metal rings punched into the wall. Modelled plasterwork depicting a hare and clover was set around the doorway leading into the fiction aisles.

Hannah wandered along the shelves, picking up a book every now and then, reading the back and the first line of some, but nothing quite grabbed her. She descended into the musty, cool smell of the basement where there was only, dim yellow artificial light. Here she discovered a hardback copy of Henry James's *The Turn of the Screw*. The dust jacket was torn and mottled with mould spots but underneath was a rough material in a lovely blush-pink with gold-embossed wording on the spine.

'Eight pounds' was written in pencil on the inside, which seemed expensive but Hannah had fallen in love with the way the book felt in her hands. When the sales assistant saw the state of the cover, she reduced the price to six and Hannah paid quickly, slipping it into her bag before the woman changed her mind.

After the cool of the bookshop, the high street was unbearably hot. They walked without speaking for several minutes, the heat robbing them of speech.

'Have you got cream on, Hannah?' Ella asked.

'Like I was going to forget,' she replied, cross

with the heat and with the difficulty she was having settling her vision. It was always harder walking in a crowd and today the brightness made her squint even with her glasses and sun hat on. She almost stumbled as Ella slowed suddenly to enter the delicatessen.

The smell of fresh bread and spicy sausages cheered Hannah up. She examined and marvelled at the foods in the trays at the counter while Ella bought Finnish pickled cucumbers, *chorizo iberico*, soda bread, olives and stuffed piquillo peppers. They drove out of town to the supermarket, armed with a list, used bags and a frown on Ella's face as they walked briskly around. They were packing the shopping into the car boot when Ella stopped still.

'Oh my God!' She pulled Hannah's arm and ducked behind the open boot door as a car pulled into the space beside them.

'Who is it?' Hannah's voice came out in a hoarse whisper. She felt a thrill of excitement seeing the odd expression on Ella's face.

'A person from the past that I don't really want to see,' Ella said with her head bent so low into the boot she practically had her face in one of the shopping bags. 'Stay down,' she hissed as Hannah peered out.

There was an ordinary-looking woman with flabby, freckled arms, a tummy that strained against a plain grey skirt, a pin-striped shirt and blonde hair cut unflatteringly short. She didn't even give them a glance as she walked by.

'She's gone,' Hannah told Ella. 'Who is she?' she asked as they watched the woman walk towards the supermarket entrance. Ella didn't reply; instead she suddenly turned and hugged Hannah but her body felt tense like Scoot's when he was stressed.

Ella unlocked the car and Hannah got in, but Ella didn't. Instead she walked around to Hannah's side and peered through the woman's car window.

Hannah wound her window down. 'What are you looking for?'

'Signs of humanity,' Ella replied and let out a weird laugh which startled Hannah. 'Ella?' she called out sharply, shifting in her seat to check whether there was anyone around. 'Please. Come on.'

'I'm coming, darling.'

Hannah turned to face the front but something about the way Ella was moving made her look back. Her mother was walking slowly and oddly close to the car, keeping her hand low as if she was holding something against it. Hannah leaned out of the window.

'What are you doing?'

'Nothing.'

Ella hurried round to the driver's side and got in. As she reversed, Hannah noticed a silver scratch snaking all the way down the length of the woman's blue car. Hannah caught her breath and glanced at Ella whose face was flushed but expressionless. She decided to say nothing.

★   ★   ★

As soon as the last of the shopping had been put away in the cupboards, Ella went into the garden. Hannah watched her follow the path down to the tool shed and it seemed as if she was visibly relaxing with every step.

'You walk like her,' Tyler said, joining Hannah at the back door. She hadn't heard him come into the kitchen.

'Do I?'

'That long-legged slide. Exactly like her.'

'Tyler, I think Ella keyed a car while we were out.'

Tyler laughed.

'Honestly. It was at the supermarket. First she made us hide from this woman and then when she'd gone Ella went over to her car. When we drove off, there was a scratch all down one side.'

'And why would she do that, squirt?'

Hannah shrugged. 'She said she knew the woman but she didn't want to see her.'

He cut a piece of bread from the new loaf. 'Do you want some?'

Hannah nodded.

Tyler took the butter and jam out of the fridge.

Hannah spoke to his back. 'I know you don't believe me.'

'It seems a bit out of character, that's all.'

'Exactly,' Hannah said excitedly. 'She was acting really weird; I mean, really weird.'

She had followed too close behind Tyler and he bumped into her when he turned round. He waited until she took a step back before speaking. 'Did the woman see you?'

32

'No. I'm pretty sure no one saw anything.'

'That's OK, then.'

'I suppose so,' Hannah said, although she wasn't sure that was really the point. She watched Tyler add a huge dollop of jam to each slice which he spread around with the back of the spoon. He handed her a piece which she had to hold flat on the palm of her hand to stop it from breaking up.

'And you don't know who the woman was?'

'She wouldn't tell me anything except that she didn't like her.'

'I think it was most probably a coincidence,' Tyler said. 'I think the car was already damaged and it had nothing to do with Ella.'

'Oh, I hadn't thought of that.'

'You wouldn't though, would you, squirt?' He placed a hand on top of her head before walking towards the door. 'Hey, Hannah.' He turned back. 'Do you fancy going to the pub this evening?'

She nodded as her mouth was full. When he had gone, she returned to the doorway but there was no sign of Ella.

★   ★   ★

'Come on, old girl,' Tyler coaxed as his old Fizzy coughed and sputtered on the rough track past Lavender Cottage. Once they were on the smoother main road into the village, the motorbike settled down and soon they were zooming along. Hannah gripped the strap on the seat between them and, cocooned in her helmet,

33

she let herself sink into the vibrating noise of it. The warm evening air flowed over her, carrying the sweet scent of wild honeysuckle from the hedges and the silage odour of the cow pasture.

Close to the entrance of the village, they caught up with someone walking on the road. He stepped up on the verge once he heard the motorbike approaching and waited for it to pass. Hannah couldn't focus clearly but she was sure she didn't recognize the young man as anyone from the village.

The pub was one of the oldest buildings in Snettersley, built in the early 18th century, the same as Spindle House. Its ceilings were low, crossed with thin, dark beams. The walls were decorated with old basket pots, an eel gun, as well as a lot of tackle and paintings of shire horses which were common all over the Fens and which used to be bred at Spindle House until Edward's parents closed the stables.

Tyler got caught up in a conversation at the bar with Colin, an old schoolfriend of Tyler's who lived with his wife, Belinda, and little boy, Jack, in one of the farm cottages a mile outside the village on the other side to Spindle House. Hannah took her half-pint of cider to the small patch of grass at the front of the pub where there were two table benches: She sat facing the road and it wasn't long before the young stranger appeared. He stopped and looked at the front of the pub and then at Hannah. He was about medium height and was wearing long, baggy blue shorts, a white T-shirt saying PLEASE. DON'T FEED THE ANIMALS, in red lettering, red baseball boots and he was carrying a rucksack.

'Hello,' he said, coming closer.

His skin was lightly tanned and his hair was reddish-brown, the colour of rain-soaked sedge.

'Hello.'

He had an unusually wide face with such a low forehead that his thick, black eyebrows looked like they were trying to creep up into his hairline. It was as if someone had pressed down on the top of his head and squashed hard. When he smiled, his whole face seemed to flatten further and all that remained of his eyes were dark slits.

'The local hostelry, I take it,' he said.

'It is. Welcome to the Black Swan,' Hannah said, feeling brave behind her sunglasses, but at that moment Tyler and Colin came outside, talking and laughing loudly, and the man slipped away.

'Did you see that lad?' she asked them. 'Do you know who he is?'

Tyler hadn't paid much attention to him, but Colin had; he said he'd never seen him before so Hannah knew he must be a visitor. Colin was the local postman so he knew everybody and a lot of everybody's business, too.

It took only a few sips of the cold, sweet cider to make Hannah feel fuzzy from her toes up. Her brother and Colin were debating the merits of satellite versus cable to which Hannah had no opinion to offer; neither could she contribute to a discussion on motorbike parts, but she was happy enough letting their talk wash over her and her thoughts drift wherever they wanted to go.

★ ★ ★

Hannah wasn't sure if it was the second pint of cider which was making Tyler weave slightly on the road, or if he was deliberately avoiding any ruts and holes for the Fizzy's sake. It didn't really matter. Once they were out of the village, there was no other traffic. They travelled along the grey strip of the road, bordered by the dark, hunched shapes of the hedges which channelled their way. Hannah felt her spirits rise until she was humming inside. In front of her was the warm, wide back of her big bear of a brother, above her the moon gleamed like a pearl in the silky sky.

3

The house that Hannah cleaned on Thursdays was her favourite house. The small, brick-built country house with its mature gardens felt more homely and lived-in than either of the others, even though it was very masculine with a lot of grey and brown decor and sturdy furniture.

She always left an hour at the end of the day for the bathroom as the client had asked her to take care of the plants in there as well as clean it. Unusually, the bath was set into a dark, wood-panelled alcove opposite a wide window. It had a wide marble surround which was filled with about thirty plants interspersed with candles. Hannah had lain in the bath when it was empty and she could imagine bathing in it at night with the window open, lit by moon and candlelight. It would be like taking a bath in a forest.

Today she moved all the pots from the surround and left them by the open window for some air while she cleaned and polished the marble. It was only when she was replacing the plant pots that she thought to look at her watch and realized that it was nearly time for Ella to pick her up.

She hurriedly finished what she was doing and then packed all her cleaning materials into her box. She sat in the kitchen where there was a view of the drive and waited for Ella's car to appear.

There was a wooden clock on a shelf of the in-built dresser and Hannah couldn't take her eyes off it as she watched each long minute go by without any sign of her mother. Although Ella was often a few minutes late, it was never by more than ten minutes and, as the clock counted out fifteen, Hannah's concern began to grow to panic. She couldn't help picturing Ella's car being nose-down in the ditch near Holme Farm because she'd overcooked the bend. Hannah's hand was trembling while she waited for someone to answer the phone at Spindle House.

'Tyler, what time did Ella leave? She hasn't got here yet.'

'I think she's still in the garden,' he said. 'I heard Scoot barking a minute ago. Hang on. I'll have a look.' Hannah heard him groan as he hoisted himself to lean out of the window. 'Yeah, she's down near the pond.'

There was a sharp whistle, then a shout, then the muffled sounds of Tyler talking.

'She forgot the time, she's leaving now. She'll be with you in fifteen minutes, she says.'

★ ★ ★

'I'm so sorry, darling. I lost track of time,' Ella said when she pulled up to the house twenty minutes later. Hannah didn't reply. She didn't know if she felt relieved or annoyed. They drove without speaking for a couple of miles with Scoot filling the silence with frantic panting.

'I hate it,' Hannah burst out and felt tears stinging the back of her eyes. 'I hate having to be driven everywhere. I hate my stupid eyes.' She pushed a finger up behind her sunglasses and wiped away a tear.

'There's no point feeling sorry for yourself — '

'That's easy for you to say,' Hannah snapped. 'You don't know what it's like. You've always been able to go wherever you want.'

They sank back into silence; even Scoot was quiet.

'You're right, Hannah, I'm sorry. It must be a real pain for you having to rely on your useless mother.' Ella gave Hannah a friendly grin and winked.

Hannah shifted in her seat and shrugged. 'I guess it's not so bad,' she said and then suddenly saw how pale Ella's face was and how dark her eyes were underneath, as if she hadn't slept for days. She leaned towards her to look more closely. 'Are you OK?'

'Of course,' Ella said sharply, sitting up straighter as if to prove the point. 'Why?'

'You look a bit, um, ill.'

'It's the heat, that's all. It's this bloody heat.'

★   ★   ★

After Hannah had changed and prepared a salad for dinner later, she went down to the dyke behind the garden. A cooler breeze had picked up and brought in a few grey clouds. It felt as if it might even rain,

A heron was picking for fish in the still, dark

39

water. All of a sudden, it took to the air and flew above the path of the dyke, its rough, croaking call still audible when Hannah could no longer see it.

A soft, splashing noise made Hannah turn her attention back to the water. She saw immediately what had scared the bird off. It was Stan, with his face like a punctured rugby ball, who had travelled the dyke in his punt ever since Hannah could remember. His punt reminded her of Ella's wooden trug that she used in the garden, but he collected eels and reeds in it, not flowers and vegetables.

Hannah called out hello and Stan nodded his greeting back without breaking his paddle stroke. Stan never spoke. Edward had told her that Stan was born mute but the story in the village was that he'd been struck dumb by lightning when he ran outside as a toddler after disobeying his mother. It was a story, Edward said, designed to scare children into listening to their parents.

Raindrops dimpled the water for a few seconds; one fell softly on the back of her hand which she licked off. She waited for more, but none came.

Stories and rumours blew in across the fields and up out of the dykes so that at times the swirling air was so full of them it was hard to know what was true and what wasn't. Hannah knew that some of these stories were about her family: that the villagers said Edward loved being with frogs more than he loved living with his family and that Ella was so obsessed with white flowers that she had produced an albino child.

4

Every second Friday evening of the month, Hannah went to the Ghost Storytelling Society meeting in Ely. At the end of the previous summer, she had come across a faded green poster on the library noticeboard with an image at the top of a black dog with piercing red eyes. It happened to be that very evening that the Society was meeting and so Hannah had decided to wait around and see what it was all about. She hadn't missed a meeting since.

The Society met in one of the back rooms of the Old Court House and Hannah, as always, was first to arrive as her bus got in nearly forty-five minutes early. She sat on the bench in the corridor outside and waited for Maggie, who was the key holder.

The air in the corridor was still and dusty; the dark, quartered oak panelling absorbed any surrounding noise and she sank into the solitude and silence until she heard the click of a door, followed by Maggie's quick steps.

They both paused in the doorway as a wave of heat rolled over them. The air in the room was dense and smelled woody, like Ella's shed on a summer's day. The windows had been nailed shut, so they closed the heavy, midnight-blue curtains against the sun. Dust particles billowed out and hung like a sparkling blue cloud before dispersing. With the curtains closed and her sunglasses on, the light was dusky and restful and Hannah realized then how badly the brightness had been straining her eyes.

Together they set out chairs in a circle; far too many in Hannah's opinion as there were only three other regulars besides themselves but, if she tried to put less out, Maggie would only ask her to add more. You never know, Maggie would say, alluding to the possibility of being besieged by ghost tourists who had come across the Society's details on the supernatural trail in the Tourist Information office.

Hannah and Maggie took their usual seats, several chairs away from each other, and waited for the others to arrive.

'It's terribly hot.' Maggie looked uncomfortable. Her salon-fresh grey hair was beginning to wilt and Hannah found it hard to believe someone would choose to wear tights when they didn't have to. Hannah had picked loose, red linen jeans and the tiniest vest top under a denim waistcoat. Looking down at her yellow flip-flops, she noticed that her toes were grey with dust.

'Its coming over from Continental Europe,' Maggie continued. 'It's so hot over there, people are dying.'

Before Hannah could respond, Magnus appeared. Hannah was a little unsure of him. Tiny eyes peered out from a face which was masked by thick facial hair like an animal's; whenever he looked in Hannah's direction, his gaze always seemed condescending.

'Evening all,' he boomed. 'Fine weather today.'

'Yes, lovely,' Maggie and Hannah chorused

42

before turning their attention gratefully towards the door as Sue strode in, her long skirt sweeping the wooden floor. Each step was accompanied by a tinkling and rattling noise produced by the many bangles and beads on her arms and, Hannah noticed with some alarm as Sue sat down, what looked like a red leather cat's collar with a bell around one ankle.

Sue was supposed to be psychic which Hannah thought ironic since she was one of the most insensitive adults Hannah knew. At Hannah's first meeting, she had turned to her and said, 'Don't your people claim to have magical powers?' If it hadn't been for Maggie's gentle but firm change of subject, Hannah might have been too embarrassed to return. Hannah suspected Maggie wasn't very fond of Sue either.

'Waiting for Kimberley again, are we?' Sue said loudly. 'Perhaps we should start without her?'

'We'll give it a couple more minutes,' Maggie said. 'There's no harm in that.'

'Did you watch *Most Haunted* this week?' Kimberley said the moment she was in the room. She stopped breathless; blonde strands of hair were falling out of her ponytail, her T-shirt was creased and there were several different-coloured stains on her beige combat pants. She always looked surprised to find herself there, as if she couldn't believe she'd managed to wrest herself away from her kids. Sometimes Hannah fancied she could see little ghost hands pulling at her which only faded away once she sat down.

Kimberley's eyes were wide with excitement.

43

'It was the best yet. There was so much activity, it was amazing.'

She was stopped short by the loud harrumph of Magnus clearing his throat.

'Oh, yes, um.' Maggie became a little flustered. 'We look forward to hearing about that later, Kimberley, dear. In the, um, usual spot.'

The evenings always took the same format: someone read out a story or an account — which were stories that were supposed to be real — then after a break they discussed anything anyone wanted to bring up, leaving the 'business' of the society, as Maggie called it, until the end.

Hannah had never read anything out although she always brought her notebook with her. She picked up her bag from underneath her chair and put it on her knee; her fingers sought and found the hard edges of the notebook inside. She pictured the words of the story she had recently finished. It was called *Paper Monsters*. Strictly speaking, it wasn't a ghost story, none of her own stories were, but it had an eerie feel. A foreboding. She watched as Magnus produced a great wodge of paper.

He cleared his throat. 'This,' he said, 'is a true story.'

Hannah, under cover of her sunglasses, glanced at the others without turning her head. She caught sight of Kimberley in the tail-end of an eye roll, Maggie was staring down at her lap but Sue was looking intently at Magnus; Hannah suddenly had the idea that she fancied him.

After ten minutes, Hannah lost track of Magnus's story. She knew how it would end though — in a bloodfest recounted in great gory detail. For some reason, her attention was drawn to the door in a split second before it began to slowly open. Hannah squeezed her eyes shut in case her vision was playing tricks but when she reopened them, the face of the young stranger from the village was peering round. She let out a gasp which made the others in the group look up. Magnus barely paused for breath before continuing with his deep voice raised a level as if defying anyone to interrupt him.

Maggie pressed her finger to her lips as she waved the young man forward. Hannah felt sorry for him as he sat marooned in the semicircle of unoccupied chairs. Any minute now and he was going to get up and walk out, she thought, so she directed her biggest, warmest smile at him.

He grinned back, slid down in his seat and rested his chin on his fist. He was wearing a dirty pair of trainers and no socks, his shorts came down over his knees and his T-shirt said 'FIT TO BUST'.

Magnus came to a halt and silence hung over them until Maggie rose to the occasion. 'Thank you, Magnus. Thought-provoking as usual.' She turned in her seat. 'And welcome to — '

'Toby.'

'Toby,' she repeated. 'This is Magnus, Kimberley, Sue, Hannah and I'm Maggie.' She gestured to each one of them in turn. 'Please just listen or share any ghost experiences or other encounters if you feel you wish to.'

'Um, OK. What? Now, you mean?' he asked, sitting up, looking startled.

45

Maggie went pink. 'Oh, well only if you want to . . . or perhaps later. We usually have a break now and . . . I think Kimberley has something she'd like to . . . '

'And me.'

'And Susan, too. So perhaps, after that . . . '

'That's fine. I'm not sure anyway — ' he petered out, giving Maggie the opportunity to jump up and start rustling in her bag.

The group wasn't supposed to use any electrical equipment in the room, but Maggie always brought along her travel kettle and everything to make tea, as well as biscuits. They had each contributed five pounds in January to cover the cost of refreshments for the year.

'I usually only listen,' Hannah said in a low voice to Toby when Maggie had passed them their tea in a plastic cup and they were returning to their seats.

'Oh, OK. Thanks — uh — '

'Hannah.'

'So,' Kimberley said when everyone was sitting down. 'I was watching on-line, and I saw this woman. She walked right across my screen, dressed in black with, like, a shawl or scarf over her head and then, right before she moved out of the picture, she turned her face and looked straight at me. It was totally amazing. The whole room went cold and there was this flicker across my computer.'

'Did you see her again?' Maggie asked.

'No, but afterwards, every ten minutes or so, this flicker — like a grey fuzzy line — would come back.'

'Did you log it?' Sue asked.

'Yes. Actually, they read it out. I've got it on video.' Kimberley barely paused for breath. 'Apparently a woman was murdered there over a hundred years ago, a housekeeper or something.'

'And you saw her,' Maggie breathed, obviously enthralled at the idea. 'Isn't that wonderful?'

Neither Magnus nor Sue looked particularly impressed so Hannah felt obliged to speak up. 'That's great, Kimberley,' she said, hoping that Toby didn't think she believed any of it.

Maggie turned to Sue. 'Didn't you have something you wanted to say?'

'I certainly do. I was at my aunt's house over in Watton and she told me about a friend of hers who was having trouble with a spirit.'

'Sue is physic sensitive,' Kimberley explained to Toby.

'Oh, right. OK.' He nodded although Hannah wasn't convinced that he knew what it meant. Sue shook out the folds of her skirt with more rattling and tinkling, straightened her glasses and then looked around the room before settling her gaze on Hannah who found herself mesmerized by her magnified blue eyes. Her lashes looked so big and thick Hannah was afraid they might be capable of crawling out from behind the lens.

'My aunt's friend has been suffering from disturbances: objects moved, strange noises in the master bedroom.'

Toby's trainer squeaked on the floor as he shifted in his seat and tried to hide a grin with his hand. Hannah looked round at the others but they were wrapped up in Sue's account. It reminded her of the times when private jokes had passed between her and her brothers in the presence of their parents. She felt herself warming to the strange-looking stranger.

'OK, thank you, Sue,' Maggie said when she had finished talking and Hannah thought one wouldn't need to be a psychic to sense the chill in Maggie's cheerful tone, but Sue looked like the cat that had got the cream when Magnus leaned forward and said, 'Very interesting, Susan. I'd like to follow up on a couple of things you mentioned at some point.'

Maggie cut in. 'It's time for the Official Sightings List.'

Official from whom, Hannah had never been sure, but Maggie always produced a printed list that she meticulously read out with dates, times and locations of all sightings and happenings in the East of the UK. This evening, there was nothing on the list that was local enough for any of them to get excited about but they patiently listened until Maggie had finished.

'Toby, was it?' boomed Magnus. 'Are you from around here?'

'No, I'm only visiting,' Toby replied and Magnus visibly relaxed; Hannah had the feeling he enjoyed his role as the only male in the group.

'Perhaps you'd like to hear one of our local legends?'

'Oh, yes,' Maggie said, going pink as she sometimes did if she spoke directly to Magnus. 'Tell him about Black Shuck.'

'Black Shuck or Old Shuck,' Magnus began, 'is the demon dog who has haunted this part of the country for hundreds of years. He runs the Suffolk coastline but in August 1577, during the most terrible thunderstorm, he came inland and rampaged through the sacred space of a church, leaving his claw marks on the outer door, which can still be seen today.'

Magnus leaned forward in his chair and Sue gasped and, even though they had all heard the story several times before, Hannah felt the back of her neck shiver as Magnus lowered and intensified his voice.

'But, Toby, the thing to remember is this: if you ever have the misfortune to be in the presence of Black Shuck, you must never, *never* look at him because the one who looks at him will be dead within a year.'

'Shit,' Toby said, then added, 'Oh, excuse me.'

'Don't worry, dear,' Maggie piped up, bright as a bird. 'Black Shuck is always shocking.'

Maggie left to empty the kettle and cups, into the toilet and Hannah stayed behind to put the chairs away with Toby who had offered to help. The others had gone ahead to the Red Horse to secure the best table.

'What did you think?' Hannah asked Toby.

'I'm not sure, to be honest.'

'It can be a rather weird experience the first time.'

'I'm glad you said it.' Toby grinned. He took the last two chairs from Hannah and put them on the stack.

'Are you going to the Red Horse for a drink?'

'Are you going?' Toby turned around.

'I don't think so.' It wasn't worth it this time

49

— the meeting had run on a little and Ella would be picking her up in about ten minutes. 'I've got a lift.'

'I could take you to Snettersley afterwards if you want. If that's where you're headed.'

'Oh, it's all arranged now. But thanks, anyway.'

'Then I think I'll give it a miss, too,' he said as Maggie came back into the room.

'Should we leave the curtains closed?' Hannah asked her. The room was getting quite dark now and Hannah pushed her sunglasses up onto the top of her head.

'I don't think we should. We're supposed to leave the room exactly as we found it.'

'I'll do them,' Toby offered and, as there was no reason for Hannah to hang around, she said her goodbyes and walked towards the door.

Maggie called her back. 'You've forgotten your bag.'

Hannah rushed over. She couldn't believe she'd almost left it behind. She hugged it in her arms, her fingers feeling for the hard square of her notebook inside.

'A precious thing, a woman's handbag,' Toby said and winked.

It wasn't until she was outside, when she needed to put her sunglasses back on, that she realized Toby had seen her eyes and that she hadn't noticed any reaction.

It was Tyler in the car not Ella.

'She said she wasn't feeling well.'

'Ella?' Hannah couldn't remember her mother ever being ill except for the time after Edward had died.

'It's probably heatstroke from being in that bloody hothouse all day,' Tyler said. 'How's squirt?' He nudged her and she jostled him back and then they put on one of Ella's old Doors cassettes and played it at full volume all the way home.

★ ★ ★

When Hannah walked into Ella's bedroom, Ella was standing in front of the dresser in her shorts and bra.

'Can't you ever knock, Hannah?' she said sharply and Hannah didn't know what to say because she had never knocked on Ella's door in her life.

'I'm sorry.'

'What do you want, love?' Ella pulled on her top and leaned her back against the dresser, her arms crossed.

'Nothing really.' Hannah stepped forward to stroke Scoot but she was unsure whether she was welcome to lie on the bed.

'I'm sorry I didn't pick you up. Did you have a good night?' Ella's softer tone encouraged Hannah to sit down but she perched on the edge just in case. She decided not to tell Ella about Toby after all. 'It was OK.'

There were shreds of pink in the evening sky visible through the window past Ella's shoulder.

'Have you got sunstroke?' Hannah asked.

'No, only a headache, darling. Did you read your story out?'

Hannah shook her head. 'Magnus read his.'

'Never mind, another time.'

'Yes,' Hannah said and then suddenly an idea rushed into her so quickly and forcefully that she felt herself being pushed upright. It was as if the ending — the true ending — to her story had been running after her all the way back from Ely, chasing behind the car out of the city, through the lanes, down the drive until it had finally caught up with her in Ella's bedroom. She knew that she couldn't wait. She had to go and do something about it.

5

Even though Hannah's eyes were tired and it was getting more difficult by the minute to keep them focused, she couldn't put *The Turn of the Screw* down. It was nearly two in the morning but there had never seemed to be a point in the story at which she could bring herself to leave it. Now, as the number of pages left to read was getting fewer and fewer, she found herself reading quicker and quicker as if she was tumbling headfirst towards the ending.

After she had read the final word, she took off her glasses, closed the book and lay there for a few minutes, her heart beating. Her attention was drawn to the window which she had left wide open with the curtains undrawn. It seemed as if the blackness outside was leaching into the room and it began to make her nervous. She forced herself to get up and, as a test against her fear, she stood at the window.

The air was cool and scented from the honeysuckle which clambered on the trellis below. The owls were quiet for once and the peace of the garden rose up, making her yawn deeply, her eyes watering.

Suddenly she saw a light. At least she thought she had, but when she looked harder, it had disappeared. Then it appeared again, slightly further to the right. It was a bobbing yellow light which was travelling slowly along the perimeter of the garden. There was a flash and then it was gone, as if it had been sucked back into the darkness.

★　★　★

In the morning, Hannah was still tired and a headache was looming. She skipped the shower, got dressed in her uniform and went downstairs where Ella was sitting at the kitchen table in her dressing gown.

Hannah glanced out of the open door, thinking only rain would keep her mother indoors but it was another dry day without a single cloud.

Scoot was lying in the middle of the lawn. He raised his head a few centimetres as if acknowledging Hannah's presence before lowering it to rest once more on his paws. He was in almost the exact spot where he had first appeared about a year after her father's death. None of them had actually seen him arrive; he was suddenly there as if he'd been pushed up out of the ground like a giant mushroom. He stayed in the same spot for a couple of hours, without moving, until they began to wonder if he was still alive. As they watched him out of the window, only a few ear twitches and a slight shift of one of his legs told them he was. After a while, they stopped thinking that he would go away of his own accord and began to discuss what they should do. Tyler suggested the RSPCA — they could see how scruffy and thin he was — but nobody volunteered to make the call.

It was Ella, who had hardly spoken since Edward's funeral, who tried to coax him into the house with bits of sausage. Gradually he came closer until she was feeding him at the back door; the next day he entered the kitchen. Day by day he blossomed and brightened and as he did, so too did Ella. Hannah had always been grateful for the little magic dog who had rescued Ella from her long sadness.

Reminded of her father, Hannah said, 'It's the Strawberry Fair this weekend.'

The annual Strawberry Fair was where Edward and Ella had first met. Of all their family stories, the Strawberry Fair was Hannah's favourite.

'Ella looked so beautiful,' Edward used to say. 'Dressed top to toe in white with her long, dark hair and big, brown eyes. She and Sadie were so young and glamorous I would never have dared go anywhere near her if it wasn't for the mutual friends they were with.'

'Your father,' Ella always interrupted Edward at this point with her version of the story, 'was the most eligible of bachelors. Handsome and shy.' It was easy for Hannah to picture her tall father, his shoulders slightly hunched with diffidence, a thirty-seven-year-old orphan with a smile like a young boy's.

'And then I found out he was obsessed with amphibians!' They would both laugh.

'She forgave me my obsession,' Edward said, followed in the next heartbeat by Ella.

'Because I had one of my own.'

'Everyone was surprised when she moved into

55

Spindle House. Including me. She and Sadie were such adventurers, sailing with rich princes and film stars and property tycoons. No one expected her to give that up and settle down here with an old man like me.'

'She wanted to do it. Because it felt right,' Hannah liked to tell him because he could look so puzzled and a little sad at this point. 'You were in love. You are in love.'

It seemed such a romantic way to meet that Hannah had day-dreams of the same thing happening to her. One year she would meet someone special at the Fair.

'Mum,' she said because Ella still hadn't responded, 'the Strawberry Fair is this week-end.'

Ella pulled a face. 'I don't really feel like going this year.'

'But we always go.'

'You go, sweetheart. I'd rather not.'

'But we always go,' Hannah repeated.

'I'm not going, Hannah, so give it a rest, please.'

Hannah swallowed down her unspoken words with the first spoonful of cereal. There was something dark about Ella, something that had been hovering around her for several days. She observed Ella through the cover of her hair which she let fall over her face and tried to pinpoint when it had started: was it from the night of the Ghost Society? Or from that odd encounter with the woman in the car park? Or perhaps even longer? She wondered with a sick feeling in her stomach if it was anything to do with her, if she had done something to upset Ella.

Ella left the room and Hannah pushed away the remains of her breakfast.

'Why the long face?' Tyler asked.

Hannah hadn't heard him come in. When she looked up, her eyes met the creased T-shirt stretched over his belly. He thudded around the kitchen, leaving misty footprints on the stone which evaporated almost immediately. He sat down with a thump at the kitchen table, placing a glass of juice and a piece of cheese on the table in front of him.

'It's Ella. She doesn't seem right.'

'She's probably still not feeling well.'

'It's not that. It's something different. She said she doesn't want to go to the Strawberry Fair. We always go. Every year.' As she spoke, a coldness passed through her. *Except for the terrible year after Edward died*, she thought, and felt a little scared.

'I'll take you,' Tyler told her. 'Don't worry, Hannah, thou shalt go to the Fayre. And besides,' he added, 'she'll probably have changed her mind by then.'

★   ★   ★

Over the next couple of days, Hannah tried to persuade Ella to tell her the story of how she and Edward had met, hoping that revisiting such a happy memory would push away Ella's dark mood. Her efforts were rewarded when, the evening before the Strawberry Fair, Ella at last

57

began to speak about it and, despite Hannah having to prompt her all the way through for the details as if she wasn't really concentrating, Hannah felt hopeful that come the morning Ella would have decided to go with them. But Ella was absent from the kitchen when Hannah came down for breakfast and it wasn't until Tyler and Hannah were about to leave that Hannah discovered her deadheading the early rose by the back door.

'We're off now.' Hannah waited a long moment to give Ella one last chance to change her mind. Hannah was wearing black pedal pushers, a white, cotton, long-sleeved top with a hood which she could put up if the sun got too hot, Ella's sunglasses, a grey silk scarf around her neck and her hair in a loose chignon. She hoped she looked a little like her mother had done on that significant day but Ella didn't notice Hannah's outfit.

'Have a lovely time, darling,' she said, but her smile didn't touch her eyes and Hannah sensed the scary darkness again so that her heart bumped when Ella called out after her, 'Oh, Hannah.'

'Yes?'

'Bring back some strawberries for me, won't you?'

This time Ella's smile released Hannah. She waved, turned and ran round the side of the house to the drive where Tyler was waiting on his motorbike, her helmet sitting on the seat behind him.

Ely was heaving. Some of the streets had been

blocked off to traffic and stalls were set up to run the length of the high street. There were street performers, a band stand and fairground rides. The smell of boiling onions from the hot dog stand filled the air; everywhere Hannah looked there were strawberries piled high.

'So, what do you want to do, squirt?' Patches of sweat were already beginning to surface on Tyler's clothes; his hair was damp at the ends. Hannah felt even hotter merely by looking at him.

They walked along the stalls on the shaded side of the street and made their first purchases: cold bottles of coke. Tyler held his against his forehead and then his neck before gulping it down in two giant swallows. Hannah sipped hers with a straw, the fizz tickling the inside of her nose.

'Hello, George, Ray,' Tyler called out.

Hannah looked up to see their neighbours from Lavender Cottage approaching. The portly figure of George and the taller, thinner form of Ray seemed to take forever to get closer as Ray shuffled slowly forward, a stick in one hand, holding onto George's arm with the other. With a shock, she remembered that Edward and Ray had been about the same age; it was impossible to imagine her father as a seventy-year-old man like Ray.

'You're as pretty as a picture,' Ray said. Each word was followed by a gasp as he struggled for breath. He looked terribly frail with his arm linked through George's for support. Hannah noticed that the sun was shining through his linen shirt, revealing the thinnest torso she'd ever seen on a man. Tyler could fell him with a single pat on his shoulder. 'You are the image of your mother.'

George had always been the hearty, jolly one of the couple but he looked exhausted in the heat and kept wiping his forehead with a handkerchief.

'Do you really think so?' She beamed at them.

'Just like the very first time we saw her,' George said and he looked at Hannah for a long moment as if she really was a creature of beauty.

'Talking of Ella,' Ray gasped out, 'isn't she with you?'

'She's not well,' Tyler said quickly and the hurried way that he'd given an excuse for her reaffirmed to Hannah that there really was something odd about her mother not wanting to come.

'Have you heard from either of your brothers recently?' George asked.

'Finn rang the other day; he's fine — you know Finn, busy making money in London. Henry we don't hear from often; he's still in Lima.'

'And are either of you interested in adventuring?'

'No,' they said loudly and simultaneously. Everyone laughed.

'It's in your bones, this place,' Ray said, his voice cracking. 'You know if you belong here. We felt it, didn't we? The moment we saw Lavender Cottage.'

'We certainly did, dear,' George said, touching

60

Ray's hand and Hannah didn't think she'd seen anyone touch another person so gently and lovingly as that.

'Now Tyler,' Ray said. 'Don't tell me you're going to wait in that house for as long as your father did before you find yourself a special young lady. How old are you now?'

Hannah giggled and glanced at Tyler who looked a little pink but she wasn't sure whether it was because of the heat.

'Twenty-seven, so I've got about ten years before I have to worry,' Tyler replied lightly. 'Anyway, it's Henry you need to have a word with. It's his turn before me. He's thirty now.'

'I remember you all as babies,' Ray sighed. 'Where have the years gone?'

'Oh no,' George cried. 'I think it's time we went. Ray is getting sentimental.'

'Indulge an old fool,' Ray wheezed but they said their goodbyes and Hannah and Tyler stood aside as they continued their slow walk down the street.

'Do you feel it's in your bones?' Hannah asked her brother.

'Well, I can't think of anywhere else I'd prefer to live, put it like that. I love that old house of ours.'

'Do you think Henry misses it? He used to know every centimetre of the area, and every creature that lived in it. Of all of us, you'd think it would be him that would find it hardest to stay away.'

'Until Edward died,' Tyler said and Hannah realized it was true; after their father died, Henry couldn't seem to stay put anywhere for long.

Only a couple of stalls further on, they bumped into Sue from the Ghost Society. Hannah introduced them. 'My brother,' Hannah said as they shook hands.

'Oh, your *brother*. I would never have guessed it but I thought he looked too old to be your boyfriend.'

Sue held on to Tyler's hand and stared at him far longer than was normal. As he stepped back, Tyler raised an eyebrow at Hannah who could only shrug in response.

'I'm surprised to see you out on such a sunny day,' Sue said, switching her attention to Hannah.

'Why's that?' Tyler cut in before Hannah had a chance to reply. She caught the tone in his voice but Sue obviously hadn't.

'I thought the sun was dangerous for albinos.' It was the sincerity of people's smiles which Hannah sometimes found upsetting. At times like these she tried to remember Edward's advice which was 'to be the bigger person'.

'Like a vampire, you mean? You think she only comes out when the sun goes down.'

Sue had finally cottoned on that she'd done something wrong but it was clear she still didn't know what. Hannah almost felt sorry for her.

'I'm fine, Sue, as long as I wear sun block,' Hannah told her, pinching hold of Tyler's T-shirt and giving it a tug. Her honey-bear brother rarely got angry but, when he did, you had to watch out for the hefty swing of his paw and the swipe of his claws.

'You should try it sometime,' Tyler added, as Hannah pulled his T-shirt again to move him away. He pointed to the shiny patches of sunburn which had formed on the top of Sue's bare shoulders. 'You're going to be sore tomorrow.'

'Bye, Sue. See you next month,' Hannah called out cheerfully, but Sue was too busy examining her sunburn to do more than mumble a goodbye.

'That was a bit mean,' Hannah told Tyler.

'She thoroughly deserved it.'

They walked in silence for a moment. 'I don't mind, you know,' Hannah said. 'But thanks anyway.'

'That's what brothers are for,' he replied. 'Oh, and Hannah, you can let go of me now.'

'Sorry!' She patted his T-shirt back into shape.

'I need a drink, squirt, or I'm going to die,' he said as they approached the Red Horse. 'I told Colin we might be coming here,' he added, as they went inside and it was Colin's dark form at the bar which Hannah recognized in the seconds it took for her vision to adjust to the grey light.

She didn't really fancy any alcohol so she chose an orange juice with ice which she crunched up cube by cube while she watched Tyler and Colin watching the football match on the pub TV; the screen was too high on the wall for Hannah to see the image in focus.

'I'm going to go,' she told Tyler.

'Give me ten more minutes, please, squirt.' His brown eyes switched from her face to the TV and back again.

'You stay. I'm going to get some strawberries for Ella and then I'll catch the half three bus back.' She couldn't resist ruffling his hair. 'And thanks, Tyler, for coming with me.'

★ ★ ★

When she got off the bus in the village, the pavement felt hot through the thin soles of her pumps. She took the short cut along the dyke but the heat in the open land was even more oppressive than in Ely. She put her hood up to protect the top of her head; her scalp felt like it was shrinking. Everything around her seemed to be reflecting the rays straight into her eyes and she felt dizzy with the intensity of the light. She screwed her eyes up as tight as possible and kept them focused on the ground in front of her.

Time seemed to have slowed down because when she next looked up, expecting to see the boundaries of Spindle House, she had only reached the group of pollarded oaks; she had at least the same distance to go again.

She walked down the bank and sat at the edge of the dyke. She pulled her pumps off and put her burning feet into the cold water. The contrast was painful but pleasantly numbing. She lowered the punnet of strawberries in at the edge amongst the reeds as the fruits on top were beginning to look mushy. She leaned forward and plunged her hands up to her elbows in the water. If you cool your wrists, Edward had once told her, you cool your whole body.

She didn't wait for her feet to dry so they

64

slipped around inside her pumps as she walked. She held the plastic punnet in one hand, away from her body to avoid the pink liquid which was dripping from the bottom.

She descended the bank to take the diagonal path that had been worn down through years of use towards the gap in the hedge. Something on her right in the carr caught her attention; an animal or object seemed to be caught up around the base of the buckthorn. She stopped in order to focus better but was still unable to recognize its shape. She started to push through the patch of cow parsley which was standing over a metre high; the white flower heads shook as she brushed past. It was only when she was a few steps away that she realized it was a tent: a small brown and green tent, round like an igloo, with its back close to the bottom of the trunk of the buckthorn. The camper had been lucky; usually even the edges of the carr got swampy but the ground had dried out over the last few weeks. Otherwise it was a really good spot with shelter provided by the carr and water close by. Henry and Tyler used to camp on the lower levels when they were kids, and Henry, when he came back for the summer after his first year at university, had done the same with her for a week. It had seemed like a different world away from the house.

'Hello. Hello. Anyone at home?'

There was no reply. She shielded her eyes to see if there was anyone nearby. She walked round to the other side of the tent. There was a line strung up between two willow saplings; on it was a towel which was dried to a crisp and a white T-shirt with a black slogan saying: 'IT'S RUDE TO ASK'.

Perhaps she could unzip the door and look inside; she had every right to, she told herself, as whoever it was was trespassing on her land. But she knew it would be wrong so she took one last glance around before leaving.

Hannah couldn't see Ella as she walked through the garden to the back door. Unusually the door was shut but it wasn't locked when she turned the handle. She called out but no one answered her and Scoot didn't come running. She walked down the hall to the front door and when she opened it, she saw Ella's car had gone.

She returned to the kitchen to put the strawberries in the fridge before going upstairs; She had entered Ella's room before really thinking about it but once inside she checked it over thoroughly, walking from end to end. Everything was the same as usual except that Ella had brought a white amaryllis in from the hothouse; the pot sat in the bowl of the china wash set on top of her chest of drawers. There were books and gardening magazines all over the floor beside her bed and so many on her bedside table that her lamp was set on top of them. Hannah opened the wardrobe doors but closed them almost immediately; it felt wrong to be looking at Ella's clothes when she wasn't there. She crossed the room to the window facing the back garden. Even standing at an angle, it was impossible to see the tent from here and Hannah was glad. For the moment, she'd rather Ella didn't know.

In her own room, Hannah stripped down to knickers and bra and lay on the bed. She drifted off to the sound of the wind chimes she'd hung in the window to catch the breeze.

Tyler's heavy footsteps running up the stairs woke her; her heart raced as he clumped closer. She turned to face her door as it began to open. He put his head round without coming in.

'Ella wants to talk to us.'

Hannah sat up. 'What about?'

'I've no idea. All she said was I had to come and get you.'

'I think it's something serious,' Hannah told him but he didn't reply. 'Give me a second.'

Hannah was cold. The sun had moved across the sky, leaving a cool breeze behind it. She dug out her jeans and a sweatshirt from the bottom of a drawer and pulled them on but she couldn't stop shivering.

Tyler was waiting for her at the top of the stairs; he was looking out of the circular window on the landing. This used to be her favourite window when she was tiny. She would wait for one of her brothers to come by and lift her up so that she could see out of it. One of them once told her that Edward lived on a plane and that the plane trails were him writing hello to her in the sky.

In the kitchen, Ella had laid out the china tea set which Hannah had never seen out of the oak dresser before. She placed a teapot in the middle of the table next to a plate of cream cakes. It made Hannah think of the Mad Hatter's tea party.

'Are we expecting the Queen?' Tyler asked, taking a seat.

'I just thought that — ' Ella looked confused; deep frown lines lay between her eyes. 'I don't know what I was thinking except to make this a bit easier, somehow.'

Hannah sat down clumsily; she glanced at Tyler who had begun to look worried. Ella hovered for a moment before joining them. She stared at her hands without speaking for what seemed like ages.

Under the table, Scoot gave a short whine and Hannah thought that it was the exact noise she could feel moving round her body, pulling every muscle and sinew tight around her heart.

'I'm going up to London, to Sadie's.'

'That'll be nice,' Tyler said in the silence that followed. 'Is Sadie OK?'

'Oh, she's fine.' Ella fidgeted. 'It's me that's . . . ' She looked at each of them in turn. 'Look, it's absolutely nothing to worry about but I've got to go to hospital. I've found something . . . a lump . . . and I need to get it checked out. Sadie's arranged for me to see a specialist. Someone she knows. He's supposed to be very good.'

Hannah felt frozen; only her eyes were capable of moving. She stared at Ella, then glanced at Tyler, then back at Ella. Tyler reached out and took Ella's hand. Their fingers squeezed together and Hannah wished that she had been the one to have made that gesture. She wished that she could have comforted Ella but she still couldn't move. She couldn't speak. She couldn't do anything.

'This specialist . . . ' Tyler said.

'He's one of the best and I'll know quickly that way. So I'll only be away a few days.'

Tyler looked at Hannah briefly. 'It's probably nothing, anyway, isn't it?'

'Probably. Almost definitely nothing.'

'When are you going?'

'Monday'

Tyler's hand touched Hannah's. 'Come on, now. It's only a test. Right, Ella?'

'And they might do a biopsy but that's only a minor exploratory operation. That's all.'

The word exploratory travelled across Hannah's mind like a space ship heading into darkness and she felt quite faint with the thought. Her vision was wobbling badly; Ella's face was a grey shape in front of her. Hannah tilted her head and everything on the table came clear. She tried really, really hard to smile and to look like she believed everything was going to be all right. She didn't know how but she managed to find the strength to reach forward and pick up the teapot. The others hastened to push their cups towards her and no one spoke while she filled each one, concentrating really hard not to spill any.

'Do you want me to go with you?' Hannah asked, putting down the teapot.

'Where?'

'To London.'

'No, darling, not this time,' Ella said and her

69

mother's immediate refusal left Hannah feeling as crushed as a little girl.

Tyler had cream on his nose from the chocolate éclair he was eating. Hannah picked up a cream doughnut and put it on her plate. Around the rim of the plate ran a thin gold band. Hannah picked at it with a nail, wondering if it was real.

'I think, I'll, I'll go and . . . ' The moment Ella stood, Scoot scrabbled up from under the table. They reached the back door at the same time but Ella let Scoot go ahead.

'Should I go after her?'

'I'd leave her alone for now,' Tyler said and when their eyes met, he offered Hannah a sympathetic smile. 'Are you OK?'

Hannah nodded. 'I knew there was something wrong. She's been acting strangely for days.'

'She would have been worrying about it, I suppose.'

'Do you think we should ring Henry?'

'What's the point? He's too far away to do anything.'

'She'll have to tell Finn. He'll be annoyed if he's kept in the dark.' 'Yes,' Tyler conceded. 'Finn will need to know.'

★ ★ ★

Hannah couldn't sleep. She stood at the open window. The owls were calling across the fields at the back. She wondered if either of the others was awake and stepped quietly outside her room to see if Ella's light was still on. It wasn't. She

70

resumed her position at her window. The moon was at the front of the house but it was so bright it gave a silver sheen to the darkness.

By the heavily shadowed hedge, Hannah saw a flash; then the bouncing yellow light she'd seen the other night moved rapidly for a few seconds before it disappeared. She had forgotten about the mystery camper and the thought filled her with a quick, hot anger. She stared fixedly ahead, willing her anger to penetrate the darkness and jab at the stranger's conscience. She would tell Tyler tomorrow, she decided, and have them moved off.

6

Hannah watched Ella from the back door. She was sitting at the garden table with her morning cup of coffee, staring into space. Hannah was unsure whether she should act as if nothing had happened or if she should try and pick up the conversation from yesterday and say all the reassuring, comforting things that she should have said at the time. Finally, she poured some muesli and milk into a bowl and went outside.

'Hello, love,' Ella said. She looked pale.

'Hello.' Hannah's heart was pounding. She hesitated for a moment and then gulped down a spoonful of cereal. She could feel Ella's eyes on her but she didn't dare meet them.

'What are you going to do today?' Ella asked.

'I'm not sure.'

Ella stood up. 'I'm going to have a sort out in the hothouse. Would you like to help?'

Hannah nodded up at her mother with a mouthful of muesli. Ella put a hand on her shoulder. 'Then I'll see you over there.'

Hannah took the remains of her breakfast and threw it in the kitchen bin, rinsed out the bowl and placed it in the dishwasher. She went upstairs and changed into an old pair of cotton combats, a long-sleeved T-shirt and trainers, and tied her hair back into such a tight bun she felt her scalp protest.

Ella's face was flushed. She wiped at her

forehead with the back of a soil-dirty hand.

'I should have done this earlier,' she said.

The first job was to take the citrus trees over to the patio. They manhandled a heavy pot onto the sack barrow, trying not to damage any of the fruit. Ella pushed it while Hannah walked alongside, keeping the tree in place; the three shallow steps onto the patio were the trickiest and they had to rest after each one, breathless and sweating. Every year they did this together but Hannah didn't remember it ever being this hot. Even Scoot didn't bother them; usually he'd be getting in their way, nearly tripping them up; instead he lay under the hebe, watching and panting.

It took them over an hour to get all the citrus trees in situ; next they filled the wheelbarrow with the smaller pots of lilies and pelargoniums and dozens of smaller plants that Hannah didn't know the names of. Hannah carefully unloaded each batch under the sycamore tree where they were to stay until Ella had time to place them in their summer spots while Ella rearranged the staging and the plants inside the hothouse for the rest of the season.

By the time Hannah had finished the last lot, she felt exhausted.

'I don't know why I always grow so many plants,' Ella said, touching the leaves of a half-a-metre-high tomato plant. Hannah looked at the lush growth of the tomatoes, cucumbers, aubergines and peppers; it was only a few weeks ago that they had spent a rainy day potting on these as tiny seedlings. 'We never eat half of it.'

'George and Ray would starve if you didn't,' Hannah said. Ella always kept their neighbours at Lavender Cottage stocked with fresh vegetables and fruit.

'I think we deserve some lunch.'

They ate cheese and pickle sandwiches at the garden table under the shade of the umbrella. Every time Hannah lifted her hand to her mouth, she could smell the musky scent of tomatoes even though she'd washed her hands.

They had exchanged few words while they were working — there had been no energy left for thought and conversation — but now that they'd stopped and she was beginning to cool down, Hannah felt all her worries returning.

She pretended to be interested in the view across the garden while under cover of her sunglasses she looked at Ella for signs of illness. Flushed from the heat, she was no longer pale and she looked to Hannah as strong and beautiful as she always did. Hannah's eyes travelled down; the skin on Ella's chest was freckled and creased where it dipped down between her breasts.

Hannah's eyes flew back up to Ella's face. Ella was looking at her.

'Better?' she asked and Hannah nodded even though she had no idea what Ella was asking.

'I'm going to go for a walk,' Hannah said and stood up clumsily, knocking into the table.

'Let your lunch go down first,' Ella said and for some reason this made Hannah feel like crying. She gulped down air and walked into the house.

By the time Hannah came downstairs, Ella had cleared the table of their lunch things and was nowhere to be seen. It wasn't until Hannah was almost at the gap in the hedge that she remembered the tent. She hoped that it had gone but as soon as she came parallel with the edge of the carr she could see that it hadn't.

'Hello,' she called again, marching straight up to it. Seeing that it was zipped closed, she bent down and slapped the material where the entrance was several times. 'Hello. Anyone home? Hello.'

She straightened up. The towel and T-shirt had gone from the line so she knew that the camper had been back. She stepped around looking for further evidence and saw a patch of burnt grass left by a fire a couple of metres away from the tent. The camper had dug a circle of earth around it as Henry had taught Hannah to do but the barrier was nowhere near wide enough. The grass was so tinder-dry at the moment one spark could set everything off. She put her hands on her hips and scanned around. No human-shaped form disclosed itself out of the wavering, sun-shimmering landscape.

Hannah walked along the bank for half a mile towards the road where the bridge crossed the dyke. Almost another half a mile further, on the other side of the bridge, was a pumping station but even at this distance Hannah could hear the boom and feel the pulse of it beneath her feet. She descended the bank and picked up the footpath which crossed pasture land over to a stile. This was at the perimeter of the nature

75

reserve which had been fenced off for the protection of the birds and animals inside. A large flock of lapwings flew up in front of her, their pee-wit cries filling the air; they circled overhead and landed back in the field behind her.

She climbed the tall, wooden stile and jumped down onto the boardwalk. The whole of the nature reserve was criss-crossed by a series of these boardwalks but Hannah was only going as far as the pond.

Ten years ago, when she had first started coming here on her own, the reeds and rushes had been much patchier and not as extensive as now. At the height of summer, some of the rushes grew as tall as Hannah but even this early on in the season they were high enough for her to feel like she was stepping into a private world cut off from anywhere else. She pulled her sun hat low over her forehead and kept her eyes level with the shorter reeds where the light was kinder. The birds were busy around her. As she walked, reed warblers — fluffy balls of feathers — flew across her path and a bunting bobbed along in front of her, enticing her away from its nest. The rushes shifted and rippled in the light breeze which was blowing through; as a child, Hannah had thought that amongst their shush-shush noise, she could hear soft voices whispering. Today, the sound was comforting.

When she reached the pond she was shocked to see it was so low that the yellow flag irises stood completely out of the water. She sat on the boardwalk with her legs over the side and her feet touched dried mud. Water mint was growing up between the slats of the boardwalk so she reached out and picked off a leaf; its refreshing scent covered her finger-tips. The good weather had brought the jewel-coloured damselflies and dragonflies out in numbers and Hannah watched two male Darters as they argued over territory, their wings crackling when they touched.

Even as kids, they'd never been allowed to swim in the pond.

'It belongs to the animals, not us,' Edward had impressed upon her brothers who had passed the ruling on to her. Spending time at the pond was one of Hannah's favourite childhood pastimes — if she could persuade one of her older, busy brothers to accompany her. She loved to catch creatures with her net and observe them in glass jars before putting them back. Frogs and fish and the tiny dragon-like newts which hung in the water in suspended animation until something tasty, or a rival, passed by when they'd be gone with a flick of their tails. Hannah loved the delicate detail of them; the long toes of the newts and their speckled orange bellies; the creepy caddis-fly larva with its weird homemade protective case built of leaves and sand and gravel; the Great Ramshorn snail whose shell looked as if it was carved out of mahogany.

A movement at the edge of the pond caught Hannah's attention. A water vole appeared to her right and sat on the bank, washing its face, its nose twitching like crazy, its eyes black and beady. She knew how to keep so still that she could become invisible, despite the hard ridges of wood that were beginning to press into the bones in her bum but the vole froze and with a flash disappeared into the undergrowth.

She lay on her back and closed her eyes. Edward always said you could hear more that way. She felt herself drifting to sleep until she became aware that the breeze had stopped, the birds had quietened and into the silence crept Hannah's worry about Ella. She got up quickly and started back to the house, her footsteps bouncing along the boardwalk.

She had been walking along the top of the bank for several minutes before she realized that the black silhouette of a person was picked out against the blue sky. It was impossible for her to gauge the distance or the direction they were walking in but as she continued the figure seemed to become clearer so she was almost certain they were headed her way.

She was almost at the edge of the carr when she realized that this must be the mystery camper and that their paths would shortly cross. She felt her earlier bravery about confronting him seeping away with each step so she dropped to the ground and, crouching low, she descended the bank where she began to run, hunched forward, breaking through the long grass, trying her best to avoid any nettles. As she came parallel with the tent, she stopped and slowly straightened up.

The camper was still approaching and, while Hannah was hesitating about when to make her break for the gap in the hedge, he came close enough for her to recognize him. It was Toby

— the new boy, from the Ghost Society. He stopped and Hannah crouched down and counted to a hundred. Slowly, slowly she stood up to find that Toby was shielding his eyes and looking in her direction. He waved to her.

She waved back and then sprinted as fast as she could to the gap in the hedge and the safety of her garden. She sprinted across the lawn, straight into the house and up to her bedroom. She threw herself onto the bed and lay there, blood booming around her body, the cloud mobile above her bed spinning in the swirl of air she had created.

When she had sufficiently recovered, she went to the window and looked down in the direction of the tent. She didn't want to think how odd her behaviour must have looked, how weird she must seem to Toby now.

7

'You mustn't worry,' Ella told Hannah, who immediately said, 'No, I won't.'

It was a lie. Of course she was going to worry and they both knew that but Hannah guessed Ella was asking her to pretend.

Tyler appeared for an early breakfast; he was taking Hannah to work once Ella had left. They ate in silence punctuated with instructions from Ella about the jobs to do in the garden and when and what to feed Scoot.

'Bloody hell, you're only supposed to be going for a few days,' Tyler joked as they all watched Scoot gobble down the remains of the scrambled egg that Ella hadn't touched.

'That really goes to show you how much I do every day that you don't notice,' Ella told him and tweaked his cheek as if he was a little boy.

'I notice,' Hannah said and felt awkward when they both turned and looked at her.

At eight o'clock, all three of them watched from the front steps as the taxi bumped down the driveway, straight into the pothole they all knew to avoid.

'I'd better give you these.' Ella handed her car keys to Tyler.

Scoot had been lying quietly on the drive but as soon as Ella was close to the taxi he leapt forward and Hannah had to run over and grab him. She held him by the scruff of his neck but he was wriggling so badly that Tyler scooped him away from her, dropping Ella's car keys. Hannah bent forward to retrieve them and when she straightened up, the taxi had already turned round and there was only the dark shape of Ella visible to her. She shielded her eyes and waved but she couldn't tell if Ella had returned her wave or not.

'We need to get you to work, squirt,' Tyler said. 'Unlock the car and I'll stick Scoot in the back.'

He deposited Scoot inside the car. 'I'll fetch your box of cleaning stuff and you get whatever else you need.'

Hannah changed into her uniform and then went to find something to take for lunch. In the fridge, the sight of her lunch box packed with sandwiches and sticks of carrots and cucumber that Ella must have prepared earlier that morning seemed to suck out her ability to move. It was Tyler's beeping of the car horn that sent her spinning into motion. Stuffing the box into a carrier bag, she grabbed her handbag, slipped her feet into her shoes and set off so quickly that one shoe wasn't on properly and she shuffled awkwardly down the hall and out of the front door.

Tyler looked enormous in Ella's car and when he wound down his window the whole car shifted with his movement.

'I don't know how Mum drives this thing,' he said as the gears gave a grinding noise and the car bucked forward but by the time they were passing Lavender Cottage the car had settled

81

under his hands and they progressed so smoothly and calmly it seemed as if they were on completely different roads to the ones she travelled with Ella.

The only time Tyler beeped the horn was at a blind bend and he slowed down when a vehicle came into sight ahead instead of accelerating until they were up close to its rear like Ella did.

Scoot was standing with his paws on the back seat, panting furiously.

'He won't jump out, will he?' Tyler asked as Hannah leaned back to wind down a window for him.

'I don't think so.' But on second thoughts it seemed quite possible that he would leap out and go running across fields and crossing dykes in pursuit of Ella so Hannah only opened it wide enough for him to poke out his nose.

'Spent a bit on this place, I'd say,' Tyler commented as they drove through the gates. 'Can't say I like it that much.'

'Nor me.'

Her Monday house was built on the site of an old piggery of the farm which had been developed into Ely golf course. The main reason that Hannah disliked the house was that it was painted white and it hurt her eyes to look at it on all but the rainiest, gloomiest days.

Once she'd checked round the property, she phoned into the office and then set to work.

Inside was stark with whites and silvers and she found the use of sheets of glass for wall partitions disorientating and excessive; even some of the furniture, including one of the baths, was made of glass. It took ages to clean and Hannah could get through almost half a bottle of glass cleaner each time. She worried that one day she would drop something heavy or walk into one of the walls and the vibrations would cause the whole interior to crack and break and come crashing down on her.

★ ★ ★

Tyler arrived to pick her up earlier than they'd arranged and by the time she'd reached the front door he was out of the car and Scoot was running loose around the garden.

'You're not allowed to come in,' she told Tyler as he advanced towards her. 'And you'll have to put Scoot back in case he poops.'

She should have rung the agency to explain that her arrangements had changed temporarily. She felt breathless, panicked, as if she had done something wrong.

Tyler peered at her. 'Who do you work for? The Gestapo? What's so great about the place anyhow?' he grumbled but headed back to the car, whistling to Scoot.

'Ella rang to say she arrived safely,' Tyler said when Hannah got in.

'Why didn't you say something before? Is she OK?'

'Yes, she's fine, and I didn't dare, after my chilly welcome,' he said and winked before starting the car.

'They're very strict about security and privacy.'

'Paranoid, more like.'

'So?' Hannah said after waiting as long as she could for Tyler to speak. He looked puzzled. 'What else did Ella say?'

'Oh, nothing much. She was about to go for her consultancy so that she's all set for Wednesday. She sent her love and asked me to remind you to water the plants in the hothouse thoroughly.'

'I was going to,' Hannah said and she felt put out that Ella had made a point of saying it as if she didn't trust Hannah to do it right.

★ ★ ★

After a shower, Hannah lay on her bed in her underwear with her notebook in front of her. She put on her glasses and picked up her pen but no matter how hard she tried the words in front of her jumped around like fleas and her mind kept drifting off to think of Ella.

Scoot was whining outside her door so she got up to let him in and returned to the bed while he wandered around the room, trying one spot after another to lie in before standing next to her bed and fixing her with sorrowful eyes.

'I feel the same,' she told him, getting up. She opened her wardrobe which she stared into for several minutes before deciding on her sailor-blue, narrow-legged cotton trousers, a pale-blue, long-sleeved voile blouse, white lace-up canvas shoes and a white crochet hat.

Scoot ran ahead of her downstairs and into the garden where Hannah let her gaze travel across the greens and colours of the plants and flowers until they alighted on the bed of irises which were in full bloom. She fetched a sharp knife from the kitchen and cut ten stems from different parts of the bed so that she didn't spoil the display. She wrapped some damp loo paper around the ends and then set off towards the gap in the hedge where Scoot caught up with her.

'That's a good boy,' she said and felt cheered by having him with her. She crept forward, expecting Scoot to dash straight to the tent and start barking but, after trotting over to inspect it, he returned to her and she set off towards the village. It was still warm even though there was low cloud and a fresh breeze which made her loose sleeves fill with air.

Hannah entered the churchyard from the top gate and walked along the back of the church to the opposite corner. The graveyard smelt dusty-sweet from the freshly mown grass which lay in soft heaps amongst the graves. Some had scattered onto the gravel pathway and her white plimsolls were soon speckled with green from grass juice. Edward's grave was in one of the older parts of the graveyard where many of the headstones were so ancient the inscriptions had worn away and they were broken and listing like rotten teeth.

Edward had one of the nicest spots. It was situated on the shallow rise of the hill before it sloped away to the perimeter wall out of which Ella had prised little rootlets of white valerian which now grew abundantly in the garden at Spindle House.

Between the wall and Edward was one of five ancient yew trees which protected the graveyard. Its trunk had grown like a giant cup and Hannah had sat in it and read a book while Edward and Ella weeded the family graves and scraped off the moss from the headstones which, Edward joked, grew like bacteria in a Petri dish. Closer up, Hannah saw the tell-tale blackened wood from a lightning hit which had split the yew open at the heart a few years ago.

Hannah placed the flowers in front of Edward's marble stone which looked as clean as when it had first been laid and sat down on the grass beside it.

'She'll be fine.' It was Hannah who had said the words out loud but the reassurance she felt was as if Edward had spoken the words through her. Scoot lay close to her, his flank heaving up and down. The white fur on his front paws was flecked with green like her shoes.

She stayed for ten minutes more until the resumption of the mower broke into her peace. The sky had begun to clear and it seemed as if the rain would fail to come after all.

* * *

They were almost home when Scoot shot forward, barking like crazy. Hannah caught him up where he stood growling at the open tent. She grabbed his collar and leaned forward but there was no one inside. She let go of Scoot and squatted down at the entrance; her eyes took a moment to accustom themselves to the green-brown light. She liked the roundness of the roof and the patterns the branches of the trees played across it. She could make out a sleeping bag which had been rolled up, clothes in a tidy pile on one side, and a small pile of books whose titles she couldn't read. She knelt down and leaned further in.

She shrieked as a hand touched her back and she spun round to face Toby,

'You scared me,' she accused, cross at being caught. She stood up and looked for Scoot who had disappeared. She whistled for the dog and glared at the young man opposite her.

'You were snooping,' he said.

'I have every right,' she told him. 'You're camping on private land. Our land.'

Toby looked unconcerned. He gazed around him. 'So that's your house then, that big house back there?'

'Yes.'

'I took a look in,' he said. 'I hope you don't mind. I was curious where that little path went to; I could see it was well-used.'

'Hey, Scoot,' Hannah called, catching sight of the dog who had ascended the bank. He turned at her voice and started to sprint towards them.

'He's not very good with strangers,' Hannah was saying as Toby crouched down to stroke him. Scoot, being contrary, rolled over and displayed his tummy to be tickled.

'At least your dog seems to like me,' Toby grinned at Hannah and she saw a flash of the piercing on his tongue. In all that made five: tongue, ear, two in one eyebrow and his lip. He pulled the one on his lip with his teeth and held it momentarily as if he was waiting for Hannah to speak.

He stood up. 'So, Hannah. Are you going to throw me off?'

'That depends.'

'It's a lovely spot, it would be rather mean of you.' He put his hands into his pockets and hunched his shoulders so his head was pushed forward slightly.

'Why are you here anyway?'

'I don't know. Exploring. Getting some space. There's a lot of space to be had here,' he added. 'At night there are thousands of stars. And the moon, have you seen it recently? Its amazing. You can see it in the sky and in the water.' They stood quietly for a moment.

'What are you doing now?'

'What, right now? I thought I'd go for a swim. Or is that not allowed either?'

She pulled a face at him. 'In the dyke? You'd better mind the eels.'

'You're kidding. Eels?'

'They grow huge,' she told him. 'Fifty years ago, when they drained the pond in our garden, there was one in it nearly three metres long and as thick as your arm.'

'Jesus.' He looked a little worriedly over at the dyke and back at Hannah. 'I've been swimming down there loads of times.'

'And there's pike. In the river. You have to watch out for them. They bit my brother Finn's toe off.'

'You're kidding.'

'Well, only the tip. And not right off. They sewed it back together but he never went swimming in the river again.'

'I don't blame him.' He pushed his hair away from his eyes; for the first time she had a fleeting glimpse of their colour, a narrow glint of green like a new shoot encased in last years sedge.

'Who would have thought such a beautiful place would be full of monsters.'

'They're not — ' Hannah stopped, realizing that he was joking. She continued anyway. 'Eels prefer to hide and pike will bite but not usually humans, although they'll take things the size of ducklings; Finn was just unlucky.'

'I feel much better already.'

'You'll be fine swimming around here. Both in the dyke and the river.'

'That's a relief, especially as it's so hot.'

'It's not usually this hot, not in June anyway.'

'I did wonder.'

'But we do get extreme weather here. When the wind comes, it's really strong; when it snows, it drifts as high as your head. There's nothing between us and Siberia.'

'Surely something?'

He was laughing at her but it was true. At least, she had always thought it was.

'So is Finn the guy whose motorbike you were on?'

'No, that's Tyler.'

'Your boyfriend?'

Hannah giggled. 'Another brother. I've got three older brothers. I'm the baby of the family. Finn's the eldest, he's married and lives in

London; Henry's the middle one and he's out in Peru; Tyler's the youngest — he's nine years older than me — and the only one who lives here with me and my mum.' As soon as she mentioned Ella, she felt the panic push against her chest. For a few minutes, she'd forgotten to worry and now it returned ten times worse.

'Are you OK?'

'I've got to go.' She turned away.

'Hannah?'

She looked back.

'What shall I do about my tent?'

'Move it to the other side of the carr, otherwise my brother might see you and make you leave.'

'What car?'

'These, um, bushes and trees. Its called carr. You'd better come forward a bit, too — its usually really boggy round here. It's only because it's been so dry that you've not sunk into the mud.'

She turned away again.

'Hey, Hannah,' he called again. 'Does that mean it's OK for me to stay?'

'For now, you can,' she called back. She had to whistle for Scoot twice before he came. 'Traitor,' she muttered as he ran past her, leading the way into the garden.

★   ★   ★

Hannah left watering the hothouse until early evening when it was cooler. She leaned over the water butt; its pond-like smell was strong but the water, as she peered at the dark circle below her, was lower than the tap outlet. She closed up the vents and then swapped the hosepipe from the water butt to the standpipe which stood on the other side of the hothouse.

There were tomatoes at all stages of growth: some still with their sun-burst flowers open, others with pale green fruits, the size of pebbles; a couple of bushes were dotted with orange and red ripening fruits. Hannah pushed her fingers gently into the soil of the cucumber grow-bag. It was dry on the surface but damp a few centimetres down. She picked off the tip of a coriander leaf and chewed it at the front of her mouth. The air looked misty with the spray from the water; daylight was leeching the light from the hothouse quickly. The flowers of the Birds of Paradise caught her eye with their flame-coloured heads.

She declined Tyler's invitation to the pub and ate supper on her own in the living room. She kept expecting Ella to appear at any moment and almost every noise made her jump. She locked up the house, leaving the key under the strawberry pot in case Tyler had forgotten his and went to bed to read.

At two in the morning, Hannah woke up. She lay still for a few minutes and then went for a pee. Instead of returning to her bedroom, she went into Ella's. Scoot was lying on the bed, curled up on the dressing gown that Ella had left there. He let out a low growl when she tried to shift him, then huffed into a tighter ball so that all she could see was a sliver of an alert brown eye in the white fluff of his tail.

She walked round and got into the other side of the bed. She reached down and touched Scoot's head and this time he licked her fingers. When she woke up to the distant sound of her alarm going off in her bedroom, he was pressed up against the back of her legs.

8

Wednesday morning, the morning of Ella's operation, was the longest Hannah had ever experienced. All the comfort she'd gained from visiting Edward's grave had left her; her stomach jumped with nerves.

The rain had finally come. The first light drops seemed to evaporate the instant they touched the hot stone of the patio but then, suddenly, as if the cloud above them had been slashed open, the water came gushing out. Dressed in pyjama bottoms and a Hello Kitty T-shirt, Hannah sat on the floor of the living room in front of the bookshelves and took out any books she could reach without getting up. She put back any which didn't contain illustrations or photographs; the others she flicked through quickly, only stopping when an image caught her eye.

The light was grey and dim and she found she was leaning closer and closer in order to see until she sighed and got up to put on the light. She wandered over to the French doors which had steamed up and wiped a patch clear; rain covered the glass on the outside, obscuring her view. She hoped Toby had moved his tent as she'd suggested, otherwise he'd be in a mud bath by now.

She made a cup of tea and sat on the settee with an old nature book she'd come across which she liked to read as a child. It was full of interesting facts. Under a photograph of the glum-looking head of an eel, she read: 'Young eels are so transparent you can read a book through them.'

The phone rang and she jumped up. Skidding on a book she'd left open on the floor, she banged against the wall, wrenching her shoulder as she put out her arm. She felt as if she'd forgotten how to move, how to breathe, as she stood over the phone.

'Hello?'

'Hannah, sweetheart, Ella's had her op and she's doing wonderfully.'

'Oh, good,' Hannah breathed down the phone, slowly finding her voice.

Sadie continued in her upbeat tone. 'We should know the results tomorrow or the next day.'

'The next day,' Hannah echoed. It hadn't occurred to her that there would be another wait before she knew that Ella was going to be all right. She felt stupid and faint. She rubbed at the muscle in her arm which felt fuzzy from where she'd banged it. Sadie was still talking. 'But tomorrow, in all probability. How are you, Hannah?'

Hannah swallowed hard. 'OK. Missing Ella, of course.'

'She misses you, too, darling, but we're having more fun than you think. Try not to worry. Have some fun yourself. There must be plenty of eligible young farmers around to distract you.' Sadie's clear laughter broke into Hannah's thoughts.

'There is this one lad I might like but he's only here on holiday.'

'A holiday romance. My favourite kind,' Sadie said. 'Oh, shoot, hang on.' There was the sound of several voices. 'I've got to go, sweetheart. So you have fun and don't worry. Ella's going to be absolutely fine.'

Hannah went upstairs to report everything to Tyler.

'You're not working?'

Tyler was sitting on the bed, playing his guitar. He put it down as soon as she came in. She spotted Scoot curled up asleep near his pillow behind him.

'It can wait.'

'She's fine,' Hannah said and added quickly, 'I mean, everything went OK today. Sadie said she'll get the results tomorrow or the next day.'

The rug slid under her bum as she sat on the floor opposite him with her back against the wardrobe door. Tyler's was the smallest bedroom but he kept it very neat. She glanced around. He'd had the same possessions for years: the guitar, the bongo drums, the ship in a bottle which came from Edward's paternal grandparents, were all things that Hannah remembered him having as a boy. The phone rang.

'It's Finn,' Tyler mouthed to her. 'Yes, Hannah just spoke to Sadie, too. Yeah, in a couple of days. I don't think so. No. No. Yes. Sure. Will do. Keep in touch, Finn, mate.'

Tyler returned to the bed. 'He wanted to know if we need him and Amy to come down.'

'What for?' Hannah said. 'Does he think we're

95

incapable of coping on our own?'

Tyler shrugged. 'Stuff like this brings out the head of the family in him, that's all. You know he's always been like it; he can't help, himself.'

'Has he seen Ella?'

'He and Amy drove over to Sadie's after they finished work. He said he offered to go with Ella to the hospital but she said no.'

'She only wants Sadie around,' Hannah said.

'He's been making some checks on Sadie's specialist friend and apparently he's pretty much top in his field.'

'Ella told him that.'

Tyler shrugged. 'He had to hear it for himself, I suppose.'

'Do you think we should ring Henry? It doesn't seem right that he's the only one of us who doesn't know. I'd want to know.'

'And then what would you do? Worry like crazy and feel awful you can't do anything because you're so far away.' Tyler stood up and walked across to his desk. He sat down and opened his laptop. He swivelled round on his chair to face Hannah. 'We'll tell him, immediately, if we need to.'

Hannah stared at him.

'But we won't need to,' he told her and swivelled back round again before she could speak. 'The rain's stopped,' he said after a moment and Hannah went over to see for herself. Leaning against his back, she could smell cigarettes and shampoo on his hair; she took a moment's comfort from the warmth and bulk of him.

'I think I'll go shopping,' she said, looking at the columns of figures, graphs and charts that populated Tyler's computer screen.

'Do you want a lift?'

'I'm going to Ely.'

'I'll drop you at the bus stop in the village if you want. Give me a shout when you're ready.'

She dressed in a light brown suede miniskirt which used to be Ella's, red flip-flops with thick white soles and a white T-shirt with batwing sleeves. She tied her hair into two long plaits; the ends tickled her neck when she twisted one way then the other in front of the mirror, imagining Ella saying how pretty she looked, like her beautiful moon child.

★ ★ ★

'Who's that lad waving? Can you see him, over by the church?' Tyler asked as he pulled up to the kerb by the village shop. The person was too far away for Hannah to be able to see his features clearly, but she could tell by his shape that it was Toby. 'Isn't he the one we saw in the pub the other day?'

'Yes. It's Toby. Was he waving at us?'

'Well, you, I should think. You'd better wave back or he'll think you're ignoring him.'

Hannah waved. 'He's not coming over, is he?' she said, panicking.

'No. Actually he's gone.'

Tyler's hand clamped down on Hannah's as she was unbuckling her seatbelt. 'Not so fast, squirt. Come on, spill the beans. How come you know his name?'

'He turned up at the Ghost Society'

'And?'

'What do you mean 'and'?'

'I have a feeling there's something else you'd like to tell me.'

'You're so nosey, Tyler,' she admonished him but she couldn't resist his twinkly, inquisitive face. 'Can you keep a secret?'

'Cross my heart . . . '

'He's camping by the carr.'

'Our carr?'

Hannah nodded.

'Why?'

She counted out the reasons on her fingers. 'He's on holiday. It's a nice spot.' She looked out of the window, checking that the bus wasn't in sight yet. 'And he's not doing any harm.'

Tyler frowned. 'Are you sure he's not casing the joint?'

'What, our place? What do we have to steal?'

'It's not only us, Hannah; there are our neighbours to consider, too.'

'No, he's not like that. I know he's not,' She didn't know how she was so sure of Toby's innocence, but she was. She met Tyler's concerned face with a fierce gaze.

He held his hands up in submission. 'OK. OK. I'll take your word for it, but the minute you suspect anything, he's gone. Deal?'

'Deal.' Glancing out of the window, she saw that the blue bus was at the top of the high street. She put her hand on the door handle and opened the door a fraction. She considered closing it and returning to Spindle House with her brother, but at the last moment she pushed the door wide. 'Thanks, Tyler,' she shouted before she ran across the road to the bus stop.

9

'I'll let you know the very moment, the absolute second after she's called if she phones while you're at work,' Tyler promised Hannah but Ella didn't call on Thursday while she was out and she didn't call in the evening either.

It was a little after eleven on Friday, when Hannah was watering the citrus trees on the patio, that Tyler yelled her name out of the window. She dropped the hosepipe and ran onto the lawn under Tyler's window.

'All clear,' he yelled with the phone in his hand. 'She's got an all clear.'

She jumped up and let out a shriek, then yelled, 'I'm coming up.' She ran towards the back door, then ran back across the garden to turn off the water at the standpipe; Scoot, thinking it was a game, chased after her, jumping up at the backs of her legs. She ran straight through the puddle of water on the patio so that she almost slipped when her flip-flops hit the stone surface in the kitchen. By the time she got up to Tyler's room, Ella had rung off.

'Everything's fine,' Tyler said. 'Panic over.'

Hannah collapsed on his bed, panting. 'That's it? Absolutely for definite? Nothing's wrong with her?'

Tyler nodded and grinned. 'Absolutely for definite.'

'I almost can't believe it.'

'Nor me. But thank fuck. She had me going for a while, there.'

'When's she coming back?'

'She didn't know. I think she might stay a couple more days.'

'A couple more days?' That seemed far too long to Hannah. She wanted Ella home, immediately, so she could see for herself. She had a feeling that she wouldn't believe that Ella was going to be all right until she actually heard her mother say the words.

★　★　★

Once Hannah had finished watering the plant pots in the garden she had a shower, carefully applied sunscreen and then opened her wardrobe. It was hard to decide what to wear; it was the hottest part of the day so she'd need to be covered up but she wanted to look nice. In the end she decided on a cornflower-blue cotton dirndl skirt which fell to a few centimetres above her ankle bones and a white silk gypsy-blouse with long sleeves. She wrapped a purple beaded necklace several times around her wrist to wear as a bracelet and added her white canvas plimsolls and hat.

Toby was sunbathing on a towel in front of his tent. He had on only a pair of baggy denim shorts and his shades. His upper arms were covered in black tattoos which looked like the symbols of an ancient language. He was getting quite tanned now and the red tone to his hair was lightening to copper.

'Hello, Hannah,' he said without moving.

'I'm going into the village,' she told him and hesitated a moment. 'If you want to come along?'

He sat up, pulled his shades down from his eyes and studied her for a moment without speaking. 'I could do with getting some supplies.' He disappeared inside his tent while Hannah waited.

'I see you moved,' she called to him. The soil beneath her feet was spongy and the tall grass was still damp at the roots; she could feel it soaking through the thin cloth of her plimsolls. She stepped forward onto the shorter, drier grass. 'Was that before or after the rain?'

His head appeared briefly. 'Oh, yeah. Before, Good tip. Thanks for that.'

He crawled out of the tent fully dressed, dragging an empty rucksack in one hand. The front of his T-shirt said 'BITE ME' and, when he turned round to zip up the tent, Hannah saw there was smaller writing on his back. She moved closer and leaned forward. She tilted her head to bring the words into focus. It read 'ON THE BUM'. She giggled.

'Something funny?'

'Your T-shirt.'

'I think there's a grasshopper in the tent,' he said. 'It sounded very loud.'

'It's probably a cricket,' Hannah told him. 'Its good luck to have one in your house.'

He looked up from lacing his red baseball boots. 'Is that so? Because I've been feeling lucky, lately.'

'Have you?' Hannah said, curious, and then smiled when she realized he was probably flirting with her. 'I don't think you've told me how long you're planning to stay for?'

'That depends whether you're going to get rid of me or not.'

'You can stay. For now. I told Tyler, so he might come and see you.'

'Is he cool about it? He won't try and beat me up, will he? He's enormous.'

'Not as long as you behave yourself.'

'What would count as misbehaving?'

'Leaving litter, not watching the fire, you know.'

'Ah,' he said. 'I thought you were talking about something altogether different.'

'Oh.' She dropped her hair forward to cover her face and stared at the ground. To her relief, Toby ended the embarrassing silence.

'Do you want to walk or shall I drive?'

'You've got a car?' She remembered then, Toby offering to give her a lift after the Ghost Society. 'Where is it?'

'On the track behind that thatched cottage.'

'Lavender Cottage? You can't go leaving it on someone's properly without their permission.'

'They have given me permission, actually. I told them I was camping here.'

'Oh, OK. Sorry.'

'George and Ray were very friendly, in fact,' he said, placing the emphasis on 'friendly' for Hannah's benefit. 'They said if you were OK with me camping, it was fine by them.'

They walked the length of the carr and turned

down the side towards a small wooden gate which was kept closed with a piece of orange rope. The gate led onto the bottom of an overgrown, narrow driveway next to Lavender Cottage's garden. A small blue car was parked on it.

'And you said it was OK with us?'

'Well, it is now, isn't it?'

Toby opened the passenger door and hot air blasted Hannah's face. She waited until he had started the engine and lowered the windows before getting inside. He reversed up the driveway, swinging left onto the track, Hannah peered past him; George and Ray would normally be in the garden on a day like today but she couldn't see any sign of them. They drove towards the village.

'Do you work?'

'I'm a student,' Toby said. 'I've just finished my second year.'

'In what?'

'Geography. But I'm specializing in cartography.'

'So what do you do after you've got a degree in cartography?'

'Lots of things: make maps, research maps.' He glanced at her. 'Lots of mappy things.'

'So you really like maps.'

He nodded. 'Sadly, I do.'

'Don't most maps already exist?'

'That's a common misconception,' he said and she wasn't sure how serious he was being. 'You'd be surprised how much of this world hasn't been mapped yet or how often maps change. Think

104

about it: a new road, a longer road, new buildings. It all means new maps.'

Hannah gave this some thought. 'You won't ever be out of a job then,' she said and felt shy when he laughed loudly. She resolved not to say anything further but found it too hard to keep quiet. 'So why have you come here? I mean, I love it, but it's not the most exciting place to have a holiday.'

'What can I say? I saw it on a map and it looked an interesting place to explore. Why are you such a big fan?'

Because it was a magical place to live, because it was in her bones, she thought but she told him, 'Just lots of reasons.'

'And what about you? Do you work?'

'I'm a Silver Maid. I clean houses for the rich and famous.'

'Round here? No way. Like who?' He faced her for so long she was afraid that they would crash.

'It's a secret. I mean it. I have actually signed a confidentiality contract; they'd probably sue me if I told.' Hannah let the outside world glide in front of her eyes in a stream of green. 'Anyway, it's no big deal; they're the same as everyone else really.'

'I bet you get massive tips.'

'Not really. One client gave me perfume for Christmas but otherwise, no. The pay's not all that brilliant actually but I like it. I like being able to think while I work.' Hannah had expected Toby to ask what it was she thought about, but he didn't; they had arrived in the village and he was too busy trying to find somewhere to park.

'You can go round the back of the church,' Hannah told him. 'There are always spaces there.'

It was a good spot, shaded from the sun by the bulk of a yew tree.

'Nice one,' Toby said and Hannah felt lifted by his appreciation.

'Shit.' She ducked down, her face was twisted to the side so she didn't miss his amused expression.

'Should I be hiding too?'

'No.' She pulled a face at him.

'Then do you mind if I ask exactly who it is you're hiding from?' He leaned his arms on the dashboard and looked through the wind-screen.

'The woman with the grey hair.'

'Her? That teeny, tiny old lady. That's who you're hiding from?'

'She was my primary school teacher.' She paused. 'She's horrible.'

'Jesus,' Toby said. 'You're shaking. I'm sorry, I didn't mean to . . . Look, she's gone now. You can sit up.' He put out his hand to help her.

'Promise?'

'I promise.'

Hannah thought she'd better explain her behaviour. 'I didn't have a very good experience at school. I was teased all the time and called names.'

'What kind of names?'

'The usual for people with albinism. Ghost. Red Eye. Vampire. Hey, Snow White, where are your dwarves? What happened to you? Did your mum bath you in bleach?'

'School is shit like that,' he said. 'I was a great target, too. A fat kid with a lisp and, I don't know if you noticed, but I'm not the prettiest boy around.'

'I like your face; it's different.'

'I've grown used to it,' he said, shrugging. 'So what's the deal with your teacher then? She didn't call you names, I hope.'

'No, but instead of standing up for me, she picked on me. People with albinism don't have the best vision in the world,' she said and stopped.

'You seem OK to me.'

She appreciated the gentle way he encouraged her to continue. 'Well, I've come off quite lightly really for someone with my condition but there are things I struggle with. Like, I'm not allowed to drive because I can't judge distances or see clearly very far — I couldn't see your face the other day in the village when you waved — and, sometimes, particularly if I'm stressed, my vision shifts and tilts and I can't always get it back in focus. That little old lady, Mrs Hibbotson, would take pleasure in asking me to read out loud and I'd get so stressed I could hardly make out a single word. She'd shout at me and say she was waiting until I was so desperate to say something that I'd make up words, any words, and then she'd shout at me even more for being insolent.'

'A classic case of a bitch of a school teacher. Where has she gone? Shall I run her over for you?'

He hunched forward, gripping hold of the steering wheel and revved the engine. Hannah laughed.

'Yes, please. Smite her down.'

'Smite her down,' he echoed and then he cut the engine. They sat quietly in the new silence. 'Did nobody ever tell you that you were beautiful?'

'Only my parents. And that doesn't really count.'

'Well, I think you're beautiful,' he said. 'If the opinion of an ugly fuck like me counts.'

Hannah's breath was caught so high up in her throat that she thought she might not be able to speak. 'It counts,' she whispered as she began to open the car door.

10

On Monday late afternoon Hannah went with Tyler to collect Ella from the train station. There were no free parking spaces as most of the station car park had been cordoned off due to subsidence of the road.

'You go and meet her,' Tyler told her. 'I'll keep circling round until you come out.'

Ella looked paler and thinner than Hannah remembered. They hugged quickly and rather awkwardly and Hannah suddenly felt shy and anxious to hurry back before Tyler had to do another lap.

'How was your journey?'

'Not bad except the air conditioning stopped working, I feel like a wilted flower.'

'Oh dear, the car is probably as hot, I'm afraid.'

'It doesn't matter. We'll soon be home.'

The word 'home' struck Hannah's heart like a pure note on a bell. She almost broke into a skip as they came out into the sunshine.

Tyler swooped the car onto the double yellow lines and Hannah quickly shoved Ella's suitcase onto the backseat and climbed in after it. She had to hold on to Scoot's collar to keep him from leaping over the front seat to Ella.

'All aboard?' Tyler yelled and pulled out into the traffic to be greeted by a blare of car horns. 'Up yours,' he shouted out of the open window.

Scoot's whining was reaching sonic heights; Hannah's heart was racing with adrenalin. She glanced at Ella who looked exhausted.

'Let him come over,' Ella said once they were out of the city centre. Scoot scrambled forward and sat in the footwell with his head on Ella's lap as if he was never going to let her out of his sight again. Hannah understood how he felt.

'How's Sadie?' Tyler asked.

'She's fine,' Ella replied and then as an afterthought added, 'She sends her love.'

'And Finn, and Amy?'

'They seemed fine. Sadie thought Amy very 'city', and that they were both very serious.'

'They always are,' Hannah said.

'But at least they made an effort to come and see me,' Ella said so sharply that Hannah wasn't sure if she should take it as a criticism.

At home, Ella sat at the kitchen table with Tyler while Hannah heated up the tomato soup she'd prepared for lunch.

'Its so lovely being home,' she repeated twice in a faraway voice.

'You haven't missed much,' Tyler told her through a mouthful of buttered bread. 'Has she, squirt?'

Ella put her spoon down. 'I'm sorry, darling, it's delicious but I really don't feel hungry.' She attempted a smile. 'I think I'll have a lie down.'

'Aren't you going into the garden?' Hannah asked. She had imagined that would be the very first thing Ella would want to do.

'Later.'

When she got up Scoot followed, his tail going furiously.

'Oh, come on then,' she told him and Hannah watched as he trotted forward, proud to be chosen.

★ ★ ★

Early evening, Hannah took Ella a cup of tea and a sandwich. She was asleep so Hannah left them on the bedside table in case she wanted something to eat when she woke up. A few hours later, when Ella still hadn't emerged from her room, Hannah looked in on her again. In the dim light she could make out Ella's form lying on top of the bedclothes, flat on her back like a carved body on top of a tomb. Scoot was lying on the floor; he raised his head and gave a whimpery greeting but he didn't move and Hannah found she couldn't go in. It was as if there was an invisible fence stopping her from going any further.

'I'll see you in the morning, sweetheart.' Ella's voice sounded wispy and distant.

'OK,' Hannah said and closed the door softly.

The next morning, Ella wasn't up by eight so Hannah knocked and put her head round the bedroom door. Ella was still in bed.

'Shall I ask Tyler to take me to work?'

Hannah could hardly see Ella's face under the mess of dark hair. 'Would you?' she said, which Hannah hadn't expected.

In the car, Hannah sat silently.

'She's tired,' Tyler said. 'The worry probably knocked her for six, she'll soon bounce back.'

★ ★ ★

After Hannah had finished work, she waited outside on the drive for Ella but ten minutes went by, then twenty, then thirty. Hannah rang the house but nobody answered. She rang Tyler's mobile.

'Where are you?'

'In the house.'

'Why didn't you answer the phone when I called a minute ago?'

'I was in the loo. What's the panic?'

'Is Ella there?'

'I don't think so. Hang on.' She could hear his feet lumping across the wooden floor; then there was a bang and then silence. A few seconds later, he said, 'Her car's not here. She must be on her way to get you.'

'I don't think so. I think something's happened to her — or to the car — maybe. Can you come anyway? You'll pass her if she's picked me up. If not, I can come back with you.'

'You won't get your box of stuff on the Fizzy.'

'Oh no! What shall I do? I'll have to leave it. What's happened to her, Tyler?' Hannah couldn't stop her voice ending in a wail.

'Don't worry. I'll come now and we'll figure it out.'

Hannah carried her box as far down the drive as her arms could take; she lowered it onto the ground and caught her breath. Then she dragged it for a few metres until it was close enough for her to manage the last part to the gate. She retraced her steps along the line which the box had scoured across the cream paving and scuffed over it with her foot so that it didn't stand out so clearly. She unlocked the house, deactivated the alarm, pressed the security button to open the gates, reactivated the alarm, ran out of the house, locked it, then sprinted down the drive where she picked up her box and stumbled out of the gate before it started to close again.

She felt exhausted. She sat on the right-hand side of the gates in the shade of the tapered conifer. She watched a marsh harrier float across the fields in front of her, only a few metres away. In the silence she could hear the sound of Tyler's Fizzy long before she could see it.

'No sign of her?'

Tyler shook his head. 'I've brought bungee cords.' He held two up. 'I thought we could tie the box to the seat and you could sit on top of it.'

It soon became clear that the box took up far too much room for that to be possible so in the end Hannah held the box on her knee as she sat back-to-back to Tyler tied together by a bungee cord tight around their waists.

The whole journey home Hannah struggled to keep the heavy box balanced on her legs. She kept a look-out for Ella's car and strained her vision so much that by the time they reached the track up to Spindle House she had a severe headache.

Ella's car was in the drive and she opened the

front door of the house as Tyler steered in beside it.

'Oh my God,' Ella said, lifting the box off Hannah. 'How resourceful, kids.' She undid the bungee cord and when Hannah got off the bike, she felt like she was floating.

'I'm so sorry, Hannah, you should have reminded me; I completely forgot it was Tuesday. I'm completely out of the routine of it all.'

The pain in Hannah's head was so acute she could hardly lift her eyes. 'So what about work on Thursday?'

'Of course, darling. Everything will be back to normal on Thursday,' she said, sounding surprised.

⋆ ⋆ ⋆

On Wednesday morning, Hannah was relieved to hear the creaking of floorboards that let her know Ella was up. Hannah decided to take a quick shower and join her mother for breakfast but when she returned to her bedroom Hannah's notebook, lying on the desk, seemed to pull her towards it. Its glossy red cover was glowing at her, filling her with such a desire to write that she hardly dared take her eyes off it while she towelled herself dry, put on knickers and a vest and picked up her glasses case.

Sitting at her desk, she placed both hands on the cover; it was almost shocking to find it cool to the touch when it had looked so charged with heat. She opened it and certain words jumped out at her as she slowly turned the pages: patter,

114

bitter, forgotten, ramble, motionless, flint. She only realized that she had been breathing rapidly and high up in her chest as her breath slowed and her body began to relax. She reached the first blank page and held her pen poised for a moment before she wrote the title: *The Silver Eel*.

She stopped only briefly to rest her eyes, to tilt her head and allow the black lines to separate and come clear before continuing on. Page after page she filled, not daring to question what she was writing, letting the words spill out of her pen onto the page. It was nearly twelve when the words started to dry up and her hunger became so acute she could picture the sandwich on a plate as if it was in front of her.

When she went downstairs, Scoot came out of the living room to greet her and then went back in. Hannah followed him and found Ella was lying on the settee facing the bookshelves with all the curtains closed. Hannah crept forward, trying to see in the dim light if Ella was awake.

'What is it, Hannah?'

'I was wondering what time we were going to Ely?' Hannah felt obliged to fill the silence that followed her question. 'Unless you want to leave it and go another day.'

'Lets leave it,' Ella said. 'There's nothing we need urgently, is there, darling?'

'No. Nothing urgent.'

'Good, because I don't really feel like bothering today.'

'Well, we'd better not bother then,' Hannah said and turned abruptly, her churlish tone

115

echoing around the gloomy room behind her.

As soon as she was in the kitchen, she sank onto a chair. Her legs were trembling and she felt teary that she should have spoken to Ella in such a way but inside she also felt angry. She made herself a sandwich and ate too quickly to enjoy it, feeling guilty for not offering to prepare something for Ella. *Let her get it herself*, she thought. *See if she can be bothered about that.*

She went upstairs and changed out of the dress that she'd put on to go to Ely into a pair of cargo pants, a long-sleeved T-shirt and her red plimsolls. She didn't stop to say goodbye to Ella as she went out.

Toby's tent was open but she couldn't see him at first. She spotted him lying on his front a little bit further away, half-hidden by the tall grass and cow parsley.

'You've frightened off all the rabbits,' he said as she came close.

'They'll come back.'

She sat on the ground next to him and in only a few minutes the rabbits emerged only a metre away from them so that Hannah could clearly see them as they shuffled along the bank, their noses ceaselessly twitching.

'Look,' Hannah said and pointed to a bare patch of soil to her right where there was a lizard sunning itself. 'In Africa, the lizard is thought to be a shape-shifter, transforming itself at will into a leopard or lion.'

'Well, I hope this one is happy staying as a lizard,' Toby said and rolled over to face her. The lizard was gone in a flash.

'Do you want to go for a walk?' she asked Toby.

'OK,' he replied, already standing up. 'Lead the way.'

They walked along the bank in the direction of the nature reserve. As they neared the road, Toby stopped and said, 'What's that noise?'

'It's the pumping station,' Hannah explained.

'Pumping what?'

'Water. This land would all be under water if there weren't any pumps.'

Hannah led the way down the bank below the bridge and they walked side-by-side through the pasture land. There was a group of oystercatchers as well as the lapwings on the far side of the field, too far away to be disturbed. A car passed on the road to their left but that was the only traffic they heard.

They crossed the wooden stile onto the boardwalk. Hannah was sure the reeds had grown several centimetres since she'd last been there. A breeze brushed past them and then dropped. Hannah could feel the boards flexing under their combined weight as they walked.

'What is this place?'

'It's a nature reserve.'

'It feels like the middle of nowhere.'

They arrived at the pond which had filled a little from the rain. Damselflies took it in turns to fly around in front of them as if they were putting on a special display.

'What are they?' Toby asked and Hannah had to hide her surprise that he didn't know before she told him.

Toby lay on his back on the boardwalk and Hannah sat down next to him.

'Can you smell something?' Toby asked.

'It's mint.' She pointed to the leaves of the plant which they had crushed underfoot. He pressed his nose into it which reminded her of Scoot. 'Wow, that's strong.'

She felt him tugging on her sleeve.

'Lie down,' he said, so she lay on her side facing him. 'Nobody can see us. We are totally and absolutely alone.'

She felt fixed in place by his eyes, like a specimen insect pinned to a display board and a shiver went through her at the thought of the danger she could have put herself in, to have come to such a lonely spot with a man she barely knew.

'Hannah,' he said and she thought her heart was going to stop as his hand came towards her. Slowly, slowly, as if time was grinding to a halt.

The air was suddenly filled with a whooshing, throbbing noise as a pair of swans flew so low overhead that Hannah could see the black of their feet tucked into their white bellies.

'Swans are beautiful,' Toby said, rolling onto his back. 'But a bit scary.'

'In medieval times, people were suspicious of swans,' Hannah told him. It seemed as if the passage of the swans had stirred up the air around them and jogged time back to normal. It even felt cooler. 'Because they believed that the flesh under the white feathers was black.'

'How do you know all this stuff?'

'Books. And my dad used to talk loads about it when he was alive.'

'Oh, he's . . . um . . . '

Hannah nodded. 'Dead. Yes. Nearly five years.'

'I'm sorry.'

'It's OK,' Hannah said but she felt tears spring suddenly into her eyes. She blinked hard. 'This was his place, his family's home for generations. He knew it inside out.'

Toby stood, held out his hand and pulled Hannah up. 'Like you do.'

She looked at him in surprise. 'Yes, I suppose I do. Yes, like me.'

★ ★ ★

As soon as she came into the garden, Hannah headed to the hothouse to see if Ella was there. The door was open but the air inside was so hot it burned her skin as if it was sticking to her. She hurried to open the vents and then looked around; in every direction there were plants wilting and dropping leaves and flowers. She put her fingers into some of the pots and found that they were dry.

'Poor things,' she said out loud, imagining their roots crackling like bleached tinder, their tendrils sucking uselessly for water from the dry-as-dust soil.

She went outside and turned on the standpipe. In the hothouse she attached the rose to the end of the hosepipe and sprayed the air and foliage of the plants to cool everything down before watering thoroughly, returning to each pot at

119

least twice to make sure that the soil was soaked through.

When she had finished she went into the house and called Ella. Tyler appeared at the top of the stairs.

'She's gone out,' he said as she walked up the stairs towards him. 'I thought you were with her.'

'No,' Hannah said and carried on past him without stopping into her bedroom and closed the door.

* * *

On Thursday, the next morning, Ella didn't appear when Hannah got up. She ate her breakfast, prepared her lunch, showered, dressed and packed everything she needed to take to work and then, having left it until the last minute and there was still no sign of Ella, she tapped lightly on her mother's bedroom door and pushed it slowly open.

Ella was already sitting up in bed. 'I've overslept, Hannah. Give me five minutes.'

'I could ask Tyler.'

'Just make your mummy a coffee in the little covered mug and we'll be off.'

They bumped down the track in silence, and it wasn't until they were five minutes from Hannah's client's house that Ella spoke. 'I'm so sorry, darling; I can't seem to find the energy for anything at the moment.'

Except, Hannah thought, she'd managed to go out yesterday in the car. Hannah couldn't hold back. 'Are you really OK?'

'What do you mean?'

Hannah tilted her head, tried to keep Ella's face as clear as possible so that she could see her reaction. 'You weren't lying — the tests were clear?'

'Darling, of course they were clear. I wouldn't lie to you about that.' Ella turned, briefly, to face her. Hannah heard the surprise in her voice and saw in her face that Ella hadn't for one moment imagined that her daughter could be worrying about her. 'I think it's the shock catching up with me,' she said, but her words fell quietly away as if she wasn't sure herself that this was the reason. 'Give me a few days and I'll be as right as rain.'

11

Although it was the afternoon and hot as a stove, Toby looked as if he'd only recently got up. He was taking a pee in the bushes when Hannah arrived at the tent and when he turned round his face looked even more squashed than normal and his hair was tangled like a dogwood thicket.

'I need a coffee,' he said, his words distorting from an immense yawn which gave Hannah plain sight of the red inside of his mouth and the round metal ball sitting in the middle of his tongue like a dark pearl inside a river oyster.

He squatted down and began to stir the ash from the previous night's fire with the remains of a partly charred twig.

'We could make one in the house.'

'You're inviting me up to the Big House? I'm honoured.'

'You might get some breakfast, too, if you're lucky.'

They ate eggs on toast in the kitchen but took their coffee into the garden. Hannah sat under the shade of the umbrella while Toby moved his chair away from the table and sat with his face turned up to the sun.

'Do I get the Grand Tour?' he asked when they'd drunk their coffee.

'Would you like to?' Hannah said, surprised.

'Why not? It looks an interesting place.' He twisted his head round and looked up at Spindle

House then back, at Hannah. 'If you don't mind?'

'I'd like to,' she told him and stood up. She picked up their mugs and carried them into the kitchen. 'Kitchen,' she announced. 'Which you've just been in.'

They passed straight through and into the hall. 'Hallway.'

'Big hallway,' Toby said, gazing up at the high ceiling and then stopped in front of the wall, his mouth open. 'Woah, Grim Reaper.'

'Its a reed sickle,' Hannah explained as Toby touched the blade with his thumb. 'Watch it. It's sharp.'

She led him into the living room and he gazed around with an expression on his face that Hannah recognized from other visitors to the house, a mixture of awe at the size of the room and confusion at the array of belongings and mixture of furnishings.

'There are a lot of books.'

'Yes.'

'A lot of gardening ones,' he said, walking along the shelves. 'I take it these are your mum's?'

'Yes. She collects them.'

He picked up a framed photograph, 'Is that your granddad?'

'That's Edward, my dad. He was fourteen years older than Ella.'

'What happened to him?'

'He got septicaemia from a cut on his hand when he was in Eritrea, working on a project to do with tree frogs.'

'So what was he? A conservationist?'

'A professor.'

Hannah opened the adjoining doors into the front room. 'It's always dark in here.' She pulled open the curtains, letting in a weak, grey light which hardly reached the corners.

'What's this?'

'A punt gun, and that's stuff from the dray horses which Edward's grandparents kept. This was my dad's.' She showed him a Victorian bag, like a doctor's bag, which contained a microscope, glass sample jars and lots of small, pointed tools. 'Edward collected antique research equipment but we donated most of it to the Museum in Ely.'

'This is a pretty amazing place,' he said as he followed her upstairs.

'I think so,' Hannah replied and she couldn't help smiling to herself.

A loud thumping preceded the appearance of Tyler above them. 'Hello, I thought I heard voices.' He leaned on the balustrade and watched them ascend the final stairs.

'This is Toby. Toby, my brother Tyler.'

'Ah ha! Our mystery camper.'

'I'm showing Toby around.'

'It's amazing,' Toby said. 'It's like a . . . museum . . . or something.'

'Definitely 'or something',' Tyler said, straightening up, and Hannah was shocked to see Toby colour slightly.

'There's only Tyler's room and a storage room on the third floor, all boring, so we won't bother going up there,' Hannah said and

124

made a face at her brother.

'We're closed to visitors today anyway.' He made a face back and turned towards his stairs. 'I'll leave you kids to it. Be good.' He stopped on the bottom stair. 'By the way, have you seen Ella?'

Hannah shrugged. 'No. She's out somewhere. Her car's gone. But I don't know where.'

When she opened her door, Hannah was confronted with the sight of her bedroom through the eyes of a stranger. After the dark wood and cool air of the other rooms, hers was bright with sunlight and there was colour in every direction you looked. The best part of the room was the cast iron fireplace under the uneven ceiling. On the mantelpiece were small stone and ceramic creatures that Edward had brought back for her from all over the world: a Japanese frog, a scorpion from Egypt, a jackal from South Africa, the tusked hog from Kenya. She also liked the way her oak desk was arranged, with all the spines of her coloured notebooks in a row across the back and her pens in a big red pot on top of the bureau drawers. She was less comfortable with the old china-headed doll which sat next to the pot and the framed illustration of Jeremy Fisher on a lily pad with his fishing rod on the wall above it.

'Can you see my tent from here?' Toby asked, looking out of the window.

'You can't see it from anywhere in the house,' Hannah said, and leaned across him to open the window wider. She heard the sound of a car on the drive. 'I think that's Ella.'

'Are you going to sneak me out?'

They held each other's gaze for several seconds. 'Don't be silly,' Hannah said. 'Come on, you can meet her.'

Ella was in the kitchen making a cup of a tea and she jumped at the sound of Hannah's voice.

'Who's that?' she asked and Hannah realized that she meant Toby, who was standing behind her.

'This is Toby,' Hannah said and moved aside to let him in. Scoot dashed forward and began to sniff around his trainers.

'Toby?'

'Hello.' Toby stuck out his hand to shake Ella's.

'Toby's on holiday here,' Hannah said.

Ella's eyes switched from Hannah to Toby. 'How lovely,' she said in a strange, flat tone after a long pause. She pushed her hair away from her face and then, as if with that movement she'd woken herself up, she came to life. 'So, would you like some tea? How long have you been here, Toby? Where are you staying?'

'A few weeks,' Toby said at the same time as Hannah said, 'In the village.' She flashed Toby a warning look.

'I hope you're enjoying it,' Ella said.

'I am.'

'We're going now,' Hannah said, anxious to get Toby away in case Ella asked more questions.

Toby turned to her as soon as they were in the garden. 'I take it your mother's not in on the location of my current residence. Why the big secret?'

'I'm going to tell her,' Hannah said, 'But I didn't want to do it with you there.'

'And?'

'And . . . she's been behaving oddly, recently. I'm not sure how she'll react.'

'You'd better do it quick before George and Ray mention anything.'

'Shit, I'd forgotten about them.' Her step faltered briefly as she glanced back at the house. 'I'll tell her when I go back. When she's in a better mood.'

'She'll be OK with it, right?'

'I'm sure she will,' Hannah replied and crossed her fingers behind her back, just in case.

12

Hannah and Toby had been walking for nearly an hour and they had finally reached the old pillbox on the river. Hannah climbed up first onto the roof which was covered in soft, short grass and wild camomile which smelt like bubblegum when she sat on it.

'This is a great viewing spot,' Toby said, turning to look in every direction. 'You can see for miles. We should come here in the daytime.'

Hannah had been to this spot in the evening once before with Edward and they had caught sight of the shadow of the biggest eel Hannah had ever seen in the river, weaving its way through the shallows before digging down into the mud. She was hoping that Toby would be lucky enough to see one too.

He sat down beside her. 'How did it go with your mum earlier?'

'OK,' she told him although she hadn't talked to Ella. There never seemed to be a good time at the moment; Ella always gave the impression she wanted to be somewhere else. 'She said you can stay,' Hannah lied. If it was OK with Tyler, Hannah was sure it would be OK with Ella.

'That's great.'

Hannah lay on her stomach and stared down at the river over the edge of the roof. 'Dusk is the best time to see the eels,' she said. Behind her, she could smell the cigarette that Toby had lit.

'What's that?' he said suddenly, crawling forward and pointing to the marshes on the other side of the river, Hannah saw the glimmer of a blue and yellow flame which seemed to hover off the ground.

'It's Will o' the Wisp,' she said, sitting up.

'It's what?'

'*Ignis Fatuus*, Foolish Fire. They're produced from marsh gases combusting — you see it a lot round here. Some people think they're ghosts or evil fairies who will hypnotise you and lead you to your doom in the treacherous marshes.'

'There's another one,' Toby said.

'Some cultures think that they're the spirits of still-born children who are caught in between worlds.'

'That's sad.' Toby lay on his stomach beside her. 'Tell me a ghost story. You must know loads.'

'I know a story about eels,' Hannah said after a moment. 'But it's not exactly a ghost story.'

'An eel story. You tell it to me and I'll keep an eye on the river in case one comes along.'

'It's called *The Silver Eel*,' Hannah began and suddenly her mouth felt so dry she didn't think she was going to be able to continue. 'Once upon a time, many hundreds of years ago, in these whereabouts, when the land was under water, there was a poor family who lived on an island reachable only by boat. The mother and father made their living catching and selling eels at the market and every one of their six children up until the age of nine helped with jobs in the house. They fetched firewood, they cleaned the floors, they prepared the turnips for supper and

129

mended the eel nets while their parents and the older children went out into the shallows and the deeps of water to catch the eels and take them to the market. Now, as the years went by, it came to pass that by their fourteenth birthday every child lost a finger in one circumstance or another: the eldest had his middle finger bitten off by an eel; the second lost her little finger to the whittling knife; the third the ring finger to an axe; the fourth the index finger to a sickle; the fifth the middle finger to a pike. Only the sixth and most beautiful child, a girl with hair so blonde it shone like silver, was unblemished. This youngest child was the only one who remained at home while the others went out for eels and all the other children would tease her and pinch her and say that a monster was going to come while they were away and take one of her fingers and they would make the girl cry.'

'Why have you stopped?'

Their faces were only centimetres apart. She had never lain so close to another person; it was as if they were sharing the same air with every breath. 'I feel a bit stupid.'

'Don't stop. I want to know what happens.'

'OK, but keep watching the water. Don't look at me.' She waited until she was sure that he wasn't going to turn round again before she continued. 'So the girl would cry and her mother would tell her off for being a cry-baby and when she said that her brothers and sisters were teasing her her father took away her dinner for being a tattle-tell.'

'Mean parents!'

'And every year, the girl became sadder and more frightened until she jumped at every noise and trembled at every shadow.'

'I don't blame her.'

'You're putting me off.'

'Sorry.' He pretended to zip up his mouth.

'And don't look at me.'

'I'm looking at the water, Hannah.'

'Years passed and no monsters came but every morning when she woke up she was filled with fear that this would be the day that something was going to happen to her. One morning, the day before her fourteenth birthday, she was sent to fetch the reeds to lay fresh for the beds which had been cut and piled on the bank to dry. As she was wrapping the first load in a sheet, she heard a voice speaking to her. It was a soft voice which seemed to slide along without breath so that it was hard to understand what was being said. Once more spoke the voice: 'Come down to the water, beautiful girl, I have something for you.' And because the voice sounded so soft and kind, the girl plucked up all her courage and went down to the water. As she stood at the water's edge, up reared the biggest eel that the girl had ever seen. Its head was silver and its body was black and it rose a metre above her and yet there was still more coiled below in the water. The girl was so scared that she fell down in a faint. When she woke up, the eel was lying on the bed of reeds beside her.

' 'If you come with me,' the eel said, 'you will no longer be afraid.'

'But the girl didn't believe the eel and she

131

jumped up and ran away home. And because she had forgotten the reeds, all her brothers and sisters laughed at her and her mother was angry and her father sent her back out even though it was pitch-dark and she was very afraid. She crept closer and closer to the bank and had reached the reeds when she saw that the eel was still lying on them. 'Don't be afraid,' said the eel and its voice was so soft and when she looked into its eyes, she saw that they were kind and she no longer felt afraid. 'Take me with you,' the girl said.

'The eel uncoiled. Length after length of its sleek, black body slid down to the water until only its tail remained on land and only its head stayed in the air. 'Hold onto my tail.'

'The girl grabbed hold of its tail and held on with all her strength as she slid down into the water. Down, down they went, and the deeper down they went, the more peaceful and beautiful it was. At first she held on with both hands, then she needed only one, then she held the tip of the eel's tail between her finger and thumb until finally she let go and she was swimming beside the eel with her hair behind her in a silver streak.'

'Is that the end?' Toby asked and Hannah shook her head.

'Three years later, on the night of a full moon, the family went out to hunt eels. The whole family waded out into the water and all the eels tried to slip away but they had laid dozens of nets earlier that day and no matter which way the eels tried to escape they were all caught up.

As the family lifted the nets, there amongst them was the beautiful girl who, when she saw all her brothers and sisters and her mother and father, struggled to free herself. The family were so afraid to see her that the father picked up a knife and drove it into her heart and killed her. As her last breath was exhaled, the biggest eel that they had ever seen rose up in front of them, its head silver, its body black, and it thrashed the water so hard that all the nets tore and all the eels escaped and huge waves rolled over everyone's heads time and again until they all were drowned. And so it is that on a full moon, the biggest eel that anyone has ever seen with a silver head and a black body, will slide up and down the river bank, in and out of the reeds, in search of his beautiful girl and if he should come across anyone, or should he touch anyone along his journey, their lungs will fill with water and they will die.'

Hannah held her breath as silence followed. If he liked it, she thought, she would tell him she wrote it. If he didn't, she would keep quiet.

'I don't think I want to see an eel now,' Toby said. 'That was creepy.' He shook his shoulders as if trying to free himself from something and Hannah smiled to herself. The story had worked.

'Its probably too late anyway. Its getting too dark.'

He stood up and stretched. 'Did you hear that story at the Ghost Club?'

'No. It's — '

'Look, Hannah. Over there. Something's going on.'

When Hannah got up all she could make out were filmy lights which curved into the sky and then dropped away.

'It's probably the farmer spraying or something.'

'I don't think so. There are loads of lights. There's definitely something happening.'

'Like what?' Hannah asked, feeling a little annoyed that his attention had been diverted.

'I don't know but why don't we go and look?' He moved right to the edge of the roof. 'Aren't you curious?' he asked, waving her forwards to join him.

A yellow glow spread upwards from the ground, into the sky. 'It does seem a bit odd,' she conceded. 'There's a bridleway that cuts across the field over there.'

The dim light made it hard to see the ground clearly underneath them; the bridleway was rough and they kept stumbling in ruts and on rocks and lumps of dried earth. As they got closer, Hannah's heart began to thump as she tried to imagine what they would find: illegal hunting, space ships, a rave?

They climbed over the gate and onto the road. There were about a dozen vehicles: several different kinds of vans, one looked like an old ice cream van, and three or four cars. They had parked in the lay-by and on the wider part of the verge and there seemed to be people everywhere.

Toby stopped a tall man with dreadlocks. 'What's going on?'

The man looked at them suspiciously. 'Who are you?'

134

'Toby.'

'Hannah.'

'Haven't I seen you somewhere before?' he said to Toby.

Toby shrugged, 'I shouldn't think so.'

'What are you doing here?' Hannah asked.

'There's been a report of a crop formation in this field. We've come to check it out.' He pointed across the road to a field which looked as if it was lit up. There was a van parked next to the gate which someone was climbing over.

'What's a crop formation?' Hannah asked as they walked with him towards the field.

'That, love, is the ultimate question.'

'Nobody really knows,' said a short man in a safari jacket and Wellingtons who was hurrying past. 'But, put simply, it's an unexplained pattern made in a field.'

'And there's one here in Jenkins' field?'

The short man stopped. 'You know the farmer?'

'Of course; everyone knows everyone around here.'

'What's he like?'

'He's OK.' Hannah remembered how Roger Jenkins had always been willing to talk to Edward about beetle banks and minimizing run-off into the waterways and that he had supported the extension of the reed beds for the nature reserve.

'He won't want us here, that's for sure,' said the first man.

'You mean you haven't got permission to go on his land?'

135

'Not many of them will give permission,' the short man told her. 'So we get in quick before they know we're here and try and stop us.'

'They don't want us on their land. They think we'll damage the crops.'

'You will if you all carry on walking through it like you're doing.'

'We're being careful, we're using the tram-lines.'

Before Hannah could say any more, Toby had taken hold of her hand and was pulling her towards the gate.

'Let's go in and have a look.' Toby had to shout above the noise of a generator which was set up in the back of one of the vans; wires trailed from it into the field.

'I don't think I should,' Hannah shouted back.

'Come on. I've seen pictures of some of these; they're amazing. We'll only stay a minute; no one will ever know you were here.'

Toby helped Hannah over the gate and they followed a woman with a torch, keeping to single file down a tramline until it opened out to a large, flattened circle of wheat which was lit by two arc lights.

The circle was much bigger than Hannah had expected — at least ten metres across — and there was a second outer ring which they must have passed without noticing it in the dark. A couple of metres of standing crop separated the two.

Hannah counted eight people inside the circle besides her and Toby. Most of them seemed to be busy measuring and photographing and marking things on pieces of paper. The short man was standing on top of a stepladder.

'What's that woman doing?'

'I think she's dowsing,' Toby said.

Hannah began to feel dizzy and queasy. It was warm in the centre of the circle and the dense air pressed on her chest. As she walked towards the edge, her body began to feel lighter and, when she squatted down, she immediately felt better. Looking at the crop underneath her feet, she saw that there was no disturbance of the soil at all, that the stem of each plant had simply folded so that it fell forward.

'Are you a believer?' A girl squatted down next to her. She had hair as white as Hannah's but cut so close to her head it looked as if it had been painted on.

'What do you mean? This is the first time I've ever seen one of these.'

'An innocent,' she said, taking hold of Hannah's hand and gently straightening her arm out towards the centre of the circle where she held it as she spoke. 'Do you feel the energy?'

'I'm not sure,' Hannah said. She was beginning to feel claustrophobic again and desperately wanted to take her hand away.

'They are messages from other beings; they use the ley-lines and the energies of the earth's spiritual history to communicate to us.'

'Oh, there's a pagan marker stone not far from here; does that mean anything?'

Hannah wobbled and the girl's grip tightened. She called out a name and the man who'd been on the stepladder came over. He squatted in front of them; he had a camera around his neck, a bag over his shoulder and a clipboard in one hand. He was sweating profusely.

'We have a link. Our friend here says there's a pagan stone not far away.'

'It's about quarter of a mile away,' Hannah said.

'Oh my God! Who *are* you?' the man said suddenly, putting his hand out as if he was going to touch her face.

Hannah stood up, side-stepped the man and walked quickly away. She stumbled across the circle, trying to see Toby. She began to feel dizzy again; her breathing constricted.

'Toby? Toby?' She saw him walking towards her from the other side of the circle and ran to him.

'What's wrong?' He caught her by the arm and steadied her.

'These people are freaking me out,' she said. 'Can we go?'

'OK.' He slid his arms around her waist and held her fast. 'But first, look at the moon.'

All that she could make out was a small white ball in the grey sky above her, but she pretended to look at it for several minutes so that she could stay leaning against him, his arms tight around her.

Ella

13

Ella had lived through some pretty scary moments over the years. There was the time when the yacht which she and Sadie were skippering lost engine power in a storm and they were being pushed towards rocks. The daylight had been wiped out by a blackness so dense it made no difference if she kept her eyes open or shut but the storm blew over as quickly as it had arrived, the waves dropped them away from the coast, the sky returned to blue, the motor kicked into life and it was almost as if the storm had never been.

Far worse than that was the phone call to tell her that Edward had died. The room had turned as dark as the storm and she felt like she was dropping faster and faster into a narrower and narrower space until all the breath was squeezed out of her body.

It was Finn who had caught her. Poor Finn, cursed by the responsibility of being the eldest son, a role he'd taken to heart ever since he was a little boy, worrying every time Edward went away. Unusually he'd been home from London for a weekend, as if, in his way of scenting trouble, he'd known something was going to happen. He'd heard the phone and then something in the tone of her voice had made him come running. He helped her onto the settee, made the first phone calls and dealt with all the arrangements.

This time there was no one to stop her falling, no one to make a phone call for her. She felt coldness creep into her very core. The only thing she could think was that it couldn't be true, that it shouldn't be true. What about Hannah, and Tyler, all the boys, the garden, Scoot? Images of everyone and everything that she loved flew through her mind.

It wasn't true, she decided. She was mistaken. With a deep breath, she ran her fingers clumsily across the bumpy, silky flesh of her left breast and after a few fumbling seconds found it again. She wasn't mistaken. A lump was there. As much as she wished it wasn't, she couldn't deny it.

She lowered her arm, only to raise it a few seconds later. Her heart was thumping so much that the pulse running through her fingers made it seem as if the lump had a little beat of its own.

She took her hand away and tried to think of everything that she had ever read about breasts and lumps and cancer. A few facts skittered across her brain. A few hopeful interpretations scuttled after them. The truth was she didn't know much at all except that lumps could be found in breasts and that they could be benign or malignant.

Several deep breaths later, she located the lump — easily this time — and probed gently, assessing its size: about that of a grape: its consistency: solid but softer than a marble. She tried gently squeezing it but quickly thought better of it.

$\star$ $\star$ $\star$

When Hannah appeared at the hothouse door to fetch her for their trip to Ely, Ella couldn't remember what she'd been doing all morning until she looked around and saw the evidence of her work. Even Hannah's bright, excited chatter couldn't penetrate the gloomy fog that draped over her every thought.

In the bookshop she waited for Hannah to go upstairs to the fiction section as she always did before heading for the 'Health and Wellbeing' shelves where she discovered spine after spine of cancer books in pale blues and pinks on white background, as if their pastel colours would make everything all right.

As soon as she heard footsteps on the stairs, she rushed back to 'Gardening'. It wasn't Hannah that time, but she remained there anyway with a book that she'd picked randomly from the shelf open in her hands until Hannah came to show off the rather battered-looking book she'd bought.

It was a beautiful day and Hannah was suffering with the brightness of the sun. She was grumpy when Ella made a fuss about her wearing sun cream which made Ella want to kiss her daughter for the sheer normality of her response.

Hannah's enthusiasm and energy always made the shopping afternoon fun and while they were in the supermarket it was almost possible for Ella to ignore the grey fear which emanated from the lump. Each time it started to creep up into her throat and towards her thoughts, she forced herself to look at Hannah who was so pretty and cheerful in Ella's old sundress that she could hardly believe her luck to have such a daughter.

It was at the sight of the midwife in the car park that Ella felt her control give way. If Hannah hadn't been with her, God knows what she would have done.

She had only ever seen the woman once since she'd attended Hannah's birth, and Ella had hidden that time too, as she knew she wouldn't be able to trust her tongue.

Hannah, always on the scent of a good story, couldn't resist bobbing up from behind the boot and looking at the woman she'd been told to hide from. Ella prayed that she wouldn't be spotted. The midwife was bound to know her. There couldn't be many babies with albinism that she had delivered in this area.

When the woman was out of sight, Ella felt a fresh wave of anger sweep through her. It seemed to power her feet round to the midwife's car. As Ella stared into the inside of the midwife's car, Hannah had asked her what she was looking for and Ella had answered, 'Signs of humanity.' But there were none. Not a single piece of rubbish, not an old jumper lying in the back or a pair of sunglasses left on top of the dash,

As Ella walked alongside the car, her keys felt hot in her hand. And, as they drove away, the sight of the long welt on the midwife's car was as refreshing as the sharp taste of lemon on her tongue.

★ ★ ★

Ella was surprised how quickly she became obsessed with the presence of the lump and yet she remained strangely incapable of doing anything about it. She found her hand wandering across her breast whenever she was alone; in the hothouse, in the bathroom where she performed a ridiculous procedure, shoving her hand up her blouse, pushing aside her bra in order to check; whenever she was in bed she had to fight not to keep touching it.

Of course she wasn't fooling herself. She knew that it was because each time she was hoping that the lump would have gone. Like the first old woman's whisker on her chin which she'd tried to tell herself was a one-off, knowing, as she wielded the tweezers to pluck it out, as she contemplated the sturdy black ugliness of the hair on the tip of her finger, that her body had betrayed her, that she had somehow lost control. That maybe not the next day nor even the next week, but soon, when she looked in the mirror, she would discover that it had returned.

So, as her fingers crept forwards across her breast, Ella's mind contemplated the lump's possible disappearance. Surely, by now, her body's defences would have done their stuff; the lump would have been nibbled away to nothing by white blood cells, blasted into bits by antibodies. *Surely*, she thought angrily, *they're in there, doing something, having a go at kicking this invader in the ass.*

One day, after she'd dropped Hannah off at

145

one of her houses, she drove into Ely and went into a doctor's surgery across the town from her own. She spent some time looking through the information racks at pamphlets and brochures on pregnancy, diabetes, heart disease, alcohol, healthy eating, giving up smoking. There was plenty of information on doing things to try and prevent you from getting cancer but, no matter how many times she spun the rack round, she couldn't find a single brochure on what happened if you got it.

The woman on reception was beginning to eye her suspiciously and the moment she called out, 'Can I help you?' Ella stuffed the leaflet she was holding back into the rack and left.

Back at Spindle House, Ella decided to spend the afternoon emptying the full compost bin and turning the other. When she lifted the piece of old carpet from the top of the heap, she revealed the curled bodies of slow worms; creatures that she valued in the garden but which always gave her the creeps as they slid silently away.

It was hot, absorbing work; her shoulders ached as she shifted spade after spade of sweet, crumbling compost into the wheelbarrow. She pushed several loads to the vegetable patch and then one to the spring flowerbed and two more to the shrubbery. She filled four plastic sacks with the remainder. She took care shifting the rougher mixture of garden waste in the second bin in case there were any more lodgers inside and once it was empty she began to remake it, layering drier, twiggy material with the greener vegetable and soft plant waste.

She heard shouting but it didn't register immediately — not until Scoot barked — that it was Tyler calling her. She was late picking up Hannah and, for the first time she could remember, she felt resentment towards her daughter that she had to leave what she was doing to fetch her.

★ ★ ★

On Friday evening when it was nearly time to pick up Hannah from the Ghost Society, Ella called up to Tyler from the landing. He came out of his room and sat on the top stair. She could see the dirty undersides of his flip-flops.

'Could you fetch your sister? I've got a headache and I really need to lie down.'

Tyler was quick to say yes. 'Can I get you anything before I go?' he asked.

His concerned face set Ella's heart spinning and she had to look away as she shook her head. 'I've had some painkillers. I think I spent too long in the sun.'

'Drink plenty of water,' Tyler called to her as he ran downstairs. 'See you later.'

Every minute between Tyler going downstairs and the car leaving dragged. She was so desperate to have the house to herself that she couldn't move from the front window in her bedroom for several seconds after the car was out of sight in case Tyler turned round at the end of the track and came back.

She calculated that she had at least an hour of solitude. She left the bedroom, walked down the stairs, out into the kitchen and then into the living room where she closed the French windows for the night. Scoot followed her every step; walked when she walked, sat or lay down whenever she stopped still. She could almost feel the energy coming from his brain as he tried to second-guess her next move, to see the familiarity of routine in her unfamiliar behaviour. But she didn't know herself. She wandered aimlessly from room to room as the house became darker, cooler, increasingly silent.

★   ★   ★

Ella was about to examine herself in the mirror when Hannah walked into her bedroom.

'Can't you ever knock, Hannah?' she asked, pulling on her top as she turned to face her daughter.

'I'm sorry.' Hannah looked as startled as if Ella had slapped her.

'What do you want, love?' Ella asked, digging deep to find some patience, knowing her daughter had come in to chat.

'Nothing, really.'

'I'm sorry I didn't pick you up. Did you have a good night?'

Hannah hovered by the bed before sitting on it. Ella was torn between joining Hannah on the bed or asking her daughter to leave.

'It was OK.'

Ella watched Hannah hesitate and her heart began to race as she had the sudden thought that Hannah *knew*. Perhaps she had been in the

148

room longer than Ella had realized and had watched Ella looking at herself; perhaps Ella had said something over the last few days to give it away. As she watched her daughter's lips begin to move, all she could hear was the rushing sound of panic in her ears.

'Ella? I said, do you think you've got sunstroke?'

'No, only a headache, darling. Did you read your story out?'

Her daughter shook her head; she looked disappointed. 'Magnus read his.'

'Never mind, another time.'

'Yes,' Hannah said and then, all of a sudden, she was gone.

Ella lay on her side on top of the bed; she drew her legs up, reached down and pulled the corner of the duvet over her feet before tucking her hands between her knees. She felt the soft bounce of the mattress as Scoot jumped up, then his heavy warmth as he nudged his body into the curve of her legs.

14

On the evening before the Strawberry Fair, Ella was in her bedroom putting away some clothes when Hannah knocked on her door. For the last couple of days, Hannah had been trying to persuade Ella to go to the Fair, so she knew what was coming. She also knew that there was no chance of Hannah succeeding. Hugged inside Ella was the thought of being alone in the house.

Hannah sat cross-legged on the bed; her hair gleamed in the lamplight, her pretty face was so symmetrical that when she was a baby she had looked like a little perfect doll. But it wasn't her face which made Hannah beautiful, it was the energy for life she had, combined with the gentleness of her spirit. It shook Ella how much she loved her daughter.

'So will you?' Hannah asked.

'Will I what?'

'Tell the story about how you and Dad met?'

'Oh, Hannah, love, you've heard it so many times. Aren't you bored of it?'

'Never. Please.'

So she sat on the bed and Hannah lay on her side and looked up at her and Ella started to tell the story.

'Sadie and I had come down to stay with family friends for the Strawberry Fair, as we did most years. I'd been hearing about Edward, the most eligible bachelor in the area, for as long as I could remember. He was considered by the family I knew to be a rather sad man — orphaned at sixteen, a solitary figure, rather awkward socially. Generally, most people thought he was crazy or at least eccentric because of his obsession with amphibians. But I thought he sounded interesting. I was with — '

'And romantic,' Hannah chipped in.

'Yes. And rather romantic.'

'Because you understood his obsession.'

'Yes. I knew what it was like to be obsessed. I had my alba plants in the London flat that Sadie and I shared, some of which I'd smuggled in from abroad.'

'Countries you'd been to when you were sailing.'

'Exactly.' Ella stroked Hannah's hair. She had been like this as a child, wanting to hear the story word for word each time, pulling Ella up if she skipped even the tiniest detail.

'I'd left my group of friends for a few minutes to go and buy ice creams for everyone but I had to wait for a marching band to pass before I could get back to them. It was a hot day and the ice creams were beginning to melt and run down my hands and I was worried that they were going to drip on my new dress.'

'Your Biba dress.'

Ella laughed. 'My Biba dress on which I'd spent my last penny for that weekend in Ely. 'Allow me,' said this dark-haired, tall, middle-aged man who had appeared out of nowhere and, before I could protest, he took all the ice creams out of my hands. 'Where to?' I led him back to my group of friends and I saw the surprise on their faces and Julia said, 'So you've met Edward then?' 'Not formally.' I turned to thank him for his help and Julia said, 'Edward Ruland, this is Ella Somers.'

'We shook hands and I thought how handsome and strong he was, nothing like the woeful orphan I had imagined. 'It makes a change from what Ella usually brings back,' someone said and the whole group laughed. 'What do you usually bring back, Ella?' Edward asked softly. 'Plants. With white flowers, mostly.' 'You like alba plants?' And I couldn't believe that he had used the word 'alba' and for the first time I really looked him in the eye. 'More than anything else in the world.' And I watched his reaction to my answer and saw him really taking me in.'

'And he liked what he saw. You knew he liked what he saw.'

'Yes, darling. We both liked what we saw.'

After a few moments of silence, Hannah knelt up on the bed. 'I think I'll go to bed.' She leaned forward, wobbling a little and gave Ella a kiss and a cuddle. Ella patted her back. 'You miss him, don't you?'

Hannah nodded into Ella's neck.

'Me too.'

When Hannah had left, Ella moved to the warm, sunken patch of duvet she'd been lying on. Edward would never have died if he'd gone into the town to get his infected cut seen to instead of making do at the camp and here Ella was, with doctors everywhere, doing the same thing — ignoring what she didn't want to see. She took Scoot downstairs to let him out for his last run around for the night and went into the living room. She hesitated for the briefest of seconds before picking up the phone and dialling Sadie's number.

'Ella! How lovely to hear from you. How are you?'

'Fine,' she said but the hesitation after her reply didn't go unnoticed by Sadie.

'Are you sure?'

'I've found a lump.'

'OK,' Sadie said slowly after listening to the details. 'And what does your doctor have to say about it?'

'I haven't been to see him yet. I suppose I've been hoping it would go away.'

'What can I do?' Sadie asked. 'Do you want me to come there?'

'No, I — ' Ella closed her eyes and lowered her head. The truth was, she didn't know what she wanted.

'Look, are you still covered by Edward's private health policy?'

'Yes, I kept it up, I thought — ' Ella sat up straight, took a deep breath. 'Well, I thought it would come in useful one day; the kids are on it too.'

'I'll make a call,' Sadie told her. 'Jimmy's son is a specialist in that field. I'll get you an appointment to see him.' Jimmy had been a longstanding lover of Sadie's; married, of course, but committed to his mistress too, as Sadie used to like to put it. They were still good friends.

153

'Oh, I couldn't let you do that; my doctor's competent enough.' Ella could hear the lack of conviction in her voice, and the bubbling of rising fear. She swallowed hard.

'I've heard, and not only from Jimmy, that his son is absolutely one of the best,' Sadie said. 'Please let me ring him. It would make me feel better at least. And you could come and stay with me; you haven't been to London for a while.'

Whilst the idea of being in the hands of 'one of the best' was comforting, what actually made Ella agree was the realization that she was thoroughly sick of living with her own thoughts; she could really do with some time in her best friend's company.

'I'll ring you tomorrow,' Sadie told her.

'It's Saturday tomorrow.'

'I'll speak to Jimmy tonight. Call in one of those many favours. No arguments,' Sadie said before Ella had opened her mouth. 'I'm going to call him. All those years have got to be worth something,' she joked. 'So I'll ring you back in the morning?'

'OK,' Ella agreed. 'Thanks, Sadie.'

'And Ella?' Sadie said, as Ella was about to ring off. 'Don't worry. Everything's going to be all right.'

★　★　★

Ella timed it so that she looked busy with the climbing rose by the back door when Hannah and Tyler were due to leave for the Fair. She had the phone handset on the kitchen window ledge which she hoped Hannah despite her usual curiosity wouldn't notice.

'Have a lovely time, darling,' she said, trying to sound cheerful and normal. As soon as Sadie's phone call came, everything would change; there would be things Ella would have to do. Hannah turned and Ella, suddenly reluctant to let her leave, called out after her, 'Oh, Hannah.'

'Yes?'

'Bring back some strawberries for me, won't you?'

She listened to the motorbike driving away before returning to work on the rose. Up close, its white flowers were marked with the occasional pink vein, a reminder of the deep pink buds which they'd blossomed out of. She worked across at eye-level, snipping off every single dead rose she could see. She didn't have to wait long before Sadie phoned.

'Can you make a consultation on Monday afternoon? If so, they can do the biopsy later this week if it's necessary.'

Ella's heart punched her ribcage. She took a deep breath before she spoke. 'OK. I'll come up on Monday.'

She sat at the garden table. Scoot came and rested his muzzle on her knee. She stroked his head, feeling the narrow ridge of his skull where his coat was thinnest. She watched how he blinked a lot which she hadn't ever noticed before; it made her eyes blink back in sympathy. She rubbed her thumb across the bumps of his eyebrows. He yawned, letting out an odour of stale meat.

'I have to go away for a few days,' she told him, practising breaking the news to Hannah and Tyler. He didn't look impressed.

★ ★ ★

Traffic crawled along on the main road into Ely; the heat built up in the car until Ella felt as if she might pass out. She was relieved to reach the turn-off to the supermarket and pick up some speed.

'Be good,' she told Scoot, parking in one of the bays furthest from the supermarket which were the only ones shaded by a small group of trees. She left the windows open as wide as she dared.

The supermarket was quieter than usual and Ella wandered haphazardly around trying to think of food to buy to leave in stock for the time she was away. She stopped at the bakery counter. It was full of pastries and cakes and biscuits. She tried and failed to remember which were Hannah's and Tyler's favourites. She decided on a selection of doughnuts and cream cakes which a woman put in a white box with a piece of gold ribbon around it as if they were to be part of a celebration.

As she was approaching the village, she heard a motorbike behind her. In her mirror she saw it flash its headlight, a yellow blink in the bright sun. It was Tyler. He followed closely behind her and, as they swung round a bend, she noticed that Hannah wasn't with him.

156

'Where's your sister?' she asked when they had both parked.

'She came home earlier by bus.'

Tyler carried both helmets in one hand and two bags of shopping in the other, leaving Ella with a further bag and the box of cakes.

'Do you want help unpacking?'

'It's OK, thanks,' Ella told him. She opened the fridge; there was a punnet of strawberries, leaking water on the middle shelf.

'Go and see if Hannah's upstairs,' she said to Tyler. 'I'd like to talk to you both.'

They came into the kitchen together. Tyler looked bemused and Hannah looked so terrified that Ella had to turn away from her. She was glad to have the cake box to open. She fiddled around, untying the ribbon instead of simply cutting it. She put the cakes on a plate, watching her hands tremble as she did so as if they weren't her own. Finally she sat at the table and began to talk.

Afterwards, when she was alone, she could hardly recall a single word that any of them had said. She knew Tyler had been kind and calm and she was glad because Hannah's reaction was worse than she'd imagined. She'd sat with her head bowed, her hands resting on the table, one cupped inside the other. When Ella looked at her, she felt as sick as if she'd touched a live cable and was reeling from the impact.

★ ★ ★

From the way her daughter kept looking at her over breakfast the following morning, Ella could sense Hannah's emotions were so close to the surface that it would take very little for them to break through. Working to move the citrus trees and rearrange the hot-house provided a useful distraction. It was so hot that neither of them had any spare energy for conversation and in the companionable silence Ella felt sucked into the tasks at hand. She fingered her plants with tenderness, took time to arrange the pots in the spaces vacated by those that they had taken outside; she marvelled at the amount of growth the vegetables had put on.

At lunch, she sat down with a sigh; her hands and clothes were filthy, her limbs felt heavy from use.

Even with her sunglasses on, Ella could feel Hannah's penetrating gaze fixed on her. She shifted in her chair and, thankfully, Hannah looked away.

'Better?' she asked Hannah, feeling the contentment of a job well done.

Hannah nodded but then suddenly announced she was going for a walk. She stood up suddenly, knocking into the table.

'Let your lunch go down first,' Ella told her but Hannah didn't pay any attention. She went into the house and passed the shed a short while later where Ella was stacking up the empty plastic pots.

★   ★   ★

158

Ella would have preferred to wait on her own for the taxi, but as both Tyler and Hannah had elected themselves as her rather gloomy send-off party, she covered the awkwardness by issuing instructions.

'You can leave the hothouse open overnight if it stays this hot, except for the top couple of roof panes,' she said, and then added, 'And water every day, please. Hannah, are you listening?'

'Water every day,' Hannah repeated. 'Don't worry, we'll look after everything.'

Ella could almost see the anxiety oozing from her daughter's pores. She found herself stepping away from Hannah, thinking irrationally that if she came into contact with these droplets of fear she would become overwhelmed and break down on the front steps and completely lose it.

By the time she was on the train, Ella felt exhausted. She slept for half an hour, woke up and then fell asleep again until the announcement and bustle in the train told her that she was nearing London King's Cross.

Ella immediately spotted Sadie in the crowd by the ticket barriers like the only bright light in a dark room; her smile shone out at her.

They hugged the moment Ella came through the barriers. They were in the way of people trying to pass but Ella didn't care, she needed that hug like a plant in a drought needed rain.

'Let's get a taxi straight back to the flat, shall we? We've got time to eat lunch there before we have to go out,' Sadie said, linking her arm in Ella's.

For the briefest moment, Ella saw her friend

159

as a stranger might see her: grey hair, feathery wrinkles under the make-up, a frailty to her slender body, but as they emerged onto the station forecourt into the midday sun and walked forward perfectly in step, she felt as if they were the girls who had worked the yachts, with bare, brown feet padding across the deck, strong, tanned legs and arms in tiny shorts and bikini tops. She looked at Sadie who squeezed her hand and smiled and Ella threw her head back and laughed like she hadn't laughed in weeks.

Sadie lived in Streatham in the same flat that she and Ella had shared over forty years ago. At that time they'd been renting but Sadie bought it when she married her first husband and managed to keep hold of the property through that divorce and the one from husband number two who had managed to screw her for every other penny during their three years of marriage.

'It always feels so good to be back here,' Ella said, looking out of the window at the back of a builder's yard and over at the edge of the park. 'It's like coming home.'

'You're the only other person who gets it,' Sadie said. 'Everyone else is always telling me that I could have moved to a nicer area for less than I've spent doing it up. But I couldn't bear to leave here. It's served me well and I know people around here. People know me, too. And, as I get older, I find it comforting that I'm known.'

'This is new.' Ella pointed to a striking, lime-green, low armchair in the corner. 'And you've decorated again.'

'What else do I have to do? Do you like it?'

Ella considered the white walls whose polished finish made her think of Lalique glass, the charcoal-grey settee, the white curtains with the green plant design, the large blue-grey abstract paintings which hung above a slender white-wood sideboard. It looked incredibly clean and new and modern. 'I love it.'

All the windows of the flat were open but there wasn't a breath of wind. Ella wasn't even aware of the noise of traffic and voices outside until there was a pause in the conversation and Sadie told her, 'Its time to get going.'

They bustled around collecting bags and keys and at the last minute Sadie fetched a small bottle of water from the fridge.

'We'll get a taxi,' Sadie said and Ella nodded because she couldn't speak; her jaw was clenched tight, her stomach was turning over.

In the taxi, she stared out of the window and wished the journey to go on for ever but of course it didn't. They walked through the glass doors of a blue building with lots of windows where Sadie did all the talking until Ella was taken into a bland office and left there on her own.

The reason you always felt so helpless in a hospital was because you didn't know where you were going and had to be led everywhere like a child on their first day at school. This was the conclusion Ella came to as she followed a nurse down a nondescript hallway, passing identical pale wooden doors on both sides. Everything had been explained to her. Not by Ian — Jimmy's son — but first by a young nurse who took care of the paperwork and next by a smartly dressed woman who introduced herself as Dr Sims, a female colleague of Dr Ian Yates. 'He'll carry out any procedure should that be necessary,' The woman had smiled as she said that and Ella had smiled back as her heart gave a small thud of hope. She hadn't even realized that the whole thing could be over that very day if the mammogram showed her lump to be a cyst.

But it wasn't over. The lump was solid so she would need to have a biopsy. Dr Sims returned to see her again, this time holding Ella's file and offering her two choices.

'A needle biopsy or an excision. The first is with a local anaesthetic, the second a general. If it's benign, there's no need to remove the whole thing, but some women prefer it that way.'

'Yes. Take it away,' Ella cut in quickly which made Dr Sims consider her for a few seconds. Ella didn't look away.

'Remember, very few cases turn out to be malignant.'

'I understand, but I would prefer — it — the lump — to be gone.'

'Fine.' Dr Sims made a note and then closed the file. 'Dr Yates will see you Wednesday. If you stop at Reception, they'll give you all the information you need about the operation.' She stood up and opened the door for Ella to pass through. She followed a nurse back down the corridor, through two pairs of swing doors and was finally deposited in Reception where Sadie

162

leapt up from a seat in the waiting area and hurried to her side.

★ ★ ★

Returning from the bathroom, Ella stood in the middle of the lounge for a moment. Sadie was sitting in the green chair with her feet up on the arm of the settee. She was watching her closely.

'What do I need breasts for, anyway? Nobody sees them, nobody touches them any more.'

Sadie looked shocked, Ella swayed a little, and then they burst out laughing. Ella thumped down on the settee. 'It's Hannah I worry about the most.'

'You should be thinking about yourself, not Hannah.'

'She's not ready to be on her own. You should have seen how terrified she looked.'

'She's much more capable than you're giving her credit for. She's a woman, for God's sake. She would be there for you, if you needed her. But you're not going to need her, not yet anyway, you old fool.'

'It scares me so much, the thought of leaving her, that I almost can't bear it.'

'Do you remember the day Hannah was born?' Sadie said. 'You were kneeling in that flowerbed, snipping away at the roots of those bloody flowers, when your waters broke.'

'Iris rhizomes.'

'You frightened the life out of me when you shouted out; I spilt gin fizz all over myself.'

'I've got a photo that Henry took of us that

163

day; we look worried but excited.'

'We were happy,' Sadie said, 'until that bitch came along and tried to spoil the party. Do you remember how she bossed us all about?'

★ ★ ★

'Don't leave me up here on my own,' Ella had said. None of her sons' births had been quick so Sadie had rounded up the boys who set up camp in her bedroom. Finn and Henry sat on the floor playing chess while Tyler read on the bed alongside Ella.

'Isn't Mr Ruland here?' the midwife had asked with a distinct air of disapproval when Sadie showed her in.

'He's on his way,' Ella said.

Finn checked his watch. 'He's probably this very minute changing planes at a small airfield in Rio,' he said in his newly deepened little man's voice. He'd memorized Edward's journey by heart.

'Will he bring any toads back with him?' Tyler asked, his eyes wide with the excitement of it all.

'No, love. Edward is researching a species of toad,' Ella started to explain to the midwife.

'Disgusting creatures,' the midwife interrupted and Ella wasn't sure whether she was referring to the toads or to the family whose life revolved around them.

Henry piped up. 'Actually, in some countries, toads are used to help in childbirth. Dad said.' He turned to Ella, frowning. 'But I think they kill them to do it.'

'This is no place for that kind of talk or for young men.' The midwife placed her hands on her hips and her big, black shoes stoutly apart. She meant business and, before Ella or Sadie could open their mouths, the boys were gone.

★ ★ ★

'I saw her the other day,' Ella cried out, sitting up. She placed her hand over her mouth. 'I did something terrible.'

'Did you slap her?' Sadie asked. 'I've always wished I had.'

'I keyed her car,' Ella said. 'I put a long scratch down the whole length of her fancy, shiny car.'

Sadie burst out laughing. 'Revenge was a long time coming, but sweet in the end.' She drank some wine. 'I suppose we should have reported her.'

'I just wanted to forget about her. It was only Hannah that mattered.'

★ ★ ★

The soft lamps in the bedroom had been inadequate for the midwife's requirements so when Hannah first opened her eyes it was under the dazzling ceiling light whose crooked shade was channelling the glare down onto the bed. The midwife let out a shriek and shrank back. The colour drained from her face so that she too became as white as snow.

The boys crowded in the doorway. Ella called them in.

165

'What's wrong?' Finn asked, holding back while his brothers approached the bed, his gaze fixed on his mother.

'Wow!' Henry cooed in amazement.

'She's got red eyes,' Tyler said.

They saw their sister's skin, beautiful in its paleness, the tufts of cotton-tail hair and as they hung over her, unwittingly shading Hannah's face, they noticed that her eyes were light blue after all. The boys drew back, a little disappointed, but Ella had already fallen in love, hook, line and sinker.

Already, a fierce protectiveness was filling her up, making her grit her teeth as she watched the midwife perfunctorily perform her duties, handling Hannah with cold, judging hands, before handing her over.

'She's an albino,' she said.

'She's beautiful,' Sadie had responded, a furious expression on her face which passed over the midwife's head, and Ella had reached out and clasped Hannah tightly, flooding her with the warmth that was her due.

It was dawn and Ella was left on her own with the baby. The boys had drifted away to their rooms and Sadie was soaking in the claw-footed bath; the scent of rose bath oil glided through the house.

Ella opened the window to the feel of fresh dew on the ground and the sight of mist draping the hunched shoulders of the shrubs and the waists of the poplars in the distance.

'Welcome to Spindle House,' she had told Hannah. 'This is your home.'

Ella knew that a lot of mothers experienced guilt mixed up with all the happiness when a child was born. To bring someone into the world simply to have another person to love had always struck Ella as an indulgence but when she held Hannah up at her bedroom window, Ella knew then, amongst all the wrenching, milky love, all the ache of her heavy vagina and the tiredness that had seeped into her bones, that this time the guilt was different.

Ella loved white flowers with an obsessive, hungry love. She was fascinated by the complexity behind their deceptively simple appearance and by their haunting, unreal air. She had wanted Hannah with the same ardent desire — a girl to go with her three dark-haired sons — so much that she had wished for her existence almost every day for seven years. It didn't seem so hard in those first absorbing months after Hannah had been born to let her imagination run and wonder if she really was to blame for the difficulties that she could see Hannah was going to experience. That the power of those twin obsessions had somehow combined together and created her beautiful alba child.

★   ★   ★

The next morning, Ella and Sadie felt hung-over so they stayed in their nightwear until nearly midday when they dressed and had breakfast in a Turkish coffee house down the road. Ella felt starved. She ate two almond pastries with icing sugar dusting while they watched the passers-by.

Time seemed to be moving slowly although all around them was rush and panic and noise and impatience as if they were in the eye of the storm. It made her feel a little breathless and dizzy. She remembered hearing that someone had proved that people were literally walking faster than they used to do a decade ago and Ella could believe it, watching them striding and shoving, their faces closed in.

Later that afternoon Finn rang to ask if it was OK for he and Amy to visit in the evening.

'If that's all right with you, Sadie?' She rather hoped that Sadie would say no as she knew Finn, unlike Tyler, would want to know about every detail. Always a relaxed host, Sadie saw no problem. 'I'll buy some tapas from down the road. Everyone likes tapas, don't they?'

Ella said yes but the truth was, Finn and Amy weren't like everyone. She couldn't see Amy licking fingers and digging around in communal dishes but she didn't feel she had a better alternative to suggest.

'Do you think they'll want to stay over?' Sadie asked. 'Bunk down in the living room? Save one of them having to drive if they want to have a drink.'

'I think it's very unlikely.'

'Of course. I forgot it's Finn we're talking about. He always was a particular little boy.'

'And they'll have work tomorrow; it would be a nightmare driving across London in the morning.'

'Are they happy, do you know? They've been married, what? Five, six years?'

'Nearly seven,' Ella said. 'They seem to be.' Whenever they came down to Spindle House, Amy always joined in and yet she never seemed quite comfortable as if the Ruland family were still strangers to her. But she suited Finn and that's what mattered.

Ella wasn't allowed to eat or drink after eight o'clock so she ate early and by the time they arrived at nine, she felt drained. She felt herself retreating and curling into a ball in her mind like Scoot did on her bed; she watched the others in the room as if she wasn't there herself.

Although he had come straight from work, Finn's shirt looked as fresh as if it was new on and Ella suspected that her son might be one of those people who always kept a change of clothes at work on the off-chance he needed them or perhaps even someone who had several new shirts lying in their packages in his desk drawer.

She noticed, not for the first time, the similarity in her son and daughter-in-law in their determined faces and sinewy bodies. *If you saw them in the street*, she thought, *you would class them as an attractive, successful couple.*

'So who is this guy you've fixed Ella up with?' Finn asked and Ella was grateful when Sadie omitted the part about him being the son of her on-off, long-term lover and instead poured out the credentials and the recommendations and awards and God knows what else; all true but pitched exactly right so that Finn, who was so terribly hard to pacify, was practically eating out of her hand.

After they'd gone, Ella persuaded Sadie to

have a nightcap. 'You deserve it,' Ella told her. 'Believe me, I'd have one if I could.'

'Finn reminds me of Edward. He has the same shape mouth.'

'Henry is most like him in temperament,' Ella said.

'Have you heard from Henry recently?'

'Not much. The odd email comes floating our way but otherwise he's pretty much out of touch. We forget how hard communication can be in other countries, don't we?'

'I don't think Finn and Amy would survive long somewhere like that. They must both have checked their phones a dozen times in the two hours they were here.'

'I don't know why they need to do it,' Ella sighed.

'Have you noticed how young people take themselves much more seriously these days,' Sadie said, breaking the silence which had fallen over them. 'And despite all this binge drinking and drug taking they're supposed to be doing, they manage to remain incredibly uptight.'

Ella smiled at her friend, thinking of their own louche days. 'Do you remember that time we brought the yacht into Antibes and we met up with those Australian boys?'

'We were only supposed to stay overnight but instead we stayed for days.'

'And then one morning we decided we were getting bored and left without saying goodbye.'

'I wouldn't want to be young now,' Sadie said.

Ella nodded. 'We've done it all before them. We've spoilt it for everyone else to come.'

* * *

Lying in bed, Ella listened to the panic in her body. The boom of her heart echoed in her head. She had to consciously swallow but her mouth remained dry. From being unable to leave the lump alone, she now couldn't bear even to look at her breast and in the shower she'd had to force herself to soap that area of her body.

She couldn't stop fear running amok in her mind. Her fingers automatically fingered her hair as her thoughts dashed through the operation, ran headlong into chemotherapy and dived straight into a sharper fear, the fear of what she would leave behind — her plants, her children and Hannah, in particular, her darling moon child — until they landed at the feet of her angriest fear: that she was absolutely not bloody ready.

* * *

Ella was shown to a small room with beige walls. A hospital gown waited on the narrow trolley-bed for her to change into. She undressed and as she sat on the edge of the bed, the flesh of her breasts and stomach hanging free, she felt the fear gearing up inside her.

Noise and the bustle of two nurses preceded the entrance of Dr Ian Yates, the son of Sadie's friend. He was a serious-looking man with a gentle manner as he once again explained the procedure she was about to undergo. When he left, she sank back onto the trolley-bed as if the

171

mattress was as soft as down. She kept her eyes closed as she was wheeled along; when she next opened them, shadowed faces with halos of white light looked down on her for a few seconds before she slid into darkness.

She woke in the little beige room which already felt like sanctuary and when a nurse came in she shut her eyes again. She didn't want to wake up. She didn't want to leave because that would mean she'd have to face whatever came next.

15

There was only one word that Ella wanted to hear when Dr Yates phoned personally to let her know the results and the moment she heard him say 'benign' nothing else mattered. She passed the phone to Sadie as soon as it was polite to do so and stood by the window overlooking the street while behind her Sadie chatted and laughed with her ex-lover's son.

In front of her lay the city but all she saw were the big skies above the flat land of her home and she felt a shifting inside her, a stretching, reaching kind of feeling. So that was that. Ella would return home and life would resume its course; she would be absorbed by Spindle House, by the children, by the plants in her garden.

'That was nice of Ian to take the time to ring,' Sadie said, standing next to her. She put a hand out and touched Ella's arm. 'Darling, are you OK?'

Ella nodded because she couldn't speak.

'It's over now. Everything's fine.'

'I don't know how I would have got through it.'

'You would have,' Sadie told her. 'But you don't need to worry about that any more. You've got your life back.'

'I've got my life back,' Ella repeated but the words seemed to lack substance.

★ ★ ★

'Welcome home, welcome home.' Hannah greeted Ella in her sweet, excited voice and they hugged briefly before Hannah pulled away.

'There's nowhere to park; we've got to hurry.' Hannah tugged her hand and she followed her daughter as quickly as she could but it felt as if she had weights on her feet.

Going outside the station was like getting off a plane in another country; the heat rose up from the pavements and even the breeze was warm. They waited for Tyler to bring the car round and then had to scramble into it as fast as they could before the anger from the cars they were blocking escalated into trouble. Even with all the windows open, it was boiling inside. Scoot was barking and choking as Hannah tried to restrain him in the back until Ella could no longer bear the noise.

'Let him come over,' she said. Scoot leaned against her legs, making her even hotter, but there was some comfort in his presence. Tyler was sweating away beside her; perspiration literally ran down his face. He looked too big for the car; he clasped the steering wheel in his large hands as if he was driving a dodgem car. Behind her, Hannah quivered like Scoot, desperate for attention.

Ella felt as if she'd been bracing herself for the bump of a hard landing only to discover that she was drifting feet-first into softly enclosing foam. She leaned her head back on the seat and felt consumed by a feeling of disappointment.

There was nothing Ella wanted to do more than to escape to her room, lie down and cool off but Hannah had prepared a nice meal. She stayed at the kitchen table for as long as she could, the effort silently screaming through her. Every word had to be coaxed out of her mouth and the food scraped like sand down her throat.

She walked cautiously towards her bedroom as if at any moment the promise of freedom could be whisked away. Relief came the moment she shut the door behind her even though the windows hadn't been opened and the air in the room was stifling. From the bed, Scoot's eyes followed her as she crossed the room to open both windows, as she changed into the first slip she found in her underwear drawer and over to the door where she hesitated. She was reluctant to leave her room so soon but she needed to pee. She opened the door slowly, peered out and then walked as quietly as she could to the bathroom.

Safely back in the bedroom, she lay on the bed with a cold, damp flannel pressed to her head. A channel of air blew across her body and she fell asleep to the sound of Scoot's breathing.

She heard Hannah come into the room and afterwards she could smell the food which Hannah had left on the bedside table but sleep drew her back down and it wasn't until early evening time — judging from the weak light in the room — that she woke up properly.

She heard someone approaching and lay as still as she could, hardly daring to breathe when

175

the door opened. It seemed as if Hannah would never go away, and so she said, 'I'll see you in the morning, sweetheart,' making her voice sound sleepy.

'OK,' Hannah whispered back.

As soon as she'd gone, Ella sat up and shared her sandwich with Scoot. She drank the cold cup of tea which was surprisingly refreshing. Using her slipper, she propped her door open enough for Scoot to escape if he needed to and got into bed. She thought she'd never sleep but it wasn't until Hannah knocked on her door in the morning that she woke up.

'Shall I ask Tyler to take me to work?' Hannah suggested.

'Would you?' Ella said sinking back into bed, her thumping heart beginning to subside.

Scoot pushed his nose into her face before jumping onto the bed. She could smell the earth on his paws and there was a crust of soil on the end of his snout where he'd been digging. A few black crumbs fell on the white sheet. She pushed Scoot away and brushed them off.

'No wonder nothing ever stays clean in this place,' she said.

Propping herself up on the pillows, she looked around the room. It had been hers alone for nearly five years and hers and Edward's for thirty years or so before that. Very little had changed since she'd first arrived at Spindle House; they'd bought a bigger bed to replace the one that Edward owned originally and they had redecorated a couple of times but always with cream walls as a base with different floral curtains and bedding. Both Henry and Hannah had been born in this room, and all her children but Hannah had been conceived here. It had been this room — maybe even this very bed — where she had imagined ending her days. A fanciful image perhaps of being surrounded by family, friends and grandchildren when she slipped from the world. The other idea she'd considered was being discovered face-down in the wild strawberries, their dense flavour crushed against her lips, having drawn a last, sweet breath. Now both these ideas seemed abhorrent and unlikely. Not the room, not the house, not the garden.

She got up and felt dizzy from standing too quickly. She walked slowly to the window which overlooked the garden. It was another day of clear blue skies. A wind was blowing strong enough to sway the tops of the poplars and to shift the taller plants in the garden but it was coming from the wrong direction to make a difference to the temperature in the room.

She stood closer to the window and looked down. The prospect of all the work which needed to be done in the garden today and every day for months to come lurched towards her. She felt her energy shrivel at the thought of the endless cycle demanded by the garden and she glimpsed, for the first time ever, the potential futility of what she had been spending most of her time on for more than half of her life.

She heard the car on the drive and five minutes later Tyler ran up the stairs and went into his room. She turned to Scoot. 'How about we get out of here for a while?'

There were clouds building up to the west, but it was already warm. Ella lowered the window for Scoot who snuffed and snorted the fresh air. Instead of taking the turning to Ely, Ella drove in the opposite direction, following the farmland boundary hedge. She pulled in by a farm gate and got out. The wooden gate was marked with notches and had splintered where rusty nails had worked their way back up to the surface. When she leaned on the top bar, she felt the familiarity of the scene flutter through her as if her soul recognized the place from centuries ago.

Scoot had wriggled through the gap between the hedge and the gatepost and he was standing at the rather bald edge of the wheat field. He dropped his nose to the ground and began to trot like a hunting dog to the right. Ella climbed over the gate. She managed it in awkward stages, first straddling the top bar where she sat for a moment before getting her second leg over and jumping down. She brushed at the seat of her trousers and rubbed the mushroom-coloured dust off her hands.

She walked in the same direction as Scoot but stopped only a few feet along the hedge. She sat on a strip of lumpy grass, hugging her knees to her chest. Looking into the stria of the dense crop was rather hypnotic as it swayed in front of her. A car swished past on the road behind her and her focus changed to the ground around her. It was uneven and hard and a couple of stunted specimens of the crop were struggling to grow alongside more vigorous thistle plants. A large, long black beetle passed in front of her toes. It tumbled off the top of a crusty ridge and landed on its back where it wriggled its legs frantically but failed to right itself. Ella picked up a twig lying close to her right hand and poked and flicked at the beetle until it was back on its feet.

Scoot was nowhere to be seen. She whistled and he came charging through the crop as if his tail were on fire, panic in his heart until he spotted Ella. He skidded to a halt, retraced a few steps and then began to rub his neck and back across the ground, having found a noxious, decaying dead animal to perfume himself with. He ignored Ella's whistles until the very last moment when she was almost close enough to touch him. He ran past and waited at the gate for her before using a shallow dip in the soil to wriggle underneath as she climbed, with better poise this time, over the top.

'Now where?' she asked him as they sat in the car, contemplating the empty road ahead. She reversed towards the gate, turned round and drove into Ely.

She parked in the short stay car park but didn't get out. She listened distractedly to a noisy play on the radio about the Battle of the Somme.

A man's face loomed into her open window, making her recoil and Scoot stand up.

'Are you arriving or leaving?' he asked, making no effort to hide his annoyance. In the mirror, she could see that he had left barely enough room for Ella to reverse past his car. His face

179

became more comically aggrieved when she said, 'Neither. I'm waiting.'

'You can't do that.'

At the sound of the man's raised voice, Scoot began to growl. The man retreated to a safer distance but he didn't go away. 'You haven't even paid,' he shouted.

'So?' Ella shrugged.

'I'll report you.'

'Go ahead,' she told him and continued to sit there for several minutes after he'd driven off, her body trembling with adrenalin.

When she got home she discovered that neither Hannah nor Tyler were there, so she sat in the cool living room with a glass of cold water from the fridge. It wasn't until she heard the engine of Tyler's motorbike that she remembered she was supposed to have picked Hannah up. She ran out of the front door and was startled to see Hannah sitting on the back of the bike with the cleaning box on her knees.

'Oh my God,' she said, hurrying to help Hannah and ignoring her face which was sharp with hurt. 'How resourceful, kids.'

Hannah put her hand to her head and staggered slightly. Ella knew instantly that she was suffering from a headache.

'I'm so sorry, Hannah, you should have reminded me, I completely forgot it was Tuesday. I'm completely out of the routine of it all.'

'So what about work on Thursday?'

'Of course, darling. Everything will be back to normal on Thursday,' she said, turning away quickly. She didn't want to give either of them the chance to ask her where she'd been or what she'd been doing. That was her business, she told herself, holding it tight inside her like a precious secret.

That evening Sadie phoned Ella. Hannah was out, Tyler was upstairs in his room.

'How are you?'

'I feel strange.'

'How?'

'I don't know. Restless. Maybe.' She paused briefly and, even though she was sure she was alone, she lowered her voice. 'Do you ever feel that you've grown timid with age?'

There was a pause in which Sadie must have been considering Ella's question. 'I think I'm more easily pleased now, if that's what you mean. Isn't contentment what we're supposed to be striving for these days?'

'We used to strive for adventure.'

'We used to be young and without ties and without responsibilities.'

'Yes.' Although Sadie didn't have children of her own, she had taken her role of step-mother to her second husband's son very seriously. 'But we could live for another thirty years, Sadie, and I'm not sure I want to spend them like I have been. And what if my time's almost up? What if this was a kind of warning?'

'It wasn't.'

'But say it was. What would you do? Wouldn't you want to find something new to fire you up?'

'I don't know. I don't think so.'

'Wouldn't you want to live each day as if it was your last?'

'Isn't that something people say rather than do?' Sadie said. 'Wouldn't it get rather tiresome after a while?'

'I don't know. But I think I might have been asleep for a long time and I never knew it.'

Ella went out to the garden when she'd finished on the phone and sat in the dark at the table. She remembered the first time she'd been to Spindle House — Edward had invited her back with him after the Strawberry Fair — and she had been amazed by the house and its grounds.

They had talked non-stop all evening and she had felt both comfortable with him and excited, too. She had stayed over, had slept with him that very first night, a fact that they had always missed out of the story they told to Hannah. They weren't embarrassed or ashamed by their behaviour — it had seemed completely natural and right to them at the time — but they were aware how rare such luck was and didn't want her to expect the same.

In the morning, there had been no awkwardness or pretence about what they had done. It was a cloudy day and not particularly warm but they sat outside, nursing mild hangovers with orange juice and a pot of coffee, and from that weekend — although she didn't move in straightaway — it became her new home: the place and the person she always returned to.

At the time, Edward had had a housekeeper which had rather impressed Ella, even though she soon discovered it wasn't at all as grand as it sounded. She was actually a cleaner who stayed over once or twice in the week so that the house didn't remain empty when he was travelling away for work. The housekeeper's name was Mrs Treacle, which sounded like a character's name in a book and although she was nothing like a ghost to look at physically, with her stout body and hair dyed jet-black, she moved as silently and elusively as one around the house, doing her best to keep out of their way when they were both there.

When Ella moved in, she came to rely on Mrs Treacle's company because, with Edward gone, the silence in the garden scared her and the noises in the house scared her and lying in bed in the pitch-black night with no street lights outside scared her. She and Mrs Treacle would spend time together, chatting over cups of tea, and Ella learned more from Mrs Treacle about Edward's family and others who lived in the village than she ever would have from him. It never seemed to occur to him that Ella would want to know.

Less than a year later, Mrs Treacle had to have an operation on her varicose veins and she never returned to work. Shortly afterwards, Edward was awarded a prestigious research grant which they'd been hoping for but by the time it came through Ella was pregnant, and they were strongly advised against her accompanying him for the six months abroad as they'd planned. At first she'd disagreed, but when she and Edward started talking about all the possible dangers, she became terrified of harming her baby.

Left at Spindle House on her own, Ella would flee to Sadie in Streatham and stay there longer than she should have — getting in the way of Sadie's complicated love life — until she couldn't put off returning to Spindle House with a heavy heart, its cold rooms and overgrown garden filling her with despair.

She couldn't find the key into the soul of the house and the garden. The more she tried, the more it seemed to reject her, like an organ in the wrong body. Tiles fell off the roof, pipes burst, one day soot fell like a black avalanche down the chimney, filling the living room with choking black dust. Even the plants which she had cherished, which were plump with health when she brought them down from London, began to wither for no apparent reason. Some of them died. Each death felt like failure. Each disaster in the house made her feel like a failure.

Gradually life improved. She got to know people in the village and George and Ray would help her with jokes and sympathy and phone calls to labourers. She came to recognize the noises which the house made and those produced by the winds in the Fens which played with the doors and windows, and she came to believe that there was no such thing as silence in the garden. By the time Edward returned, the house was holding up, the vegetable garden was taking shape and she was big and slow with Finn, feeling more settled and at peace. Edward was home for nearly a year after Finn was born and by the time he had to leave again, they were married and she had begun to feel properly at home, as if she had been accepted.

But now it seemed that while she was away for

those few days the connection had broken again, and this time she didn't know if she wanted it back. This was the kind of summer she always dreamed they'd get, a chance to spend hours outside enjoying the garden. Instead, wherever she looked she saw death: wilting plants, crisping leaves, blooms fading and buds failing.

The lump had definitely gone — she had been brave enough to gently test the tender spot of her breast — and yet she could still feel it there, or rather the ghost of what might have been, pressing her flesh, making her wince, catching her thoughts.

The slow drift into dusk had started and the birds were making their last flights of the day. A robin flew past with pulpy, spiky creatures gathered in its beak. A blackbird flew up, chattering in alarm. Scoot raised his head. It was a perfect summer's evening. Shouldn't she be happier? Shouldn't she be full of the desire to live now that she'd been given this second chance?

★　★　★

On Wednesday, Ella jumped at the chance to forego their usual trip to Ely in the afternoon when Hannah suggested they leave it until another day, but on Thursday, despite sleeping late, she got up and took Hannah to work.

She felt dazed driving and tried to drink her coffee at the wheel when it was too hot, she was so desperate to clear her head.

They were almost at Hannah's client's house

when she realized that they hadn't exchanged a single word. She stole a glance at her daughter, whose face said it all; she could never hide it when she was upset.

'I'm so sorry, darling, I can't seem to find the energy for anything at the moment.'

'Are you really OK?' Hannah asked immediately.

'What do you mean?'

'You weren't lying — the tests were clear?'

'Darling, of course they were clear, I wouldn't lie to you about that.' Ella was shocked that Hannah should even imagine that was possible. 'I think it's the stress catching up with me,' she said and wondered how true that was. She would have to pull herself together, she thought. She would have to stop making such a meal of this. 'Give me a few days and I'll be as right as rain,' she told Hannah, and hoped that she sounded convincing.

16

Driving back from the village, Ella decided that she didn't want to go home straightaway and so she turned off the main road in search of the field she'd visited a few days ago. After several miles she realized she couldn't remember exactly which one it was. She drove slowly down several roads, looking out for the old wooden gate but the ones she passed were either metal or looked unfamiliar and she felt sure she'd recognize it as soon as she saw it. She drove a little further and took a right turning. This led her down an unsurfaced track which crossed a dyke and emerged onto a road she thought she knew. Somewhere around here was a very pretty stone cottage with an ancient mulberry tree in the front garden but, five minutes later, she realized she was still in the middle of farmland and probably going round in circles. She stopped the car at the next pull-in and got out.

It was only mid-morning and the sun was already intense. Scoot immediately started panting which made her feel hotter. She needed to pee but the gate to the field wouldn't open; it had been tied with wire and there was a coil of barbed wire on top. It was an oilseed rape field and the crop's smell was pungent, the colour of it strident. She noticed what looked like a stile across the hedging of the field opposite but, as she approached, it turned out to be a section of dilapidated, old wooden fence. It had rotted at the bottom so that Ella was able to lift the whole piece up and tug it far enough towards her to give a sizeable gap to get through. She turned, expecting to find Scoot pushing against her legs in his haste to be ahead of her, but he had stopped on the road. She whistled to him and then went in, leaving the fence propped open for him to follow.

Scoot pushed his face up near the fence and began to growl. He ran from side to side, growling, then ran back onto the road where he started barking so hard his legs were lifting off the ground. Ella stood at the edge of the field. All she could see was a full crop of wheat; the heads were a little green but it was tall and healthy looking.

Scoot's ears went up and he shot towards her like a fuzzy white and black torpedo, letting loose a string of high-pitched, strangled barks as he jumped up against the fence. A sinister feeling shivered through Ella and, before she was able to rationalize the feeling, a fear crept in and solidified. There was someone in the field watching her. She began to edge backwards towards the fence, towards Scoot who was still growling. She didn't dare turn round. She focused on moving backwards until she'd reached the gap. Once there, she pushed her way through, catching her arm on something sharp, and ran towards the car with Scoot ahead of her.

Feeling safe with the doors locked and the windows up, she advanced slowly towards the fence but as soon as they came close Scoot went into a frenzy, his front paws banging against the glass. Ella accelerated quickly past before he did himself some damage.

When Scoot had calmed down, Ella stopped the car and waited until her hands had stopped trembling. As soon as she felt able, she drove as fast as she dared; she didn't even slow down to look for her shades, driving half-blind with the sun shining off the road. After a few minutes, she realized that she was much closer to home than she'd thought.

In the kitchen, Ella ran the cold tap. She filled Scoot's bowl with fresh water and put it outside for him before filling a glass for herself and switching the kettle on. When she turned round, Hannah was standing in the doorway. Ella jumped.

'You scared me.'

'Sorry.' Hannah stepped forward and then in the shadowy hall Ella could make out that someone else was behind her.

'Who's that?'

'This is Toby,' Hannah said and moved aside to let him in. Scoot dashed forward and began to sniff around his trainers.

'Toby?' The boy was slightly taller than Hannah and he had a pumpkin-shaped head with squashed features and rather more piercings than Ella liked. The way his small eyes peered through a mass of wavy brown curls made him look rather sly but he had a ready, broad smile and he held his hand out to shake.

'Hello.'

'Toby's on holiday here,' Hannah said.

'How lovely,' Ella said, wondering how long Hannah had known him. They seemed very comfortable together and yet she hadn't mentioned him before. Ella looked sharply at both of them. 'So, would you like some tea? How long have you been here, Toby? Where are you staying?' She found herself firing questions at him but none of them were the ones she really wanted to ask.

'A few weeks,' Toby replied at the same time as Hannah said, 'In the village.' Ella caught a look which passed between them and this made her pay even more attention. 'I hope you're enjoying it,' she said, glancing at one, then the other.

'I am.' He seemed very polite and well-spoken but Ella knew that didn't really mean anything.

'We're going now,' Hannah said and she went first out of the back door.

Toby turned as he was leaving. 'Nice to meet you.'

'You, too,' she replied and, as their gaze held for a brief moment, she saw something in his expression which let her know that he was Hannah's boyfriend. Her breath caught as her eyes travelled back to where they had come from, 'Oh no,' she said quietly to herself.

At Hannah's age, she and Sadie had travelled across Europe, thinking nothing of sleeping with young men with the aim of obtaining a comfortable bed for the night, a meal paid for or, the best of all, a decent shower which in those days was harder to come by than hen's teeth. But, still.

She stood in the doorway and watched them

walking across the lawn together. It was hard to take her eyes off Hannah. She was wearing pale blue cotton trousers, a bright yellow top and yellow flip-flops. Ella's gut recognized the way Hannah was dressed, the way she moved. It was how Ella used to feel. How she used to be. Ella had never felt old before but now she felt herself sagging and thickening and slowing every second as she stood there while Hannah seemed to grow more luminous.

17

On Monday, once she'd dropped Hannah off for work, Ella took the opposite direction to home. She'd driven several miles before she decided that her destination was the coast.

She recognized the names of the larger coastal towns but none of them appealed to her until, about five miles out of Kings Lynn, she saw the name 'Saltmarsh' on a turning signpost and swung across the opposite lane at the last minute.

She followed a winding, narrow road, unsure if it was taking her closer or further away from the sea. She was at the point of giving up and heading back when she came to a sign, saying: 'Welcome to Saltmarsh. Please drive carefully through the village.'

She passed several houses and buildings and had travelled about half a mile further between fields before she realized that she had driven right through the village. She turned in the empty road and drove back. This time she spotted a sign for car parking which she followed, bumping into one of five parking bays in a sandy area with a brick wall at the end and the sea beyond it.

She got out of the car. The air felt clear and the heat was dense but a sudden, welcome breeze blew her hair across her face and skimmed her bare legs and arms. Behind the car park were several houses, a SPAR and a little further up the road was a pub. There were very few people around and hardly anyone on the beach that she could see.

Scoot had already found his way onto the beach so she followed him down the three shallow brick steps. The sand was very fine and pale and there were clumps of thick brown seaweed everywhere which squeaked and crisped under her feet. In one direction, the beach opened out, in the other it formed creeks between marsh beds. In the distance she could make out the masts of beached boats like white nicks in the blue of the sky.

She walked towards the open beach; it took longer to get there than she'd thought it would. The sand was dry and loose, making it hard going; it trickled through her toes with each step and rubbed the skin on her heels under the leather strap. Scoot was in his element, running after the seagulls and rounding up a flock of little, dashing birds with pencil strokes for legs.

She walked down to the edge of the water and took her sandals off to cool and clean her feet before continuing parallel to the bank of low sand-dunes past other visitors who had set up camp at intervals along the foot of the dunes, until she arrived at an empty spot.

Here it was sheltered from the cooling breeze so after only a short while, the heat became intense. Scoot's tongue was hanging sideways out of his mouth, his whole body was heaving as he panted. As Ella didn't have any water, sun cream or food with her, she decided it was wisest to head back to the village. She would be better prepared next time.

She found Scoot's lead on the back seat of the car and tied him up outside the SPAR while she went to buy a bottle of water. She poured it into her cupped hand and he lapped up handful after handful until there was only a little left in the bottom which she drank. She passed her tongue over her dry lips and pulled her hair back off her face.

She untied Scoot and they walked along the road towards the pub. She didn't hold out much hope of it being open for business but as she got closer she could see that the front door was wide open.

She tied Scoot to the leg of the table outside and he immediately lay down under its shade. The pub seemed incredibly dark after the brightness outside and it took Ella's eyes a moment to adjust.

She was surprised to see from the clock behind the bar that it was not quite twelve o'clock; she felt she'd been out on the beach for hours.

'Are you still doing breakfasts?'

'Until twelve-thirty,' the girl said. 'Do you want to order one?'

'Yes, a full English please, with orange juice.'

'Where are you sitting?'

Ella looked around the empty pub and back at the girl. 'Outside.'

She moved Scoot to a table with an umbrella; she felt tight-skinned from the heat. There were salt marks on the leather of her sandals.

The food was surprisingly good and there was a generous amount of everything. She ate slowly, feeding Scoot bits of bacon and sausage which he snapped down hungrily. The salt from the bacon stung her sun-sensitized lips.

She took her empty plate in and ordered a coffee. She needed the caffeine but she didn't have great hopes for it being nice, judging from the sachets stacked on top of the machine behind the bar. The coffee was rather weak but it wasn't the worst she'd tasted, and the fresh brandy snap that accompanied it was a nice touch.

Her eyes felt bleary as she drove home, but there was a warmth of a contented tiredness deep in her bones which she hadn't felt for a long time.

★　★　★

Ella hadn't imagined she would return to Saltmarsh so soon but the following day, after she'd dropped Hannah off, she found herself driving to the motorway with that intention. She wasn't sure if she'd remember where the turning was and in fact, almost missed it. But by ten o'clock she was parking in the village.

It was a cooler, cloudier day than the one before but as Ella stood by the wall, looking out to sea, she felt a moment of pure happiness at being back. She liked the mix of colours here: blues and browns and gold and white.

This time Ella chose to follow the line of sand which ran through the marshes. The sand was

195

firmer and damper here and it narrowed and widened at various points where low, shrubby vegetation spilled forward or receded. The plants were twiggy with small, hard leaves, a little like blueberry bushes. She would look them up in her books when she got home.

The sand tapered to such a point in one place that she had to walk a few feet across the plants until she reached a wide area of wet sand. It looked as if the sea had only recently retreated from here, leaving a strange crop exposed; rounded lumps of fine, light-green seaweed stood about four inches high, like hundreds of tiny ghosts which had been draped in green sheets. Trailing through them was the brown line which led to a white buoy at the far end of the patch of sand. She had expected the seaweed to be firmer but it was soft and squashed easily under foot. She felt bad about standing on the bumps, as if she was crushing the life out of them.

Ella looked behind her. The village was out of sight but further to her right was a single house next to a line of trees. She wondered what it would be like to wake up there with nothing between you and the ocean and the sky. It didn't look very far away but the landscape made it hard to judge distances. She considered walking across to it but it was impossible to discern a route ahead. For a moment she felt panicked, as if she were caught alone in the middle of a maze. She whistled to Scoot and turned to retrace her route back to the village.

18

Every day that Ella came to the village, there was a different atmosphere to the place. It might be a change in the tide, the wind, the marooned boats, or lack of boats, an impenetrable blue sky, the greyer, cooler light, but she felt the same — as soon as she got out of the car she felt she could breathe. The feeling was addictive.

From the moment she got up it was as if she was covered in plastic from her head to her feet, which made her feel both shielded and trapped. When she pulled into the little car park by the SPAR shop, she felt as if she was ripping the covering from her and stepping outside. Nothing was required of her here.

Scoot ran ahead; birds flew up from the shrub cover to the left, his pawprints criss-crossing their spiky tracks. A group of waders twittered and rose up in perfect synchronicity. When they landed further up the beach, their thin legs were moving so fast they looked as if they were floating in the air.

Ella followed a shallow snake of water where boats waited in meagre pools, banked on the mud. She walked up to a small, wooden rowing boat, its outboard motor pulled up. In the stern was a yellow plastic box and a coil of weathered, blue nylon rope. She took off her sandals and got in. She sat on the wooden seat that ran across the middle of it; it rocked and swayed under her weight.

Scoot put his paws up on the edge but he backed away when the boat tipped towards him. Ella threw him a piece of her banana which he ate despite it being coated in sand. She leaned out of the boat and gave him some water to drink from the palm of her hand.

When she got out, she picked up her sandals and carried them as she walked through the water. It had warmed in the sun and the sand seemed to melt away under her feet. She wondered how far down she would sink if she stood in the same spot for a long time. She imagined herself gradually disappearing, being sucked down and down until she was gone.

She remained barefoot all the way back to the car park; the steps were hot on her bare soles so she sat on the wall and put her sandals back on. It seemed much hotter walking along the road to the pub. She noticed that the edges of the tarmac looked tacky so she put Scoot on the lead and made him keep on the grass verge so that he didn't get any tar on his paws.

She tied Scoot to the leg of a table and went inside. It was a different girl serving today. Ella bought a bottle of mango and passionfruit juice and a bag of beef-flavoured crisps and ordered a ploughman's which the girl wrote carefully on a small slip of paper, handing Ella the bottom portion with the number seven scrawled across it.

Ella shared her meal with Scoot as usual; they both seemed to get very hungry on these trips.

She noticed how dry and crinkled the skin on the back of her hands was looking when she passed the barmaid her empty plate.

'Would you like something else?' The girl leaned down and stroked Scoots head.

'A coffee would be lovely.'

She ordered it only to give herself an excuse to prolong the time there; in the back of her head was the thought that she had to pick up Hannah later. But later wasn't now. For now, she had nowhere else to be.

Before she left, she paid a visit to the Ladies, casting a glance at her reflection in the mirror. The glass was speckled and blurry with age but it was probably better that way. She was surprised to see her face so tanned; she loosened her hair from its ponytail and tied her scarf in a gypsy knot around her head.

She stopped at the first petrol station she came to and bought some mints from the counter as she paid; the raw onion she'd eaten was coating her tongue. She was halfway across the petrol forecourt when she heard someone shouting her name. When she turned, the sun was bright in her eyes, making it difficult to see. A man was hurrying towards her, smiling. She waited. As he approached, she thought he looked familiar but she couldn't place him.

'Denis,' he said, putting out his hand. He was a good foot taller than her, slightly wrinkled, slightly tanned, an angular, rather noble face. He had thick, wavy hair which was cut short; it was peppered with grey, like hers. 'We met at a party or two. I knew Edward. I came to his funeral.'

'Ah,' she said. 'Yes, of course.'

As soon as he had mentioned Edward, Ella's instinct was to run away and maybe she would have if it hadn't meant pushing past him to get to her car.

'What are you doing in these parts?'

'Enjoying the scenery, walking.' She pointed to Scoot who had his front paws on the dashboard and was watching them. 'And you?'

'I live around here. I moved here about three years ago.'

'How lovely.'

'I wanted to get out of Ely, be somewhere more open, be able to look outwards.' He frowned slightly as he finished speaking.

'Its good for that,' Ella said, and they both turned their faces as if they were expecting to see something different to the busy road and industrial warehouse on the other side.

'You look incredible,' he said and even though Ella knew he was only flattering her, she felt it was a generous thing to say. 'How about, well, what do you say, we have a drink? I know a nice wine bar not far from here.'

He seemed so awkward, and yet so bright and happy that she found herself agreeing. She followed his car into the town and parked at the back of Sainsbury's.

'Scoot, stay,' she said, raising the window so that there was no chance of him wriggling out.

Denis led her under a stone archway and then down the street to a wooden-fronted wine bar called Blake's. Inside, the bottom half of the walls was painted a plum colour and the top half, a light green. There was an obvious French theme going on, with rather good fake vines growing up the wooden poles at the bar and a liberal sprinkling of carafes and paintings and photographs of the vineyards and scenes of the *vendange*.

'There's a garden,' Denis told her and she stood by the door to look at it while he bought the drinks. It was a small, white-painted courtyard with topiary box and bay, giving structure to the slightly raised beds which were spilling over with fuchsias, euphorbia, lavender and pelargonium.

There was one free table but Ella was happy to stay indoors in the cool.

'Still busy with your plants?' Denis asked when they were seated. Perhaps noticing Ella's surprise, he explained, 'We had a long conversation once about obsessions. Edward's, yours and mine.'

A vague memory flitted through her mind of them standing at a party together, watching Edward gesturing passionately, discussing seriously — overly seriously — never understanding small-talk. He had been happy to let Ella do the circulating while he talked to the few people he wanted to. She had always found it hard to take her eyes off him; she was greedy for her husband's attention and liked nothing better than to catch his eye across a room.

'I'm terribly sorry, I don't remember what yours was.'

'I'm not surprised. It was very boring.' He

shrugged apologetically. 'Work. A total workaholic, I'm afraid. Cost me my marriage.'

'Well, Edward's cost him his life,' Ella said and, to her great surprise, she laughed. 'Not directly, of course, but, you know.'

'Yes,' Denis said and she felt that perhaps he did understand.

'I've been thinking recently that mine seems pretty much a waste of a life, too.'

'How can you say that? Your garden's a thing of beauty. I think it must be wonderful to have created something like that.'

'You've seen it?'

'After the funeral,' he said.

She didn't remember much about that day and found it odd to think of this man being there, perhaps meeting her family, seeing where she lived.

'So what is it about white flowers that you like?'

'Lots of different things,' she said. 'I like the contrast they provide. They make green look greener, they make brightness in the night when everything else fades. If you see a white form of the bluebell in the wood, it makes you notice the blue even more.'

She remembered that she had always been drawn to white flowers but it was when she was travelling through the Greek islands and she came across the Cretan cyclamen on the island that she began to see how special they were. Up until then she hadn't been looking closely. She hadn't seen the different tones and shades, the velvet and smooth textures, the veins and streaks and flushes of colour on the petals and sometimes the sudden flash of colour on the secret inside.

'What do you do, Denis?'

'I'm retired now but I owned a vending machine business. I started off doing repairs when I finished school and it got bigger and bigger until, before I knew it, it was worth millions. Only trouble was, I never had time to enjoy what the money bought me. My son runs it now but he has a healthier attitude.'

'You have a son?'

'And a daughter. You have two sons and a daughter, don't you?'

'Three sons and,' Ella said, looking at her watch, 'one daughter who I have to pick up.'

'Have you time for another drink?' he asked.

She shook her head. 'It's been nice, Denis. Thank you.'

'Do you think we could meet up if you're ever over this way again?'

She didn't tell him that she made the trip every day; that she couldn't imagine not doing so at the moment. 'I'm not sure.'

'Have you got a pen?'

She passed him the biro she used for her shopping list and he wrote on the back of a card he took from his wallet.

'Give me a ring, if you ever do want to.'

Ella turned the card over. It had the name of his plumber on the front with a picture of a plunger under the line: 'No job too big or small.'

Denis walked her to her car and, feeling self-conscious as he watched her back out of the driving space, she drove off quicker than she meant to, making the tyres squeal on the road like a boy-racer, and bumping the corner of the kerb.

★ ★ ★

Hannah opened the gates as soon as Ella buzzed to go through. She got out to help Hannah put her box into the boot. Her daughter looked hot and tired; her hair was limp and was escaping from her hair clips and falling into her face.

'Good day?'

'All right,' Hannah said. 'What have you been doing?'

'Nothing much. I went for a walk.'

'Have you been drinking?' Hannah asked and leaned towards Ella as if she was going to smell her breath.

'For God's sake, Hannah,' Ella said, putting out a hand in front of her. 'I had a drink in a pub with my lunch, that's all.' She felt her anger continue to spiral as she looked into Hannah's surprised face. She turned away quickly and got into the car.

Hannah didn't speak when she got in. She held her body turned towards the window, her shoulder blocking her mother out.

Driving subdued Ella's anger; she glanced at Hannah. 'There are some gypsies camping out on Jenkins' land,' she said. 'I came past them earlier. Jenkins isn't going to be happy.'

'They're not gypsies, they've come to see

the crop circle,' Hannah said. 'There's a big difference.'

'OK. So tell me.'

'They travel wherever there are formations in crops and some of them do scientific tests and others simply enjoy being close to them.'

Ella was puzzled. 'So why are they here?'

'Because there's one in Jenkins' field.'

'Is there? How do you know?'

'I've been to see it.'

'What's it like?'

Hannah thought for a moment. 'Incredible really, but weird, too. It felt a bit creepy.'

Ella felt a chill come over her as she remembered Scoot's odd behaviour the other day in the field and the sensation she'd had of being watched. She'd become disorientated driving around the small roads that day but it struck her that the field could well have been on Jenkins' land. She pushed the thought aside — she was getting as bad as Hannah.

'Did you go with Toby?' She tried to sound casual but Hannah wasn't fooled.

'Yes, Ella, With Toby,' Hannah replied, giving her a small, tight smile and although Ella wondered what else her daughter hadn't told her, she knew she had no right to ask, not when she had her own secrets to keep.

★　★　★

That evening Ella went down to the hothouse. The mossy tank which filled with rainwater off the roof of the greenhouse was almost empty

205

although she hadn't used it recently. She hovered in the open doorway, waiting for the usual bubble of excitement she felt whenever she came here but it refused to materialize.

She stepped inside. There were a lot of red tomatoes; some had split open but the flavour of the cherry ones was rich and deep. She ate several, one after the other. She passed her fingers over the basil; she admired the aubergine plants which each had several fruits: some deep purple, one a creamy colour with streaks of violet on its skin.

She walked alongside the staging. The amaryllis were ready to be given some air, the Hot Water plant and the dove orchids were doing much better than they should, considering her neglect. A thought occurred to her. She leaned down and pushed her fingers into the compost of one pot, then another, then another. All of them were damp. Hannah must have been watering them.

She sensed someone behind her. Hannah was standing in the doorway as Ella had done only a few minutes before.

'It smells wonderful in here,' she said.

It should have been easy to welcome her in. It only required a word or a look from Ella. She could have thanked her for watering and Hannah would have been inside in an instant but somehow Ella couldn't.

For once, Hannah wasn't wearing her big, dark sunglasses and all Ella could see in the perfect face of her daughter was an expectant expression which changed to puzzlement.

206

Ella reached out and plucked a flower from the dove orchid and held it, feather-light in the clenched palm of her hand unable to move or speak.

After Hannah had gone, she found that she'd squeezed so hard that her knuckles were aching and when she opened her hand, the flower was as limp and colourless as if she had crushed the very essence of light out of it. She let it drop to the ground and walked out of the hothouse.

★ ★ ★

It was several hours later before Hannah returned home. Ella was sitting at the garden table, with only the pale light filtering through the living room windows to brighten the night.

'Where've you been, darling?' Ella asked her gently.

If Hannah was surprised to find her mother waiting for her, she didn't show it but although she came closer, she didn't attempt to join Ella at the table.

'Nowhere really. Just at the dyke.' She moved her feet as if she was preparing for flight. Her face was closed, suspicious and secretive. 'Toby's camping down there.'

'What do you mean?'

'He's staying there, camping.'

'No, Hannah. He can't do that. You don't even know the boy.'

'I know he's a student and that he's on holiday and that he's all right.'

The anger that lay congealed in Ella's chest,

waiting to erupt, spewed out. 'For God's sake, Hannah. Don't be so naïve.'

'Tyler said it was OK. George and Ray are fine with it; he parks his car in their drive.' Hannah's voice was tearful but defiant.

Ella drew a long breath. 'How long has this been going on?'

'A few weeks.'

'Good of you to tell me now.'

'You weren't here when he arrived and I didn't want to worry you when you came back and ever since then . . .'

'Ever since then, what?'

'Nothing.' She stared at the ground. 'Tyler said it was OK.'

'Why doesn't he stay with the others?'

'What others?'

'The travellers. Or whatever you call them.'

'He's not one of them. We only met them the other day.'

'And he parks in George and Ray's drive?'

'He cuts their grass for them in exchange,' Hannah said eagerly as if offering it as evidence of Toby's good character.

Ella felt a sudden rush of affection for her daughter but when she spoke her words failed to match. 'Well, seeing as it's all arranged, there's nothing much I can do about it.'

Ella continued to sit outside after Hannah had gone in. The conversation could have ended with a hug and maybe a shared moment making cocoa together. It could easily have ended like that if only Ella had let it.

She phoned Sadie.

'I think I'm going mad.'

'Join the club, darling.'

'Seriously, Sadie, I don't know what's happening to me.' She closed all the doors to the living room and sat on the settee facing the French windows. 'I feel angry all the time and I keep taking it out on Hannah.'

'You've been through something.'

'But it was nothing. A false alarm. It's over.'

'Maybe it's still something you've got to come to terms with.'

'I want Hannah to stand on her own two feet and yet I'm worried to death about her. She's got this dubious-looking boyfriend who I don't trust as far as I can throw him.'

'Do you think you might be jealous of her?'

'No, that would be awful. And ridiculous.' Ella stood up and paced around the room.

'It would be quite understandable . . .'

'No, it wouldn't.' The idea of it made Ella feel quite sick. It would be totally unforgivable. 'It's like I want to hold on to her so tight but at the same time I can't bear her near me. I feel so trapped by her, by this place, by everything.' Ella peered through a gap in the curtains. There was nothing to see but the light from the room reflecting back at her.

'I meant it might be something you're feeling temporarily,' Sadie said. 'Have you tried talking to her?'

'I don't know if I can.' Ella sat on the chair behind her and rubbed her forehead with one hand. 'She's wary of me already and I don't want to say anything to make her hate me. I couldn't

209

bear it if she hated me.'

'Hannah won't ever hate you, darling. She adores you as much as you do her.'

'I'm not supposed to feel like this. I'm supposed to feel relieved and grateful and happy that I'm going to be all right,' she said and she remained sitting for a long time after she'd finished on the phone, staring across the room, wondering why she didn't.

19

One evening, around midnight, Ella was reading in the living room when she heard Hannah go into the kitchen. Moments later, the phone rang.

'Are you expecting a call?' she called to Hannah who put her head round the door.

'No.'

They looked at each other in alarm. Ella reached for the phone. The line crackled and hummed and at first Ella thought that there was no one there but then, loudly, clearly, came Henry's voice.

'Hello, Mum.'

'Henry.'

Hannah's face lit up when Ella said his name but Ella felt breathless. Like all her children, he rarely called her 'Mum' and so she knew immediately that something was wrong. Hannah came and stood next to her, expecting to take her turn talking to him.

'Good news, I'm coming home.'

'That's great.' She mouthed to Hannah, 'He's coming home.'

Hannah grinned broadly.

'But I've had a bit of an accident. Nothing serious, nothing to worry about.'

Ella's blood felt chilled. 'What happened?'

'A car accident. A few broken bones and bruises. They wouldn't give me the all-clear to fly home until now. I've got a flight to Madrid tomorrow and then I'm flying into Stansted the day after. Do you think you or Tyler can pick me up?'

'Of course, darling.' Ella wrote the flight date and time on the message pad. Hannah picked it up. When she looked at Ella, her face was a mixture of emotions reflecting Ella's own worry and pleasure at having him back.

'And you're sure you're OK to fly?'

'Yes, I'll be fine. I'm looking forward to coming home,' he said but there was something odd in his tone which made Ella wonder.

'We're looking forward to seeing you, darling,' she told him and the two days until he arrived seemed to stretch in front of her as long as infinity.

★   ★   ★

Henry was first off the flight, courtesy of being in a wheelchair pushed by an air hostess. Through the glass partition, Ella watched how the woman chatted away to him but Henry didn't seem to be responding in his usual sociable manner. There were two bags piled on top of each other in his lap and the one arm she could see was in a sling. As they came out, she was struck by the pallor of his face and her heart turned over to think of him in pain. She waved at him and the relief on his face as he grinned at her and waved back with his good arm brought tears close. She wanted to rush through the barrier and give him the biggest hug he'd ever had. She walked quickly forward so that she reached him at the

212

very moment the hostess pushed the chair through.

In fact, obstructed by his bags and his bad arm, it was almost impossible to touch him. Ella had to content herself with putting her hands to his face and kissing him on both cheeks.

'I have to take the wheelchair back,' the hostess told her. 'Sorry.'

'Of course.'

Ella and the hostess removed the bags so that Henry could get out. He pushed himself slowly upright. They thanked the woman as she turned to leave.

'I'll take these,' Ella said as Henry took two stiff and careful steps towards his luggage. The bags were heavy but the fact that Henry hadn't argued about Ella carrying them told her all she needed to know.

It was a relief to finally reach the car. She put the bags in the boot while Henry eased himself into the front passenger seat.

'Have you got painkillers?' Ella asked, handing him a bottle of water. He drank thirstily.

'Here.' He fished a small plastic bottle out of his shirt pocket and took two. 'Nice to see the old land again,' he said when they eventually made their way out of the airport perimeter.

'You don't have to talk,' Ella told him, sensing that he'd used the last of his energy to get through the journey.

'Thanks,' he said, closing his eyes. Within a minute, he was asleep.

When they were on the motorway, Ella took the opportunity to have a better look at her son.

He was unshaven, his hair messy; his clothes were dirty and smelled a little sweaty but he was a handsome young man. He'd always been handsome. *A heartbreaker*, she used to say to Edward when Henry was a little boy. *One day he'll break some poor girl's heart.* It struck her suddenly how strange but wonderful it was that she was this man's mother. That she was the mother of four amazing people. She would never have imagined herself capable or lucky enough to have achieved something as great as that.

About half an hour from home, Henry woke. He drank the rest of the water and then stretched his neck from side to side.

'It's hot,' he said. 'I didn't expect it to be hot.'

'It's been like this for weeks.'

Henry shifted in his seat. 'I am so fucking uncomfortable,' he said and Ella knew that he must be feeling rough because Henry didn't complain about anything. He was like Edward, he could sit for six hours in the same spot without moving, in order to catch a glimpse of a beetle.

'Won't be long now.'

So, what's new, Ella? Fill me in on everything. How's Hannah and Tyler?'

'Tyler's fine. Hannah I hardly see. She has a new friend, Toby.'

'A boyfriend?'

'I think so. They spend all their time together or over with the Crop Circle Followers.'

'The what?'

'Apparently there's one of those mysterious crop patterns in Jenkins' field. A whole group of them have camped up next to it.'

'I bet Jenkins is pissed off about that.'

'And the rest of the village. There's bloody uproar; you'd swear the whole of Glastonbury had moved in, the way they talk. I've driven past a number of times and it's always looked fine to me — no litter or anything.' Ella indicated right to move into the middle lane and overtake a slow-moving lorry. 'It doesn't stop them making the most of things, though. The prices in the village shop have gone rocketing up since they arrived. Do you know, they actually charged me a secret 'locals' rate' for the bread when I went in there.'

'And Hannah's hanging out with this group?'

'She and Toby go over there. She says all they do is sit and talk. You know Hannah, she's interested in anything vaguely mystical or spiritual. I can't stop her, Henry. She's old enough to look after herself. I can't wrap her up in cotton wool for the rest of her life, even if I wanted to. Which I don't. At her age, Sadie and I were travelling around Europe. You were, too. She can't live like a fairy princess in her castle forever.'

'She loves Spindle House, she always has. More than any of us. And besides, it's different for Hannah. She's different.'

'It shouldn't be. It can't be. It isn't what real life is about. She should be able to fend for herself.' Ella's hands were trembling. *I can't look after my moon child forever*, is what Ella wanted to say but she couldn't.

'It sounds like that's exactly what she's

beginning to do — showing a bit of independence,' Henry said, and Ella could understand why he was looking at her, puzzled. 'What's Toby like, anyway?'

'He seems nice. Very polite. He's a student.'

'It's about time she had a boyfriend,' Henry said and his words made everything sound so normal that she leaned back and smiled.

'Have you heard from Finn lately?'

'Yes, I saw him and Amy the other week when I went up to London.' She paused. 'To see Sadie.' He didn't need to know about the cancer scare right now.

'Still our family capitalist?'

Ella laughed. 'He tried to get Sadie to invest in some shares.'

'That's our Finn.'

'Oh, Henry, it is good to have you home,' she said and reached across and patted his leg. 'Even if it's not in the best of circumstances.'

There were roadworks before the motorway exit and so Ella was back later than she had anticipated. She called up to Tyler but he wasn't home so she had to quickly sort out Henry before going to pick up Hannah. She poured him a cold drink of orange juice, made a cup of tea and a ham and cheese sandwich. She put them on the coffee table beside the settee, switched the TV onto the news channel for him and gave him the remote controls. Scoot was lying with his back pressed against the bottom of the settee. He had always liked Henry.

'I'm sorry I have to rush off.' She would have liked to have sat for a while with Henry, taken time to be together and let the conversation happen. She felt a rush of irritation towards Hannah and then was embarrassed when Henry said, 'Well, you can't leave her there. I'll be fine, anyway; I've got all I need.'

She bent down to kiss him on the forehead.

★   ★   ★

Ella took the turns and junctions that she needed to without registering her route until she came to the final turning that led to the house. All the way she'd been thinking how awful she must sound to Henry over Hannah — no wonder he'd been looking at her strangely in the car.

Despite her determination to be more patient with Hannah, the moment Hannah's face dropped when she saw that Henry wasn't in the car, Ella's irritation reignited.

'I thought he might come with you.'

'Don't be ridiculous,' Ella told her. 'He's been travelling since this morning and he's in a lot of pain.'

'Is he badly hurt?' Hannah asked, sounding alarmed. She held the clip of the seat belt suspended in front of her chest.

'No, darling,' Ella reassured her. 'I think the flying wasn't too good for him. He'll soon be fine after he's rested.'

'I can't wait to see him.'

'He may be asleep,' Ella warned her, feeling as if she was preparing a small child for an unpleasant event.

'I bet he's glad to be home,' Hannah said.

217

'I know I would be.'

'How was your day, darling?'

'Good,' she said. 'I thought of an ending for my story. It came to me when I was cleaning the windows. I'm going to write it tonight.'

'Aren't you seeing Toby tonight?'

'Yes, I suppose so. At some point.'

'Are you going to introduce him to Henry? He wants to meet him.' She twisted to look at Hannah, her arm leaning out of the open window.

'You told Henry?'

'He asked for news about you. What was I supposed to say?'

'I suppose you told him about the Crop Circles, too?' Hannah accused.

'A little. Not much.'

'I wanted to tell him myself, that's all.'

Ella placed the fingers of her right hand on her forehead and counted to ten while she massaged her brow. 'He only knows that Toby and the circles exist. There's still plenty for you to talk about, Hannah.'

Henry was asleep when they arrived home but he woke up the moment Hannah went in, before she had even spoken to him. Ella watched from the door as Hannah pressed her face against her brother's and hugged him round the neck.

He groaned and she jumped back.

'What hurts?'

'Everything,' he said and they both laughed.

'Can I get you anything, Henry?' Ella called over.

'I'll get it,' Hannah offered. 'Whatever he needs.'

Ella went out into the garden. Scoot followed. He stretched and yawned, his backside up in the air. It made Ella want to stretch, too; her legs and back felt stiff and tired from the driving. She walked around the flowerbeds and then headed down to the pond where she hadn't been for a while. No matter how hot and dry the weather was, that area of the garden always remained damp. Ella maintained that there was a hidden spring around there somewhere but she'd never been able to find it. She had kept a patch of carr behind the pond to soak up some of the moisture and planted a giant gunnera which she had to push past now to get to the back of the pond. The pale green, young leaves had prickles as soft as the spines on the hoglets the kids had rescued one autumn but the mature ones scratched her skin.

It was worth it though. The giant Himalayan lily which had taken four years to mature was now a couple of feet taller than she was and in full flower. She stood on tiptoe and breathed in the strong scent of honeysuckle mixed with incense.

She heard Hannah and Henry's voices as they came out into the garden and then caught a hint of cigarette smoke. In a moment she would shout to them to come and see this amazing sight but for a few seconds longer she wanted to keep it all to herself.

20

Ella placed a cup of tea on the coffee table near Henry. He moved his head slightly and said, 'Thank you,' but he didn't look at her or take the opportunity to start a conversation even though she remained there long enough to give him the chance.

She closed the living room door and then walked quietly up the stairs. There was no need to walk quietly; no one would have cared if she'd run up them, singing at the top of her lungs, but she was going up to talk to Tyler about Henry and so she felt secretive and obliged to be a little discreet.

She knocked on Tyler's door.

'Come in.'

Tyler had swivelled in his chair to face the door and he watched her as she crossed the room and sat down on his bed. Tyler looked like a contented, scruffy bird surrounded by his shiny, precious possessions in the middle of his immaculate nest. His hair was too long and stuck up on the top like a crest; his feet were grubby, his toe-nails needed cutting. These details were things most people noticed but not Tyler; he'd never put great store by his appearance. What about a girl for Tyler? Would he ever find one stuck up in his room, beating a track from the house to the pub and back? *His head's in the clouds*, his teachers had always said, *but he's a sweet boy.*

'You should get out more,' she said.

'I'm fine, Ma.'

'It's stuffy in here,' she said. 'It's not healthy.'

'You get used to it. It's like living in a different climate,' he joked.

She stood up and squeezed between the wall and the end of the desk so that she could get to the window. Tyler's was the only room where you could catch sight of the cathedral on a clear day. She felt a yearning to be out there, away from the house, further than the city. She hadn't been to the coast for days now, not since Henry came home, and it felt like grief each time she remembered it.

'What is it, Ella?'

'It's Henry. I'm worried about him. I thought he'd be better once he'd rested but he seems to be getting worse; he's so down. I wondered if he'd talked to you?' She knew that Henry and Tyler had spent time together and that one evening they had walked to the pub. Tyler's friend Colin had given them a lift back.

'You mean about his accident?'

'I think something else happened, too. Have you noticed how he hasn't mentioned a single thing about this trip yet, or shown us any photos? It's not like him at all.'

'You're really worried, aren't you?'

She nodded.

'It's not really my place to tell you, but there was a woman,' Tyler said. 'Henry said something the other night. They split up after the accident.'

'A woman? A girlfriend?'

'Yes. She was Spanish, I think. But that's all I know.'

Ella took a moment to digest this. 'Was she in the accident too?'

'No. They'd argued before it. Henry was on his own.'

'He doesn't normally take it badly,' Ella said, thinking of the countless ex-girlfriends Henry had left in his wake. 'Was she special?'

Tyler shrugged. 'He didn't say.'

'Thank you. For telling me.' She leaned forward and kissed him on the forehead before slipping out from behind the desk.

'You won't let on I said anything, will you?'

'Of course not.'

She combed her fingers through his hair and gently turned him to face her. 'And Tyler, sweetheart, how are you doing?'

'You know you don't have to worry about me.'

'Thank God.' She smiled at him and then asked, seriously, 'Are you sure?'

He nodded. 'Or Hannah. Toby's all right, you know.'

Ella stepped back. That was the trouble with Tyler; he noticed more than you'd expect from someone who was stuck at the top of the house all day and most of the night.

'She didn't tell you about him because she thought you might make him leave. She wasn't going to tell me either.'

'We can't let any old person turn up and make themselves at home a couple of feet outside the garden. It might set a precedent.'

Tyler laughed. 'I can't see them queuing up to camp there.'

'I suppose not,' Ella said, happy to leave it there and get out before Tyler turned his wise gaze on her.

★ ★ ★

Later that evening, Ella drove into the village to pick up milk. There were several people already in the shop who carried on talking when she went in. She went straight to the fridge and picked up two litres of milk. She stood for a moment, listening to their conversation.

'They had the police out there the other evening.'

'What for?'

'Drugs, no doubt.'

'I won't drive that way now. They try and block the road and they're aggressive. One of them came at Trevor with a baseball bat.'

'I don't know how you can let your daughter go running around with them.'

Four unfriendly faces were looking in Ella's direction. Three of them she knew well, one only by name. It wasn't a nice atmosphere. She walked towards them.

'She's not running around with them. But even if she was, I wouldn't be worried. They're not doing any harm.'

'Tell that to Annie Potter. She's had her car stolen.'

'The Smiths' shed was broken into and their lawnmower was stolen.'

'What makes you think it was them? What on earth would they want with the lawn-mower?' Ella walked over to the counter and counted out the correct change.

'They'd sell it for drugs. They'd sell their grandmother for drugs.'

Instead of going straight home, Ella decided to drive to the camp. It was early evening and there were only five or six vehicles parked there; quite a few less than when Ella had passed before. There were lights on in two of the vans and three people were sitting around an unlit fire, drinking out of mugs and smoking cigarettes.

She left her car on the road and walked over to them with Scoot at her side. Out of nowhere, two dogs ran up to him. There was some posturing and peeing on the grass before they trotted off again.

'I'm looking for my daughter, Hannah.'

They shook their heads but didn't speak.

'She might be with Toby?'

'I know Toby,' one of them said. 'But he's not here.'

'The really blonde girl, you mean?' a redheaded young woman said.

'Yes.'

'She's not here either.'

When Ella got home, she knew Tyler was out because his motorbike had gone. Henry seemed to be asleep on the settee. She went up to Hannah's bedroom. There was no light on so she knocked quietly on the door before pushing it open.

Hannah's bed was made and the rest of the

room was reasonably tidy apart from a large pile of clothes that she had left hanging over the back of her desk chair. The clothes were a mixture of Ella's old ones, some from the second-hand and charity shops, and the odd item she had actually bought new. She must have been having a 'trying on' session before she went out.

Hannah's notebook was on the desk. It wasn't open, but her pen was slotted inside, marking the current page. Ella picked it up and then put it down almost immediately.

*   *   *

Ella crossed the lawn and passed through the gap in hedge. The boys had made this shortcut years ago by pushing through a narrow space until Ella was so fed up with snagged and torn clothes that she cut the branches back on either side. It became useful to her when she wanted to call them in for dinner and, as she emerged now, it was easy to remember those days.

She shouted, 'Hannah,' but received no reply. She walked over to the tent. It was zipped up and seemingly empty when she gave it a tap. Scoot started sniffing around the remains of a fire and she whistled him away.

Ella walked up the high bank. The sky over the fields and the marsh beds was growing dim. She thought she spotted a bright light further down but in an instant it was gone. She felt nervous. Even though she was only a few feet outside the boundary of her garden, it felt strange. Somewhere out there, she thought, was her

225

daughter. Hannah wouldn't be nervous; she was as comfortable in the open countryside as she was in Spindle House. All of this was her home, she belonged here much more than Ella ever had.

21

As Ella approached the turning for Spindle House, her guilt at not returning earlier to make lunch for Henry became acute. He'd been asleep when she'd set off to Ely and she'd intended to be an hour at the most in the shops but it was such a lovely day that she couldn't resist sitting on a bench on the riverside, watching the ducks and swans. Then, because she was hot, she'd gone into the nearest café and ordered an iced tea. Of course she knew that she was delaying going home but at least, she justified it to herself, she hadn't disappeared to Saltmarsh for the day.

She sighed. She had stayed away from the village for so many days now that the image of its wild, quiet beach had become so faded there were times she doubted its existence. The house and Henry's dark mood dragged her forwards, as if her car was hurtling towards a black hole.

There was a car in the drive which Ella didn't recognize. When she came round the side of the house, she saw the back of a brown-haired woman sitting at the garden table with Henry. Scoot ran up to the woman, pushing himself against her leg. She let out a shriek.

'Down, Scoot,' Ella called and hurried towards the table.

'This is Kirsten,' Henry said.

'Hello, Mrs Ruland.' She bobbed up from her chair, her hand outstretched, and plumped down again when she noticed that Ella's hands were full with shopping bags.

'You remember Kirsten, Ella?' Henry said.

Ella was pleased to hear the animation in his voice and to see a new brightness in his face. She turned with greater interest towards Kirsten whose face she now recognized. She was pretty in a bland kind of way; she had freckles on her nose and her eyes were big and wide-spaced, giving her face an openness that Ella didn't naturally trust. She thought she might be the kind of person who didn't appear to be paying attention but who was taking everything in. Kirsten had dropped her gaze as if she'd been observing Ella but now she slowly raised her eyes to meet Ella's.

'Oh, Henry, of course Mrs Ruland won't. It was years ago.'

'It's Ella. Please.'

Kirsten's smile made her face light up. 'Ella.'

'Kirsten? Aren't you Joy and Clive's daughter?'

'Yes, that's right.'

Ella remembered. She was the only child of older parents and she had seemed a lonely little girl. One year, after seeing her dressed in frumpy clothes like a mini-Joy at the school gates, Ella had gone straight over to Joy and invited Kirsten to Henry's birthday party which was coming up. Joy had looked surprised and strangely annoyed, and Ella thought that Kirsten probably wouldn't come. But she had — in a terrible pink satin dress — her eyes wide with excitement.

'We were just working out how long it was since Henry and I went out.'

'It's over ten years ago,' Henry said and gave a rueful, playful smile which was clearly for Kirsten's benefit.

Of course. How could Ella have forgotten? Kirsten had been Henry's girlfriend for a short time when they were in the sixth form and she vaguely remembered Kirsten as one of the many girls who would ring for Henry only to be told he was out.

'Your garden is beautiful,' Kirsten said. 'It's been my dream garden ever since I first saw it.'

'Oh, that's very kind.'

'Are you going to join us?' Henry asked. 'Kirsten made some food.'

'I hope you don't mind. Henry said he hadn't had lunch so I prepared a light tea.'

The light tea consisted of a tomato salad, bread and cheese. Kirsten had also filled a bowl with some crisps, as you would for a child's picnic.

'Of course I don't mind; I'm grateful. I'm sorry, Henry, I got held up in Ely,' she mumbled lamely. 'It looks lovely but I must put the shopping away.'

Kirsten jumped up, taking the bags from Ella. 'I'll do it. If you sit down, I'll bring a plate and a glass.'

She trotted across the patio and into the kitchen. She was a short woman, a little plump, with big boobs and a small waist. Her clothing wasn't as old-fashioned as she'd been made to wear as a child but it was pretty conservative. She was thirty, the same age as Henry, but from a distance you could easily think she was in her forties.

Ella sat down opposite Henry. 'You look better, darling. Did you have a good sleep?'

'Not bad,' he replied but she felt as if his attention was on hold, waiting for Kirsten to return. They both turned as she bounced out of the back door towards them, hair flapping, boobs jiggling, a broad smile on her face. Ella didn't dare look at the expression on Henry's face.

'There.' Kirsten laid out a plate, glass, knife and a paper napkin in front of her. The napkin was a surprise; even Ella wouldn't have been able to say where they were stored right now. As Kirsten poured juice into her glass, Ella noticed that she wasn't wearing a ring on her wedding finger.

'Shall I get something for you?' Kirsten asked Henry as she sat down beside him. Henry, who hated to be waited on, said yes, another slice of bread and cheese would be great, thanks, Kirsten, and why did food taste so much better outdoors on a lovely sunny day?

'Oh, it does, doesn't it?' Kirsten enthused. 'Especially in such a beautiful place as this.'

Ella felt as if she were in the middle of a scene which was moving too fast for her to keep up. She closed her eyes for a brief moment until Henry spoke,

'I've been catching up on all the gossip.'

'Henry, of course, is the gossip,' Kirsten said. 'I mean, the big news in the village is that he's back home.'

It had been the same when Edward returned from a trip. Ella couldn't move two steps in the village without being stopped by people wanting to ask about him. In a way, it had made her feel proud to be part of the excitement and it had helped her to feel as if she belonged.

'You know, Ella, this stuff about the crop circles sounds like it might be getting a bit out of hand. Maybe we should talk to Hannah?' Henry said.

'I was telling Henry there's been a lot of trouble with the Travellers.'

'I think we should leave her alone.' Ella looked first at Henry and then at Kirsten.

'The villagers aren't very happy, that's all,' Kirsten said quietly.

'Let them be unhappy. Hannah's not any of their business.' Ella held Kirsten's gaze until she lowered her eyes and began to gather a few spilled crumbs into the palm of her hand.

'Hannah's not stupid,' Henry said after a brief silence. 'I'm sure there's nothing to worry about.'

'Where do you work, Kirsten?' Ella asked.

Kirsten lifted her eyes and sat up straighter when she saw Ella smiling at her. The happiness in her face was as obvious as Scoot's eagerness to please after he'd been told off.

'A solicitors in Ely.'

'And do you live in Ely too?'

'Yes. I've got a flat. It's on the second floor so it hasn't got a garden,' she said. 'That's why it's been so lovely sitting out here.' She smiled. 'But, all the same, I'd better be going.'

'You'll have to come again,' Henry said. 'Won't she?'

'Really?' Kirsten stopped quite still, her eyes fixed on Ella.

'Yes, it's been great to see you,' Henry said, sounding as if he really meant it. For the first time since he'd been home he seemed relaxed, as if he'd been relieved of something. Ella wondered what it was about Kirsten that she should have managed that so quickly.

'Of course,' Ella said. 'Anytime.'

'Well, thank you. I'll pop round after work.' She stood up. 'It was lovely to see you, Mrs Ruland, and you too, Henry. Don't get up, either of you.'

'Don't forget to come and see me again,' Henry called out and she waved at him before disappearing round the corner of the house.

'She seems nice,' Ella said once the car had turned off the drive onto the track.

'Yes. Kirsten will always be Kirsten,' Henry replied immediately, but Ella couldn't tell from the tone of his voice if he thought that was a good thing or not.

'Has she got a boyfriend, did she say?'

'She didn't mention one,' Henry said and Ella wondered how long it would be before Kirsten was back.

★ ★ ★

On Wednesday evening, as soon as Ella heard a car on the drive, she knew it was Kirsten. She was relieved. The day after Kirsten's visit Henry

232

had seemed much more spirited; he had begun to strip the outside frame of the kitchen window where the paint was flaking badly. It took him a long time as he was only using one hand and because, whenever Ella looked up from the bed she was weeding, he had stopped — whether in thought or to rest, Ella wasn't sure. But when Ella went to call him for dinner, she found that he'd left out all the tools and sandpaper and was asleep on one of the garden loungers. He ate only half his meal and hardly exchanged a word despite Hannah's efforts at conversation, and went to bed early.

Today, the frame remained untouched and Henry, apart from coming outside for a smoke, lay on the settee in the living room with the curtains closed. Ella felt annoyed every time she went in or passed the room; the air was stuffy and dusty like a forgotten room in a museum. It made her desire to drive to Saltmarsh harder to live with — she could almost feel the soft wind blowing through her clothes and the sand sifting across her bare feet. She even missed sitting outside the pub with a cup of weak-tasting coffee. Yet she knew she couldn't go. At some point, without really being conscious of how, she'd tied herself to a promise that she wouldn't go back there until Henry showed signs of improvement.

Ella walked round to the front of the house. Kirsten was locking her car.

'I've come to see Henry,' she said, as if Ella wouldn't know that.

'How lovely,' Ella called back and told her to

go straight in as the front door was unlocked.

She returned to her weeding and for a while managed to fall into the spell of what she was doing so that, when she stood up, she saw with some satisfaction the progress she had made.

'Would you like a cup of tea?' Kirsten called over from the kitchen doorway. 'I'm making one for me and Henry.'

'Yes, please.' Ella walked towards her, beating off the soil from the glove she'd been using on the leg of her shorts.

'It must be quite a job keeping on top of such a big place,' Kirsten said as they stood together, looking out across the lawn.

'It is.'

'But you love it,' Kirsten said. 'So it doesn't feel so much like work.'

'I suppose not.' Ella looked behind her into the house. 'Where's Henry?'

'He's gone up to his room to get changed. I thought it might make him feel a bit better. We're going to sit out here with our tea when it's made.'

'When are you next coming over?'

Kirsten seemed flustered. 'Oh, I don't know. I hadn't thought.'

Ella laughed. 'I'm sorry, I realize I'm sounding rather odd. I've been worried about Henry and he seemed much happier after you were last here. You really cheer him up.'

'I'll come back whenever you want. If you think I'm helping.'

'Can you come tomorrow?'

'I'm sorry, I can't tomorrow. I go . . . I have

something to do on Thursdays.'

'Friday then?'

'Yes, Friday is fine.'

'Shush.' Ella put her finger to her lips. She could hear the thump of Henry's feet on the stairs. 'So, Friday then,' she whispered. 'Thanks, Kirsten.'

★ ★ ★

On Friday Ella had toast for breakfast and then, as she was sitting in the kitchen drinking a cup of coffee, waiting for one of the children to get up, she realized that she wasn't obliged to tell them she was going out, she could simply leave. The decision made, she hurried to get herself ready before any of them appeared and delayed her.

As she got nearer to the coast, the sky began to grey over and a few spots of rain fell on the windscreen, creating a smeared arc when she put the wipers on. The screen washer seemed to be out of liquid or blocked again and so every time the sun made an appearance she had to angle her head to see clearly.

There was one other car in the village car park but she couldn't see anyone on the beach. The wind whipped up sand into her face as she came down the steps and she felt cold until she'd been walking for a few minutes.

The tide must have gone out recently as there was a wavy line of seaweed and shells on the sand, dotted with brightly coloured things: a punctured blue plastic ball, a white trainer, lengths of orange and blue rope.

She looked out at the horizon. It was hard to see the difference between sea and sky. She looked behind her where the wind was lifting trails of sand at the foot of the dunes and felt the pressure lift and her spirit float free, as light as the air around her.

It was too cold to sit outside the pub for very long. She ate a bowl of ham and pea soup with toasted garlic French bread, warming her hands on the sides of the dish until all the soup was gone.

It had never been her intention to call Denis but, as soon as she opened her purse to pay for the meal, the edge of the white card he'd given her seemed to shine out at her. She left a tip for the girl behind the bar. It was the girl who had served her the very first time but she was friendlier today and offered her a bowl of water for Scoot.

Ella returned to the car and turned the heating on to warm her feet. The sea was getting rougher, the waves were cresting further out but the sky was clearing.

She didn't often use her mobile phone and she decided that if, when she got it out of her bag, there was any battery left, then she would phone Denis. If there wasn't, she would go home.

She turned on the phone. It beeped into life and she peered down at the dim display. There was both battery and reception. She took the card out of her purse and carefully pressed each digit.

'Denis, it's Ella.'

'Ella, How lovely. I had begun to lose hope.'

'I — uh . . . ' She stared dumbly out of the window and felt hot with humiliation.

Denis came to the rescue. 'Are you in my neck of the woods by any chance?'

'Yes. Not far away.'

'Shall we meet? At Blake's?'

'Yes. What time?'

'Well, I have the luxury of only walking down the street so it's as soon as you can get here.'

'Half an hour?'

'Half an hour it is.'

Ella leaned over and pulled the passenger sunshield down to look in the mirror. With only the narrow view it offered her, she had the impression of a wind-blown and weather-beaten face. She looked down at the damp patch in her lap where Scoot had lain his wet stomach across her and brushed ineffectively at the sand sticking to the wet bottoms of her trousers.

She got out of the car. She scraped her fingers through her hair, dusted her trousers down with Scoot's towel, fished out a dry pair of faded blue canvas shoes and a cream linen blouson jacket that she kept in the boot. She felt there was some improvement but she wasn't sure it was up to the standard of Blake's or Denis.

It took her only twenty minutes to reach the car park behind Salisbury's and every minute that she sat in the car waiting made it harder to get out. Suddenly her mother's words came to her, words that she hadn't thought of for years: 'She was making a production out of it.' It was true — she was going to meet someone, that was all. Something that the younger Ella wouldn't have thought twice about.

Denis was already there and she apologized for being late although, when she glanced at the bar clock, she saw it was only by a couple of minutes. He stood up to kiss her hello and insisted on going to the bar for her drink.

'How do you usually spend your day?' she asked him when he returned.

'Let me see. I have a leisurely breakfast, I go for a swim — in the local pool not the sea. In the afternoon I read, or go for a walk or play bowls. In the evenings, I might watch a bit of TV, or have a drink here. Sometimes I look after my grandson on a weekend morning.'

She thought how unlike Edward he was. Edward was intense and restless but Denis was as calm as the sea on the turn. She felt her confidence slip — she hadn't wanted to think of Edward.

'I see you were shocked by my mentioning bowls.'

She laughed.

'I hope to convince you that it's a wonderful game. And very sociable; I've made lots of friends.'

The word 'friends' echoed in her mind. She felt her face flush with the realization that, apart from Sadie, her life was bereft of friends.

'It's not terribly exciting but it makes me happy.'

'You're happy?' she asked but she knew the answer already. He had the relaxed, confident features of a contented man.

'Yes. For the most part.'

'Don't you get lonely, Denis?'

'Yes. Sometimes. Do you?'

She nodded. She couldn't speak, finding herself choked with sudden tears. She pinched the top of her nose hard and sniffed. She felt so embarrassed she couldn't look at Denis. 'I'm sorry.'

'There's no need to be.'

'I don't know where that came from,' she said and managed a laugh.

'It happens to us all,' he told her and went back to the bar, giving her time to find a tissue in her bag and get herself in order.

'I've taken the liberty of ordering avocado and prawn *crostini*. They are very good here,' he said when he sat down.

The *crostini* were delicious and Denis kindly persuaded her to have the last one. She felt a little drunk even though she'd only had two small glasses of wine. She wondered if she was over the limit. She had never understood how units of alcohol worked and usually kept to her own rule of only one glass of whatever she was drinking.

It would have been easy, she thought, to have stayed on and drunk a little more. She felt safe in Blake's with Denis; she felt protected from whatever the winds of the Fens were blowing at her. But of course it was impossible to stay. She slid her arms into her jacket, she picked up her handbag, she pushed back her hair and stood up. With each movement, she was preparing, arming herself for her return to Spindle House.

Denis walked her to her car and there was a

moment as he leaned forward and held the door open for her when she thought that he was going to kiss her. He didn't, but instead of feeling relieved, she felt the non-kiss hovering near her lips and wished that she had had it to remember on the journey home. She wondered how it would have tasted. *Like salt*, she thought. *A briny kiss, full of the sea and sunshine.*

22

Less than two weeks after Kirsten had first visited, Ella came down and found Henry and Kirsten in the kitchen. It was a pleasant tableau of a couple in love — talking and laughing over a shared breakfast, but for Ella it was a shocking moment. She stopped quite still, her skin chilled. She would have turned around and left except that Henry saw her and so she had no choice but to join them.

'I've made coffee,' Kirsten said. 'If you'd like some.'

'Yes, please.' Once she was sitting, she began to feel much better, although the waves of aftershock continued to hammer her heart. For that brief moment, it had been like seeing Edward and herself. But it was Henry of course, not Edward, and it was Kirsten who happened to be wearing an old robe of Ella's.

'I hope you don't mind,' Kirsten said, gesturing to the robe. She must have caught Ella looking. 'Henry got it from the linen cupboard.'

Henry said, 'Of course Ella doesn't mind, I told you.' And Ella was grateful that she didn't have to reply because she wouldn't have known how to.

A couple of minutes later, Hannah appeared. She was wearing Ella's suede miniskirt with a purple voile tunic which came to a couple of inches above the hem of the skirt. She had tied back her wet hair and her head looked small and fragile.

Over the rim of her mug, Ella watched her daughter taking in the scene.

'Isn't that Ella's . . . ?'

Hannah knew all the clothes Ella owned and was probably more possessive of them than Ella herself.

'Kirsten's borrowed it.'

'Of course I don't look anywhere near as good as you would in it. You always look so elegant in whatever you wear.'

Ella found Kirsten difficult. She had lost count of the times that Kirsten had mentioned her elegance or her good taste or her glamorous past. At first Ella had felt quite flattered, but it had become embarrassing after a while. She didn't know how to respond — it sounded clumsy and false to reciprocate with a compliment each time — because Kirsten, of course, was anything but elegant. She was gauche and frumpy like her mother who, Ella remembered now, she had first mistaken for Kirsten's grandmother. And Kirsten had a strange way of always pausing before she replied to a question, as if she was holding back the real answer and supplying the one she thought Ella wanted to hear instead. This gave Ella the impression that she didn't know anything about her, which was odd considering how much time Kirsten spent at Spindle House and her constant stream of chatter.

'You're a different shape, that's why,' Hannah piped up when Kirsten was standing at the toaster. When Kirsten turned round, Ella noticed that she was flushed and was pulling the robe tighter as if to make herself smaller.

'Hannah is always borrowing my clothes. Or adopting them as her own,' Ella said, feeling a little sorry for the woman. Hannah could be honest to the point of insensitivity sometimes.

'This is one of Ella's.' Hannah lifted up her tunic to show Kirsten the skirt underneath. Ella glimpsed her daughter's concave stomach and the jut of hip bones under the waistband. 'And these.' She pointed to the sunglasses on top of her head.

'Very trendy,' Kirsten said. 'I think I've seen you with those on, Ella, in a photograph somewhere.'

'If this is about clothes,' Henry stood up, 'it's my cue to excuse myself and get dressed.' He stretched, winced and swore.

Ella glanced at Kirsten who seemed to be feasting her eyes on her son's bare torso. A lot of his bruises had faded, although the worst one across his diaphragm was still purple-black in the centre.

'What are you doing today, Hannah?' Ella asked, switching her attention away from Henry. Hannah stopped dead still.

'Why? Did you want to go into Ely or something?'

Ella looked at her in surprise. 'No, I was only wondering . . . '

'I didn't think so,' Hannah said and with that she was gone, leaving Ella and Kirsten sitting in silence for several moments.

'Do you want me to take Henry to the hospital for his check-up?'

Ella had forgotten all about the appointment. 'Aren't you supposed to be at work?'

'I could take the day off. I'm owed holiday.'

Although it would leave her free to go to Saltmarsh and to see Denis, Ella felt inclined to refuse precisely because she wanted to go so badly.

'It would give you a chance to work in the garden. It must be hard keeping up such a big house as well as the garden.'

'Well, I don't always manage it, as you can see.'

'I could help. I don't mind. I'd like to.'

'That's very kind but — '

'You like to do it yourself.'

'Yes, that's it,' Ella agreed although it was a lie. It would be wonderful to have the work done for her. Her heart wasn't in it at the moment and she knew she was only skimming the surface of what should be done and drifting along on the back of the work she'd put in over the years. But help would have had to come in spirit form because there wasn't a single real person she could imagine herself allowing to do it. Not anyone she knew, not Hannah, not a stranger and she didn't want Kirsten of all people helping her. The unbidden phrase echoed in her head. Kirsten of all people. Her attention swerved back to the woman in front of her. Now, Ella wondered, why should she think that?

'Have you ever thought about having a conservatory?'

'Not really, no,' Ella replied, feeling wrong-footed by Kirsten's question.

'You get very tasteful ones now. I was looking at some in the magazines and the best thing is that they really add value to your house.'

'I hadn't really considered — '

'They're brilliant in winter; you can still enjoy your garden without being out there.'

'It sounds nice but — '

'You know, this place could be amazing . . . Well, I mean it already is.' Kirsten smiled.

Ella forced a smile in return. 'I like to think so.'

'I'll bring some information for you to have a look.'

'Oh, all right. Thanks.'

'So shall I take Henry?'

'OK. Thank you.' Ella sighed and decided that agreeing was the easiest thing to do.

Kirsten

23

It wasn't that Kirsten didn't love her parents, it was the thought of having to spend the whole Sunday afternoon with them where every minute was accounted for. She often got this feeling and sometimes, like today, she even held the phone in her hand with an excuse ready. She had to get the balance right, not too light otherwise it would seem as if she simply couldn't be bothered, but not serious enough to worry them. 'I've got a cold starting' was the best, 'and I really don't want to pass it on to you.' She was hopeful that her thoughtfulness would neutralize the bad marks against her for not turning up.

In the end, it was easier to go. But the fact that it was she who — in a small way — had made the decision to do so revived her mood. It was a beautiful day: hot and dry with the sky an immense blue dome curving above. She would have felt too guilty to do anything but stay indoors anyway; tidying up, washing out undies, having a slow, quiet day, getting ready to go to work the next day.

As soon as she opened the front door, her mother appeared, a wide silhouette hurrying down the narrow, dark hall towards her. As her mother leaned in to place a dry kiss on Kirsten's cheek, her fingers almost — but didn't quite — touched her daughter's bare arm. Kirsten had often wondered whether she would receive a more enthusiastic greeting if her parents didn't see her so often.

She followed her mother towards the weak light emanating from the open kitchen door which they stopped outside. Joy had an apron tied around her church clothes, her polished shoes gleamed, her hair was freshly done. She looked like a woman in an advert for gravy from the 1950's.

Kirsten was also wearing a skirt and short-sleeved blouse but she had on sandals and she knew her mother would be thinking that she looked cheap with her bare legs and arms, especially on a Sunday. Kirsten waited for Joy to mention her transgression but her silence after the way she looked her up and down was enough to lower Kirsten's spirits.

'Your father's in the lounge. I'll make the tea.'

Clive had on slacks and a shirt and tie even though it was eighty degrees outside.

'Aren't you hot?' she asked him but he said not and, in fact, the living room was quite dingy and cool; you would be hard-pressed to know it was summer out there. Kirsten had a theory that these houses were purposely built at an aspect which minimized the amount of sunlight inside, making it hard for expectations and aspirations to rise out of the grey and gloomy atmosphere and so keeping the occupiers in their place.

She stood in front of the window and considered the little garden. It looked like a painted scene, perfect and unreal. It was immaculately ordered with groups of pots surrounded by clean, grey gravel. The wooden bench was alive with sunlight and she would have loved to have been able to suggest that they sit and drink their tea on it but she knew it was futile. The garden was somewhere to keep neat and tidy but not to enjoy.

She had never been encouraged to play outside as a child and as she got older she wasn't allowed to help in the garden either. She was more of a hindrance than a help, she'd been told on many occasions.

Kirsten could have done so much with the garden. She would have filled it with colour; beds would brim with flowers, fences would be festooned with climbers, birds would fly in, bees buzz, butterflies teeter on perfumed cushions.

'Sit down, love. You don't look like you're stopping.'

She sat on the sofa opposite her father's armchair.

'How's work going?' he asked through the newspaper he held up in front of his face.

'Well,' Kirsten said.

'Good, good. Any chance of that promotion?'

Kirsten didn't know why her father had got it in his head that she was due for promotion. In all honesty, she'd gone as far as she probably could with the company without getting more qualifications. 'Maybe. We'll see.'

There was a loud crash from the kitchen. Kirsten's father was out of his chair in a second. Kirsten didn't think she'd ever seen him move so fast. She followed him into the kitchen where she saw her mother kneeling down over the smashed milk bottle.

'That was the last,' Joy said. 'I used the rest for the sauce.'

Her parents looked at each other as if their world had come to an end.

'I'll go and get some from the shop,' Kirsten said and you would have thought she'd suggested she was going to fly to the moon.

She walked slowly down the road, enjoying the warmth on her skin. The shop was busy, bustling. She picked up the milk from the fridge but let an elderly lady go ahead of her in the queue as she was in no hurry to get back.

'Hey, Kirsten.'

Someone touched her on the shoulder. She turned to see the smiling face of her old schoolfriend, Jasmine.

'Visiting your parents?'

'Sunday lunch.'

'Stuff that today,' Jasmine said. 'It's much too hot. We're taking the kids to the beach.' She was clutching bags of crisps, some chocolate bars and a pretty, dark-haired little girl at her side was holding two packets of pasties.

'Lucky you,' Kirsten said, feeling a rush of jealousy which she immediately felt guilty about.

'They like their routines, though, don't they? The oldies,' Jasmine said sympathetically, which Kirsten thought was nice of her as she knew for a fact, from the disapproving comments Joy had made, that since retirement Jasmine's parents had eschewed their old routines like Sunday church-going and instead were 'gallivanting on golfing trips' all over the world.

'Oh, Kirsten.' Jasmine stopped her as she was

about to leave. 'Did you know Henry's back? Henry Ruland. He's been in an accident or something and come home to recover.'

'Henry?'

'He's still single, I hear,' Jasmine said over her shoulder as she passed her shopping to the woman on the till. 'You should go and see him.'

'Maybe.'

'You never know.' Jasmine winked and Kirsten glanced around, embarrassed, sure that everyone was listening.

'I've got to go, Jas,' she said, walking away, calling back, 'Nice to see you. Have fun on the beach.'

★ ★ ★

'You were gone a long time. The tea's cold. I'll have to make a new pot.'

'Isn't it a bit late now? We'll be eating soon,' her father said.

'The shop was busy. Everyone's having picnics and barbecues.'

'Typical,' Joy said. 'There was hardly anyone at church today. Fair weather worshippers, that's what they are.'

Kirsten didn't bother to point out her mother's misnomer. She watched her disappear into the kitchen, not to return until the dinner was served up, and flicked through the magazine of her father's paper. There was an article on a country house in Essex in the Home section which looked beautiful.

She glanced around the lounge but she could

have described it in detail with her eyes closed. Her parents had hardly changed anything from when they bought it. They had the same brick fireplace, virtually the same cream anaglypta wallpaper with its repeated pattern of beige grasses, the display cabinet of china thimbles, a single framed photograph of their wedding day and one of Kirsten's christening in the local church. Her bedroom was the only room which they had ever altered substantially with a new carpet and curtains and new MFI furniture only weeks after she'd left home; as if they couldn't wait to eradicate her.

They squashed into the stuffy, drab dining room. Kirsten took her usual seat with her back to the window; there was barely enough room to push the chair away to get in. A patch of sun burned on the middle of her back which in other circumstances might have been pleasant but in the airless room it made her cramped body feel more tortured. If she went to see Henry, Kirsten thought, she could have a look round Spindle House and see if it was as lovely as she remembered.

The meal was exactly the same as it always was, winter or summer. Beef, Yorkshire pudding, roast potatoes, cabbage, carrots and onion gravy. She tried to feel grateful but the food was too heavy to be eating on a hot day like today.

'I saw Jasmine in the shop. She said that Henry Ruland has come home.'

'Which one is he?'

'The one in the same year as Kirsten at school,' Joy explained. 'The one that travels.'

254

'Another one shirking his responsibilities, like his father,' Clive said. 'When he should be out earning money.'

'Mr Ruland was earning money. Travelling was part of his job,' Kirsten said.

'Left her to bring up those kids on her own. No wonder they came out wrong. She just let them run wild.' Her mother pursed her lips. 'She could barely look after herself; she used to turn up in old, dirty clothes to fetch them from school like she didn't own a penny, I could never understand the fuss they made about her.'

'Who's they? What fuss?'

'People. When they got married. You'd swear they were Prince Charles and Lady Di back then. You couldn't move for photos in the papers.'

'Why?'

'He was the eligible bachelor, the one all the girls were after, especially after his parents were killed in a car crash. She was the glamour girl of the Sixties.'

'The Kennedy Curse,' her father interrupted. 'Bad blood. And the luck to go with it.'

'You can see it coming out in the girl. She's an albino.'

'I heard she's a little simple.'

'She's nothing of the sort,' Kirsten protested, remembering her as quiet and gentle; a sweet girl.

Her parents maintained their silence while Kirsten flushed with shame and anger. 'Anyway, I thought I'd go and see Henry.'

'Why would you want to do that?' Joy asked.

Kirsten had never told her parents she was going out with Henry when she was at school — an instinct which she understood better now. 'He was in a car accident and he could probably do with some company.'

'An accident? I told you,' Clive lifted his knife and waved it in the air. 'They're cursed.'

'I wouldn't bother,' Joy said. 'They won't want to know you.'

After they'd eaten, Kirsten and her father returned to the lounge while Joy got on with the washing up — she liked to do it straightaway so she could relax. She never accepted Kirsten's offer to help, maintaining she was clumsy and would only break something.

Clive put the TV on and they watched it in silence.

'Have you heard about the Travellers?' Kirsten's father asked her when the credits of the programme were rolling.

'No. Who are they?'

'They're a disgrace is who they are,' her mother said, rubbing cream into her hands as she came into the room. 'Thieves and vandals, the lot of them.'

'They've come to see a circle or some such nonsense in a field. They believe aliens made them.'

'They were talking about it at work. I didn't realize it was around here.'

'It's not far from the village over by Wicker's bend. On Jenkins' land.'

'Everyone's got to lock their doors now. Mrs Lambert won't leave her house once it's dark.

We're like prisoners in our own homes. Show her the paper, Clive.'

Kirsten's father leaned down to pick up a newspaper. He passed it to Kirsten. It had been folded on the page where there was an aerial photograph of two rings, one inside the other, in the middle of a field. It looked quite beautiful. Underneath was a shot of a group of people with several vehicles behind them.

'They're only alien watchers,' Kirsten said.

'The police should move them on,' Clive said.

'They're nothing but trouble,' Joy added and Kirsten could tell that they had been talking this over for days.

The volume on the TV was turned up for *Songs of Praise* — their favourite programme — and all hope of conversation ceased immediately.

Kirsten could feel her mother's warmth close to her skin and hear her heavy breathing. Every now and then her father cleared his throat, a habit of his which had driven her to distraction when she lived at home. Kirsten glanced out of the window. Her whole body felt as if it was screaming.

'I'd better be going.' She stood up.

'Aren't you staying for tea?' Joy asked, her eyes flicking between Kirsten and the TV.

'I've got some extra work to do for tomorrow.'

'That's a good girl. You want to show them you're keen,' Clive said without turning his head.

★ ★ ★

257

She beeped her car horn even though she knew her mother didn't like her doing it but drove away slowly instead of hurtling the car down the road as she would have liked to do. She shivered with pleasure as cool air from the air-conditioning began to circulate. She drove through the top of the village and then doubled back towards Spindle House but when she came to the turning, she drove straight past it and onto the bridge where she stopped.

Kirsten had first visited Spindle House when she was nine years old and went to a birthday party of Henry's. Joy had bought her a party dress especially for the day but had given the dress to the Salvation Army a couple of weeks later. It was the only children's party she'd ever been to as her mother had told her that you shouldn't accept other people's invitations if you couldn't give invitations of your own. Kirsten had never understood why they couldn't invite people to their house, but she knew better than to ask.

At the end of the party, Henry was giving kisses to all the girls along with the balloons and party bags and that was the closest Kirsten got to him for years until they began to travel on the same bus to the grammar school in Ely. In the sixth form a couple of their mutual friends paired off and Henry and Kirsten ended up spending time together, talking, then kissing, until everyone started calling them girlfriend and boyfriend.

They only really saw each other on the bus and during some lunch breaks at school. A few times, Kirsten had walked down to see Henry at the house but it was difficult for her to get away for long and Henry was never at home. Henry finished their relationship one day when he told her he was going out with someone else. It wasn't a surprise; Kirsten hadn't believed Henry could really like her anyway. But it was still the worst thing she'd ever lived through in her life and at the time she didn't know how she was ever going to get over it.

Of course she did get over it, and the break-up of a couple of other relationships since, but every now and then something would make Kirsten think of Henry and wonder where he was and what he was doing.

It seemed to her that of everyone she had known, Henry was the only one who had made it. Not in terms of money, she didn't mean that. Some of the other boys they were at school with were loaded now but they worked for fifty hours in an office all week like Jasmine's husband and then played golf all day on Sunday. Henry was an adventurer. Henry was romance.

There was a tractor approaching behind Kirsten and, because the bridge was a single track, she had to drive forward. She kept going until she was home.

Kirsten's flat always seemed extra light and airy after she'd been to her parents' house. She had originally wanted one of the ground floor garden flats but she couldn't afford one in the end. She was glad now, because she'd noticed how much more shaded the bottom of the Old Corn Exchange was, with their smaller windows and the high walls around the gardens. Up on the second floor, there was nothing to impede the sun and she had a good view of the cathedral and the nice part of the city.

She was given the choice of the fittings and décor as part of the price and it had taken her ages to choose, finally deciding on the Country Cottage look. She was pleased on the whole. She liked the cream-painted units in the kitchen and the polished pine flooring throughout. She loved her living area the best with its thick, cream rug, the chandelier with white and pink glass beads like a dream catcher over the dining table and the window sill of flourishing plants.

She changed into her lounge pants and T-shirt and, after watering her plants and dusting the ornaments and collection of candlesticks on the shelving unit, she settled on the settee with a cup of tea, a bar of chocolate and one of the binders containing some of the glossy house and garden magazines which she'd been collecting for over five years since she started looking for her flat.

24

On Monday, Kirsten was first to arrive at work as usual. She shared her office with Emma and Valerie but she liked to get everything switched on and the coffee going for when the other two arrived. Together they formed a pool of secretaries for the partners of the firm although each was assigned a particular one for whom they did priority work. Although there wasn't officially a senior secretary among them, Kirsten had been there the longest and it was generally she who covered any emergencies.

Valerie was next to get in and Emma the last. Valerie was married with two teenage children but Emma was only twenty-three and single and she had a very active social life which seemed to consist of drinking and clubbing the whole weekend and some week nights too. Kirsten suspected that she was still drunk on occasions when she came to work but she had never brought it up with Emma or mentioned it to Valerie, although she suspected Val thought the same.

Kirsten had been to pick up any early mail from the post-room and she came into the office as the other two were talking about their weekends.

'Wasn't it gorgeous weather?' she remarked, and the others agreed with her. 'My friend Jasmine went to the beach but I bet the traffic to get there was terrible.'

'I wouldn't fancy sitting in a jam in that heat,' Valerie said.

'Nor me,' Kirsten replied and quickly turned her attention to her PC and began to type.

In the afternoon, when Emma brought Kirsten the biscuits to have with her tea, she asked, 'Is it all right, Kirsten, if I leave a bit early today?'

'It's your turn to do the late cover, isn't it?'

'Yes, but I've made plans and . . . '

Kirsten looked at the biscuit she had poised in mid-air and then up at Emma's impatient, expectant face. 'I'm sorry but I've made plans too,' she said, and took a bite out of the biscuit.

Kirsten could see in Emma's eyes that she didn't believe her. She chewed slowly while Emma watched. Finally she swallowed and said, 'A friend of mine who's been travelling has come back home injured and I'm going to see him. Why don't you ask Val to do it?'

Emma turned to look at Valerie.

'No,' Valerie called over. 'Sorry, Emma. I've made arrangements.'

'Sorry.' Kirsten shrugged and shuffled papers until Emma had returned to her desk.

During the rest of the afternoon, Emma made several telephone calls where she talked quietly and urgently into the phone, flashing Kirsten an occasional dirty look whenever their eyes met. Emma didn't look up as Kirsten was leaving, so on impulse she called a cheery, 'Have a nice evening,' before closing the door.

The car bumped and bounced up the badly potholed track and it was a relief to turn into the open gate and onto the gravel drive. There it was — Spindle House — prettier than she'd remembered, with white flowering climbers in full bloom, bright against the honey-coloured stone. She'd forgotten how grand the front door was with pillars either side and the stone steps leading up to it and she'd never noticed the brick buildings on the right which were almost entirely covered in ivy. There were no cars in the drive so she parked next to a rusty motorbike.

When she got out of the car, she was surprised by how quiet it was. Whenever Kirsten had thought about the house, she saw it full of people and noise and laughter, and yet, as she stood on the front steps, the atmosphere of absorbing silence seemed to be both familiar and right.

She rang the doorbell but no one answered. She pressed it again, putting her ear against the door to see if it was working. She couldn't hear anything. She turned round quickly, thinking someone was watching her but there was nobody in sight. The door knocker was made of heavy cast iron in a twisted rope design and looked as old as the house. She knocked a few times but it sounded embarrassingly loud.

She realized, of course, that they would all be in the garden — how silly of her not to think of that before. Taking a deep breath, she walked round the side of the house, calling ahead of her. She regretted not going home to change now;

she was hot in her tights and her work clothes seemed totally inappropriate for wandering around someone's garden.

Kirsten stopped. In every direction there was something beautiful to see: a bed of white and blue flowers of all shades caught her eye, an archway covered in a white rose led enticingly to a dark, secret area; further off, she could see pink, blue and yellow flower heads sprinkled like scraps of coloured paper blowing in the tall grass. It looked absolutely lovely but, if it had been Kirsten's, she would have chosen deeper, richer colours: buttercup yellow, purple-blues and all shades of red: crimson, maroons and cerise.

She looked over at the house and noticed that the back door was open. On either side, the heads of a white hydrangea nodded as she approached and white sea campion spilled over the edge of the stones.

Suddenly a head appeared at the top of the house. It was Tyler. All grown up with a goatee and lots of hair.

'Hey,' he called down.

'Hi. I came to see Henry. I heard he was home.'

'Come on in,' Tyler said. 'He's in the living room. Hey, don't I know you?' he asked.

'I'm Kirsten, I used to — '

'Yeah, Kirsten. Of course. Nice to see you again. I don't know if Henry's awake but, you know, go right ahead. You know where it is.'

She didn't see Henry in the room at first. She was so busy taking in her surroundings that she didn't spot him lying on the mustard-coloured settee with a plaid blanket over him. The TV volume was on very low and the curtains were drawn so that the light in the room was dim but restful, not gloomy like at her parents'. How could it ever be gloomy, with its generous proportions and high ceilings?

There were so many treasures she didn't know what to look at first: the silver-grey rug in front of her with cascading flowers; the two occasional tables filled with vases and heavy-based metal lamps; or over at the fireplace where a mahogany fireguard with a needlepoint tapestry of a Golden Chinese pheasant was illuminated by a splice of light from behind the curtains. On the walls were various photographs, the details of which were hard to see in the light; above the mantelpiece was a large oil painting of a fenland landscape with Ely cathedral in the distance; to her left, on a narrow piece of wall, was a cluster of abstract paintings with blocks and stripes of greys and sand and bronze.

'Who is it?'

Kirsten's heart bumped as she replied.

'Kirsten. Kirsten.' Henry's head swivelled in vain to get her in his sight and she quickly stepped forward. 'Well, bloody hell, Kirsten. How great to see you. Take a seat.'

'I heard you'd been in an accident,' she said.

'Nothing dramatic,' he told her, struggling to sit up. 'Just a bit of a bash around, a few broken ribs and arm.'

Henry looked like someone you'd see in a magazine with 'extreme' in the title or posed in a travel magazine with a little-known, idyllic place in the background which he'd been coming to for years.

'Where were you?'

'Peru. Not the best place for an accident.'

'How did it happen?'

'I overturned a jeep,' he said. 'It could have been worse,' he added. 'I'll tell you about it one day.'

He leaned his head back for a moment and then straightened up and looked directly at her. 'It's so nice to see you.'

She smiled and, to cover her embarrassment, asked, 'Can I do anything for you?'

'I'm dying for a cold drink and something to eat. Would you mind? I'm not so good with knives right now.' He raised his arm in the cast slightly.

They went out to the kitchen and Kirsten waited while Henry took out a plate of cold beef from the fridge, and a packet of cheese, and fetched a partly used loaf from the breadbin.

Kirsten felt along the edge of one of the kitchen units; they seemed to be real oak although they were a little tired and grubby. The difference would be amazing, she thought, if they were stripped down and bleach-cleaned. The brown flagstones were probably original but they were rather dirty too. In fact, the whole kitchen was a bit of a mess. The area next to the back door swelled with hanging coats and underneath lay a mish-mash of boots and shoes; every available surface was covered in all sorts of bits and bobs like plants, pots of utensils, appliances, open books, bills and papers. One shelf was dedicated to a row of ornate tea caddies. Only the big table remained reasonably clear apart from an open newspaper and a large plant in a green glass bowl in the middle of it.

Henry watched her as she sliced the meat and cheese and put it on a plate. 'Do enough for yourself,' he said and, although she wasn't hungry, she liked the idea of sharing the meal so she cut some more.

She looked in the fridge and found a carton of apple juice and a couple of fresh lemons. 'Can I make up a jug?' she asked.

'By all means, if you can find one.'

They opened and closed cupboard after cupboard until, in an overhead one, Kirsten spotted a thick, red glass jug at the back.

'Why don't you go on outside?' she suggested to Henry, peering at the dusty bottom of the jug. As soon as he'd gone, she washed and wiped it clean before pouring in the juice.

She found a tray behind the toaster and carried the food outside. Henry stood up and awkwardly pulled out a chair for her to sit down. She noticed that he was very thin. 'No meat on his bones,' her mother's shrill voice cut in and Kirsten pulled her stomach in tight.

'Where's your mother?'

'I'm not sure.' Henry looked around as if expecting to see her somewhere in the garden. 'Probably shopping.'

'I expect she's happy to have you home.'

The flowerbed closest to them was full of herbs and so busy with bees their accumulative buzzing was loud enough to intrude on their conversation.

'Ella? I suppose so.'

'Of course she is.'

'Yes, yes she is,' he said quickly. 'She's had a lot on her mind recently, that's all.'

Kirsten waited for a minute to see if Henry was going to add anything more but he didn't. Instead, he took out a rather squashed packet of cigarettes and laid them on the table.

'It's even lovelier here than I remember.'

'How long has it been, Kirsten?'

She shrugged although she knew exactly how long. 'A few years.'

'You look different.'

'How?'

'I don't know but it suits you.'

She laughed.

'I'm serious. You seem very calm. Like there's a serenity about you.' He gave her a sideways glance and smiled. 'It's quite charming.'

He had her again from that moment. If ever she had imagined herself to be free from him, she wasn't any more. She took a mouthful of sandwich for something to do and then regretted it as he watched her chew.

'What do you do?'

She swallowed hard. 'Oh, nothing much. I'm a legal secretary.'

'Is it interesting?'

'It's OK, I suppose,' she said, trying to sound serene and wondering what that entailed.

'That's Ella's car,' Henry said, although Kirsten hadn't heard a thing.

Kirsten waited nervously for her to appear. She got flustered by the dog jumping up but Mrs Ruland was so beautiful and gracious when she came over; she smiled warmly at Kirsten and made the dog behave.

Kirsten got up from her chair to shake her hand and was embarrassed when she saw that Mrs Ruland's hands were full of shopping bags but neither she nor Henry seemed to think anything of her mistake.

'You remember Kirsten, Ella?' Henry said. Kirsten was shocked to hear him address his mother by her first name but then she could see why — no epithet like 'Mum' seemed suitable for her.

'Oh, Henry, of course Mrs Ruland won't. It was years ago.'

But she did remember her and her parents and for a heartbeat Kirsten thought Ella was going to say something bad about them, something which she didn't know if she'd have the strength to stand up against. Kirsten's fears were unfounded; the conversation moved on and Kirsten had the chance to compliment Ella on her garden which was what she had wanted to do from the moment Ella had come home.

'Your garden is beautiful,' Kirsten said. 'It's been my dream garden ever since I first saw it.'

'Oh, that's very kind,' Ella said and Kirsten thought how gracious her quiet response was.

'Are you going to join us?' Henry asked. 'Kirsten made some food.'

'I hope you don't mind. Henry said he hadn't had lunch so I prepared a light tea.'

Kirsten felt rather ashamed at the remains of the food; all the beef was gone, the salad was wilting and the cheese looked as if it was turning in the heat. She wanted to make amends so much that she startled Ella in her haste to fetch a plate and glass.

In the kitchen she tried to breathe calmly. She found a plate, a glass and a knife and then stood with her eyes closed, trying to visualize where she'd seen the napkins in their earlier hunt through the cupboards. She found them on the second attempt.

She peered outside. Ella was sitting with Henry and, while Kirsten watched, she placed a hand momentarily on his arm. That was how it was supposed to be: where a mother's touch was a casual part of everyday life, not where it had to be earned and bargained for.

'There.' Kirsten put the plate, glass, knife and a paper napkin down on the table and was on cloud nine when Ella called her 'darling' as she thanked her.

She was so nervous that she didn't know how she got through the rest of the time with them. She felt dizzy with the effort. It wasn't until she was at the Ely turning that she felt she was able to breathe properly. She couldn't remember all the conversation but, thinking back, she must have done OK; Ella had asked her to use her first name and they had both invited her back. Henry had made a particular point of it. 'Don't forget to come and see me again,' Henry had called out and her heart sang with the memory.

The next morning, Kirsten was first into work as usual. She turned on the lights, got the coffee machine going, sorted the mail for the other secretaries and had already begun to work on hers when Valerie and Emma arrived within five minutes of each other. Kirsten had to take minutes for an early meeting so it wasn't until morning break-time that she had the chance to catch up with the others. They stood in the little kitchen for ten minutes until, finally, Emma turned to her and said, in a rather sneering tone, 'So, how was your evening, Kirsten?'

'Oh, yes,' Valerie said. 'Spill the beans.'

'His name's Henry and I went out with him years ago and he's been travelling and now he's back.'

'And, what's he like?'

'He's every bit as gorgeous as he used to be. And we got on really well.'

'Are you going to see him again?' Emma wanted to know.

'Yes,' she said but she felt sick at having spoken about Henry in such a gross way, as if she'd somehow betrayed him. She threw the remains of her coffee away and hurried back to her desk. For the rest of the day, every time she looked at Emma she felt annoyed, as if she had dragged Kirsten down to her level, and she worried that through some convoluted set of coincidences Henry would hear about it and think badly of her.

In the afternoon, after a lunchtime of

replaying the conversation at Spindle House in her head, Kirsten decided to ask Valerie when she thought she should go back to see Henry. She hadn't intended Emma to get involved in the conversation but, before she could stop her, Val had called her over to Kirsten's desk.

Both of them wanted to know — in minute detail — who had said what and, once she told them, they seemed to look at her in a completely different way.

'I think you should leave it today,' Emma said. 'But go tomorrow. You don't want to seem too keen.'

'Go this evening,' Val suggested. 'Henry's not well — he needs the company.'

She decided to go with Emma's opinion in the end. Emma, she thought, would have had much more dating experience than Val. Besides, she didn't want to seem pushy to Henry or Ella.

She spent the whole of Tuesday evening trying on clothes that would be more in keeping with the house and finally chose a printed cotton skirt with a white blouse and heeled sandals. She tried her hair several ways: with a clip, without, up and then down. Frustrated almost to tears, she was finally inspired to leave it free like Ella's.

Before she left work on Wednesday, both Val and Emma wished her luck, which didn't help Kirsten's nerves.

★　★　★

When Kirsten was parking, Ella appeared from the side of the house. She had on a floppy hat,

272

held a trowel in her hand and was wearing baggy shorts and a shirt; her hair was pulled back into a loose bun. Even with soil everywhere, she looked beautiful and elegant. The dog dashed forward and then sat down a few metres away from Kirsten and stared.

'I've come to see Henry,' Kirsten called over. Standing with the sunlight bright upon her, she knew that her outfit was all wrong; it was much too neat and formal. She leaned down, patted her knees and called the dog which didn't budge.

As Kirsten started to walk towards Ella, she waved her back. 'Go on in. The front door's open.'

Henry was lying on the mustard settee again. Kirsten glanced around as she walked towards him. She thought how wonderful it was to be able to lie on one settee in the room and be too far away to see if someone was lying on the other.

Henry pushed himself upright. He had obviously been asleep — his hair was all over the place and he looked grey. To give him time to wake up properly, Kirsten started to scan the bookshelves.

'Are all these your father's books? I didn't realize he'd written so many.'

'Yes, most of them are out of print though. Except those two on the left. They're the ones that are on the university reading lists. They're the ones that bring in the money.'

'I remember him coming to school to talk to us once,' Kirsten said, pulling one of the books out and holding it in her hands. It was heavy.

'About amphibians.'

'I can still remember how many native species of amphibians there are in the UK.'

'Could you name them though?' Henry laughed.

'He was a very charismatic man. He made you really want to listen.' She slotted the book back and turned to face Henry. 'I'm sorry, is it OK to talk about him?'

'Yes. In fact, it's nice to talk about him sometimes.'

'So will you write a book? About your travelling?'

'Me? No. I'm too lazy. Hannah's the writer in this house.'

'Hannah?'

'She writes these weird tales — she calls them fables. But don't ask her about them.'

'Why not?'

'She's superstitious.'

They were silent for a few moments. Kirsten hadn't seen Hannah for years; she remembered a thin girl, tall for her age and, of course, you couldn't help but notice how pale her skin and hair were. She'd worn thick glasses that looked too old for her.

Henry had shoved aside the blanket that was covering him. He was wearing only a pair of black boxer shorts.

'Why don't you get dressed?' Kirsten suggested, trying not to look too closely at Henry's bare legs. 'We could take a walk round the garden.'

'I could do with a bit of air.'

'I'll make some tea, if you like,' Kirsten called after him.

'Whatever you fancy,' he called back.

You, she thought, and then told herself off. She'd been listening to Emma talking about men so long that she'd ending up thinking like her.

She stood at the back door waiting for the kettle to boil and watched Ella walk towards her. Puffs of dust and soil floated off her as she beat a glove against her shorts.

'It must be quite a job keeping on top of such a big place,' Kirsten said.

'It is.'

'But you love it,' Kirsten said. 'So it doesn't feel so much like work.'

'I suppose not,' Ella peered into the kitchen. 'Where's Henry?'

'He's gone up to his room to get changed. I thought it might make him feel a bit better. We're going to sit out here with our tea when it's made.'

'When are you next coming over?' Ella asked suddenly, taking Kirsten completely by surprise. Her first thought was that she wasn't wanted here, that she had come back too soon, but Ella saw her face and laughed.

'I'm sorry. I realize I'm sounding rather odd. I've been rather worried about Henry and he seemed much happier after you were last here. You really cheer him up.'

'I'll come back whenever you want. If you think I'm helping.'

'Can you come tomorrow?'

Kirsten helped out at the church Kids' Club in

275

Ely on Thursdays and so she'd said no to Ella before she realized she could easily have phoned up and told them she couldn't go. She felt a little consoled by Emma's words — best not to seem too keen — but hated the thought that she was letting Ella down.

'Friday then?'

'Yes, Friday is fine.'

'Shush.' Ella put her finger to her lips. Kirsten glanced guiltily behind her. She couldn't see Henry but then the door from the hall began to open.

'So, Friday then. Thanks, Kirsten,' Ella whispered and touched Kirsten's arm, leaving a dusting of brown soil on her skin. Kirsten's fingers hovered over it for a moment before she wiped it off.

After they'd drunk their tea, she and Henry walked slowly down to a pond and then back again to the garden table where Henry said he had to rest. He seemed in worse shape than a couple of days ago and Kirsten could see why Ella was worried about him. She went inside to fetch his cigarettes and lighter which he'd left in the living room and when she came out, a young woman was standing beside him, pressing her cheek against his.

She realized in the next instant that it was Hannah, but that didn't stop Kirsten feeling a quick pulse of jealousy.

'Do you remember Kirsten?' Henry said.

'I think so.' Hannah took such a long time to look at Kirsten that she felt rather embarrassed, especially as she couldn't see half of Hannah's face under the over-large, dark sunglasses she had on. She was going to say, 'I remember you,' but thought it might be taken the wrong way.

'It was quite a few years ago,' Kirsten said.

'You came round here,' Hannah said. 'A couple of times.'

'Yes, yes, I did,' Kirsten said, surprised and even more embarrassed. Henry hadn't been there each time she'd called and she'd had to turn round and go straight home again.

'Hannah notices and remembers everything, don't you, my little spy?'

Hannah leaned over Henry, hugging him round the neck. 'Have you come to cheer Henry up? He's been a bit miserable.'

'In that case, I hope so.' Kirsten handed Henry the cigarettes and lighter. He smiled at her.

From nowhere, Scoot appeared next to Kirsten, making her jump again. He pushed his nose into her lap and then rested his chin on her leg. She found the look in his eyes unnerving. She desperately wanted to push him away but she was aware that Henry and Hannah were both watching her. She moved her leg slightly and Scoot jumped up, placing both paws on her knee and panting his hot, smelly breath into her face.

'Down,' she said, feeling self-conscious, but he didn't move.

'Down,' Hannah commanded and Scoot immediately dropped to the ground. 'You have to be firm with a dog,' Hannah told her. 'Otherwise he won't respect you.'

But this advice seemed contradictory to

Kirsten seeing as, all the time she was talking, Hannah was bent over, playing with Scoot's ears and scrunching up the fur on his back while he tried to lick her face.

'I've never had a pet,' Kirsten said after Hannah had left, with Scoot following. Pets were dirty, smelly things and a waste of time and money according to Joy. 'I took a hamster home from school once as it was my turn and Mum freaked about it.'

Kirsten had watched her name getting closer and closer to the top of the rota and had put off telling her mother until it was too late. One Friday, Joy came to pick up Kirsten and found Kirsten with the teacher, the hamster cage and a sheet of instructions.

'Kirsten's been looking forward to this for ages,' the teacher said for no reason that Kirsten could think of other than she'd seen the look on her mother's face and was trying to make the best of it. 'It does them good, you know, to care for something.'

'My husband's allergic.'

The teacher became flustered. 'Oh dear. It's too late . . . '

'We'll just have to keep it in a separate room, I suppose. But if you'd make a note.'

'Of course.'

'What a cheek,' her mother had said afterwards. 'They shouldn't assume everyone can do it. What if we'd been going away?'

'Are we going away then?' Kirsten felt her heart leap; they never went away. Only once to see her dad's brother in Shropshire.

'Don't be silly, Kirsten. Of course we're not going away.'

★ ★ ★

'Mum told the teacher my dad was allergic so that I never had the chance to look after it again.'

'She lied?' Henry asked.

'Yes.'

'Poor Kirsten.' He rubbed the back of her hand with his fingers. Cigarette smoke curled straight up her nose but she didn't care.

★ ★ ★

On Thursday evening, when it was time to go the Kids' Club, Kirsten found she wasn't looking forward to it at all. In fact, she was dreading it. She'd been going for nearly a year and up until she had started to visit Henry at Spindle House it had been the highlight of her week.

The trouble was, she'd been having an on-and-off kind of thing for several months with Paul, another of the helpers, who coordinated the activity programme. They always took their coffee break together and often stayed behind to tidy up. On several occasions — more than she wanted to admit — he'd come back to her flat with her and they'd had sex.

She didn't know quite how it had started, they'd never been on a date together, but she had liked the attention he gave her. She could see now, as she walked down the street to the community centre, that she had been lonely

279

and easily flattered.

She opened the door, walked across the reception area and through the second set of doors into the hall. Ange and Geoff were there, wheeling the computers on the trolleys across the room and putting out the chairs and tables. Because they shared the centre with other groups, they had to pack everything away at the end of the evening and they couldn't let the kids put anything up on the walls, but it was a large room with plenty of area for them to play games and do some artwork as well as use the computers. There was a small kitchen which they could use to make teas and coffees, although it was only the adults who bothered, the kids bought fizzy drinks out of the vending machine.

She was just starting to feel hopeful that Paul wasn't there when he appeared from the storage cupboard with his arms full of boxes and the tarpaulin they put on the floor if any of the little ones did some painting.

'Give us a hand,' he called over to Kirsten and she felt obliged to do so.

'So how have you been?'

'Great.' She knew it was wrong to compare him to Henry but she couldn't help it. Paul had thick, curly hair which often got too bushy and made him look effeminate; he had very large feet which he had told her he had difficulty getting shoes to fit and which, like a clown, seemed to make him rather unstable, liable to trip and stumble. His voice turned shrill when he tried to get serious with the kids and she knew that they laughed at him.

She turned round as the first of the children arrived. She waved at them but only one little girl waved back. She suspected that some of them laughed at her, too.

For the rest of the evening, she managed to avoid being near Paul and when she got the chance, she told Ange that she had to leave promptly that night and couldn't stay to help pack away.

'No worries,' Ange said. 'I'll ask one of the older boys to give a hand.' Ange was an ex-social worker who, since she took early retirement, seemed to have done nothing but work. She fostered children and was a school governor, as well as running this and a sports club. Kirsten liked Ange. She had once said to Kirsten that she was glad she was there, that it was important for the kids to have younger people around for them to relate to. It had surprised but pleased Kirsten that Ange should see her as young; Kirsten had never felt young, she'd never felt like a real child.

Shortly before eight o'clock, Kirsten fetched her bag out of the locked cabinet and called out goodbye.

She tried not to notice Paul bob up from where he was crouched down by the computers but even though she hurried, he caught up with her in the reception area.

'Off early?'

'Yes.'

'I could come round afterwards,' he said, playing with the cross he wore on a chain around his neck.

'No. I don't think so.'

'Got your monthlies?' he said loudly. She blinked with the shock and went bright red.

'Yes,' she said, turning and walking quickly out of the door. She felt so humiliated that tears prickled her eyes.

*   *   *

The next day, when she arrived at Spindle House, there was neither Ella's car nor the motorbike in the drive, and no reply as usual at the door. She walked round the side of the house and saw Henry and Hannah at the garden table.

They watched her approach but didn't speak to her until she was closer. She looked at each one in turn. 'I'm sorry, have I interrupted something?'

'No, not particularly,' Henry said. 'Come and sit down.'

She pulled out a chair and smiled at Hannah who looked a little put out.

'So,' Hannah said, sounding impatient, 'you really don't think it's odd that she disappears all the time?'

'She's busy, that's all.'

'I'm worried about her,' Hannah continued. 'It's ever since . . . ' She glanced at Kirsten and then back at Henry. 'Since she came back from London. Up until then, she hardly used to leave the garden.'

'It's probably this heat. I wouldn't want to be working outside in it either.'

'But where does she go? What does she do?'

'Maybe she meets someone. A friend or

something.' They both looked at Kirsten, shocked. She wasn't sure if it was because of what she'd said or if they'd forgotten she was there.

'Kirsten's probably right,' Henry said, lighting his cigarette and blowing the smoke in a long stream out of the corner of his mouth, away from them.

Hannah looked cross. 'She hasn't got any friends. Not around here. There's only Sadie in London.'

'They've always been very close, Hannah and Ella,' Henry said as they watched Hannah walk across the lawn to the hedge where she suddenly disappeared from view.

'But not any more?'

'Oh, no. They still are. Very,' he said, sounding annoyed. He squashed the end of the cigarette so hard on the stone with his foot that she didn't dare open her mouth again for several minutes.

25

'Come closer,' Henry said. 'Bring your chair closer.'

It was dusk. They were alone in the garden. Tyler had gone to the pub, Hannah was out with Toby somewhere. She had no idea where Ella was — no one ever did.

She stood up and moved her chair alongside his but, before she had chance to sit down, he grabbed hold of her, pulling her awkwardly on top of him. He groaned and she tried to struggle up because she thought she was hurting him, but he held her tighter and then he started to kiss her and his hands started to feel their way across her stomach, between her shirt and her skirt.

'Don't move,' he said as she tried to wriggle away.

'What if somebody comes?'

'There's no one here.'

She felt his penis harden under her hand, she felt the hairs on his legs against the bare skin of her thighs. She opened the fly of his shorts. He didn't have any underwear on.

'Sit on me,' he said.

'OK, wait a second.' She stood up, went to the kitchen and switched off the outside light, then, with her back to Henry, she fished around up her skirt and took her knickers off. She carefully straddled him, her hands found his penis again and gently pulled it out of his shorts. She raised herself up and then, holding his penis in place, she lowered down and felt Henry sliding inside.

'Hang on,' he said. 'Shouldn't we use — ?'

'I'm on the pill.'

'Well, I'm clean,' he said.

'Me too.'

'Of course you are,' he whispered into her ear. 'Of course you are.'

When she opened her eyes, she was surprised to find how light the evening was; she could see Henry's face quite clearly, the slits of his barely opened eyes, the way he was pressing his lips together. He had his hands either side of her hips and was helping to rock her back and forth, move her up and down. Kirsten was tiring, her legs were at awkward angles. She wanted to look beautiful for Henry but she was beginning to sweat and she thought she might be grimacing with the effort. She leaned forward, pressed her face against his neck.

She felt him come and then felt his groan vibrate in his chest. Over his shoulder, Kirsten could see moths fluttering around a pot of tall white flowers, she could smell a sweetish perfume.

'Kirst, you'll have to move,' Henry said. He helped her off him and brushed her skirt back into place. She moved her chair a little further away and sat with her knickers clenched in her hands in her lap.

It seemed that only minutes after they'd finished, Ella came round the corner of the house.

'Why haven't you got the lights on?' Ella asked.

'We've been watching the bats,' Henry replied.

'And the moths,' Kirsten added and she glanced at Henry before smiling up at Ella as she walked past.

'Do you want to go out for a drink?' Kirsten suggested.

'Not really.'

'Don't you want to be seen with me?' she joked.

When Ella switched on the kitchen light, it brought out shadows and strange depths of light so that it was impossible to see the expression on Henry's face.

'Let's just stay here tonight. Is that OK, Kirst?'

'Yes.'

'Thank you.'

'Will you go back to Peru when you've recovered?' She tried to speak lightly, as if the question was insignificant, purely conversational. She kept her face turned away from him, out towards the garden.

'No.'

'Didn't you like it out there?'

'I did but it's over with now. I've finished with the place. I never want to go back.'

'But somewhere else? You'll be going somewhere else.'

'I really don't know. I think I've finished with it all. Are you trying to get rid of me already?'

She turned to find him grinning at her. 'Never,' she told him.

'Kirsten, can you do me a favour?'

'Of course.' Her heart started pounding; she had no idea what he was going to ask but she knew she'd say yes, whatever it was.

'Can you help me have a bath? I haven't been able to wash properly since I got home.'

★ ★ ★

The bath had clawed feet and steep sides. Kirsten could see that with the slow water flow it was going to take ages to fill. She sat on the edge of the bath while Henry stood with his back against the door.

'Isn't there somewhere more comfortable we could wait?' she asked, so he took her across the hall into his room.

Henry's room was obviously normally used as the guestroom. It had pale-blue walls and matching golden-coloured wood furniture. The bed linen and curtains were tan and cream but on the walls were two bright screen prints of poppies and cornflowers. In the corner by the window was a cosy tweed armchair with cushions next to a round wooden table with a little drawer in the front.

Scattered in various places were Henry's possessions. He didn't seem to have much: a laptop, camera, a few books, a pile of clothes on the floor at the end of the bed and a large, green and brown rucksack hanging on the back of the door.

She helped Henry off with his T-shirt and then he wriggled out of his shorts using one hand. He

287

stood there completely naked while Kirsten looked at him and at his penis which she had earlier had inside her. Half-erect, it was long and slim. Henry was tanned and too thin, she thought again; she could see his ribs, but his arms were muscular and his legs too. She felt desire building. She felt like she was feasting her eyes on him but he didn't seem to mind.

He lay back on the bed, propping himself up on the pillows. 'Why don't you take your skirt and top off, save you getting wet in a minute.'

She wanted to be the kind of woman who was unselfconscious about undressing in front of him but all she could think of were the knickers she'd tucked into her bra in a panic when she was walking up the stairs.

She unbuttoned her blouse and turned away as she took it off. She caught a glimpse of herself in the mirror; her breasts were squashed into an old white bra and her peach-coloured knickers were protruding from between her breasts.

'Take your skirt off,' Henry ordered from the bed and so she undid the zip and let it fall, her back still towards him.

'Where are your knickers, naughty girl?'

'In my bag,' she said. 'From earlier.'

In one swift movement, she undid her bra and let her knickers fall on top of her skirt. She turned around.

'Lovely.'

She got on the bed and lay beside him. He twisted awkwardly, jiggled sideways trying to position his broken arm before he leaned over her and began to kiss her. She ran her hands across his back, down his buttocks, feeling how his skin changed from smooth to the rough of short hairs. She felt she could lie there forever while he played his tongue around her mouth and across her lips.

'Oh my God, the bath!' he said, kissing her on the nose and rolling away. Kirsten quickly pushed herself upright and picked up his T-shirt to put on.

'Nobody will see,' he said behind her as she peered out of the door but she waited until Henry had the bathroom door open before she ran across.

The water was running cold but the temperature in the bath was warm enough. Henry sat in it and Kirsten soaped his back while he propped his arm on the side.

'Don't you have a shower?'

'In the bathroom Hannah and Ella use. This used to be the old family bathroom before it was cut in half to make another bedroom.'

While Henry dunked down in the water to wet his hair, Kirsten imagined how she would decorate the room. She'd have the old sink and bath refurbished, put in an antique pine towel rack and laundry box, and she'd paint the walls the palest green. She realized Henry had spoken.

'Would you mind?'

He was holding out the bar of soap to her and, although he was perfectly able to wash his own privates, she took the soap from him. She lathered up well and then knelt on the floor beside the bath, delving both hands in the water until she found his penis and balls. They felt silky with soap as she caressed them; she could feel him hardening under her hands but she didn't stop. She watched his face. He was so good-looking. His face was made for people to stare at, for people to enjoy. It was amazing that he should want her. But he did. She could feel the evidence growing and hardening under her hands, she could see it in the intensity of his face in front of her very eyes.

He reached out and touched her face, pushed her damp hair back, revealing her breasts which were propped on the edge of the bath. She looked down at her nipples which were like two mushroom buds begging to be touched.

★ ★ ★

The next evening, when Kirsten arrived at Spindle House, both Ella's car and Tyler's motorbike were absent. She didn't bother to knock on the front door, instead she walked straight round the side of the house. There was no one in the garden that she could see and, unusually, the back door was closed. When she tried the handle, however, it opened.

She went into the living room but Henry wasn't there. She opened the door to the front room, a room that she had never been in before. She could see why it wasn't used much. It was dark with heavy, old furniture and the air felt damp and smelt rather musty. She shut the door quickly — it was a little too reminiscent of her parents' house. She made her way upstairs, calling out as she went.

She had the definite feeling that she was alone in the house but checked to see if Henry was in his room before knocking quietly on Hannah's door.

It was surprisingly girlish. The walls were painted very pale pink apart from one which was dark like cranberry. The matching wardrobe, bed, dressing table and bedside table were in cream with ornate legs and decorative edgings — they were either French or in a French style, Kirsten didn't know which. There was an odd mix of quite childish items like the line of little animals on the mantelpiece above the attractive fireplace, the toy rabbit on her bed and the child's painting of a dragonfly, as well as possessions which Kirsten would have expected a young woman to have: a bookcase filled with books, a CD rack and a wardrobe absolutely stuffed with clothes. Kirsten could hardly believe the amount Hannah had managed to squeeze inside — it took her several flustered attempts to close the doors.

The only non-matching piece of furniture was a small oak bureau over by the window. On it was an amazing black-and-white photograph of Ella sitting on a yacht; she looked absolutely beautiful. Lying open was a notebook covered in large, erratic writing: words sloped down, others crawled upwards, some jumped off the line as if the writer had hiccoughs. She could hardly make out a single word.

Kirsten took a final glance around before making her way to Ella's room. Again, she first knocked before slowly opening the door. She peered in; there was no one there. She went to the top of the stairs and called out into the silence. No one replied.

She returned to Ella's room, leaving the door ajar. It was a large room with windows at either end — they were both open, so it felt much cooler than Hannah's. The walls were cream, as were the chest of drawers and one of the wardrobes. The bed and the other wardrobe were wood. Maybe oak, Kirsten thought, giving the end of the bed a quick rap. The flower print curtains were lovely, if a little faded, and Kirsten adored the combination of blues and creams of the handmade quilt on top of the bed. She walked over to the chest of drawers. On the top was a poppy-pattern wash jug and bowl next to a group of antique perfume bottles: an atomizer with a tasselled leather pump bulb, a tall, clear crystal bottle with a gold ball stopper and a round one with a silver and enamel inlay and a blue glass peacock tail stopper.

Kirsten wandered over to the cream wardrobe. She glanced through the dresses and skirts and tops, none of which she'd seen Ella wearing. She expected to find more of Ella's everyday clothes in the second wardrobe but she closed it quickly when she discovered it was full of men's suits and trousers and shirts. She turned round. On either side of the bed was a matching table; on one was a lamp with a glass base and large cream shade, a pot-plant with a big white flower standing on a blue saucer and a pile of books which Kirsten saw were gardening ones as she approached. She fingered the contents of a tiny, shallow plate: a thin gold ring and a gold chain with a locket; there was a sepia photograph of a woman who didn't look a bit like Ella, and a glasses case. She walked round to the other side — Edward's side. His lamp had a round brass base and a cream shade; there were a couple of books and a set of drawers about twenty centimetres high. She slid the top drawer open to reveal several pairs of cufflinks laid out on a piece of black velvet; the second contained a watch and lighter, the bottom, deeper drawer held some paperwork and a pile of passports with their corners cut off. She took out the top one and flicked to the photograph. It looked so much like Henry that she checked the name at the front. Edward Finnegan Ruland.

She caught the sound of a car engine and stood still to listen before crossing to the front window, her heart fluttering. It was impossible to see anything but a small section of the track near the house but she couldn't risk getting caught.

She was filling the kettle when Ella and Henry came into the kitchen.

'I've just got here,' she said, and hoped they didn't notice her breathlessness. 'I thought I'd make tea.'

'Lovely,' Ella said.

'Hello, you.' Henry leaned down and kissed her on the mouth.

★ ★ ★

'What is it you do on a Thursday again?' Henry asked and Kirsten, who had been trying not to think about the next day, said, 'Help out at a Kids' Club.'

'That's very community-spirited of you.' As Henry stretched, his T-shirt rose up and revealed his stomach. They were all so thin, she thought — except Tyler, she remembered; Tyler was cuddly. She didn't feel like she had to hold her stomach in so tightly when he was around.

'I thought I might give it a miss.' Kirsten wasn't sure she could face Paul ever again. She wished she'd made it clearer that evening that their arrangement, or whatever it was, had finished. It should never have started, she thought, as a sickening image of Paul lowering himself on top of her came into her mind. He had always stared at her breasts, she remembered; he'd never once looked at her face. She put her hand out and touched Henry's, his fingers immediately reached out to hold hers.

'Oh, shame. I was thinking of going with you.'

'You were?'

'It might do me some good to get out of this place for an evening.'

'Seriously?'

'Yes. Why not?' Henry said laughing.

★ ★ ★

At four o'clock on Thursday when she phoned Henry to make arrangements to pick him up, he said. 'I'm sorry, Kirst. I think I'll give it a miss tonight.'

She couldn't speak,

'I don't think I'm in the mood to face a bunch

of kids,' he told her. 'Kirsten? Are you there?'

'I don't think I'll go then.'

'Won't you be letting them down?'

'There are other people there. They can manage without me.'

'You should go,' Henry said. 'I feel bad, now.'

'To be honest, I don't really feel like it either,' she said. When it was a choice between an evening in the garden at Spindle House or having to deal with Paul, she knew which won, hands down. 'Shall I come over?' she asked.

There was a prolonged silence before Henry spoke. 'If you want to.'

'It's OK, Henry,' she reassured him. 'It's what I'd prefer to do.'

'Well,' he said, 'if you're sure.'

She phoned Ange. 'I'm not going to be able to make it tonight, I'm afraid.'

'Are you poorly, love?'

'I think I'm coming down with something,' she said. 'And I've got a pile of work to do for tomorrow as well.'

'Well, don't over-do it,' Ange said. 'Get an early night.'

'Thanks, Ange.'

'It won't only be the kids who are disappointed, wink, wink.'

'Oh. Um. Bye, then,' Kirsten murmured hurriedly. Her face stayed hot for several minutes after she'd rung off.

26

Kirsten loved being with Henry at Spindle House. When she wasn't with him, she was thinking about him, and at lunchtimes at work she pored over house and garden magazines. She was determined to learn about some of the plants and flowers in Ella's garden so that she could be of more help. She couldn't fail to notice that all the house and garden work fell to Ella — Hannah was never around, Tyler seemed totally unaware of the need and Henry was still incapacitated with his arm. Either Ella did it or no one did.

So Kirsten had taken it upon herself to help with the meals and have a little tidy-up whenever she got the chance; Ella hadn't said anything about it, but Kirsten hoped that meant she was pleased. Kirsten was also researching conservatories for Ella; she had a good idea of Ella's tastes because she'd been paying close attention to anything she said and did and, of course, she was also bearing in mind the character of Spindle House.

Kirsten tried to get out of bed but Henry woke as soon as she moved.

'I'm getting up,' she said. She was late. She had stayed over a couple of nights before but always left early, before anyone else was up.

'I'd better get up, too. I've got the hospital this morning.'

He stepped into the boxer shorts he picked up from the floor, his bum a perfect curve as he leaned forward. He left the door open behind him and Kirsten hurried over to push it shut but Henry was still in the doorway.

'What are you waiting for?' he asked. 'Bathroom's free.'

'I'm getting dressed. I can't go down like this,' she said, standing in front of him; her slip barely covered her secret parts.

'Hang on,' Henry said and he reappeared a minute later with a dark-brown, satin robe.

'Wear this. It's an old one of Ella's.'

'Oh no, I shouldn't.'

'She won't mind.'

Henry practically pushed it at her and, even though Kirsten took the robe, she still hesitated.

'Hurry up, Kirsten,' he said a little impatiently.

She slipped it on and went into the bathroom where she was confronted by a more glamorous version of herself in the mirror. She mussed up her hair, shook it out and smiled at herself.

They were first down for breakfast. The air was cool in the kitchen and the stone floor was cold under her bare feet. Henry opened the back door to let Scoot out while Kirsten began to lay the table. Henry fetched the newspaper from the hallway and skimmed through the pages as he watched her placing cereals and milk and sugar on the table and prepared a pot of coffee and toast for them both.

When Ella came into the kitchen, Kirsten saw immediately that the robe had been a mistake. She wished that she'd listened to her instinct;

she was normally so sensitive to people's feelings but Henry had distracted her. He'd been so insistent that she'd assumed he knew his mother better.

She wanted to run and change but that would have made it worse. She looked sorrowfully at the table which she'd taken such pleasure in preparing. She felt so awkward she wished she could disappear but then Hannah came in and it seemed that Henry was right — Ella didn't mind other people wearing her stuff, Hannah did it all the time.

Kirsten pulled the robe tighter in case she was exposing anything she shouldn't and felt a rush of pleasure. It was little things like that which made Kirsten feel she was being accepted. For a brief moment, she saw herself living here, permanently. She saw her and Ella sharing the house duties, a bit like a communal life only much better, especially when Kirsten's own children came along. She found she was staring at Henry who was standing up and stretching, his bruises on show for all the world to see.

'What are you doing today, Hannah?' Ella asked.

Kirsten didn't catch their brief exchange of words, all she caught was the rude tone in Hannah's voice and how upset Ella looked after she'd gone.

'Do you want me to take Henry to the hospital for his check-up?' Kirsten offered.

'Aren't you supposed to be at work?'

'I could take a day off I'm owed holiday,' The other two were always doing it; ringing in at the last minute. And she was owed holiday. She had carried over nearly a week of unused leave again this year.

'It would give you a chance to work in the garden. It must be hard keeping up such a big house as well as the garden.'

'Well, I don't always manage it, as you can see.'

'I could help. I don't mind. I'd like to.'

'That's very kind but — '

'You like to do it yourself.'

'Yes, that's it,' Ella said but Kirsten could tell she found the idea appealing; it would probably happen as Ella became more comfortable with the idea that Kirsten wasn't really a guest.

'Have you ever thought about having a conservatory?'

'Not really, no.'

'You get some very tasteful ones now. I was looking at some in the magazines and the best thing is that they really add value to your house.'

'I hadn't really considered — ' Ella said, but she definitely looked interested.

'They're brilliant in winter; you can still enjoy your garden without being out there.'

'It sounds nice but — '

'You know, this place could be amazing . . . Well, I mean it already is.' Kirsten smiled to show her how much she meant it.

Ella smiled back. 'I like to think so.'

'I'll bring some information for you to have a look,' Kirsten said, and thought how surprised Ella would be to see the cuttings from the magazines and the sample brochures she'd collected.

'Oh, all right. Thanks.'

'So shall I take Henry?'

'OK. Thank you.'

Kirsten excused herself to leave a message for Val when she got in. It hadn't taken Ella much persuading in the end and now she had a whole day with Henry ahead of her. After they'd been to the hospital, they could spend some time in Ely. Her heart leapt at the thought of bumping into Emma or Valerie during their lunch breaks. 'This is Henry,' she'd say. That would be all she needed to say.

27

'Did Ella say how long she'd be?'

Kirsten looked up from her breakfast. Hannah was wearing her Silver Maids uniform. She looked annoyed.

'I didn't see her. She must have left before I was up.' Kirsten found she was getting slower and slower in the mornings. Spindle House seemed to demand a more leisurely approach to the start of the day. She liked to sit in the garden to eat her toast and drink her tea. There were a couple of bold sparrows who hopped around on the patio close by, waiting for her crumbs.

'She's supposed to be taking me to work.'

'I can give you a lift, if you like.'

'Could you? I have to leave in about ten minutes.'

'That's fine. I only need to clean my teeth and fetch my bag from the bedroom.'

When she came down, Hannah was waiting by her car, her plastic box of cleaning products at her feet.

'Don't they have this stuff at the houses?' Kirsten had always thought it strange that Hannah took it all with her.

'We're not supposed to leave anything there.'

'That seems a bit silly,' Kirsten said and Hannah shrugged.

'You'll have to direct me,' Kirsten told her as they bumped down the track.

'OK.'

'Do you like what you do?'

'It's OK.'

'I hear you write stories.' Kirsten turned her head slightly to find Hannah facing her. She was frowning.

'Who told you that?'

'Henry, I think,' she dissembled remembering too late that Henry had told her Hannah didn't like to talk about it.

'He had no right to tell you.'

'I'm sorry,' Kirsten told her and they fell into a silence which Kirsten didn't know how to break.

When Hannah's mobile rang, it made Kirsten jump so much that she swerved slightly in the road.

'It's Ella,' Hannah mouthed. 'With Kirsten. Yes. We're nearly there now. I didn't know where you were. I know. It doesn't matter.'

Even though Kirsten suspected it was unnecessary, Hannah had directed her through the Travellers' camp. She had to slow right down as there was only a narrow passage between the vehicles which were parked on both sides of the road and a couple of dogs kept running out in front of the car. Her hands tightened on the wheel. She felt eyes all around her. She glanced at Hannah who snapped her phone closed and buzzed down her window.

'They're still in bed,' Hannah said and Kirsten saw that there were curtains in the vans and cardboard on the inside of most of the car windows.

'Even your friend, Toby?' Kirsten had only met

Toby a couple of times and she railed to see how such a pretty, friendly girl as Hannah could be interested in such an ugly, morose boy. She always tried to find the good in the kids but the surly, restless kind like him really made it hard.

'He's not one of them,' Hannah said. 'He was here before them. He's on holiday here.'

'Oh, I thought — '

'That's what everyone seems to think.'

'I've heard they've ruined the crop,' Kirsten said once they had left the camp behind.

'Who said that?'

Kirsten shrugged not wanting to say.

'It's not true. They're very careful. They're respectful of the land.' Hannah's girlish voice rose higher in protest.

'They've been stealing things from the village.'

'Who says?'

'People in the village.'

'People in the village say a lot of things that aren't true, don't you know that?' she said softly and tilted her head as if she was assessing Kirsten.

'What do you mean?'

'I mean, they're not at all like others make out — they're nice people, mostly.'

'I didn't mean to upset you,' Kirsten said, feeling bad.

'Have you been in the Circle?' Hannah smiled at her. Her smile was an echo of Ella's in the photograph in Hannah's bedroom. 'It's pretty amazing; you can definitely feel an energy there. You should try it.' Hannah looked behind her. 'If we went back now, I could go in with you.'

'I don't think so . . . '

'Are you afraid?'

'No.' But she was a little. Not of the Circle but of the villagers, and the chance that her parents would hear about it. It would cause a lot of trouble and for what? Just to look at some beaten-down crops in a field.

'Aren't you curious?'

'No. Not really.'

Hannah stared at her. 'Not at all?'

Kirsten shook her head. 'You know, I've only ever been in one field and that's the one they open for Bonfire Night.'

'The Paddock?'

'Is that what it's called?'

'That can't be possible. You grew up in the middle of the countryside, you must have been through fields on walks.'

'I've walked on the roads to get somewhere but I've never been for a walk round here, you know, simply for something to do.'

'Never?' Hannah shook her head. 'Don't tell Henry that.'

'Why not?' Kirsten laughed but stopped the moment she saw Hannah's serious expression.

'Well, it's Henry. That's what he does,' she said, sounding incredulous, as if Kirsten should know this. 'The natural world is all he's ever been interested in.'

'He hasn't shown any inclination towards going for a walk while I've been with him.'

Hannah looked at her lap. 'That's because he's different to how he used to be.'

Kirsten's heart was thumping. 'He's not been well — '

'It's not that.' Hannah raised her eyes, fixed them on Kirsten. 'Something happened in Lima. I mean, something more than the accident. Hasn't he told you?'

'No. What happened?' She held her breath and stared out of the window, trying to prepare herself for what Hannah was going to say. Her eyes followed the white line down the middle of the road until it ran to a point out of sight. She didn't feel connected to her body, her hands didn't feel real enough to be turning the wheel and changing the gears as they appeared to be doing.

'He's not talked to any of us about it. I was hoping you'd know.'

'He said he's not going back there. It's over. He said he's not going to travel any more; he's going to stay here, at Spindle House.' She felt buoyant with relief and a small stab of pride that she was deemed Henry's confidante.

'He really said that?'

'Yes.'

'Then it must be worse than I thought.' Hannah spoke quietly, as if that was going to make her words easier to bear. Kirsten felt the blood flooding into the skin on her face. She wanted to deny what Hannah had said but part of her, the deep, instinctive part of her, recognized it as true.

★ ★ ★

That evening, Kirsten suggested to Henry that they go for a walk. He blinked slowly before agreeing. 'Where do you want to go?'

'Anywhere. Wherever you usually go.'

She helped him put on his trainers and tie his laces but, as they were about to leave, he caught hold of her arm and stopped her.

'You're not going in those?' He looked at Kirsten's sandals and then at her face. She had called into her flat after work specifically to pick up the ones with the lowest heel. 'You'll break your bloody ankle.'

Kirsten hadn't even noticed that there was a wooden chest in the kitchen below the swell of coats and jackets and buried under the numerous pairs of shoes and boots. He grunted with the effort of lifting the lid and called her over.

'Put those on.' He was pointing to a pair of red, ankle-length Wellington boots. She pulled them out — they smelled of rubber which had been left out in the damp too long. She upended them to release anything that might be living inside and cautiously pushed one foot in, then the other. They pinched her toes and she thought she looked ridiculous, but Henry seemed to approve.

He strode so fast across the lawn that Kirsten had to break into a jog to catch him up. They passed through a narrow gap in the hedge and came out onto a flat area of grass with the bank of a dyke straight in front of them. To the left was a small group of trees.

'There's a tent there,' Kirsten said.

'It's Toby's,' Henry told her, as if it was normal to have your sister's weird boyfriend camping in your back garden. She checked the back of her leg where she had felt something snag and saw that there was a huge ladder running down the length of her calf. She'd have to buy another pair of tights in the morning before she went into work.

'Let's go to the pond,' Henry said and he set off at his quick pace again so that Kirsten had to alternate between walking and jogging to keep up.

'Jesus, Kirsten. They'll hear you a mile off stomping along like that.'

'Who will?' She felt hot and breathless.

'Everything. Birds, animals, insects. There won't be anything around to see at this rate.'

'What do you expect to see?' she asked.

Henry stopped and looked at her. 'What do you want to see? You suggested the walk.'

'A fox,' she offered tentatively, the first thing which came into her head. She'd had no idea a walk would involve hunting out creatures; she'd imagined they'd find somewhere pretty to sit and watch the sun go down.

Henry spun away and set off again but this time he kept to a slower pace so that Kirsten could walk beside him. They walked along the bank, across a field. Her second field, she thought to herself, and smiled. She followed Henry under the bridge which she didn't know was possible and up another bank. She noticed how he kept to a worn path through the grass and so stayed behind him until they arrived at a stile.

Henry climbed over it first.

'Your turn,' he told her and laughed as she struggled to get one leg over without tearing her skirt or losing her dignity.

'I see we'll have to get you kitted out properly next time,' he said and reached up to help her. Even when she was safely back on land he didn't let go until he'd finished kissing her.

'Walk in the middle,' he told her. A long stretch of narrow decking snaked ahead of them through tall reeds. 'And step across the gaps; that way you'll keep the vibration to a minimum and hopefully we'll see something interesting.'

She did as he'd told her, trying to place her feet as lightly as possible. It was a beautiful evening with a soft, orange light; the warm breeze blew across the reeds, making them shiver and sigh. She glanced at Henry; he was carrying his arm tucked across his chest but it seemed as if the tension had dropped from his face the moment he had climbed over the stile.

'It's very low,' he said, peering down at a pool of brown water with bits of slimy weeds draped up the sides. It smelt like bad drains.

Henry sat cross-legged on the boardwalk. 'I've spent many happy hours here,' he said.

'Doing what?' Kirsten lowered herself carefully down, hitching up her skirt as discreetly as she could. She sat sideways, leaning heavily on one hand.

'Just watching. Looking out for things, like one of the native amphibians.'

She couldn't have been happier that he'd remembered what she'd told him and he was using it to tease her.

'We used to come here all the time when we were kids.'

'All of you?'

'Me and Tyler mostly. It was before Hannah was born and Finn wasn't into nature much either.'

They fell silent again. It felt easy to not talk in a place like this. It wrapped you up like a dream world. 'It's very peaceful,' she said, but she wouldn't have wanted to be out here on her own.

28

Kirsten was barely through the office door when Emma called out, 'What have you bought, Kirsten?' That girl could smell a shopping bag from a mile away.

'Some trainers.' It was the first pair that Kirsten had ever owned. She had been bewildered by the array of them in the shop and the assistant hadn't been much help when she'd told him she needed them for walking.

'You mean walking boots,' he'd said and led her to a different area where gloomy green and brown and black boots with thick soles like a workman would wear were displayed.

'I had something more elegant in mind,' she'd said firmly.

'Ooh, lets see.' Emma and Valerie stood over her as she peeled back the tissue paper in the box to reveal the trainers.

'Nice.' Emma reached in and held one of them aloft. Kirsten had tried to imagine which of the many trainers Ella or Hannah would choose but the closest she'd seen either of them wearing were canvas shoes that looked like the plimsolls she'd worn for sports when she was little. There didn't seem to be any of those in the shop, so she'd chosen a white pair with some pink on the sides and a silver star on the heel.

'Are you joining a gym?' Valerie wanted to know.

'It's for when me and Henry go on walks,' Kirsten told her and blushed, which didn't go unnoticed by Emma.

'It's me and Henry now, is it?' she teased, returning the shoe to the box. 'Good make.'

Hannah had been right, Henry was different when he was out in nature. On their walk he'd seem more relaxed, more present. As soon as they got back to Spindle House, he seemed to withdraw. He didn't want to sit outside in the garden as Kirsten would have liked to do — it was such a lovely evening, it seemed a shame to waste it. Instead, he wanted her to stay with him in the living room where they sat with one of the curtains pulled across to block out the light and the TV on. Kirsten couldn't settle, her attention was drawn to the window through which she could see the herb bed and the front of Ella's hothouse. She had never been inside the hothouse. When Henry had shown her round, they'd stood in the doorway, gazing at the damp, tropical lushness of plants crammed in together. There were yet more of Ella's beloved white flowers but it had been nice to see other colours standing out: the red of the tomatoes, the purple aubergines, some orange flowers which looked like birds' heads with long beaks.

Henry twitched and sighed. He'd fallen asleep, slumping sideways onto the arm of the settee. She slid away carefully and gently draped the throw over him.

Outside was a lot cooler than earlier — the air felt damp as if it was going to rain. Ella's patchy lawn could really do with it. Kirsten couldn't understand why Ella didn't give it a soaking at the same time as she was watering the beds. She headed towards the hothouse and was surprised to find that the door was closed. She was reluctant to open it as she was afraid it would upset the temperature; Henry had told her that Ella had some very rare plants inside. The windows were obscured by steam and droplets of water so it was impossible to tell if anyone was in there. If Ella was, she reasoned, she'd open the door and call Kirsten in. She walked around the side of the hothouse and back again in case she could catch Ella's attention but felt silly after a minute of waiting and so she returned to the kitchen where she discovered Tyler making a sandwich.

'Where's Henry?' Tyler asked.

'Asleep. We went for a walk in the nature reserve. It seems to have tired him out.'

'Really?' He glanced at her, then almost as an afterthought offered her a cup of tea. 'I'm making one.'

'Yes, please.'

She sat at the kitchen table and looked at Tyler's back. He was much wider than Henry and whiter, too, from spending all that time up in his room.

'What is it you do, Tyler? I don't think anyone's ever said.'

'I analyze research data,' he told her. 'Mainly for Cambridge University but for some commercial companies, too.'

'It sounds interesting.'

'Thanks for pretending, Kirsten.' He laughed.

'Well, I like it anyway, so that's what matters. How about you? You're a legal secretary, aren't you?'

It surprised her that he knew. In fact, she was finding Tyler quite surprising in many ways. Despite his bulk and all his hair, he seemed very gentle. He was quite good-looking, too, in a more ordinary way than Henry, but his face was friendlier, more open.

He joined her at the table, plonking down his plate and an open packet of ginger cookies which he pushed towards her. 'Help yourself.' She took one, dunked it in her tea, then she took another two. She didn't mind eating in front of Tyler like she did with the others; they made her so self-conscious of her weight and manners that she only ever ate the minimum she could get away with without seeming like she had some eating disorder.

'What I like about my job is that there is right and there is wrong and all sorts in between, but there is always a path through it which is dictated by rules and I like helping to find it.' She paused for a moment. 'I don't know why people say lawyers are boring. You're witness to people's most important moments: birth, death; marriage, buying a house, divorce. I like being a trusted part of that.'

'People at all their highs and lows in life,' Tyler said. 'There is something fundamental about it.'

'Yes,' she said. *Fundamental*, she thought. That was a good way of expressing what she felt, 'Can I ask you a question?'

'Will I be able to answer it?'

'I don't know. It's about Henry.'

'Aah.'

Tyler's tone of voice and the way he shifted his eyes down made her think he knew something. 'Has Henry spoken to you about what happened in Lima?'

'About the accident, you mean? A little.'

'Hannah said the accident's only part of it. That something else happened out there. She said that he seems like a different person since he got back.'

'What you've got to realize is that Hannah worries about everyone.' Tyler smiled. 'And that she is a bit of a drama queen.'

'Is she?' Kirsten said. 'Because when I told her that Henry says he's not travelling any more and that he's going to stay here, Hannah seemed to think that meant he was really unhappy or something.'

Tyler frowned. 'I do think he's feeling rather traumatized,' he said slowly. 'So it might be a bit early for him to be making those kinds of decisions.'

'So you think he'll go away again?'

'I don't know.'

'And you don't know anything else that happened in Lima?'

'I think you should talk to him yourself,' Tyler told her and he pushed his chair back so quickly that it crashed to the floor and set Kirsten's heart booming. As he righted it, he turned his head. 'Henry's calling you,' he said, and she heard the sleep-muffled sound of Henry's voice coming from the living room.

'Coming,' she shouted and stood up. Tyler gestured for her to pass ahead of him through the door. So she hurried into the hall, feeling his presence following closely behind, but when she hesitated outside the living room and turned to look round at him, she saw that he hadn't even crossed the kitchen threshold. The hallway was too dark to see his expression but she knew he was watching her.

She heard Henry's voice, stronger, closer now, calling her, and she gave Tyler a quick, apologetic smile before going in.

29

Kirsten felt as if she was walking on air in her new trainers as she went round the side of Spindle House and into the garden. She was pleased to see Henry sitting at the garden table and that he had a bottle of wine in front of him.

'A glass of wine on a summer's evening. How perfect,' she said as she sat down, but got up immediately when she noticed that there was only one glass.

'You'd better bring another bottle, too,' Henry said, drinking down the remainder of his wine in a large, loud swallow.

'What are we celebrating?' she asked him when she returned.

'Whatever you want, my darling,' he told her and grabbed hold of her hand clumsily. She slowly removed her fingers from his grasp and poured them both a glass from the new bottle.

'So what excitements have happened at the office today, my little secretary?' Henry said and Kirsten sipped at her wine, taking a few moments to think. She had never seen Henry drunk and she didn't really like his loud enthusiasm or the mocking tone in his voice.

'Come here,' he said, pulling at her arm, 'I want to whisper you something.' When she leaned towards him, he put his hands on either side of her head and brought his mouth close.

She felt the warmth of his breath and then recoiled when he suddenly jabbed his wet tongue inside her ear. She pushed him away and he laughed loudly.

He got up, tugged at her hand until she stood up, then he held her close against him with his good arm across her back.

'Lets go to bed,' he said.

'I'd rather stay here and unwind with a drink for a while,' she told him, trying to step away. He held her tighter.

'Oh come on, Kirsten, you know that's what you've come here for.'

She twisted out of his hold. Her white trainers flashed on the ground as she ran towards her car. She reached it, breathless, only to be greeted by Tyler's astonished face as he stood beside his motorbike ready to leave.

'Kirsten? Are you OK?'

She was too shaken to speak. She got into the car and drove off quickly. Looking behind in her mirror at the house, she could see Tyler still standing by his motorbike watching her, but there was no sign of Henry.

★   ★   ★

She couldn't think about what had happened without feeling upset. Henry's words had been so ugly, so embarrassing. When her mobile phone rang shortly after lunchtime on Thursday, she was both hopeful and anxious about seeing his number on the display.

'Kirst, it's Henry.'

'Hello, Henry.' She had to whisper so that Emma and Valerie wouldn't overhear; it made it harder to keep the wobble out of her voice.

'I'm so sorry for being such a pig yesterday.'

'Did you . . . did you mean it?' She closed her eyes as she asked the question and bowed her head as if she were awaiting execution by his reply.

'Kirst, no, God,' he stumbled in his rush to deny it and she felt some satisfaction at his evident surprise that she had had to ask. 'Of course not. It was the drink talking, that's all. You know I think a lot of you. You do know that, don't you?'

She took a breath as if she were about to launch herself head-first into dark water, 'I'm sorry I ran away.'

'I would have too, in your shoes. Believe me.' He laughed and then switched instantly back to a serious tone. 'Do you forgive me, Kirst?'

'Yes,' she said after a short pause, but she'd said yes twice already: once in her head and once in her heart, she thought, placing the palm of her hand on her chest to calm herself.

'Will you come over this evening?'

'I can't. I've got the Kids' Club, I've already told them I'm going.' Even if Henry had asked her to cancel it, she knew she couldn't avoid Paul any longer. Now that she and Henry had made up, she felt stronger about talking to him and finally clearing the air.

* * *

Despite her resolve, when Kirsten walked into the Community Centre her heart was beating so rapidly and her face was so red from embarrassment all she could manage was a quick, blind wave to whoever was in the hall before heading straight through to the kitchen. She pretended to be busy by the sink until her skin had cooled. When she turned round, she almost knocked Ange over.

'Gosh, Kirsten,' Ange said. 'Are you all right?'

Over Ange's shoulder, Kirsten was watching Paul and Geoff manoeuvring the computer trolleys into place. Geoff had his back to her but Paul had fixed her with such a weird expression that it made her feel nervous. When he tripped, she had to look away.

'I'm sorry I haven't been for a while,' Kirsten said. 'I've been spending time with my boyfriend; he's been in an accident and can't get around much, so . . . '

Ange's big, blue eyes widened. 'Your boy-friend?'

Kirsten nodded.

'Does Paul know?'

'About Henry? No.'

'I think you'd better tell him.'

'I was going to,' she said and, made brave by irritation at Ange's bossy tone, added, 'I don't know what Paul's told you but there was never much between us.'

'I thought it was only a matter of time before you two became an item.'

'No. That was never going to happen.'

Ange stepped aside as Kirsten pushed past

her. She felt Ange's hand on her arm. 'I didn't mean to say anything out of line, Kirsten.'

'I know.' It was too hard to stay angry at Ange. Kirsten looked in Paul's direction and then at Ange. 'Wish me luck.'

It wasn't until the end of the evening that Kirsten had the chance to speak to Paul. Ange and Geoff hurried off, giving Kirsten the impression that Geoff had been filled in on the situation. Paul leaned against one of the tables and watched while Kirsten began to stack the chairs.

'I saw your mother the other day. It seems like you've been lying.'

She'd forgotten how small a world it was around Ely, Paul was the son of a couple who went to her parents' church.

'She said you haven't been ill at all, Kirsten.'

Kirsten stared at him. His voice was beginning to sound shrill and she knew now why the children made fun of him; they could sense that when he got angry he was on the edge of being out of control. Kirsten sighed and continued to stack the chairs.

'I don't owe you any explanation because it's none of your business what I do in my free time, or what I say I do.'

'We fucked. In case you don't remember.' He spat the words across the room and for the briefest moment she felt afraid that she was alone with him, but the fear died when she saw that he couldn't meet her eyes.

'Oh, I remember. But that's all we did, Paul.' A chair fell out of her grip and it crashed against the others like an emphatic end to her words. 'An hour of sex on a Thursday evening every now and then hardly constitutes a relationship.' With each word her voice got stronger and the internal voice inside her head chattered like a happy monkey, cheering her on. 'You were never interested in seeing me.'

'I have commitments on other days,' he said primly.

'Exactly.'

'From what your mother said, you're out of your league, Kirsten.'

She could picture the scene clearly: Paul and her mother standing in the street discussing her, tutting and sighing over her behaviour as her parents had always done. She had never been able to do anything right. A bubble of relief rose from her chest, up her throat and into her mouth, making her want to laugh out loud at her lucky escape.

'Well, one thing's for sure, I wouldn't ever want to be in yours.' She turned away from him and crossed the room to collect her handbag and then she kept on walking straight out of the hall without looking behind her. Her heart was beating so violently she thought she might be having a heart attack but the moment she got out into the air she felt a rush of euphoria.

★   ★   ★

'You're back then.' Kirsten twisted round to see Tyler in the obscurity of the shadowed front door.

'Yes.' She smiled in his direction.

'Have you talked to him, Kirsten?'

'No, not yet.'

'You should,' he said, and there was something in his tone which made her uncomfortable. She leaned into the car and reached across the seat to get her sunglasses and pick up her trainers from the floor of the passenger seat. When she stood up, Tyler had gone.

Her trainers were warm in her hands from the heat of the car and she continued to hold them for several seconds more before deciding to put them back. She walked around the side of the house, nervous about how they would be with each other. She was relieved to find that Henry wasn't sitting at the garden table. She passed quickly through the kitchen and into the hall where she took a slow, deep breath to calm herself, her fingers resting on the handle of the living room door.

The door moved away from her hand, she blinked as light flooded over her.

'I thought I heard you,' Henry said and he stepped forward and held her in a long, tight embrace which said everything Kirsten needed to hear.

30

It was Henry who suggested that they go for a walk. They took the same route to the nature reserve that they had before. It was easier to keep up with Henry this time and he glanced approvingly at her new footwear. The sun was still high in the sky and it was so hot that the horizon shimmered and danced in front of her eyes as they walked on the top of the bank.

At the stile, she hoped that Henry would kiss her again as he had before, but he turned his back while she climbed over by herself and stared down the boardwalk.

The air seemed denser here and the light stronger. Even with her sunglasses on, she found she was squinting against the force of the rays. Everything seemed bleached of colour except for the sky which was so saturated in blue it looked liquid.

'It's even lower,' Henry said, looking worried when they reached the pond. 'I hope this weather breaks soon.'

He lay on his back and looked upwards; Kirsten did the same but had to sit up after a minute as the wood was hard under her spine.

'What's wrong, Henry?' she asked him. 'Why are you so unhappy?'

He didn't speak for so long that she thought he was never going to answer her. He sat up, pulled his knees towards his chest and rested his bad arm on top.

'I don't know how to begin,' he said. 'I don't know how to talk about it. I've never talked about it to anyone.'

'Who was she?'

He faced her. 'How did you know?'

She hadn't. Until that moment. 'Call it women's intuition. Tell me about her. Tell me what happened.'

'I love it here. Don't you think it's gorgeous?' He gave a small, sad smile. 'It's like a gentle watercolour, a pastel perhaps. Easy on the eye. Over there, the beauty can stun you. But there's a harshness to it, and it's rotten, too. There's all this poverty and violence and cruelty all played out in this beautiful place. It's mind-blowing.'

She tried to picture it even though she knew she wouldn't like what she pictured.

'And in the middle of all this confusion comes Sophia.'

'She was your girlfriend?'

He nodded. 'I fell in love,' he said. 'We both did. Heavily. We drenched ourselves in it.' The way he spoke chilled her right through. An insect landed on her hand and, as she watched it crawling across her skin, she imagined squashing it between her fingers until it popped. She shook her arm and was relieved when it flew away.

'It wasn't sustainable, I see that now. It was too intense, like that place. Beautiful but rotten inside.'

'What happened?' she asked.

'She had an abortion,' he said. 'Without telling me.'

The horror of hearing Henry's words brought blood pounding to her face.

'We were always arguing but of course this one was the worst; it was horrible. I got drunk after she'd gone to bed and half a bottle of bourbon later it seemed like a good idea to take the jeep and leave. The next thing I remember is being in hospital with the worst headache in the world and Sophia telling me it was over.'

Kirsten touched his arm and he grabbed at her hand. 'That's why I'm so happy to have you, Kirst. You've got a calm, quiet loveliness, just like this place.'

She shifted towards him and they leaned against each other, his good arm pulling her close.

She knew that what he had said to her should have been the best thing she had ever heard and that she should have been grateful for what amounted to the most romantic words anyone had ever used about her, and yet she couldn't shake off the picture of Henry and Sophia with their riotous passion in a place which was brighter and larger than life. What she feared was that Henry would come to see what they had together as a pale, watercolour version — soft on the eye and on the heart.

'And it's over between you?'

'Oh yes. It's definitely over.'

31

The women in the shop resumed their conversation as soon as they saw it was Kirsten who had come in.

'Jenkins has had enough. And I don't blame him,' said a woman whom Kirsten recognized but whose name she couldn't remember.

'It's about time something was done.'

'All the crops are ready anyway,' Mrs Barker added. 'This sun's brought the harvest on early.'

'I heard they're expecting trouble.'

'More trouble.' Margery Greene's voice was painfully squeaky, like a little girl's. 'They brought it with them from the start.'

'They've got extra police coming in from Cambridge.'

Kirsten stopped what she was doing and listened.

'Once the field's cut, they'll have no reason to stay.'

'Are you talking about the Crop Circle followers?' Kirsten asked, coming out from behind the shelves. The women all turned to look at her.

'Yes. And good riddance,' Margery squeaked.

'I expect that Ruland girl will get mixed up in it now she's with that boy.'

'He's not one of them,' Kirsten said. 'He's here on holiday.'

The women stared at her. It was obvious that

326

they didn't believe her.

'Why's she always over there then?' one of them asked and it sent a flurry of agreement around the group.

'I heard she's out of control,' Margery said. 'Her mother can't do anything with her.'

'I bet her father's turning in his grave.'

'He was never at home when he was alive,' the unknown woman said.

'The family name went downhill the moment his parents died,' Margery said.

★ ★ ★

Kirsten was making a drink and a snack for her and Henry's supper when Hannah and Toby came into the kitchen from the garden.

'Hi, Kirsten,' Hannah said. 'Are you having a nice evening?'

'Quiet,' Kirsten replied. On the floor behind Hannah, lined up with the other boots and Wellingtons, were Kirsten's trainers. There was a little dust on the toes but otherwise they were still as white as when she'd bought them over a couple of weeks ago. They hadn't taken a walk since the day Henry had told her about Sophia; they hadn't talked about anything since then either. Henry had become withdrawn and a little bad-tempered; he hardly ever moved from the living room. Kirsten would have liked to ask Hannah or Ella for some advice but they were hardly ever around and, when they were, it never seemed to be the right moment.

'Where's Henry?'

'Watching TV.'

She caught Hannah looking at her. It was a surprise to see her without her sunglasses on. Her eyelids looked reddened and sore, as if she'd been rubbing them.

'What does he do during the day, when I'm not here, Hannah? Do you know?'

Hannah took out the loaf of brown bread from the breadbin and started to cut thick slices straight onto the wooden work surface. The butter was too cold to spread, so crumbs were flying everywhere. Kirsten resisted the urge to wipe up while Hannah was there, she could do it later.

'I'm only asking because I'm worried about him,' Kirsten said, which was true but she was also worried for herself. She knew how easy it was to end up thinking badly of someone simply because you'd shared your secret with them.

'He doesn't really do anything. He stays in bed until the afternoon and then he sits around the house or the garden waiting for you to come.'

Kirsten saw a look pass between Hannah and Toby but she didn't mind. She had heard what she'd wanted to hear — Henry wanted her at Spindle House, he was just having difficulty showing it.

Hannah had begun to accumulate various packets and containers of food: crisps, biscuits, cherry tomatoes, baby cucumbers, spring onions, the slices of bread packed with cold meat.

'Could you leave the butter out?' Kirsten asked and Hannah handed the dish to her. 'You've got enough there to feed an army.'

'Its for a couple of days,' Hannah told her.

'Is this something to do with the Crop Circle?' Kirsten looked at Hannah who wouldn't meet her eyes, and then at Toby. 'I heard they're going to cut the field.'

'Where did you hear that?' Toby asked.

'In the village shop.'

'The hub of the world,' Toby said and laughed a not very nice laugh, Kirsten thought.

'Did they say when?' Hannah asked.

'No, only that it's soon and that they're expecting trouble. They're bringing in extra police.'

'Fascists,' Toby pronounced and stood up. 'We'd better get going.'

'It's a vigil,' Hannah told her. 'They only want to delay it for a short while.'

'Be careful,' Kirsten said.

'I will.'

'Does Ella know you're going?'

'No,' Hannah said and began to pack everything neatly into a carrier bag. Toby leaned against the door frame, waiting.

'Shouldn't you . . . tell her?' Kirsten had been about to say, 'ask her if it's OK'. It was sometimes hard to remember that Hannah wasn't a child.

'She won't care anyway. If she even notices I'm not here,' Hannah said, looking up. 'But don't tell her, will you, Kirsten?'

Kirsten shook her head. 'As long as you promise to leave if there's any sign of trouble.'

'I promise.' Hannah laughed and then the next second she was gone. Kirsten wiped the work surfaces down and carried the mugs of tea with a plate of cheese on toast balanced on top of each. She pushed the door open with her hip and felt her heart sink when she saw that Henry had already closed the curtains, blocking out the gentle evening light.

★ ★ ★

Kirsten slept in late the next morning and when she got up she was certain that neither Hannah nor Ella had been home the previous night. There was no trace of anyone having eaten breakfast, the curtains in the living room were still closed and the back door was locked.

She reported her findings to Henry when she took breakfast and the Saturday paper up to him in bed.

'They'll be around somewhere,' he said dismissively, through crunching toast and rustling newspaper. If she were to cut a hole in the paper and look through it, it wouldn't have surprised her to discover her father's face there instead of Henry's.

Kirsten wandered out into the garden in the afternoon when Henry fell asleep during the film they were watching. Kirsten was relieved; she was desperate for air and bored beyond belief. She walked over to the hothouse and was surprised to find it closed up.

She hesitated for a moment before sliding one side of the door open — a wave of hot air hit her face. She stepped inside. The heat was so dry she found it difficult to breathe properly. It took her a few minutes to work out how the top vents opened, but she managed in the end although it didn't seem to make any difference to the temperature at all. Everywhere she looked, plants were drooping and wilting. She went outside to the water butt but the hosepipe was disconnected from the tap and, when she looked inside, there was only a few centimetres or so of stinking water at the bottom. She spotted a watering can about two-thirds full on the other side of the door and set about watering those plants which looked the most desperate.

There was an empty Tupperware container lying on the floor next to the tomatoes and so she picked any ripe ones she could see until the box was overflowing. She wiped clean a cherry tomato on her shirt and popped it into her mouth, its sweet flavour seemed to explode on her tongue.

When she returned to the living room, Henry hardly stirred when she sat down. The film barely seemed to have moved on, even though she felt as if she'd been away for hours.

Henry woke at the sound of Ella's car coming into the drive. He yawned stale breath over Kirsten who had been dozing too. They wandered into the kitchen where Ella had already made a start on the dinner. Onions, garlic, rice and a box of fresh brown shrimp were laid out neatly beside a chopping board.

'Would you like some help?' Kirsten asked.

'No. Um. Thanks.'

Kirsten hovered in case Ella was only being polite and changed her mind. 'You don't know where the small frying pan is, do you?'

'Oh yes.' Kirsten went over to a cupboard and pulled it out. 'I put it in here with the bigger ones — it seemed more logical.'

'I like to keep it out on top because I use it to start off the onions and garlic,' Ella explained. Kirsten didn't think that was very hygienic but she handed the pan over without saying a word.

'Perhaps you could set the table?' Ella said.

'The one in the garden?' Kirsten asked, desperately hoping Ella would say yes.

'That would be nicer, don't you think? We'd better make the most of eating out before the weather breaks.'

'Can I pick some flowers for it?'

'Which ones?' Ella looked at her, the spatula poised in her hand.

'Well, those roses in front of the patio are looking lovely.'

'No,' Ella said. 'I never cut those.'

'Oh, I'm sorry, I think I did the other day.' Kirsten blushed furiously. 'I'd better leave it, then.'

'Cut some of the zinnia,' Ella told her. When Kirsten didn't move, she turned off the heat under the pan and told her to follow. She pointed out which flowers they were and left Kirsten to cut 'enough to fill a large vase' while she went to pick some salad stuff. Each time Kirsten looked up, she could see the top of Ella's head. It was a moment like this which Kirsten had been hoping for ever since she'd first come to Spindle House to see Henry.

* * *

'Henry? Could you call Hannah at the back please?' Ella stood at the back door, her face a little flushed from the hot cooker,

Kirsten put out a hand to stop Henry getting up. 'She's not . . . ' Kirsten glanced behind her to see that Ella hadn't returned to the kitchen and was watching them. She lifted her hand away and let Henry get up and walk slowly across the lawn towards the gap in the hedge. When he had disappeared, she turned her head and caught Ella still looking at her.

Henry was back a couple of minutes later. 'No sign of her.'

'We'll have to start without her,' Ella said as Tyler appeared behind her. He kissed his mother on the forehead and caught her in a hug which she pretended to struggle out of.

'Put me down, you big idiot,' she said and it was the happiest Kirsten had ever heard Ella sound.

Tyler's T-shirt had pulled up, exposing his round, hairy belly. She noticed that he tugged it down the instant he realized. He clumped a hand on Henry's shoulder, causing his brother to let out an oomph of surprise and pain. 'For fuck's sake, Ty.'

'Oh shit mate, I forgot.' Tyler stood blinking like a child who had made its first mistake in public. Kirsten was relieved when Henry shrugged and made a joke of it, releasing Tyler from his mortification.

'This is delicious, Ella,' Kirsten said. 'The

333

shrimp are so fresh. Where did you get them?'

'In Ely.'

'At the fishmongers? Or the delicatessen?' She'd seen a lot of Worldwide Delicatessen products in the kitchen so she knew Ella shopped there.

'You can get them anywhere, Kirsten,' Ella said. 'At Worldwide's, at the fishmonger, in every bloody supermarket.'

At first Kirsten thought that Ella must be making a joke that she didn't understand, but as she looked first at Ella's face, then saw that both Henry's and Tyler's were like a paused scene on a film, she realized that, without meaning to, she had really annoyed Ella.

As if someone had pressed play, all three of them began to talk. Tyler started to tell them about someone he'd been chatting to in the pub, Henry was sharing facts about the rarity of river oysters, and above them both Ella was apologizing.

'I'm sorry. It's because I'm rather worried about Hannah. Is it only me who thinks it's odd she hasn't been back yet this evening?'

'She's probably with Toby.'

'But is that a good thing? I know it doesn't seem fair but I'm not sure I trust the boy.'

'I don't think she was here last night,' Henry said. 'But then again, who was?'

Everyone's eyes we're drawn to Ella who blushed lightly.

'She's at the field,' Kirsten said, hardly daring to lift her eyes as she felt all attention redirected towards her. 'I think, anyway.'

'What field?'

'The one with the Crop Circle. The Travellers are going to try and stop them cutting it.'

'Why didn't you say anything before?' Ella threw out.

'She asked me not to,' Kirsten said, looking at Henry for some back-up.

'They won't stop it,' Henry said, stabbing several shrimps onto his fork. 'They'll arrest them for trespassing.'

'I don't understand what the attraction is with that lot,' Ella said.

Kirsten was quick to agree but felt chastened when Tyler reminded them gently but firmly, 'They are her friends.'

'She'll be fine,' Henry said. 'Getting out and meeting new people does you good, don't you think, Ella?'

Kirsten couldn't understand why Ella was blushing again but Henry hadn't seemed to notice — he was busy eating the last of his food as if there was nothing going on.

*   *   *

Henry and Kirsten had gone to bed when the phone rang, then stopped, then rang again. Only a few minutes later, there was a soft tapping at the door.

Henry called, 'Come in.'

Kirsten didn't know who was going to open the door as she tucked the sheet tight around her. Ella's white, worried face appeared.

'Hannah's at the police station in Ely. I'm

335

going to pick her up.'

'I'll come with you,' Henry said and in two moves he was out of the bed and pulling a clean pair of jeans out from a pile of clothes sitting on top of the chair.

Kirsten and Ella watched him for a moment as he shook them out and proceeded to struggle into them, using one arm.

'Hang on, Henry.' Kirsten got out of bed. She couldn't bear watching any longer. She grabbed hold of the waistband of the jeans and hoisted them up; turning Henry to face her, she did up the button fly for him.

He grinned at her. 'Thanks, Kirst.'

'Is she all right?' Kirsten asked, hiding behind Henry.

'She's upset but she said she was fine.'

'You might as well come too,' Henry said. 'Now that you're up.'

'Well, I — '

'We've got to go right now,' Ella said and Kirsten didn't know if this was an attempt to put her off going with them or to make her hurry. She pulled on the dress she had been wearing earlier and picked up a sweatshirt of Henry's.

'Can I borrow this?'

As they were walking down the stairs, Kirsten whispered to Henry, 'What about Tyler? Shouldn't we tell him that we're going?'

'He's not here,' Henry told her and Kirsten wondered how they ever managed to keep track of each other's comings and goings in a house as big as this.

Hannah

32

When Hannah answered the phone, the silence on the other end seemed to approach her ear like ripples thrown out when a pebble lands in water. The line had that different quality of sound that she used to hear when Edward phoned from abroad.

'Hello,' she said again and this time a woman spoke.

'Is Henry there please?' Her voice was heavily accented but clear.

'Hold on a second, I'll get him.'

'Wait,' the woman said imperiously. 'Who am I speaking with please?'

'Hannah, his sister.'

'Ah, Hannah. He's told me about you. Wait. Before I speak to him . . . he is OK, Henry?'

She walked to the French windows. Henry was sitting at the garden table, smoking, otherwise he would have been in here, he would have answered the phone.

'He's OK,' Hannah told the woman because she didn't think it was her place to say anything more than that. 'But who are *you*?'

'Sophia.'

Hannah opened the French windows and stepped outside.

'It's for you, Henry.'

'For me?'

'It's Sophia.' His face looked as shocked as if

she had struck him. He stared at her silently and it seemed like ages before he took the phone that she held out to him.

'Sophia,' he said and his voice didn't sound like Henry. Hannah knew then that this woman was the reason that the light had gone out in Henry and why he looked out at the world he loved and felt nothing.

Hannah walked back into the living room. She had lost count of the number of girls and women whom Henry had brought home to Spindle House, never mind those who had phoned or turned up out of the blue even after Henry had told them it was over. But up until now Hannah had never seen Henry on the receiving end of a love affair gone wrong and she felt a little shaken.

Henry came in to put the phone back on the base.

'Hannah?'

'Yes.' She turned to face him. He looked exhausted.

'Don't mention this to Kirsten, will you?'

'I won't.' The fact that Henry felt the need to ask told her everything.

She returned to the French windows and watched Henry carry a bottle of wine and a glass to the table. He poured out a full glass, drank it straight down and lit a cigarette. As she watched him, she felt she was looking at the future and she knew that it was never going to work with Kirsten and that first Kirsten, and then Henry, would soon be gone.

⋆　⋆　⋆

Toby was waiting for Hannah by his car. It was weird, Hannah thought, how only a few weeks ago she would have been sitting next to Ella driving into Ely on a Wednesday afternoon and now it was Toby beside her. He had arrived and stepped in like a substitute for Ella the moment she went off the pitch.

Of course it was different with Toby; they still went to the bookshop but he followed her around chatting, so that the books didn't have the chance to speak to her and she ended up buying nothing or something silly that she regretted the moment she came out of the shop.

Toby was a better companion to walk through the streets with. He noticed things that she couldn't and he would stop every now and then to give her time to focus on what he was looking at: like a squirrel running along the top of a high stone wall or a hedge cut into the shape of a teapot where they sold cream teas.

Today Hannah was wearing her black cigarette pants and her long gypsy blouse which Toby had mentioned he liked before. She glanced at him and he took her hand and laced her fingers into his.

They walked along the river and felt guilty for not having any food for the ducks. They walked back into the town and went into a pub called the Drummer's Arms which Hannah had never been to before. She knew immediately that she didn't like it. She didn't like the unfriendly way the men in there stared at her when she took off

341

her sunglasses but she wasn't quick enough to stop Toby from going to get drinks.

She sat in a dark corner with her back to the bar and waited for Toby to return.

Hannah tried not to talk so that they would both finish their drinks quickly and get out, but Toby hadn't noticed anything was wrong, so she had to explain.

'It's not very nice in here,' she whispered.

'Why?' Toby said, rather too loudly, 'What's wrong with it?'

'Shush.' She gave him a little tap on the shin with the toe of her pump. 'They don't seem very welcoming.'

'They seemed all right to me. They're just a bunch of locals having a drink. You're a local too,' he said and grinned. 'So you should be fine.'

She gave him a fake smile and let it pass, but she knew what people were like. She knew without having to look behind her that they were talking about them and that there was nastiness in their words. As a girl, she used to try and intuit from people's eyes whether they'd be the kind of person to poke at her or to let her be. Now she'd fine-tuned that sense and could tell from the moment she came into their presence.

'Let's hurry up anyway,' she suggested.

'OK,' Toby said, shrugging. He took a long drink of his pint and licked the froth from his top lip. 'I needed that.'

While they drank, she told him about the phone call from Sophia.

'Well, well,' Toby said. 'Sounds like Kirsten

is the rebound girl.'

'Do you really think so?'

'I'd put money on it.'

'Poor Kirsten.'

'Poor Henry more like. She's not the most exciting person to hang out with.'

Hannah tilted her head. Toby had a habit of tapping under his chin when he was speaking and the flutter of his fingers sometimes made it hard for her to focus on his face.

'Well, who is exciting really?' she asked.

'You are.'

'Me?'

He nodded. 'You take me to places where I might get eaten by eels or damned to death by a red-eyed ghost of a dog.'

'Stupid.' She laughed and poked her finger into his arm.

'You're a very interesting woman, you know. Different,' he told her. 'Different — but in a good way.'

They smiled across the table and Hannah felt so lit up inside that she almost forgot about the people behind her.

She made Toby leave their empty glasses on the table rather than returning them to the bar as he often did, and they walked towards the door. The hairs on the back of her neck were prickling but their exit seemed to have gone unnoticed.

It wasn't until they had opened the door that a man shouted out, 'Where are you going now? Back to your coffin?'

'Keep walking,' Hannah said and pushed Toby forward.

'I'm going back in,' he told her but she barred his way. 'The stupid, fucking bastards.'

'It doesn't matter.'

'Of course it matters.'

'Not to me. Not any more.'

Toby shook his head but he turned round and she followed him down the street, looking at the words 'ON MY BUM' on his T-shirt dancing in front of her. She caught up with him and slid her hand into his.

'You don't have to defend me,' she said and he stopped her, pulled her towards him. He leaned in and kissed her for so long that she was surprised by how bright the day was when she opened her eyes.

★   ★   ★

On Friday evening, Hannah was coming down the stairs as Tyler was coming up.

'Whose car pulled up a few minutes ago?' she asked.

'Kirsten's.'

'So she's come back.'

'Yes.'

'I wonder how long for?'

'Why do you say that?'

'Henry had a phone call on Wednesday from someone called Sophia.'

'She phoned?'

'Do you know about her?' They both instinctively looked over the edge of the banister and began to move up the stairs to the landing where the round window was.

'Only that he's been trying to get hold of her ever since he got back.' Tyler spoke in a lowered voice. 'So that's why she went running off on Wednesday.'

'Did she? I thought he wasn't going to tell her. He asked me not to say anything.'

'Well, something upset her because she legged it from the garden, into her car and drove off, and when I went round to see Henry he was pissed out of his brain and mumbling to himself about bloody women.'

'Poor Kirsten.'

'It's good that she knows,' Tyler said. 'She seems really nice; she deserves to be treated better than that.'

★ ★ ★

On Saturday morning, when Hannah walked into the kitchen, Kirsten sang out, 'Just in time,' and asked her if she wanted any breakfast. She stood proudly over the cooker while Ella, Henry and Tyler sat at the table. Hannah exchanged a look with Tyler who gave a half-shrug but when she glanced in Henry's direction, she found he was staring at her. He put his finger to his mouth, shook his head and glared.

Nobody spoke while Kirsten served up the food. The table was properly set with everything in jugs and bowls and plates instead of their packets as usual and there was even a vase of fresh flowers in the middle. It looked like a picture from one of the magazines that Kirsten always had her nose in.

'Kirsten went out to buy it all this morning,' Henry said, as Kirsten passed over plates of a full English breakfast. His tone made everyone turn to face him, even Kirsten who then smiled shyly as if he'd paid her the greatest compliment in the world.

'It's the least I could do, seeing as I've been here so often.' Kirsten beamed her smile around the kitchen and it bounced around like a playful kitten, full of the joy of living, while the members of the Ruland family sat like morose party poopers.

'Well, there's no need but it's — uh — lovely to — uh. Thank you.' Ella seemed confused, as if she had stumbled across alien proceedings and was now trapped against her will. Hannah noticed that she was wearing a new blouse — in a pale grey silk with a drawstring neckline. She leaned her chair back a little to get a better view of the rest of her clothes: both Ella's jeans and her sandals were new too. When she glanced up, Ella was watching her. Something flickered then faded across Ella's face, then she frowned and began to eat.

Hannah's heart was bumping. She picked at the food in front of her but she didn't see it, instead she was replaying Ella's face through her mind. She wanted to ask her mother why she'd bought new clothes and where she disappeared to for hours, but it was as though the questions were surrounded by an invisible barrier which would send a warning shock through her body if she came too close. She

346

glanced up at Henry and Kirsten and thought how the house was creaking with secrets.

★ ★ ★

Ella left shortly after breakfast and Hannah hovered around the kitchen, trying to find a way to get Tyler on his own. She offered to stack the dishwasher, volunteering Tyler's help which thankfully Kirsten agreed to while she and Henry took a second cup of coffee out to the garden.

Carrying the stack of plates from the table across the room, Hannah paused by the back door. Henry and Kirsten were wandering round the garden like visitors to a National Trust property, pointing out the pretty flowers. Kirsten was wearing one of her old-fashioned dresses, pulled in at the waist and which came to a few centimetres below the knee, She was bare-footed and looked very short standing next to Henry.

At that moment, Kirsten let out a shriek and clung onto Henry's arm as he waved off some attacking insect; Kirsten gazed up at him and he leaned down to kiss her.

'It looks like they're back on,' Hannah said, turning away.

'Do you think he really likes her?' Tyler asked. He was standing so close behind that it startled her.

Hannah shrugged. 'Did you see those weird signs Henry was making at me at breakfast? I don't think she knows about Sophia.'

'You should ask him.'

'Maybe you could?'

'No,' Tyler said. 'I think it's best you do it.'

'Why?' Hannah asked.

'Because I do,' he said, sounding a little cross with her. When their eyes met, his slid away as if he too had a secret to keep.

★ ★ ★

It wasn't until a few evenings later that Hannah had the chance to talk to Henry. She was surprised how nervous she felt approaching him. From a distance, he looked fit and healthy but up close she was reminded how thin he was, and his face was tired and weighed down even though he smiled at her when she sat beside him on the settee.

'Kirsten's gone?'

'Yes.'

'Will she be back tomorrow?'

'I suppose so. That's what we arranged.'

'Does she know about Sophia?'

'Yes,' he said and in his eyes she caught a glimpse of the darkness which had got its claws into the old Henry and was keeping him locked away from them. 'But not that she's been phoning. I don't want her to know about that.'

'What was Sophia like?' She pulled her legs up and rested her chin on her knees. She spoke casually although her pulse was racing.

'Beautiful, funny, very intelligent, adventurous.' Henry's voice brightened and darkened, swooped and sighed and Hannah wished she could see what this woman looked like who Henry had fallen for so badly. Instead, an image of Kirsten appeared: a woman who couldn't truthfully be called any of those things.

'Did you love her?'

'What's that, anyway? It's only the short, good bit before it all goes bad.'

'And what about Kirsten?' she asked softly. 'Is that how you feel about her?'

'Kirsten's a nice woman,' he said.

'She is,' Hannah agreed. 'And thoughtful and kind.'

'And peaceful.'

Not far away, in the kitchen, were Kirsten's white trainers — left amongst the family footwear like flags planted at their destination — and Hannah felt bad that she had played a part in encouraging her to feel at home. Despite what Toby had said about her being boring, she knew that Kirsten wouldn't want Henry to find her peaceful. What person would? In their own way, didn't everyone want to be found exciting, interesting, absorbing? Kirsten would want to be another Sophia for Henry because that was what he meant to her.

'Are you OK?' When she put her hand on Henry's arm, she was surprised to feel how solid he was.

'Of course I am,' he said and flashed a smile at her. 'Don't worry about me, Hannie. I really am fine.'

★   ★   ★

The night seemed darker once Hannah was away from the house. The sky was full of clouds, so there wasn't any moon or starlight. Toby had his gas lamp on. He was reading *The Turn of the Screw*, which Hannah had lent him.

'This would have been a very different story if they'd had mobile phones,' he said, putting the open book face-down on the ground when she sat next to him. Its spine cried out to her for help.

'The pages will get damp.' She picked up the book and closed it.

'You've lost my page.'

'You'll find it again,' she told him.

She felt Toby touching her hand and she froze, struck suddenly by the desire for his fingers to explore further. As if he sensed how she felt, he began to move his hand lightly up her arm. When she closed her eyes, she felt heat travel in waves across and through her body.

'Let's go in the tent,' he suggested.

They got up together, without speaking. Toby's hand slipped down to hold hers even though it was awkward to walk; both of them seemed reluctant to let go of the other.

It was dark inside the tent and as Hannah crawled forward she felt like a bat using echolocation to avoid things that she could sense close by but couldn't see. The silky material of Toby's sleeping bag slipped underneath her knees.

'Hang on.'

Toby was lit up suddenly in torchlight. He was fishing around in a bag at the top of the tent.

'Shall I?' he asked, holding something up.

Hannah leaned forward to see what it was, then drew back quickly, feeling embarrassed. It was a condom.

'Hannah?' He shone the light onto her face and she closed her eyes and nodded. At school, a rumour had circulated that she would drain the blood from any boy who slept with her to fill up her own veins, and she would blush pink in front of their eyes before they died. Well, that second part had been the detail she herself had added.

The boys at school hadn't interested her but Toby did. He pulled off his T-shirt and then turned to her.

'Let's lie down,' he said and he balanced the torch on top of the bag so that yellow light filled the top part of the tent but left a more gentle, grey light at ground level as they slid and wriggled out of their clothes.

The more he touched her, the more she wanted him to. It was the heat and heaviness of him which surprised her the most. She found she liked the way she was trapped beneath him so that there was nothing left for her to do but concentrate on kissing.

'Are you ready?'

She took a big gulp of air as if she was about to plunge herself into deep water and she didn't know when she'd have the chance to breathe again. Toby arched over her and then pushed inside her and it hurt at first but then, as he kept moving and kissing and stroking, she found herself sinking into the pleasure of it.

She didn't come, but she was close; her climax

kept slipping away from her when Toby changed the rhythm or she became aware of his hand pressing too heavily against her leg or a lump in the ground working into her spine. Afterwards, they lay on their backs a few centimetres apart as their skin was too hot and sticky to touch.

'That was nice,' Toby said, holding her hand.

'Yes.' She looked along her body which had remained as white as before. Her mind felt sharper but her body drifted as if she was floating on water.

Toby tensed at the sound of rustling close by but Hannah knew that noises became amplified in the dark and it was only a small creature on its nightly round.

'What if it's one of your brothers?' he said when Hannah giggled, which made her laugh more. 'Oh God, is that a spider's web over there?'

'Don't worry. It's just your dream-catcher,' Hannah said.

'What's a dream-catcher?'

'You hang them in your bedroom to separate the good dreams from the bad; some Native American tribes based them originally on spiders' webs.'

Toby fell asleep first and Hannah listened to him breathing. It was a privilege for someone to trust you enough to sleep beside you. She waited until she was sure he was fast asleep and then she crawled carefully out of the tent, clutching Toby's T-shirt in her hand, which was the first item of clothing she had come across.

The breeze cooled her skin immediately as she

walked naked over the bank down to the dyke. The water was icy as she stepped in and squatted down. The clouds had cleared and the moon gave the water a mercury sheen which she plunged into. She spluttered with the shock of the cold as she surfaced and rose up in one smooth movement. Strands of her wet hair slapped like black weeds against her skin and dribbled trails of cold down her back. She hurried up the bank and pulled on Toby's T-shirt which felt as warm as if it had been on a radiator.

She walked back towards the house, hesitating for a moment as she came level with the tent, but she felt drawn to her bedroom where her notebook lay closed on the desk, the pen at its side. She would put on a pair of pyjamas and some thick socks and set some of the words inside her free onto the page.

The garden was in darkness as she ran across the lawn. No lights were on and the back door was locked; nobody had realized she wasn't home. She fished out the key from under the strawberry pot and opened the door as quietly as she could.

The wooden stairs creaked and cracked like gunshot no matter how lightly she tried to tread. She heard the bump of Scoot jumping off Ella's bed and then he appeared at the top of the stairs to greet her. He followed her as far as the door to her room as if he was making sure she was safe inside before returning to Ella.

Hannah was trembling with cold. As she wrapped herself in her dressing gown, she thought how, if she had returned to Toby, she could have dried herself against his hot body as if she was lying down on a slab of stone warmed by the sun. She got into bed, pulling up the quilt from the end to snuggle around her. Her notebook still lay on the desk but the urgency to write had fallen away.

33

'They think the harvest will be this weekend.' Toby put his phone down and turned to Hannah.

She felt a spark of excitement. 'Bridget said she was going to lie in front of the combine harvester.'

'Bridget's full of crap. I bet she doesn't do anything,' Toby said. 'The plan is to hold a vigil on the field from tonight until the farmer arrives and then Trevor's going to ask him to delay harvesting until after the autumn equinox.'

'He won't. That's a few weeks away.'

'I know but I said we'd go along anyway.'

'What for?' Hannah pulled the seed heads off a stalk of grass and threw them into the air. The breeze blew one back onto the arm of her blouse. She picked it off and nibbled on it with her front teeth.

'Moral support.'

'I'm not sure.'

'It's only a bit of fun.' He pushed her over and held her down by the wrists.

'Maybe, then. If you insist.'

'I do.' He dropped his body on top of hers and began to kiss her. As she kissed him back, she felt one of his hands running down the length of her side and over her hip.

'We shouldn't.'

'Why not?'

She twisted her head away and caught sight of the end of Toby's sleeping bag poking out of the tent half a metre away. They had made love every day since the first time but she hadn't yet stayed overnight with him.

'I don't have a good reason,' she said, smiling up at him and she shifted to release the material of her skirt which was trapped underneath her so that Toby could find his way inside it.

'Skirts are great,' he mumbled into her ear. 'I forbid you to ever wear trousers again.'

A small pulse that she thought had faded built quickly and she found herself squeezing Toby with her thighs as she came, letting out a cry of surprise and pleasure which Toby caught up, yelling out as he pushed one urgent, final time before he became still. He rolled off her and they lay there for a few seconds in silence and then first Hannah, then Toby began to laugh.

'I hope nobody heard us,' Hannah said.

'Who is there around to hear anything?' Toby said and then shouted up to the sky. 'Hello, hello.'

They sank back into silence.

'I'm starving,' Toby said suddenly when Hannah thought he had drifted off to sleep.

'I could make us a meal.'

'We should take something with us. We ought to get going soon.'

'Let's go to the house and see what we can find.'

Kirsten was in the kitchen when they got there.

'Where's Henry?' Hannah asked. She really

hoped that Kirsten wasn't going to tell her that he was wandering around the garden some-where.

'Watching TV.'

Hannah tried to keep her back turned away from Kirsten while she brushed her skirt down in case she had grass all over it.

'What does he do during the day, when I'm not here, Hannah? Do you know?'

Hannah felt caught. She busied herself making sandwiches and collecting anything she could think of that would keep for a couple of days out of a fridge.

'I'm only asking because I'm worried about him,' Kirsten said.

'He doesn't really do anything,' Hannah told her. 'He stays in bed until the afternoon and then he sits around the house or the garden waiting for you to come.'

She couldn't help glancing at Toby as she spoke — she hoped he'd keep quiet about what she'd told him the other day, about how Henry spoke to Sophia every day on the phone.

Kirsten commented on the amount of food she had collected together.

'It's for a couple of days,' Hannah told her, feeling like she owed her some truth at least and Hannah was surprised when Kirsten knew exactly what it was for. Toby wanted to know where she'd heard about the field being cut.

'In the village shop.'

'The hub of the world,' Toby said. He often made a joke about it being a very small world around here.

'Did they say when?' Hannah asked.

'No, only that it's soon and that they're expecting trouble. They're bringing in extra police.'

Hannah felt shocked. She hadn't imagined there would be any police at all, never mind extra ones.

'Fascists,' Toby said and Hannah was surprised by the anger in his voice.

'It's a vigil,' Hannah tried to explain because Kirsten was looking increasingly worried and she didn't want her telling Ella or Henry what she was up to. 'They only want to delay it for a short while.'

'Be careful,' Kirsten said.

'I will.'

'Does Ella know you're going?'

'No,' Hannah replied.

'Shouldn't you . . . tell her?'

'She won't care anyway. If she even notices I'm not here,' Hannah said; most nights the back door was locked before Hannah was in. Behind her, she could sense Toby's impatience to be gone. 'But don't tell her, will you, Kirsten?'

'As long as you promise to leave if there's any sign of trouble,' Kirsten said.

'I promise.' Hannah laughed at Kirsten's motherly tone but it was sweet of her to care.

'You should tell her,' Toby said when they were near the gap in the hedge. Hannah turned to look at him.

'I can't, he's my brother.'

'She's a nice woman.'

'Shall we walk?' Hannah asked, partly because

it was a beautiful evening and she wanted to savour it and partly because she was feeling rather nervous about what she was getting involved in.

'It'll take too long,' Toby said. 'It's already getting dark.'

* * *

Animals seemed to be having a universal death wish that evening: rabbits, a fox, even a stoat leapt out in front of the car, setting Hannah's heart racing each time Toby braked. The ghost-white body of an owl landed in the road ahead of them. Toby braked sharply before slowing to a halt.

'It's watching us.' Hannah felt the bird's spectral, magnetic eyes drawing her in. 'A lot of people believe owls are a symbol of death.'

'Do you?'

'I like them,' Hannah said. 'But they can be a bit creepy.'

'I think it's dazzled,' Toby said. 'I'd better cut the lights.'

As soon as the headlights were off, the bird lifted into the air and swung leisurely over the hedge across the fields, melting into the sky.

Hannah let out her breath and Toby glanced at her.

'I have a feeling its going to be one of those weird nights,' he said.

* * *

'How many people do you think are here?' Hannah asked as Toby drove past the lay-by where the main camp fire was burning and down a long line of cars and vans and bumped the car up on the grass behind a converted bus.

'I don't know but it looks like they've called in the cavalry,' Toby replied.

They walked back along the road. In one hand, Hannah held a bag of food, in the other, she gripped hold of Toby's hand. She didn't recognize anyone at first but gradually familiar faces began to emerge from the shadows and through the flickering orange flames. She spotted Anita and Trevor whom she'd always thought of as the leaders of the group. They had been following and researching crop formations for years; Trevor had shown her photographs from 2001 — Cambridgeshire's vintage year for the Circles — when the Angel and the Big One were created: much more elaborate and beautiful patterns than the one in the field.

Hannah was really hungry now but she felt too embarrassed to get out her plastic containers and start having a picnic in front of everyone. She dug around in the bag for a couple of packets of crisps for her and Toby, and a packet of chocolate biscuits which she opened and then felt obliged to offer to her neighbour — a man whom she'd never seen before, with tattoos on his bald head.

'Nice one,' he said, taking the whole packet and she watched it being passed round the circle until it was out of sight. It never made its way back. A constant stream of spliffs came by which she handed straight to Toby. She'd tried smoking one one night, but the unpredictable effect it had on her vision scared her.

She was relieved to see their friends, Piper and Frank, with Smith the Labrador dog, and called out to them.

'We've been on field duty,' Piper said, sitting next to Hannah. 'Everyone's taking a turn in front of the gates.' She handed them each a can of cider; they were warm but Hannah was grateful to have anything to fill her stomach. The moment the alcohol touched her insides she felt pissed. She looked behind her — the circle around the fire had broken up into smaller groups like their own. A woman with long, dark hair danced in front of the flames, a cigarette or spliff in one hand, a litre bottle of beer in the other.

When the cider was gone, Toby produced a quarter bottle of whisky from a pocket of his shorts which she drank neat like the others were doing, the liquid burning her mouth. She remembered the bag of food and they fell on it, cooing and exclaiming as treasure after treasure was revealed. Hannah devoured two pieces of bread, taking such big bites she could feel the lumps travelling down her throat. Each time she looked at Toby, she felt happy; each time he touched her — even the slightest touch — her body sang with pleasure.

It was turning light by the time they stumbled back to the car. They adjusted the seats back as far as they could go and lay facing each other. Toby leaned towards her and they started to kiss but they fell asleep before it went any further.

When Hannah woke up her back was aching, her head was throbbing, and she didn't know which she needed most — a pee or a drink of water.

She walked down to the camp fire to see if there were any bottles of water around. Some people were curled up asleep by the remains of the fire, others were still awake, hunched forward, their eyes fixed on something that only they could see.

She found an open can of coke and tipped some into the palm of her hand to check it out before drinking the rest in one go as she walked away from the camp. She climbed down into the ditch at the side of the road and squatted amongst a patch of wild angelica.

She heard shouting and dogs barking. She climbed up the side of the ditch and began to run back towards the camp. Everyone was running in the same direction — towards the field gate — like children running to a fight in the playground.

She spotted Toby waving at her and he jogged over to meet her.

'They're coming,' he said, taking her hand.

Now she had stopped running she could feel the ground rumbling underneath her feet and the low growl and clank of heavy machinery approaching. There was a police car parked a little way down from the gate where some of the followers were perched. The dancing woman from the night before was lying on the ground in front of them. Hannah glanced around. There were about twenty other people besides her and Toby; there had seemed to be many more than that last night.

The combine harvester loomed into view, preceded by another police car which stopped in front of the gate. Three policemen got out. Someone yelled, 'Fascists,' but the police ignored the group. Joined by the two officers from the first car, they approached the people by the gate and, after a few minutes of talking, all but the dancing woman moved. They returned to the group, shrugging and swearing, but their defeat was inevitable. Even stationary and silent, the combine harvester was an enormous, awesome machine; its wheels were taller than Hannah. She recognized the farmhand driving it. It was Neil who used to be at school with Tyler. He'd had a photograph taken with Bill Oddie for the local paper when he'd found a pair of bitterns breeding somewhere around here. Neil didn't see her. He was too removed from them in his metal eyrie; smoking a cigarette, he looked out across a view that no one else could see.

Two policemen remained squatting next to the dancing woman who was still lying on the ground, while the other officers approached the group.

'Going to have to move you back, lads and lassies,' one of them said, with a Scottish accent. 'Back about six feet please.'

'Come on, now, please. Move back.'

Hannah and Toby shuffled backwards like the rest of them. Hannah noticed one of the policemen was videoing everyone in the crowd so she tried to stay out of sight behind a tall man.

'Whose is this car?'

Leon stepped forward.

'You'll have to move it, mate, unless you want it flattened by that thing.'

They had to stand aside to let Leon drive through and, when the gap closed again, Hannah saw that the dancing woman was being lifted by her arms and carried towards a police car.

Shouts and whistles went up from the crowd but they were drowned out as the combine juddered into life and the engine roared and the machine inched forward. A couple of people knelt down as if they were praying; a man broke out of the group but one of the policemen stepped in his way and pushed him back as the combine gathered momentum. It swung out to turn into the field, the road crunched and trembled under its weight and then it passed through the open gate, followed by a tractor pulling a red baling machine.

Hannah and Toby stayed there for a couple of hours although there was nothing to do but sit around and chat. Toby went to fetch Hannah's sun cream and hat from the car. The air smelt of diesel and, when Hannah looked up, it seemed like the light was being filtered through golden dust. Hannah watched Piper take cups of tea over to the two policemen who had remained behind in one of the cars. They got out, took their jackets off and leaned against the side of the car, soaking up the sun.

'Do you want something stronger to go in

that?' shouted a man clutching a can of lager.

The Scottish officer shouted back. 'Aye. Let's see the measure of your whisky.'

Hannah and Toby returned to the car to sleep for a few hours. They opened all the windows as wide as they could and covered the windscreen with two of Toby's towels to block out the sun. Hannah sank onto the car seat and closed her eyes. She drifted off immediately and then twitched into half-wakefulness. She felt the car shifting as Toby moved, then he began to snore. She spun down into such a deep sleep that when she woke she was in the exact same position lying on her back, her arms crossed over her stomach.

She struggled upright and her movement must have woken up Toby.

'What time is it?' His voice was muffled and sleepy.

Hannah checked the car clock. 'Nearly half past six.'

'Can you smell food? Or am I having a nasal hallucination?'

Hannah sniffed the air. 'It smells like curry. Maybe Pam's cooking something.'

Toby went for a pee while Hannah changed her top and then went to the toilet in the ditch with Toby standing guard. By the time they'd reached Pam's catering van, Hannah felt faint with hunger. They bought two cans of coke and paid a couple of pounds each for a big dollop of rice and curry and carried the plates over to the main camp area. They sat on the ground and ate without exchanging a single word. After they'd finished, Toby stretched out on the grass with his arms under his head and looked at Hannah.

'Better?'

She nodded. 'I think the combine's stopped,' she said, listening hard.

'Frank said they've finished. We slept through them leaving.'

'I'd like to see what it looks like.' Hannah stood up. 'Are you coming?'

They sat on top of the gate for a few minutes before jumping down. The field looked pale and bare except for the fat barrels of wheat which had been left here and there.

They walked forward, the spiky stubble crisped under Hannah's pumps. It was impossible to tell if they were walking in the direction where the Crop Circles had been and Hannah was about to suggest they turn back when she noticed a green patch ahead. As they got closer, they saw that fresh green shoots had started to grow where the Circles had been. There were now two perfect green circles, as if they had been reborn.

Hannah walked across the inner circle and back to Toby.

'What shall we do now?' he asked.

Hannah looked around. 'Go back, I suppose.'

The fire had been lit and a car had been parked up behind it. Loud music was coming out of the open boot.

'I think it's party time,' Toby said. 'I'd better fetch my cider.'

Hannah watched people come and go, crossing and re-crossing the camp area. She waved to Piper who was collecting up rubbish in a big, black sack and said hello to Leon as he walked past carrying an armful of wood which he piled close to the fire; even people she didn't know seemed to have a task to do. Louie stopped to ask her how she was just as Toby came back.

'It was some day,' Louie said and Toby agreed. Hannah listened but she wasn't concentrating; the purposefulness of others around her had made her feel useless and with it had come a wave of longing to be back in her room in Spindle House. She glanced at the urine-coloured liquid sloshing around in the flagon that Toby was holding and felt sick at the thought of drinking it. But when Toby sat down beside her and held out the plastic cup full of cider that he'd poured for her, she took it.

As it grew dark, someone began to juggle with fire. Hannah found the spinning balls of light mesmerizing; they trailed silver, blue and gold tails behind them like mini meteors chasing across the dark sky.

Toby got up to go to the toilet and Hannah instantly missed the warmth of him where he had been leaning against her. She tried to keep him in sight but he was swallowed up by the night the moment he stepped away from the reaches of the fire.

She heard shouting and turned round as others near her stood up; some started running towards the road. She got up and tried to see Toby but there was no sign of him.

'It's an attack,' she thought she heard someone say.

She saw the bald tattoo-headed man pick up some of the wooden sticks from the pile and hand them out to other men as he ran towards the road. She wondered if Toby had gone back to the car and started to head that way but stumbled as her foot caught against a rut in the ground. Someone ran into her and she fell, spinning and rolling onto the grass. She crouched there, believing that she was going to get trampled on, but she was too dazed and winded to get up. When she did, there was no one else around but she could hear shouting and screaming and dogs barking from the direction of the field.

As she approached, she saw men fighting; some kicking and punching, others with sticks; the noise of crunching and groans was horrible. She looked around frantically for Toby, shouting out his name. Her vision was jumping all over the place, she barely recognized Piper who caught hold of her.

'Come to the van,' Piper said. 'It'll be safe there.'

'I've got to find Toby,' Hannah said, pulling away.

Police sirens were getting closer but the men continued to fight. Hannah spotted someone lying near the gate so she ran across the road and along the verge next to the hedge until she reached him. He groaned and rolled over and tried to get up. It wasn't Toby.

'Stay still,' she told him.

A policeman pushed her as she started to stand up and she landed heavily on her bottom next to the injured man. A moment later, she was wrenched up and dragged away.

'That man's hurt,' she told the policeman but she was disorientated by the blue-white dazzle of headlights. She shielded her eyes and staggered and then someone grabbed her under the arms and pulled her up into a van. There was a bench running down each side and she slid onto the end which was free, keeping her head bowed while she tried to calm herself and catch her breath.

The doors were slammed shut and it went completely dark. The van bumped around as it reversed and then began to travel smoothly, quickly gathering speed.

'Fucking bastards,' a man's voice said but nobody else spoke. As Hannah's eyes got used to the darkness, she caught glimpses of the other passengers' faces but there were none that she recognized. Her legs were shaking and she had to concentrate hard not to cry.

At the police station she gave her name and address but, before she had finished, the officer stopped writing.

'Hannah Ruland. What are you doing mixed up with this lot?'

She wanted to say that they were her friends but even in the lit building she still hadn't known any of the people she'd been brought in with. She burst into tears.

She was ushered into a small room where a woman was sitting at a table. She was introduced as a police officer although she wasn't wearing a uniform. Hannah tried to describe what she had seen but she kept confusing the two nights with each other and she couldn't stop crying.

'Is there someone you can call, to pick you up?' the woman asked, and Hannah nodded.

She was given fifty pence and shown to a phone on the wall. She dialled the number for Spindle House. It rang once before she cut the call. The coin rattled down to the metal slot where she scooped it up. Should she use it to ring Toby's mobile phone instead, she wondered? But she didn't know where he was and she desperately wanted to go home.

'Have you finished?' A very large woman with black whiskers on her chin peered at Hannah. She smelt strongly of BO. Hannah tried not to wrinkle her nose so that she didn't hurt the woman's feelings, although she found the smell quite awful.

'In a minute,' Hannah replied and redialled her home number. She heard Ella's voice answer and for a moment couldn't speak.

'It's Hannah.'

'Hannah? Where are you? Is everything all right?'

'I'm in Ely. At the police station.'

'Why? What's happened?'

'There's been some trouble. Can you come and pick me up?'

'Of course I can, darling. I'll leave now. Are you all right though, Hannah?'

'I'm OK. A bit shaky,' she said. 'I just really want to get home.'

34

Hannah woke late. She lay for a few minutes listening to the voices through her open window. She lay there until she realized that one of the voices she could hear was Finn's, then she got out of bed and went over to check. The garden table was out of sight but listening closer, she heard Amy's unmistakable, high-pitched, slightly American accent.

Hannah groaned. She was convinced that Finn possessed a super-ability to sense whenever something important happened to Hannah even if he was miles away in London. When she decided not to go to university, down he came. When she got the job at Silver Maids, down he came.

He meant well, but he really didn't get Hannah. He couldn't understand why she'd chosen to stay at Spindle House when she had the chance to leave. He couldn't understand that she didn't mind cleaning other people's houses because she saw it as a way to get paid while writing her stories.

She looked around for her notebook, suddenly fearful that she'd lost it somewhere in the events of the night. She was relieved to see it lying on her desk where she'd left it behind. She placed the palm of her hand on the cover and felt the warmth of the words rising to meet her.

She was about to sit down at the desk when

she heard someone thudding up the stairs and along the landing. There was a soft tapping on the door and then Tyler peered in.

'Only me,' he said. 'Can I come in?'

She nodded and sat on the bed where he joined her. 'I believe I have you to thank for bringing Finn and Amy down upon us.'

'I didn't ask them to come.'

'Apparently Ella did. Although she regretted it the minute she'd stopped panicking.'

'Was she worried about me?'

'Of course she was, squirt. We all were.' He gave her a hug. 'So was it horrible?'

'Yes. It was awful. And I lost Toby. Oh my God.' Panic flashed through her. 'I've got to find out if Toby is all right.'

'He's fine,' Tyler said. 'He came to see you but you were asleep, so I said you'd catch up with him later. But you'd better keep him away from here — Ella and Finn are mightily pissed off with him.'

'Why?'

'They think he should have looked after you.'

'It wasn't his fault.'

Tyler held his hands up. 'Don't blame the messenger.'

Hannah got up and paced around the room. 'I must go and see him. He's my friend.'

'You have to deal with your family first.'

'I don't have to do anything,' Hannah said.

'Be reasonable, squirt. Finn's come down 'specially to know you're OK and Ella did rescue you from Ely. You only have to spend a few hours with them and then you'll be free to do whatever you want.'

'I suppose,' she agreed reluctantly.

'And besides, you can't leave me on my own out there. You know how argumentative Finn and Henry are, and I get the feeling Amy and Kirsten aren't going to be best buddies either.'

Hannah never could resist Tyler's doleful face; she put her arm around his neck. He smelt of cigarettes and his hot, wooden room. She kissed him on the cheek.

'I'll have a shower and come down.'

In the shower, she noticed she had several bruises on her arms, a couple on her legs and a large, very tender one on her right side. Her mind spun her back to the disorientated panic she'd felt the night before and she had to put her hand out to the wall to stop herself keeling over.

She pulled on her combat trousers and a blue and white, striped, long-sleeved T-shirt. She combed her hair out, tied it back into a ponytail and then looked around for her sunglasses. Her stomach felt as if it had turned to molten liquid as she realized that the sunglasses were missing. She sat on her bed. Second to her notebooks, the sunglasses were the most important thing in her life — she couldn't imagine being without them.

She tried to picture when she was last wearing them and felt a little calmer when she remembered putting them on the dashboard of Toby's car when they were sleeping there in the afternoon. That decided it. She stood up. She would go and see Toby first; the others could wait. She would make her escape out of the front door and go the long way round past Lavender Cottage.

She had barely stepped onto the drive when Finn appeared.

'Where do you think you're going?' he said.

Hannah squinted to look at him. He was dressed in his version of casual: a pair of very smart jeans, a pale lemon shirt and brown brogues. He gave her a hug as if it was a secondary thought.

Amy appeared behind him. 'Hannah,' she exclaimed, giving her a brief kiss on the cheek. 'You're looking very thin,' she added in a rather disapproving voice. Hannah thought it was a bit of a cheek coming from a woman who had so little body fat she could be used as an illustration for the vascular system.

Without speaking, without actual physical contact, Hannah found herself being drawn away from where she intended to go, round to the garden.

'There she is. How are you feeling?' Hannah was grateful for Kirsten's exuberance.

'Where's Ella?' Hannah asked, looking around for her mother. She noticed Tyler had also made his escape and she sank onto a chair, feeling cross at their abandonment.

'She'll be back in a minute,' Kirsten said, leaning forward. She put her hand on Hannah's. 'She's only gone to get some shopping.'

Finn's mobile on the table gave an insistent beep, beep and he snatched it up and headed off across the lawn.

Nobody spoke as they watched him criss-crossing the lawn, talking and gesticulating. He ducked when a blackbird broke cover close to him, rattling its alarm call.

'I think I'll go and start on some lunch,' Kirsten said.

'Oh, Kirsten, don't worry about anything for me.' Amy dug around in a bag which was as big as her torso. 'I'm on this crazy no-whatever diet and I've brought mine with me.' She waved a container with a foil lid in the air. 'If you wouldn't mind putting this in the fridge?'

Kirsten's face sagged as she took the container from her.

'Did I say something wrong?' Amy asked.

Henry shrugged. 'Making meals is Kirsten's thing.'

'Oh, she's that kind of woman,' Amy said. 'Very different for you. You usually go for the alternative types, don't you?'

'I thought I'd have a change,' Henry said and grinned at Amy who smiled and flicked her hair. Neither of them had seen Kirsten behind them. She strode forward with bowls of olives and crisps, blushing.

'So how did you two meet?' Amy asked, looking inside the bowls and taking nothing.

'We went out together when we were at school,' Kirsten told her.

'How sweet.' Amy turned to Henry. 'I'm learning a whole new side of you, Henry.'

'I always said I was a complicated man.'

Hannah had forgotten how flirtatious Henry and Amy were with each other. It had never

375

seemed to bother Finn but she could see that Kirsten was struggling. She stood next to the table, torn between leaving them together or getting on with the meal.

'Can I help you in the kitchen?' Hannah offered.

'No, you rest,' Kirsten said after a moment's hesitation. 'After your ordeal.'

'I'll help,' Amy said, getting up.

'I don't need . . . ' Kirsten was saying as Finn returned to the table.

'Girls' talk, is it?' Finn joked.

Henry laughed and Amy made a face at them both while Kirsten looked bewildered. She turned and headed back to the kitchen with Amy following. From behind, it could have been daughter following mother and Hannah was glad that Henry was looking in the other direction.

'There's Ella,' Finn said, but Hannah had already heard her car. Last night, Ella had been nice to her, but after what Tyler had said about Toby, she wondered if she was in for a telling-off today.

Ella rounded the corner in a flurry of bags. Finn immediately got up to relieve her of them.

'Where to?'

'In the kitchen, darling. Thanks.'

She touched Hannah on the head. 'How are you feeling today?'

'A bit tired,' Hannah answered. She thought it best not to mention her bruises to her mother.

'Where are your sunglasses, darling?'

'I think I might have lost them.'

'Have mine for now.' Ella took off the ones she was wearing. Hannah immediately put them on and instantly felt more relaxed with the cooler light on her eyes.

'They suit you,' Ella said approvingly and Hannah's worries lifted.

Amy came out of the kitchen. 'I'm not really needed,' she said, sitting down. 'I think I was getting in the way.'

'Join the club,' Ella said, and everyone left it a little too long to comment as they stared at Ella who picked out an olive and ate it without looking up. Hannah glanced at Henry who raised an eyebrow in response.

Finn cleared his throat. 'Shall I call Tyler?'

'I'll do it,' Ella said, getting up. 'I'm going upstairs anyway.' But instead of going through the kitchen, she made her way to the front of the house.

'She probably needed something from the car,' Finn suggested, making it clear to Hannah that he also thought her behaviour odd. She was glad that others had been witness to an incident; she'd begun to think she was imagining it.

Ella came back out from the kitchen though, along with Kirsten and Tyler, each carrying dishes of food.

'This is nice,' Ella said and everyone agreed.

When Kirsten said thank you, Hannah noticed that Ella looked sharply at her. *She doesn't like her,* Hannah thought suddenly. *Ella really doesn't like Kirsten.*

'So where next, Henry?' Finn asked.

'Nothing's planned.'

377

'Perhaps see where the mood takes you?' Amy said.

'Well, I — '

'Henry's become quite a home bird these days,' Kirsten said. 'He's given up travelling.'

Finn and Amy laughed and Kirsten looked confused.

'You're like your father,' Ella said. 'You can't stay in one place for any length of time.'

It had been a while since Ella had offered a comment about Edward; Hannah caught Ella's eye and smiled.

'Edward said that you can tell everything you need to know about a place if you experience it at dawn and at dusk.'

Henry and Tyler groaned. 'That's just a load of rubbish,' Henry said.

'I think it's true,' Hannah replied, feeling a little put out.

'So where do you fancy, Henry?' Finn asked and Henry shrugged.

'The day Henry gives up travelling is the day Finn gives up money,' Amy said.

'I'm only repeating what Henry said.' Kirsten turned to Henry. 'Aren't I?'

'Yes,' he said and he took hold of her hand.

Tyler stood up abruptly, mumbling about having something urgent he had to do.

'What's up with Tyler?' Finn asked.

'Nothing.' Ella and Hannah both spoke at the same time and their eyes met briefly before they turned to watch Tyler walking back into the house. Hannah remembered thinking he had behaved out of character another time recently but she couldn't remember when it was.

'Who the fuck!' Finn was up on his feet.

'It's OK. It's only Toby,' Kirsten said.

Toby was cutting across the lawn towards them.

'He's my friend,' Hannah said, and she nearly knocked over her glass of water in her haste to reach him before he got too close. Behind her, she could hear Finn's angry voice.

'I don't want you to go out this evening,' Ella called out.

'I take it I'm not flavour of the month round here.'

'They'll get over it,' Hannah told him and she touched his hand. 'I'm so glad you're all right.'

'I went back to the car; I thought that was where you'd be and, when you weren't, I went round asking everyone but nobody had seen you. Tyler said they took you to the police station.'

'I was on my way to the car when I saw a man lying on the ground. I went to see if it was you and that's when the police grabbed me and took me.'

'Did they charge you?'

'No, they let me go. One of them knew my family which was pretty lucky, I guess.'

'I'm sorry I wasn't with you.'

'The police probably wouldn't have let me go so easily if you had been.'

'They're all watching us,' Toby whispered and Hannah glanced behind her.

'You'd better go,' she said, feeling herself tilt

towards Toby as if her body completely disagreed with her words. 'I'll come see you as soon as I can.'

'I brought you these.' He handed her something wrapped in toilet paper.

'My sunglasses!'

'I thought you'd be needing them but I see you've got new ones.'

'They're only borrowed from Ella.' She looked at the sunglasses. 'I can't tell you how great it is to have them back.' As if to prove it to him, she took off Ella's and put on her own, then she kissed him. She didn't care if anyone was watching — he deserved it. It was the second best present she had ever been given.

★ ★ ★

Hannah had decided to wait until everyone was in bed before she went to see Toby. It was easier that way, with Ella and Finn still on his case. Scoot growled softly as she passed Ella's bedroom.

'It's only me,' she whispered.

He followed her into the kitchen but she didn't let him out of the house. She locked the door behind her and slipped the key under the strawberry pot. It was a windy night and colder than she'd thought. Her bare feet were already freezing.

It was really dark. Even though she knew the way with her eyes closed, the density of the night was a little unnerving and she was glad to reach Toby's little tent.

'It's me, Hannah,' she called out to him.

He unzipped the tent. 'You frightened the life out of me. I've been waiting for all your brothers to come and beat me up.'

'Finn and Amy have gone.'

'Oh, so it's only two of them I need to worry about now.' Toby switched on the torch and she crawled inside. It smelt of earth and dried reeds and Toby.

'Jesus, you're freezing,' he said as one of her ice-cold feet touched his leg. 'Quick, get in.' He slid his legs into the sleeping bag and held it open for her to do the same.

'Will we both fit?'

'I don't see why not. There's nothing to you.'

They wriggled and jostled each other to get comfortable, ending up pressed front to front. Hannah's nose was pushed into the base of Toby's neck and his leg weighed heavily on hers but it felt good to be so close to him. Her feet were tingling as they warmed up.

'Frank got his finger broken,' Toby said.

'Oh my God. How?'

'He doesn't remember. He woke up with it all turned black and at a funny angle. Piper freaked when she saw it.'

Hannah tried and failed not to giggle. 'I shouldn't laugh.'

'Everyone else did.'

'I can't believe it was only last night. It feels like ages ago.'

'Were you scared?'

'A little.'

He squeezed her.

'Who were they? The ones that came?' Hannah asked.

'Vigilante idiots from one of the local villages.'

'My village?'

'I don't know,' Toby said. They fell into silence and Hannah felt herself drifting towards sleep.

'I've got to go away,' Toby said, and Hannah felt the air squash out of her as if he had sat down hard on her stomach. 'Only for a couple of days. Maybe three.'

'Is it something important?' she asked and immediately wondered if she sounded too nosy. She suddenly thought how little she knew about Toby and how much he knew about her.

He didn't answer immediately. 'A duty visit,' he said in the end. 'I've got an uncle who lives in Cambridge who I said I'd go and see. My mum's been on my back about it for days now.'

'When are you going?'

'Tomorrow.'

'Tomorrow,' Hannah echoed.

'I should have left a couple of days ago but I wanted to stick around until they'd cut the field.'

Not because he didn't want to leave me, Hannah thought, and she instinctively tried to pull away from him but she was trapped in the sleeping bag and Toby was holding her tight.

'I'm going to miss you,' he said.

'I'll miss you too,' she replied and she thought how quickly she had got used to him being there and how different Spindle House would feel when he was gone. For a long time now, it had been just her and Ella and Tyler in Spindle House, doing the same things day after day, week after week. She wasn't sure she liked change. It seemed only to bring you something new by taking something old away. Scoot for Edward. Toby for Ella. Kirsten for Henry. She pressed her lips against Toby's skin and tasted the salt on him. *Don't leave me*, she wanted to tell him. But she didn't.

★ ★ ★

Hannah woke in a panic. The air in the tent was stifling and her head was stuffy as if she'd overslept. Her vision wobbled badly but after a few moments she managed to make out the time on Toby's watch. It was only ten past seven.

Toby yawned and stretched.

'Will you be gone before I get back from work?' she whispered, kneeling over him.

'Yes.' He propped himself up on his elbow. 'I'll be back soon, Hannah.'

'I know,' she said but she couldn't look him in the eye. She gave him a quick kiss but he pulled her back.

'A proper one,' he demanded.

Although she tried to do what he wanted, her heart wasn't in it. Goodbye kisses were sad kisses, she thought, marking the end of something good.

Kirsten was in the kitchen eating breakfast when she went in. She didn't seem surprised or make any comment about where Hannah had appeared from.

'I've made a pot of tea,' Kirsten said. 'If you want to grab yourself a mug.'

Hannah took a mug out of the cupboard and sat down opposite Kirsten.

'Mondays are always the hardest,' Kirsten said.

Hannah nodded. She felt too dazed to speak.

'Another beautiful morning,' Kirsten continued. 'It's almost getting annoying now. Especially as my office is like an oven.'

Hannah glanced at Kirsten's clothes. She was wearing a skirt suit as usual with a blouse and tights. 'Aren't you allowed to wear something, um, looser or more casual?'

'Oh, you don't have to dress so formally,' Kirsten said, looking down at her blouse. 'But it helps me get into the right frame of mind. It's a bit like a school uniform, I suppose. I always loved my school uniform.'

'I know what you mean. As soon as I put on my Silver Maids uniform, I feel different. The day feels different.'

They smiled at each other.

'Can I talk to you about Henry?'

Hannah looked at her in alarm. 'Well, I've got to get ready . . . '

'I know about Sophia,' Kirsten said. 'I take it you do, too?'

'A little,' she dissembled.

'She broke his heart. Henry had his heart broken and then his body got broken too, and he came back to Spindle House to mend.' Hannah stared as Kirsten raised her chin and looked defiantly at her. 'I'm willing to help him do that,' she said. 'All I want to know is what I'm dealing with.'

'I'm not sure what you mean.' Was Kirsten aware, Hannah wondered, that Henry was in touch with Sophia every day? Merely talking to Kirsten felt like lying and she didn't like lying to Kirsten. Hannah was sure that she was one of those people who took lies badly.

'Do you think he's over her?' Kirsten said quickly.

'I don't know.' Hannah suspected he wasn't. But that wasn't the same as knowing and in that way, at least, her response was truthful.

'Henry's not as tough as you think,' Kirsten said.

Hannah had never imagined he was but she was interested to hear Kirsten say it. She wondered what Henry talked to her about. She tilted her head and Kirsten's face came into focus. When Henry said she was peaceful, maybe he meant that he trusted her to care about him, maybe that would win against whatever chaotic passion Sophia had to offer. She thought of Toby and how he wouldn't be there this evening when she came back and felt that she missed him already.

'He wants us to go away.'

'Travelling?' Hannah was surprised; more about the 'us' than that Henry was ready to leave.

Kirsten looked annoyed. 'No, no. On holiday. I don't know where. I haven't been abroad for a few years and it seems a shame to waste the nice weather we're having here.'

'It won't last though.'

'I always feel like I'm on holiday at Spindle

House — I'd be happy to spend a week off here.'

'It does you good to go away though sometimes,' Hannah said, remembering something Edward had told her. 'It makes you appreciate what you have at home.'

'Oh yes. Of course.' Kirsten's face lit up as she smiled across the table. 'Thank you, Hannah.'

She collected her bowl and plate and mug together and stood up at the same time as Ella entered the room. Ella had pushed back her hair behind a white headband and was wearing a fitted white shirt with dark blue jeans. She looked fresh and happy until she spotted Hannah.

'You're not ready,' she said, checking her watch and dumping her bag on top of the table. 'We'll be late.'

Hannah hadn't even had breakfast but she didn't dare mention it to Ella who stood over her as she got up slowly.

'Are you going out, Ella?' Kirsten asked as she ran her dishes under the hot tap. Hannah watched how Ella flushed.

'I'm taking Hannah to work as usual,' she said.

'I meant afterwards,' Kirsten said over her shoulder. 'Are you going to see your friend?'

'What friend?' Ella said sharply. Her eyes grazed across Hannah's face and then fixed on the back of Kirsten's head.

'I thought you had a friend,' Kirsten continued, turning round. She wiped her hands dry on a kitchen towel. 'Henry said . . . ' She stopped and looked at mother, then daughter.

'Get a move on, Hannah,' Ella said. 'I'll see you in the car.'

35

Tyler moved the chair opposite Hannah and plonked it next to Henry. He hunched over his packet of tobacco and only spoke when he had taken the first drag. 'Missing Toby, squirt?'

'Has lover boy gone?' Henry asked, pushing the ashtray across the table so that Tyler could share it.

'Only for a few days,' Hannah said. 'He's coming back.'

'That's what they all say.' Henry was the only one to laugh. The last time Toby had texted Hannah he'd said he was thinking of staying on for a couple of days longer than planned.

Tyler leaned forward and tapped his roll-up on the lip of the ashtray. 'Not everybody lies like you,' he said, addressing Henry.

'What do you mean?'

'Think about it. I'm sure you'll work it out.' The chair creaked as he eased himself back on it. He continued to hold Henry's gaze. Henry, after a moment, shrugged and took out another cigarette even though he hadn't finished the one he was smoking.

'Don't you ever take this up,' he warned Hannah when he caught her looking.

She shook her head. 'I'm not stupid.'

'There's another crop formation,' Tyler said. 'A few miles from the last one. Near Waddlesworth.'

'How do you know?'

'They were talking about it in the pub.'

'I wonder if they know at the camp?'

'Probably,' Henry said. 'Jungle drums are in good working order around here.'

'But the Followers don't go into the village any more.'

'Why don't you go and tell them then?' Henry asked.

'I, um . . . ' She hadn't been over there since the cutting of the field and she was reluctant to do so without Toby.

A gust of wind blew across the table. Henry and Tyler made a grab for their packets of cigarettes and tobacco while Hannah shook her hair back off her face. Ash was scattered over the tabletop.

'I could give you a lift over there?' Tyler offered, stubbing out his cigarette.

Henry turned to her as she and Tyler stood up. 'Do you actually believe in this stuff?'

'I don't know. But I like the way they appear out of nowhere and that nobody can pin down the reason they exist.'

★   ★   ★

At the top of the long road which led towards the camp, Hannah tried to lean round the side of Tyler. She couldn't see any sign of vehicles ahead but she didn't trust her eyes enough to believe they weren't there. The sun was slanting across the road which made it hard to see anything other than splashes and smears of colour in the distance. The motorbike wobbled and Tyler tapped her on the leg to make her sit back.

He cut the engine when they reached the lay-by opposite the field. They took off their helmets and looked around.

'It was here, wasn't it?' Tyler asked and Hannah nodded, although it was hard to believe it. They got off the bike and wandered around. On the wide verge nearest the lay-by was a blackened circle from the main camp fire; there were patches of flattened and yellow grass outlining where some of the vans and cars had been.

'They've done a good job of clearing up,' Tyler said.

With her foot, Hannah nudged a pile of unburnt sticks which had been left in the longer grass. She recoiled as they shifted and she caught sight of the darkened end of a stick. Her pulse raced at the thought that it could be someone's blood from the fight.

'I take it they've already heard about the new one,' Tyler said.

'Do you think that's where they've gone?'

'I thought that's what they did — follow wherever these things appear?'

'They like to, but a lot of them have jobs and they can't get the time off.' She watched Tyler take this in. 'You thought they were all permanent travellers?'

He shrugged. 'I don't know them like you.'

'Do you want to see the Circle?'

'I thought it had been cut.'

'You can still see where it was. Come on, I'll show you.'

The motorbike puttered behind as she walked across to the entrance to the field. She waited on top of the gate while Tyler secured the bike. The gate swung a little under Tyler's weight as he climbed over.

Weeds were already beginning to colonize the field and Hannah began to worry that she was leading Tyler on a wild goose chase but a few metres in, she caught a glimpse of a film of dense, dark green on the ground where the weeds were more populous — like a pool of green water.

'It's much bigger than I imagined,' Tyler said. He walked around it. 'There's another ring, around the outside.'

'That happens a lot apparently.' Hannah walked to the centre of the Circle a little apprehensively. 'Do you feel anything?'

'No. Do you?'

She turned a full three hundred and sixty degrees and waited to see if the claustrophobic feeling descended on her. 'No.'

'The wheat's rooted here; it's started to grow again.' Tyler was squatting down.

'It's because it was only bent over, not broken,' Hannah said, joining him. 'When it was fresh you could see that it was laid down in a sort of swirling pattern.'

'It's actually pretty amazing,' Tyler said, standing up and brushing off his hands and Hannah felt pleased.

★ ★ ★

Feeling dusty and hot from the field, Hannah ran upstairs to change into her bikini.

'Are you coming?' she called to Tyler who was behind her on the stairs.

'Got work to do,' he said. 'Sorry, squirt.'

Her excitement sank and she had almost decided not to bother going herself when she remembered that she had always enjoyed swimming on her own before Toby arrived. She hurriedly changed into her bikini, putting Ella's maxi dress on top. Although it was evening, the sun was still quite powerful.

She forced herself not to look at Toby's tent as she came through the gap in the hedge and walked quickly in the direction of the village.

'Hey,' she heard. 'Hey, Hannah. Wait.'

Toby was jogging to catch her up. His hair was bouncing all over the place and she could see the flesh of his stomach jiggle as he thumped the ground with each step. Before he reached her, she turned away and continued walking.

He appeared alongside her, his arm brushing against hers. 'Why didn't you wait?' He panted each word next to her ear.

'I'm going swimming.'

'Are you pissed off with me?'

'No.'

She felt his hand on her shoulder, then across her stomach. 'Stop,' he told her. 'Look at me.'

He was grinning at her. She felt like thumping him. 'I'm back now.'

'Good for you.'

'Hannah. Please.' He pulled a pouting face at her. 'Be nice to me. I missed you.'

She hung her head.

'Did you miss me?'

She shrugged. 'Maybe.'

'A teeny, tiny bit? Or a big bit?' He poked at her waist, her arm, her stomach, grinning.

'Big,' she admitted.

'Good. Come here.' He pulled her against him but she twisted out of his hold.

'No,' she said. 'I'm going swimming.'

She took a few steps forward before she realized that he hadn't moved. She shielded her eyes as she looked at him. 'Aren't you coming?'

'I haven't got my swimmers on,' he said.

'We'll go to a spot that's really quiet. No one will see.'

When he drew next to her again, she took hold of his hand and led him to a place on the bank which had good coverage from rushes and grass although there was an awkward, deep step into the water.

'No eels around here, are there?' he asked, sitting down and experimentally putting one foot in. He pulled it out quickly. 'Yuck, it's all soft.'

'It's only a bit of mud,' Hannah said, pulling off her dress and wading in. The mud squelched up between her toes and the water reached her thighs after only a couple of steps. She turned round just in time to witness Toby belly-flop into the water from a standing position. His body made a loud smack as it touched down, sending a huge spray of water into the air. He surfaced, shaking his hair free from his eyes, blindly looking around for her. He lunged forward but she dived away from him and swam a steady breast-stroke for several metres before floating on her back. The evening light gently glinted off the water; she could hear Toby splashing around and then silence.

He was back on the bank with his legs pulled up, chin on his knees, watching her. She swam towards him. She glimpsed his penis and balls nesting on the grass as he shifted his legs.

'The camp's gone,' she said, treading water opposite him.

'When?'

'I don't know. There's a new crop formation near here; they might have moved there.'

'A new one. Great. Do you know where it is? We could go and find them.'

Hannah moved closer to the bank, waiting for Toby's head to emerge from his T-shirt as he pulled it on. 'Not tonight though,' she said. 'I've got work.'

He held out his hand to help her up and tugged her sharply at the last minute so that she stumbled against him.

'I'm soaking,' she said, struggling to get free.

'I don't care. I'm not going to let you go until you kiss me.'

She felt shy, hardly daring to look at him. His face was shadowed but water sparkled in his hair like fireflies, making her squint. She closed her eyes and let him kiss her.

'That's better,' he said. 'Now I'm beginning to think you're pleased to see me.'

36

Hannah was walking through the Tuesday house doing her initial security check before she phoned in when she heard voices coming from a bedroom. She froze, her heart thumping. She was about to creep downstairs to alert the security company when a man came out of a bedroom and stood in front of her in the hallway. It took her a couple of moments to recognize him as the owner; he looked older than in the photographs around the house.

'Who the fuck are you?'

'I'm the maid. From Silver Maids.' She pointed to the logo on her tunic.

'The maid, huh?' He took a step towards her and looked her up and down so intensely it made her uncomfortable.

'Yes.' She thought about adding 'sir' but didn't. 'I'm sorry, the Agency didn't say you'd be here.'

'Change of plans. Last minute. The Mrs is in there.' He jerked his thumb back towards the door. 'I wouldn't go in if I were you.'

'I won't,' she told him, turning to leave. 'I'll carry on as usual. Downstairs.' She heard the click of the door behind her and looked round; the man had returned to the bedroom. Downstairs she phoned in to the Agency and explained that the owner was present.

There was a short silence. 'Don't bother them.

Do any urgent jobs and then leave.'

She had no intention of bothering them or going anywhere near them. She didn't like the house and it wasn't a surprise to discover that she wasn't getting a good feeling about the owners either.

The large windows in the lounge were smudged with handprints and grease from being opened and closed so Hannah set to work to clean them up. As she worked, she tried to concentrate on a story but the words jumped around in her head, slippery as fish.

'Are you sure you can see to do that properly?' the man asked. She hadn't heard him come up behind her.

'I've got sensitive eyes,' Hannah said when she realized he was talking about her sunglasses which she still had on. 'It's actually better for me to wear them in bright light like this.'

'Take them off,' he told her. 'You're making me feel nervous.'

The threatening expression on his face seemed at odds with the joking tone of his voice, which made it hard for Hannah to know how to react.

'I'd rather not,' she told him.

'You have to do what I say. I'm your boss,' he said and his hand flashed out towards her face as if to snatch the sunglasses away. Hannah instinctively put out her arm and felt her nails catch against his skin.

'You're a fiery little bitch, aren't you?' he said, examining the nick on his hand.

'I'm sorry,' Hannah said, moving sideways, but he stepped across to block her way and then walked forwards, forcing her up against the glass.

'What's going on?' Hannah was relieved to hear his wife's voice.

'Just checking up on Miss Maid here,' the man said over his shoulder and then, quickly and viciously, he pinched her nipple before walking away.

Hannah turned round quickly. She squirted cleaner on the glass and wiped at it randomly. She bit her lip to stop the tears which were gathering; her breast was throbbing with pain. She heard the tap of the woman's heels crossing the floor towards her but pretended to be absorbed in her work. It wasn't until the woman was beside her that Hannah stopped what she was doing.

'I think it's better if you leave,' the woman said in a low, urgent voice.

Hannah nodded. She hurriedly began to pack up her things. Out of the corner of her eye, she could see the woman standing in front of the windows which she'd been cleaning a moment ago. Her arms were folded and she appeared to be looking at something outside but Hannah had the feeling she was watching her instead.

'Will you buzz me out of the gates?' Hannah's voice shook as she spoke.

'Of course,' the woman said.

Although the awkward weight of the box made Hannah's arms ache, she was determined to reach the gates without stopping. As she got close, she heard the click and hum as they opened in front of her.

She collapsed on the grass behind the conifer; the whole of her body was shaking. She dialled Spindle House but there was no reply. She tried Ella's mobile but that went straight through to voicemail. Next she tried Tyler's mobile but that rang on and on. Finally she called Toby and he answered immediately.

Her voice came out in a squeak and she began to cry.

'Hannah. What's wrong? What is it?'

'Something horrible has happened,' she managed to say. 'Can you come and get me?'

'I'm on my way. You just tell me where.'

It seemed to take Toby forever to arrive but, when she checked her mobile phone, it was less than fifteen minutes before his car was heading down the road towards her. They didn't speak until her box was loaded in the back and Toby was driving away from the house.

He listened to what had happened without interrupting, but when she glanced at him, his jaw was clenched so tight she could see a big vein surfacing on his neck.

'I'm OK,' she said.

He looked down at the hand she'd put on his knee to reassure him. 'I'm so fucking angry,' he said.

'I don't want to think about it,' she told him and the determination she felt must have come through in her voice because, after a brief pause, he suggested that they drive into Ely.

'I'll need to go home and get changed,' Hannah said.

The back door at the house was unlocked even

though there appeared to be no one at home, not even Henry who rarely went out. It was as if someone had waved a wand and made them all disappear.

They went up to her room where Toby stretched out on her bed.

'I'll have a quick shower,' she told him.

'No rush. I'll enjoy a bit of luxury while I wait.'

There wasn't a mark where the man had pinched her, but her nipple still felt tender when she touched it.

She put her underwear back on before returning to the bedroom. Toby was reading something and her stomach dropped when she thought it might be one of her notebooks but it was a collection of ghost stories. When he wasn't looking, she slipped the notebook from her desk into her handbag.

'Very nice,' he said. She had put on Ella's sundress with a short, cream cardigan on top and her blue canvas shoes.

Kirsten was coming into the drive as they were leaving, so Toby waited for her car to pass first. Hannah called out from her window that the key was under the strawberry pot. When Kirsten started to speak in return, Hannah told Toby to drive off.

'I don't want Kirsten to ask me about Henry,' she told him. 'I don't know where he is and I don't think I want to know.'

★   ★   ★

They wandered a little aimlessly around Ely before drifting in the direction of the river. They sat on a bench and watched an old lady feed a whole loaf to the ducks and geese. Some of the geese got out of the water and pecked at the woman's legs but she didn't seem to care.

The temperature had dropped and a chilly wind was making Hannah feel cold even in her cardigan.

'It's going to rain,' Hannah said, looking at the dark clouds gathering and no sooner had she said it than several big drops landed on the ground in front of them. They ran to the car and bumped into Leon in the car park.

'Hey, do you know anything about the new crop formation?' Toby asked. They all looked up as the rain began to fall more heavily.

'Yeah, we've all moved there. You should come along.'

Hannah hooked her arm in Toby's and he gave her hand a squeeze. 'Where is it?' she asked.

'I'm going now. You can follow me if you want.'

★   ★   ★

The new camp was in a lumpy meadow. The farmer was charging five pounds a night per vehicle to camp there.

'We didn't have any choice,' Trevor said. 'The roads are too narrow to park on and the new formation is a nice one.'

They crowded into Bridget's van. The rain was coming down steadily and the grey light made it seem much later than it really was. Trevor passed them an aerial photograph. This time, there was a large main Circle with a smaller one about a quarter of its size a short distance away. When Hannah looked carefully, she could see no connecting line or passage between the two.

'Clockwise pattern in the larger one,' Trevor said. 'Anti-clockwise in the small.'

'They're warning us about genetically modified food,' announced a girl whom Hannah hadn't even noticed curled up in a colourful blanket on the floor beneath the table.

'It's too late for that,' Frank called out before he was hushed by Piper.

The girl sat up. She had the rough-cut hair and surly face of a teenage boy but the round breasts of a woman showed clearly under her tight T-shirt.

'Who are you?' she asked and somehow managed with the tone of her voice and the way she looked at Toby to make Hannah feel excluded.

'Toby,' he said. 'And this is Hannah.'

'I'm Imogen. Gin for short.' She barely glanced at Hannah. 'Are you staying?'

'I've got work,' Hannah said quietly. She hadn't phoned the Agency, she realized, her heart pressing against her chest. She should have phoned the Agency. 'Although, I suppose I might have been sacked.'

'For what? You didn't do anything wrong.' Hannah liked how Toby was indignant on her behalf. She shrugged.

'Why don't you quit?' he suggested.

'Quit what?' Frank wanted to know.

'Her job. This bastard assaulted her and then his wife kicked her out.'

Hannah had to explain about her job and go through what had happened at the house all over again. Everyone had something to say about it, apart from Imogen who stared into the distance.

'You should definitely quit,' Piper said and several others agreed.

Hannah took a deep breath as the decision to do so bubbled up through her chest, making her feel light-headed. 'OK. I'll quit.'

They all cheered and Toby hugged her and kissed her on the mouth. She couldn't help glancing to see if Imogen was watching, but she had resumed her position under the table and had pulled the blanket over her head.

Trevor opened the door and announced that the rain had stopped, so they got out of the van and began to build a fire with the dry wood that had been stored underneath. The grass was wet but the soil still felt solid. It would take a good soaking, Hannah thought, before it softened up properly.

The fire was slow to give off much heat and Hannah sat as close to it as she could to keep warm. Without Hannah noticing, Imogen had come out of the van and was standing on the other side of the fire as if she was rising out of the flames. Suddenly she pulled off her top and began to dance her way around the edge of the group, her bare breasts bounced and shone in the firelight. When she approached Hannah and Toby, she stopped in front of him and swayed like a cobra hypnotizing its prey.

Toby shifted, leaving a sudden, cool gap between their bodies. He gave a short, soft laugh and glanced at Hannah before turning to face Imogen who came closer and closer and closer.

'I'm going to the loo.' Hannah touched Toby's shoulder as she stood up. He jerked backwards as if he was surprised to find her still there. Imogen was moving off, continuing her journey round the fire.

When Hannah returned, she felt a stab of shock to see someone had taken her place beside Toby, but it was Piper, who was sharing a cider with him.

'I'd like to have a piercing,' Hannah said, looking at the ring in Piper's lip.

'Ask Anita,' Piper told her. 'She's qualified. She owns a tattoo shop in Glastonbury.'

Before there was time to change her mind, Hannah was sitting in Trevor and Anita's van with Toby holding her hand.

'Are you sure about this?' he asked her. She looked up at his and Anita's faces and nodded.

It hurt like crazy. The pain built and built until it had reached a pitch where she was beyond it.

Afterwards, when they returned to sit by the fire, the ring felt heavy and her lip throbbed with a deep pulse of its own.

Ella

37

'I think I could look out at this view for ever,' Ella told Denis. 'It really is quite lovely.' Denis's flat was on the third floor and the little wooden balcony stood proud of the building so that it caught the sun and the wind from three sides. It reminded Ella of sitting right at the tip of a boat moored in the middle of the sea.

'I'd like that,' he said, and then as she held herself still, nervous of where the conversation was heading, he pointed to the muddy patch of sand where they often watched birds gathering and said, 'What are those, do you think?' He picked up the binoculars that sat ready on the table. 'Sanderlings, perhaps?' He showed her the picture in his *Birdwatchers' Guide Book*. Neither of them were good at identifying the birds but they enjoyed sharing the attempt.

'Both Hannah and Henry would be able to tell you the species in an instant. Edward got them interested when they were tiny.' Denis handed her the binoculars. 'I really don't know,' she admitted. 'They could be.'

'Another piece of cake?' he asked.

Not many people realized that she had a sweet tooth as she didn't often indulge it. But Denis liked desserts too, so he always bought one when he knew she was coming. Today's treat was coffee and praline. She was sure she'd put on several pounds since she'd met Denis but the sea air gave her such an appetite she found it hard to refuse any food on offer.

Scoot lifted his head when he heard them eating; he yawned and sat up. He'd be getting bored soon and it was nearly time to pick up Hannah anyway.

The thought of how Hannah had looked at her clothes that morning made her shiver. She knew about Denis, Ella was sure of it. Well, not Denis specifically, but she knew that she had met someone. Hannah wasn't stupid — what other reason would there be to explain Ella's behaviour? She had tried to read the expression on her daughter's face but it was impossible. She should have told her, rather than let her work it out for herself, but Hannah's knowing was a relief, nevertheless. It was the coward's way. Ella was a coward. She looked at Denis and wondered if he would like her as much if he knew how cowardly she'd been.

'Are you going?' Denis asked. He must have sensed her restlessness. She nodded. 'I'll walk you down.'

She wandered around the living room while she waited for Denis to put his shoes and jacket on. The room was simple but personal and comfortable. He had photographs of his children and two grandchildren displayed on the sideboard next to a carved wooden bowl; there was one settee and a leather chair with a footstool which was shaped like a horse's saddle. He had apologized for the bare walls when she first came to the flat. He hadn't, he said, been able to find anything to compete with the natural

406

beauty outside his window.

They linked arms as they walked down the street to where Ella had parked her car. The lack of parking was the only complaint Denis had about his home.

'Martha would never let me do this,' Denis said.

'What?'

'Link arms, hold hands. She said it was childish. To be honest, I think it was because she didn't really want to touch me.'

'I like it.' She touched his hand and smiled at him because even though he'd spoken lightly she knew that he often got sad when he talked about Martha. He had said once that he felt a little diminished by the failure of his marriage.

On the drive home, she thought how clever Denis was not to try and stop her leaving; that by not pushing her, he made staying over seem increasingly tempting. She smiled to think that he had used the same patient technique to get her into bed. She hadn't slept with anyone for years, literally for years, and the idea of it had terrified her, but gradually, gradually, the thought began to seem quite lovely.

It felt special to be close to someone again, to be naked with a man, to feel his strength and solidity. It had happened one afternoon without any fuss or drama. A breeze blew into the bedroom, a Beach Boys track played on the radio by the bed and she'd been spun back to a time when she was young and comfortable to share the gift of her body as he was sharing his with her. They made each other happy. In the end it seemed such a wonderfully easy thing to do.

She opened the car windows and the damp evening air entered, waking up Scoot who caught the familiar scents as they got closer to Spindle House.

By the time she was passing Lavender Cottage, Ella's certainty about what she was doing had evaporated.

She was relieved to find Henry sitting on his own at the garden table. 'I think I'll join you,' she said, but she regretted it the moment Kirsten appeared from the kitchen.

'I'll get you a glass,' she said, looking delighted to see Ella there.

'Don't worry. On second thoughts, I'd better go and water. The plants must be parched.'

'Kirsten's done the hothouse,' Henry told her. 'We weren't sure when you'd be back.'

'Oh, well, that's great, thanks,' she said. 'I think I'll take a stroll down to the pond anyway. Stretch my legs.'

On the rare summer evenings when Edward was home from a trip and the children were in bed, they would suddenly discover that they had the garden to themselves. Their favourite place to sit was down at the frog pond and invariably their conversation would centre around Edward's trip or the kids or her plants but sometimes their talk turned to what-ifs.

'What if,' Edward had asked more than once, 'I don't come back, Ella. What will you do?'

She had always assumed he meant what would she do with Spindle House, and she had assured him that she wouldn't run off to London but

408

would continue to live there until the children were ready to take it on themselves. Now she wondered whether he hadn't been talking about the house at all but about the possibility of a Denis that he hadn't dared to voice.

Illuminated by the patio light were the dark shapes of Henry and Kirsten still at the garden table. One day — and, with the speed the days ran past her now, that day would arrive very soon — Spindle House would no longer be hers. When Hannah became twenty-one, the house legally passed to all the children. Ella felt burdened by the house and garden but she also felt an intense possessiveness towards both and the idea of relinquishing them spun her into confusion.

It was silly but she had never really considered the reality of her future. Yes, she was protected and could live in Spindle House until she died, but you heard about children playing all sorts of tricks on elderly parents so that they could get their hands on the house. Not that she doubted her own kids for an instant, but it was their wives and husbands you could never bargain for. Not Amy, she had her own money, and probably not Kirsten, either; Kirsten loved the house and she was a kind girl. Only Ella didn't think it was likely Henry would stick with Kirsten and so there would be other girlfriends for Henry, and Tyler, too, and boyfriends of Hannah's who would look on the house as an asset, who looked at her children as asset-rich.

There were no guarantees, Ella thought. And

she'd been so cosily wrapped up in her life at Spindle House she'd forgotten that.

★　★　★

The next day Ella had arranged to watch Denis play in a bowls match. She liked the black and white, timber-framed club house with its walls of trophies and club photographs dating back to the Thirties. She had been pleased and a little proud to find Denis appearing in the team photographs for the last two years. He looked like a captain of a ship in his smart blazer and handsome face.

She sat at the tables overlooking the green with the other spectators and sipped a gin and tonic. Denis's team lost. She hoped it had nothing to do with the fact that Denis kept looking across at her when he should have been concentrating on the game.

'How does a chap like this find a woman like you?' a bushy-browed man bellowed at them after the match. Everyone laughed, including Denis, but she thought she caught a glimpse of uncertainty underneath so she slid her hand into his and squeezed his fingers.

'Do you want to have a go?' he offered.

It was a chance to touch which they both knew was engineered but that made it more fun; she was finding Denis increasingly attractive.

'I think we'll stop now, otherwise you'll be showing me up,' he said when she turned out to have a good eye for the game.

'It's beginners' luck. Or a wonderful tutor,' she

said and felt good at the sight of Denis's smile.

They walked home, hand in hand, and when they got in, she followed him into the bedroom and sat on his bed.

'Thank you for coming today,' he said, sitting beside her once he'd hung up his blazer and stored his bowls bag away.

'I'm scared,' she said.

Even though this wasn't the first time they'd slept together, it felt like there was more to lose.

'There's no need,' he said, pushing her hair off her shoulder and placing a kiss there. 'It's only me.'

He was extra tender with her, undressing her as if her fragility was physical. At first, the way he didn't take his eyes off her face was unsettling until she realized that he was offering her sight of his own emotions. She touched his gentle face and saw it contort and strain with the effort of his love-making and she felt her chin jut forward, her mouth open as she approached orgasm and he dipped low, pressing his face hard into her neck, groaning and pushing deep inside her until he came.

Hunger got them up. Ella sat in the kitchen while Denis baked a fish and served it with stir-fry vegetables: the quickest meal they could think of for which he had ingredients. Afterwards, they ate thick slices of cheese on biscuits with the most delicious pickle Ella thought she had ever tasted. It turned out to be Branston's. Denis had put some into a cut-glass bowl as he'd been too ashamed to admit he preferred that brand above all others.

Scoot started fidgeting. They walked him on the beach over the road, huddling together in the cold night wind.

Ella was only supposed to be going back to Denis's flat to pick up her keys and handbag, but instead she said yes to his offer of a cup of tea and they settled in the living room with only the moon for light.

'Stay,' he said, at the precise moment she was losing her nerve to ask if she could.

38

'Would you like some help?' Kirsten asked.

'No. Um. Thanks.' What Ella really wanted was to be left in peace. She couldn't remember the last time she'd made a whole meal without Kirsten popping in and out several times. She looked around for the small frying pan she kept on top of the oven to sweat onions and garlic and knew immediately that Kirsten had put it somewhere else. Sure enough, Kirsten pulled it out of a cupboard, announcing that it was a more logical place to keep it.

'I like to keep it out on top because I use it to start off the onions and garlic,' Ella had explained but the notion of a different kind of logic seemed to pass over Kirsten's head.

'Perhaps you could set the table?' Ella offered, to get her out of the kitchen.

'The one in the garden?' Kirsten asked.

'That would be nicer, don't you think? We'd better make the most of eating out before the weather breaks.'

'Can I pick some flowers for it?'

Ella stopped what she was doing. For the last few days, vases of flowers had begun to appear all over the house: the kitchen, the living room, the hall, even in the bathroom. The garden would be bald by the time Kirsten was finished.

Kirsten went bright red when Ella told her that she couldn't cut the rose by the patio. *It's a bloody ancient, rare rose,* she wanted to say, but she took pity on the girl. She offered Kirsten the zinnia elegans instead. Kirsten stood there like a lemon until Ella took her out to the flowerbed and kept a covert eye on her to make sure she didn't get carried away.

When Ella asked Henry to call Hannah in, she saw Kirsten put a hand out as if she was going to stop Henry getting up. What was the point of that? Ella wondered. It was as if Kirsten couldn't help involving herself in everything. Henry slouched across the garden, his jeans scraping along the ground. Ella worried about him: he was so passive these days it was as if he'd been brainwashed.

'We'll have to start without her,' Ella decided when Henry returned saying that Hannah wasn't there.

Tyler grabbed hold of her from behind. He was as hot as toast and smelled of his evil roll-ups and fresh deodorant. He had always been the most demonstrative of the children, seeking comfort in physical contact, and so she hugged his solid, big body as hard as she could before he let go.

He greeted Henry clumsily and Ella could hardly bear Tyler's hurt expression when Henry made a fuss. 'Boys,' Ella warned as if they were children.

She glanced up to catch an affectionate, consoling smile pass from Kirsten to Tyler and thought suddenly how Kirsten would have been perfect for Tyler if she hadn't fallen for Henry like all the girls did. She felt her heart squeeze with sharp affection for her youngest son. He was such a home-body; she feared he was never going to find a girlfriend hidden away in Spindle House.

As usual, there were twenty questions from Kirsten under the guise of compliments. She seemed to have made it her quest to observe and study Ella and everything she did. The next thing she knew, Kirsten would be styling her hair like Ella and wearing the same kind of clothes. She paused — a forkful of food before her mouth — as she saw that Kirsten was, in fact, wearing loose linen trousers, a cotton shirt and flip-flops instead of her usual prim skirts and heels.

'You can get them anywhere, Kirsten. At Worldwide's, at the fishmonger, in every bloody supermarket.' *Find your own way*, she thought, with a biting petulance. *I had to find mine*. The trouble with young people was that they wanted it all handed to them on a plate. Ella had worked for what she had — it might not seem like it — but she had worked bloody hard to get to this point in her life.

It was the look on Tyler's face which made her feel bad.

'I'm sorry. It's because I'm rather worried about Hannah,' she said to Kirsten and hoped she'd take that explanation as an apology for her rudeness. 'Is it only me who thinks it's odd she hasn't been back yet this evening?'

'She's probably with Toby.'

'But is that a good thing? I know it doesn't seem fair but I'm not sure I trust the boy.'

'I don't think she was here last night,' Henry

415

said. 'But then again, who was?'

Ella felt herself blushing but hoped that nobody would notice in the dimming light. She'd been stupid to think that it would only be Hannah who knew. Shame burned through Ella at the idea of them talking about her. She was so busy with her own thoughts she didn't realize Kirsten was saying that she knew where Hannah was.

'Why didn't you say anything before?' Ella asked. Sometimes she really found Kirsten hard to understand.

'She asked me not to.'

When Ella expressed her misgivings about Hannah's involvement with the group, neither Henry nor Tyler seemed concerned.

'Getting out and meeting new people does you good, don't you think, Ella?' Henry said and this time, although she felt herself redden, Ella was determined to look her son in the eye. Henry met hers with an even gaze but she hadn't a clue what he was thinking. He turned his attention back to his food and in that movement Ella saw Edward. She looked at Tyler and saw, running through him, a core, a seam of Edward, too. In fact, wherever she rested her eyes, anywhere in the house or garden, she was reminded of her husband. Even the fork she was eating with was from the set Edward's parents had received for a wedding gift. She felt her head spinning. At Spindle House, Denis hardly seemed possible at all.

Henry and Kirsten went into the house, leaving Tyler and Ella alone together.

'Tyler, love,' she asked him, 'are you happy?' It suddenly seemed important to know.

'Not bad,' he replied. He pressed the tips of his fingers together to form a prop on which to rest his chin.

'But?'

He darted a look at her. 'It's something I need to let run its course.'

'A girl?' She quickly rephrased her question. 'You mean a woman?'

He nodded. 'I'm afraid so.'

'Oh, love.'

'I'll get over it,' he told her. 'Don't worry.'

They sat in silence for several minutes. The others hadn't thought to turn on the outside light and so only a pale light from the living room touched the edges of their table; the descending darkness felt comforting.

'And you, Ella? Are you happy?'

She felt something like longing mixed with laughter bubble up through her body. 'I think I might be.'

'Are we going to meet him?' Tyler asked softly.

'I don't know. I'm not sure I'm ready for that.'

'We're happy for you, you know.'

'Even Hannah?'

There was a short pause before Tyler answered. 'I'm not sure Hannah knows.'

'She doesn't know?' Ella echoed, feeling confused.

'She's so wrapped up with Toby and, well, I think it's a case of not being able to acknowledge it yet.'

'She adored Edward,' Ella said flatly.

'But she loves you too.'

'I should have told you all but I didn't — I still don't — know where it's going.'

'Does he have a name?'

'Denis.'

'Denis,' Tyler repeated. 'Well, when you're ready, I look forward to meeting him.' He stood up. 'The pub calls.'

'You won't say anything? To Hannah, I mean.'

He shook his head.

'Thank you, Tyler.' She took his hand and let it slip out of her grip as he walked away. 'And I hope it works out for you, my darling,' she said, quietly, offering it up as a wish on the night air.

★ ★ ★

Ella was asleep on the settee with Scoot lying across her legs. His claws dug into her flesh as he leapt off in shock at the sound of the phone. Ella scrambled up and clutched the handset to her ear, hearing only her pounding heart for the first few seconds.

'Hello?'

'It's Hannah.'

She heard the panic in Hannah's voice. 'Hannah? Where are you? Is everything all right?'

'I'm in Ely. At the police station.'

'Why? What's happened?'

'There's been some trouble. Can you come and pick me up?'

'Of course I can, darling. I'll leave now. Are you all right though, Hannah?'

'I'm OK, a bit shaky,' she said. 'I just really want to get home.'

Ella stood for a moment, her hand trembling, then without thinking she dialled Finn's number. He answered on the first ring.

'Ella, you're ringing late.'

'It's Hannah. She's been picked up by the police and I've got to fetch her from Ely.'

'What on earth for?'

'Oh, I don't actually know. That was stupid of me not to ask.' She paused for a couple of beats. 'I'm sorry, Finn, I'm in a bit of a flap; I thought you might know if I'll need to find Hannah's passport to show as identity or anything?'

'No. Just go,' he said. 'Take Henry or Tyler with you. I'll come down in the morning.'

'There's no need. I'm sure it's nothing to worry about.'

'We're coming,' Finn said firmly. 'We were thinking of paying a visit soon anyway.'

Ella ran up the stairs and knocked softly on Henry's door. She heard his voice call out and she put her head round and told him she had to pick up Hannah at the police station. Without asking any questions, Henry got straight out of bed. After watching him momentarily struggle, Kirsten got up and helped him pull on his jeans. Ella's eyes were drawn to the joggling flesh of Kirsten's bottom under the silky material of her nightdress.

'Is she all right?' Kirsten asked.

'She sounded upset but she said she was fine.'

'You might as well come too,' Henry said to Kirsten. 'Now that you're up.'

'We've got to go right now,' Ella said quickly. She didn't want Kirsten with them. It was a family thing, surely, she thought, not entertainment for strangers. But Kirsten was already beginning to get dressed.

In the car, Ella turned to Henry and said, 'I don't know why, but I phoned Finn a few minutes ago and told him about Hannah.'

'Christ, Ella, what did you do that for?'

'I panicked. Pure panic. And now I feel bad for worrying him.'

'Oh well. He'll live.'

'The trouble is — ' there was a pause while Ella started the car ' — he's coming down tomorrow.'

'Who's coming?' Kirsten asked.

'My brother, Finn.'

'And Amy,' Ella added.

'And Amy? You're in for a treat tomorrow then, Kirst.'

★ ★ ★

Ella had imagined finding Hannah locked in a room or a cell but she was sitting in reception with a plastic cup of tea, looking tear-stained and frightened. She wobbled a little when she stood up and was squinting so badly under the bright strip lights that Ella could hardly see her eyes. Her daughter's body felt as light as cardboard when Ella folded her into her arms.

'Do we have to do or sign anything?'

Hannah shook her head. 'No. They didn't

420

arrest me. They've been very nice, particularly Peter.'

'Oh, well, thank you, Peter.' Ella looked at the police officer who was sitting at the desk behind Hannah. 'We really appreciate it.'

He leaned on his elbows and smiled. 'You're welcome. I knew your late husband, ma'am,' he said. 'And the young lady's been no trouble. Wrong place at the wrong time, let's say.'

In less than five minutes the group of them were traipsing back out to the car. Ella sank into the driver's seat and leaned back against the headrest for a moment. Hannah was sitting bolt upright in the passenger seat.

'OK, love?' Ella started the car and began to reverse out of the parking spot.

'I'm worried about Toby,' Hannah said. 'We got split up in the fight.'

'There was a fight?' Ella said, braking sharply.

'It's been brewing for weeks,' Kirsten said.

Hannah turned in her seat. 'It was some men from one of the villages who started it. They came with sticks and one of them had a knife, I saw it. We were only trying to defend ourselves.'

Ella glanced in her rear-view mirror at Kirsten who looked rather shaken by Hannah's outburst.

'I'm sure Toby will be fine,' Henry said. 'The police would have mentioned it if anyone had been hurt.'

'There was a man lying on the ground.'

'And you think it might have been Toby?'

'No. I checked. I don't know who it was. I'd never seen him before.'

'Well, I'm sorry, but right now I don't care

421

about Toby,' Ella said. 'As far as I'm concerned, he should have been looking after you.'

'I'm afraid I agree with Ella,' Kirsten said.

'I don't care what you think,' Hannah shouted at her, tears running down her face.

'Don't be rude, Hannah,' Ella said but she darted a look at Kirsten, warning her to keep her mouth shut. 'You're safe and that's what matters. We can talk about all the rest tomorrow.'

★   ★   ★

Finn and Amy arrived before eleven the next day and Ella could practically see Kirsten sagging the moment she saw Amy's precision-toned body, and withering under Finn's harsh scrutiny when they were introduced.

'Scoot, down,' Finn commanded and Scoot sidled off under the table.

'Hey, man,' Henry said and they clasped hands and hugged each other.

'Hello, Henry.' Amy stood on tiptoe to kiss Henry on the cheek. 'Still gorgeous, I see.'

'Oh,' Kirsten said, looking alarmed. 'I'll go and make coffee.'

When they were settled at the garden table, Ella glanced around. Despite the circumstances, she suddenly felt pleased to have Finn home. She leaned forward and touched his arm. 'Hannah's fine,' she told him. 'She's having a lie-in.'

'I told him not to worry,' Amy said. 'But you know Finn.'

Ella looked at her daughter-in-law and found

422

Amy smiling at her. Surprised, she smiled back.

'So, Henry,' Amy said, 'would you recommend Kenya for a holiday? We were thinking of going there this year.'

'I didn't know you'd been to Kenya, Henry,' Kirsten said, returning with a loaded tray. 'How exciting.'

Without replying to Amy, Henry stood up and took the tray from Kirsten.

'What do you do, Amy?' Kirsten asked.

'I'm in commodities.'

'She's the top woman in her field,' Finn announced proudly.

'Oh, how lovely,' Kirsten said, cutting up a cake that she had baked that morning.

Amy put her hand up to block the plate that Kirsten was trying to pass to her. 'Not for me, thanks.' Ella would have felt sorry for Kirsten if she didn't think she'd rather brought it on herself by playing mother hen.

'How about you?'

'I'm a legal secretary.'

'Good steady job, that,' Finn said, managing to sound both pompous and patronizing. Ella caught Henry's eye and they smiled knowingly at each other.

'I don't know how you can stand working in an office,' Henry said and, although the comment was meant more generally, Ella could tell by the way Kirsten flushed that she had taken it personally.

'I think the law is incredibly interesting,' Tyler said, walking round to kiss Amy and shake Finn's hand. 'You see people at all their highs and lows in life,' he continued and winked at Kirsten, who lowered her head as if she was embarrassed, but Ella could see that she was smiling.

It crept up on her. Only a few moments before, Ella had been enjoying the company of her children, the warm sun on her legs, the taste of good coffee and, she had to admit, a really delicious piece of lemon cake, and the next it was as if someone had shrouded her in plastic. The conversation was muffled, their faces were blurry. Hot springs of panic spurted inside her and she began to struggle for breath.

She stood up suddenly, 'I've forgotten to get eggs.'

'I'll go.' Kirsten leapt to her feet.

'No.' Perhaps she had spoken more firmly than she intended because she could feel everyone's eyes on her. 'I need some other bits and bobs; I meant to go yesterday, but — ' She didn't finish the sentence.

Scoot scrambled to his feet as soon as Ella pushed back her chair. 'Hold Scoot, would you, Tyler? I won't be long.'

As soon as she was out of sight of the house, her breathing became easier. She drove slowly along the road in the direction of Ely and then took a short cut to the main road towards the supermarket. She bought bread, milk, eggs and bacon for breakfast, wine, fruit juice, fresh fruit for Amy, a free-range chicken and two large packs of ready prepared stir-fry vegetables. She looked for whitebait but the fresh fish selection was meagre and uninspiring. As she surveyed her shopping trolley, she could see that she was making rather random choices but she was out of touch with what she'd got in stock.

Ella was back in good time to make lunch but the moment she rounded the corner of the house she knew from the food smells that Kirsten had already made a start. Finn immediately stood to help her with the shopping bags and she handed them over, feeling deflated. Scoot bounced around her; she nudged him aside with her foot as she took a chair next to Hannah.

'How are you feeling today?'

'A bit tired,' Hannah replied.

'Where are your sunglasses, darling?'

'I think I might have lost them.'

'Have mine for now.' She hated to see Hannah struggle in the sun and was annoyed with the others for not noticing. 'They suit you,' she told her, although they looked strange after seeing her so long in the old pair.

Amy appeared from the kitchen. 'I'm not really needed. I think I was getting in the way.'

'Join the club,' Ella said before she could stop herself.

She offered to call Tyler to dinner which gave her an excuse to pick up her mobile phone which she'd left in the car. She switched it on as she went up to her bedroom and, although she wasn't expecting any, she couldn't help feeling disappointed that she had no missed calls.

'This is nice,' Ella said when they were all sitting down to lunch. Nice was a safe, compromising word to use; what she really wanted to say she was afraid might sound crazy or slightly hysterical. What she wanted to say was: *I can't tell you how wonderful it is to have you all here together, how happy it makes me to see your dear, precious faces.* Then Kirsten spoilt it by saying 'thank you' as if Ella had been referring to the meal; now none of them would realize how important their presence was to her at that moment.

'So where next, Henry?' Finn asked.

'Nothing's planned.'

'Perhaps see where the mood takes you?' Amy said and before Henry had the chance to reply, Kirsten piped up that Henry had given up travelling. Not surprisingly, Finn and Amy laughed.

'You're like your father,' she said to him but her words were meant for Kirsten. She needed to realize the kind of person Henry was before she got in any deeper. 'You can't stay in one place for any length of time.'

Hannah came out with a saying of Edward's that she liked to quote. It made her brothers groan, which in turn made Hannah sulk. *How little things change*, Ella thought, and she had to smile.

'The day Henry gives up travelling is the day Finn gives up money,' Amy said.

Kirsten wouldn't have it. 'I'm only repeating what Henry said,' she insisted and Henry, gallantly, Ella thought, backed her up. But she recognized the slightly confused expression on his face — she would bet anything that his thoughts were already elsewhere.

'What's up with Tyler?' Finn asked when he

426

left the table suddenly.

'Nothing.' Ella and Hannah had both responded so swiftly that Ella was sure Hannah knew about Tyler's mystery woman and might even know her identity. She hoped it wasn't Colin's wife; she'd always suspected Tyler had a thing for her and his friendship with Colin was too important to mess up.

Finn shouted out and sprang to his feet. Toby was standing on the lawn.

'He's my friend,' Hannah said. She was in such a hurry to get to him, she set the whole table rocking.

'Is that the guy she was with last night?'

'He's all right,' Henry said. 'It's not his fault it kicked off.'

'He looks a piece of work to me.'

'I don't want you to go out this evening,' Ella shouted over to Hannah but she knew she had no power to stop her.

'I don't understand why she's hanging around with that kind of person, and working as a cleaner, for God's sake. She has a brain, she should use it. I could get her something in the city, if she wanted it.'

'She wouldn't want it,' Ella told him.

'If she gave it a chance she might find she liked it.' The way Amy said it made Ella think that she and Finn had discussed the idea before.

'I loved London when I was her age. But I can't imagine Hannah living there. She's not that kind of person.'

'She can always come back,' Kirsten said. 'Like Henry has.'

'He won't stay, Kirsten,' Hannah said, returning to her seat. 'As soon as he's better, he'll get bored and then he'll get itchy feet. He always does.'

'Hannah . . . ' Ella warned. Once again she felt sorry for Kirsten even though only a few minutes ago she'd been trying to get the woman to see exactly that.

'It's true. We all know it.'

'They always say everyone returns to the Fens if it's in your blood,' Finn said.

'Do you believe that?' Amy asked, looking surprised.

Finn shrugged. 'I don't know. I do think this is an awesome place. This house, I mean.'

'It's nice to hear you say that. Edward would be pleased,' Ella told him and touched his hand. He looked so much younger when he smiled.

'Actually, when you think about it,' Henry said, 'Edward spent more time away than here.'

'That's not true,' Hannah protested. 'It only felt like that because you missed him.'

'You should go to university,' Finn told her. 'Instead of wasting time.'

'I don't want to. I'm happy here.' Hannah spun to face Ella. 'Tell him.'

'In the end, a career in cleaning — or writing — ' Finn added, quickly pre-empting Hannah's protest, 'isn't going to pay the bills.'

'Oh, Finn. I think there's plenty of time before she need worry about that.' Ella looked across at Hannah who was staring into the candle in the middle of the table. When did the candle appear, Ella wondered? She looked at Kirsten who was following the conversation like a spectator at a tennis match.

'If she loves the place so much, she should take some responsibility for it.'

'What do you mean?'

'A listed house like this costs money, Hannah.'

'Do you pay for it? Is that what you mean?' Hannah looked at Ella. 'Is that true?'

'Yes,' Ella admitted. 'Finn pays for the upkeep of the house. Edward's money, I'm afraid, doesn't go very far these days.'

'I didn't know. Did you, Henry?'

Henry shook his head.

'He never wanted you to know before, that's why.' Ella looked around. Everyone, including Finn, seemed stunned.

'I'm happy to do it,' Finn said slowly. 'That's not why I brought it up.'

'It's because he worries about you. He just wants the best for you,' Amy jumped in, and Ella suddenly saw that behind her awkward, odd ways, she was a kind person and that she did really love Finn.

Hannah got up and pushed her way onto Finn's knee. She put her arm around his neck and pressed her face against his. 'Lovely Finn,' Hannah said. 'I'm really grateful that you care enough to worry about us.'

39

Ella managed to squeeze into the little car park at Saltmarsh between a white van and the wall. It was the busiest she had ever seen it. The tide was in and the only way onto the beach was by a sandy footpath to the right of the car park which Ella had never noticed before. Even though it was a blowy day and not as hot as recently, it felt warm on the path: it was sheltered from the wind by clumps of marsh mallow covered in pink flowers. She stopped to touch the soft-looking leaves and was surprised to discover they felt like fur.

There were several families on the beach, which she had expected to see as it was the middle of the school holidays, but there also seemed to be quite a number of people up on the marshes. An elderly man came over to make a fuss of Scoot and he told her that they were harvesting samphire. His eyes and nose were watering in the wind and he constantly wiped at his face with a huge, white handkerchief.

'Don't they call it poor man's asparagus?'

'Yes, that's right.' He looked pleased with her. 'Have you tried it?'

She nodded. 'A while ago.'

'I come here every year. It's the best time to pick it if you're thinking of taking some yourself.'

'I wouldn't know how,' Ella told him.

'You snip it off at the bottom and leave the

root. Some of the greedy ones pull the whole thing up because it's quicker, but then it can't regrow, see.'

'People don't think,' Ella said.

'You're right there.'

She watched him for a while as he made his slow journey across the marsh and then she walked Scoot down to the edge of the sea where he dashed towards the waves, barking indignantly when they chased him back up the sand.

★ ★ ★

Ella was sitting on the edge of the open boot of the car, changing out of her walking shoes, when the owner of the van next to her appeared with a carrier bag of samphire. He began to pack the contents into a cool box which he had taken out of the back of the van. Ella was pleased to see that he had cut his plants like the old man had said.

'Would you sell me some?'

'It's for my restaurant,' he said, staring at her as if he hadn't noticed her before.

'I only want a small amount.' She knew Denis would appreciate not just the food but the story behind it. The man looked at her, then at the cool box.

'OK.' He brought out a handful. 'Have you got a bag?'

She grabbed the plastic container which she used as Scoot's water dish and the man placed the bundle inside.

'How much?'

'Forget it,' the man said, sliding the box into the van and slamming the door. 'Enjoy.'

'What's the name of your restaurant?' she called out but he didn't hear her.

★ ★ ★

'Well done, you.' Denis received the samphire enthusiastically. 'I love this stuff.'

He cooked it the traditional way: boiled and served with butter, lemon juice and black pepper on thinly sliced rye bread.

'I saw Martha today,' he said. Denis had been looking after his grandson at his daughter's house in the morning. 'And I told her about you. She didn't seem very happy for me.'

'Oh dear.' Ella felt herself frowning. 'What does that mean?'

He laughed gently at her. 'It doesn't mean anything except that today I annoyed Martha, which I have to admit gave me a certain amount of pleasure.'

Ella sighed. 'You always make everything sound so simple.'

After lunch, they took a pot of coffee into the living room.

'You shouldn't feel guilty, Ella.'

'How do you always know what I'm feeling?' she asked. It was true that he had a knack of picking up on her emotions.

'I see it in your face.' He poured the coffee and handed her a mug. 'But I also know that everyone of our age carries guilt around along with the rest of our baggage: ex-spouses, deceased spouses, children, grandchildren. We have to try and remember that we don't have to please them all.'

'I still can't bring myself to tell Hannah. I thought it would be easy after I'd talked to Tyler but it isn't. She was so close to her father and she still thinks the world of him.'

'I'm not trying to replace Edward.'

'I know.'

'Maybe you should trust her to be happy for you.'

Ella sat with her feet up in Denis's lap, watching how fast the clouds were rushing across the sky. Every now and then, the weak sun peeped through and then was gone. On and off for the last hour she'd been thinking about how to talk to Hannah about Denis.

'All right,' Ella said. 'I've made my mind up. Would you like to come to Spindle House the day after tomorrow?'

Denis lowered the book he was reading. 'I would. Thank you.'

'That gives me time to speak to Hannah.'

'Prepare her for the shock.' Denis twinkled his eyes at her but Ella was already feeling nervous. 'It'll be fine,' he said and gently squeezed her toes. 'Don't worry.'

★ ★ ★

When Ella arrived to pick Hannah up from work, she couldn't see her waiting on the drive as usual. She passed the key-card under the scanner and drove through the gates. She parked and

433

beeped the horn and looked at the house. Blank windows stared back at her; it looked deserted but then again, it always did. She got out and went up the steps to the front door. She rang the bell. Inside, it chimed loudly like a church bell. She scanned the front garden while she waited. She wondered if she had come to the wrong house but, no, it was definitely where she'd dropped Hannah in the morning. She remembered commenting to Hannah that the plants never seemed to get bigger in their garden. They're stunted by the wind, Hannah had said. It seems to be a wind trap here.

Ella took her mobile out of the glove compartment and saw that there was a missed call from Hannah in the morning. She dialled the house phone first but there was no reply. She tried Hannah's mobile which didn't even ring before it went to voicemail.

She gave the house one last look before driving away. She decided to take a short detour to the camp, thinking Hannah might be there, but she was shocked to find that the camp had gone.

She got out of the car and Scoot snuffled around and peed on the grass. It looked as if they had left a few days ago and she wondered why Hannah hadn't mentioned them going.

Henry was in the living room when she arrived at the house, but he told her that he and Tyler hadn't been home long.

'Where did you go?'

'Only to Ely.'

'Not on the back of his bike, I hope. How

434

could you hold on properly?'

'My arm's fine now, Ella. This thing is coming off in a couple of days.'

'I'd forgotten.' They both looked at his arm. 'I bet you can't wait.'

'Freedom,' Henry said, picking up the magazine supplement from last weekend's paper. 'Finally.'

Ella went up to Hannah's bedroom. She was relieved to see the Silver Maid uniform lying crumpled on the floor; at least she knew Hannah had been back. She picked up the uniform and selected other dirty clothes from the laundry bin in the bathroom and went downstairs to put on a wash.

Ella stayed up even after Henry had gone to bed but Hannah still hadn't returned by one o'clock. She locked the back door, leaving the key out of the keyhole so that it could be unlocked from the outside, and went upstairs to bed.

She didn't feel able to sleep so she spent some time trying to find the pea-like flower that she had seen that day on the coast in her wild flower book. She found it quickly: it was yellow vetch as she had thought. She was, she decided, always going to be much better at identifying plants than birds.

She fell asleep with the light on and woke as dawn was breaking. She got up and stood in the doorway to Hannah's room, looking at her empty bed. It was silly to worry, she told herself. Hannah could be up to much worse on a gap year trailing round Australia or drinking herself

435

stupid at university. She had to get used to the fact that Hannah was growing up.

Ella went down for breakfast. After a half-hearted attempt at a piece of toast, she tidied up the kitchen, stacked the dishwasher and hung last night's washing out. Eight o'clock, then nine o'clock went by and Hannah still didn't appear. Neither, she realized, had Kirsten. She walked round the side of the house and when she saw Kirsten's car wasn't there she turned back across the lawn and went out of the garden through the gap in the hedge. She called ahead to give Hannah and Toby plenty of warning that she was coming. The tent was closed up and she slapped several times on it before unzipping the front. Warm, musty air greeted her but there was nobody inside.

Henry came shuffling out of the back door as Ella approached the house. He didn't have a top on and she saw that his jeans were far too big for him; they hung low and precariously on his hips.

'Where's Kirsten?'

Henry pulled out a cigarette from the packet and held it, unlit, in his fingers. The shadows under his eyes showed black in his tanned face. 'At home or work, I suppose.'

'You don't think Hannah's with her, do you?'

'No. Why would she be?'

Ella shrugged. 'It seems odd that neither of them were here last night when they're both usually around.'

'Kirsten's not being here has nothing to do with Hannah,' Henry said slowly, blowing a plume of smoke into the air where it drifted towards the house. There was something in the way he hunched his shoulders, something about the tightness of his jaw which made Ella stop, pull a chair out and sit down opposite him.

'What's happened?'

'We fell out over Sophia.'

Ella's mind churned over the name. She had never heard her mentioned before. 'Who's Sophia?'

'You know, the girl that got me into this mess,' Henry said, holding up his arm.

Henry seemed to think that she should know all about Sophia so Ella did her best to pretend that she did. 'But that's all over, isn't it? I mean, you're here, after all.'

'But I didn't tell Kirsten that Sophia and I have been talking and Sophia rang yesterday when I was out.'

'Kirsten answered the phone?'

'Yes.'

'Poor Kirsten.'

'Come off it, Ella. You don't even like her.'

'I do like her,' she protested. 'It's just . . . ' She hesitated but not for long. There were too many things being left unsaid in this house at the moment, too many secrets. 'Oh, Henry. All those compliments, all that enthusiasm, it's too much. It makes me uncomfortable.' She wasn't surprised when Henry laughed; her reasons did sound rather feeble.

'She was only trying to impress you, Ella. She thinks you're completely wonderful. And she loves Spindle House.'

'Well, as for that,' Ella said pointedly. 'It is still my home.'

'Of course it's your home, Ella. Whatever are you on about?' Henry dropped the cigarette end on the stone paving and then, glancing guiltily at her, he quickly leaned down to retrieve it and put it in the ashtray.

'So there's Sophia,' Ella said, raising first one hand and then the other. 'And there's Kirsten.'

'I'm not sure there is Sophia — I don't think I could go through that again.'

'Then why are you talking to her?'

He shrugged. 'I don't know.'

'And Kirsten?'

'I don't know about her either.'

'Oh, Henry.'

'I know this makes me sound like a complete shit, Ella. Tyler's already given me a hard time about it.'

'Things aren't always black and white, love. I'm not judging you,' she said quickly, thinking fleetingly of Denis. She wasn't sure what Henry thought about Denis, but it wasn't the moment to ask.

'Well, you might do when I tell you I bought a flight to Almeria today. I've got a friend there who needs some help running his villa business.'

'When are you going?'

'Soon. I was thinking of asking Kirsten to go with me.'

Ella tried not to look surprised. 'How likely do you think it is that she'll say yes?'

'She might if she likes me enough,' Henry

said. 'But . . . ' His words drifted off with another shrug.

'Do you really want her to go with you?'

'I feel I should at least ask her,' he said after seeming to give Ella's question some thought. 'Don't you?'

40

Ella was in Hannah's bedroom putting away some clean clothes when Hannah appeared in the doorway. Ella peered at her.

'What's that?' As she stepped towards her daughter, she could clearly see her lip swollen around a thin, metal ring.

'It's a piercing,' Hannah said. 'Anita did it for me.'

'Not the woman from the camp? For God's sake, Hannah, you could have caught anything.'

'She's licensed. It was done properly.' Hannah walked towards the mirror on her dressing table and studied and prodded at her lip, turning her face this way and that. 'It'll go down soon.'

'You missed work,' Ella said to her back.

'I've quit.'

Ella let a couple of beats of silence go by to give Hannah a chance to speak. 'So you've given your job up so you can run around with Toby for the rest of the summer. Honestly, Hannah, I thought you had more sense than that.'

Hannah turned round, her eyes wide with surprise.

'I'm beginning to think Finn was right,' Ella continued. 'It's about time you grew up and started taking some responsibility for yourself.'

'I do.'

Ella dropped the pile of clothes she was holding onto Hannah's bed. 'I'm sorry but I don't see much evidence of that.'

When she looked across at Hannah, she saw that her daughter had begun to cry. She rushed to hold her but Hannah's body remained taut in her arms. She pulled her towards the bed and made her sit down.

'The man . . . ' Hannah sobbed. 'The man attacked me.'

'What man? Oh my God, Hannah, sweetie. I'm sorry. Come on, love, tell me what happened.' She stroked Hannah's hair, trying not to think about how angry she was as Hannah gasped and heaved and sobbed the words out.

'He wasn't supposed to be there. In the house. There was a change of plan.'

Ella reached out and passed Hannah the box of tissues from her dressing table. She put them in her lap and blew her nose. 'It wasn't anything serious but he was horrible and his wife knew it but she made *me* leave, not him.'

'I'm so sorry, darling.'

'It's not your fault,' Hannah said.

'I'm sorry for jumping to conclusions.'

Hannah blew her nose loudly again.

'And he didn't hurt you?'

'He pinched my nipple!' Hannah exclaimed and her shocked, indignant face was such a picture that Ella had to hug her again. They fell backwards onto the bed and lay facing each other, only a few inches apart.

'Why didn't you call me?' Ella tucked a wayward strand of Hannah's hair behind her ear. She tried not to look at the blue-black swelling that was marring her daughter's

441

beautiful face. Her moon child.

'I tried. I couldn't get hold of you.'

'Oh, yes.' Ella sat up quickly. Of course, she had been over at Denis's place.

'Where do you go, Ella?' Hannah said, at the very moment Ella heard a car draw up in the drive. 'Who's that?'

Ella's heart was thudding as she said, 'It's someone I want you to meet.'

'Who?' Hannah sat up and tilted her head as she peered at Ella.

There was a loud knock on the door.

'It's a friend of mine, a good friend.' Ella stroked the top of her daughter's head and noticed her hair was slightly greasy. She cast a swift glance over the rest of her and saw that her nails were filthy and there was a grey film over her feet and ankles. Denis knocked again, louder this time. 'Why don't you have a shower and come down when you're ready. I'll explain later.'

Denis had started to walk back to the car when she opened the front door.

'Is this a bad time?' he asked the moment he saw her face.

'No. Come in, come in.' She was shaking as she filled the kettle. Behind her, she could sense Denis looking around. Then she felt him come closer. He brushed the hair away from her neck and kissed her shoulder. She turned round and stepped out of his reach.

'I haven't had a chance to tell Hannah yet.'

'Tell me what?' Hannah crossed the kitchen. She was wearing Ella's old sundress and her wet hair dripped water, making a dark spot on the

442

material at the back.

'About Denis, that Denis was coming.'

'Hello, Hannah.' Denis stretched out his long arm towards Hannah who only hesitated for a second before shaking his hand.

'You told me upstairs you wanted me to meet your friend.'

'Yes.' Ella felt flustered. 'That's right.' She turned to Denis. 'Would you like coffee or tea?'

'Coffee, love, please,' Denis replied. 'Oh, I've brought some cake. I'll go and get it from the car.'

As she poured water into the cafetière, Ella could feel the intensity of Hannah's eyes fixed on her.

'So who is Denis exactly?'

Ella wiped her hands on a piece of kitchen towel and turned to face her daughter. She glanced out into the hallway. She reckoned she had a few minutes before Denis was back. 'He's the person I've been going to meet. You asked me where I went and that's where — to see Denis.'

'Why didn't you say anything before?'

'Well, it was hard for me to, I suppose. I thought you'd guessed, until Tyler said you didn't know.'

'Guessed what?'

'I wanted to tell you but I didn't know how you'd take it.'

'Take what, Ella? I don't understand what you're talking about.'

Ella heard the front door close. With Denis's long strides, she had only a few more seconds.

443

'Hannah, don't be obtuse. About me and Denis. I didn't know how you'd take it because of Edward.'

Denis appeared in the doorway, holding a cake box aloft. When Ella next looked in Hannah's direction, she'd gone. Ella rushed to the open back door and was in time to see Hannah running towards the gap in the hedge. Scoot was chasing behind her, thinking it was a game.

'She's gone.'

'Oh dear.' Denis slid the box across the surface and came towards Ella. 'I'm sorry.'

'She's upset.' Ella should never have mentioned Edward. That's where she went wrong.

'She'll come back,' Denis said. 'It'll be all right.'

They took the coffee and cake out to the garden. Ella was trembling so much she thought she was bound to spill something before she reached the table.

'Are you hiding your sons from me, too?' he asked and she saw that, despite what he said, Denis was a little nervous. She touched his hand gently.

'No. Tyler's taken Henry to have his cast off at the hospital. I'd forgotten the date of the appointment.'

Denis let out a sigh and looked around. 'It's so beautiful, Ella. It's even lovelier than I remember. Maybe you can show me around when we've got our breath back.'

After they'd finished their coffee, Ella took him to the hothouse. She hesitated before sliding the door open, unsure of what she would be

444

faced with inside, but the plants were flourishing.

'Ah-hah. So this is where you keep your special ones,' Denis said, looking over the top of her head. At the back, the moon flower and grape had both reached the roof.

'Can I pick one?' Denis asked, pointing to a tomato. All the vegetable plants were heavy with fruits.

'Pick whatever you like.'

'Delicious,' he said with his mouth full as they walked along. 'Your fingers don't stop,' he added. It was true, Ella couldn't help pinching off dead flowers and dying leaves, testing the soil in the pots, encouraging an errant tendril back into place. Everywhere she looked, she saw tweaks and tidying to do.

'What is that amazing smell?' he asked.

'It's the sea lily.' She led him over to it. 'It grows in the wild on the seashore in Turkey.'

'It looks too delicate to produce such a scent.'

'I wish I could ask you to stay tonight,' she said suddenly.

'It's OK. I understand.' He touched her face, kissed her lightly on the mouth. 'Next time, perhaps.'

She nodded and stood on tiptoe so that she could kiss him back.

'You know, Ella, all this that you've done, it couldn't possibly be considered a waste of time.'

★　★　★

445

Ella was lying on her bed with the bedroom door open, waiting for Hannah to come home. Shortly after midnight, she was relieved to hear the back door and then the stairs creaking as she came up. Scoot gave a low-level growl and wagged his tail.

'Shush,' she told him. Hannah's shadow flitted past and Ella called her back.

'Come in, Hannah, please.'

It was a shock to see her pierced lip again but Ella tried not to show it. She patted her bed. 'Come and sit with me a moment.'

Hannah walked slowly over and sat on the edge as if she were an uncomfortable guest. She was wearing a T-shirt saying 'FIT TO BUST' over the top of her dress.

'Can we talk about things?'

'It's OK, Ella. I'm OK with Denis,' Hannah said. A furrow appeared between her eyebrows as she tilted her head and looked earnestly at Ella.

'Thank you, darling. That means a lot to me.' She touched Hannah's hand. 'You're freezing.' She began to rub Hannah's cold hand between her own until Hannah slipped it away.

'I wish you'd told me though. I hate all these secrets. Everyone seems to have secrets.'

'I didn't want to upset you.'

'I know.' Hannah got up. 'I'm going away for a few days, Ella.'

'Away? Where?'

'The camp's moved.'

'I saw they had gone,' Ella interjected. 'I went looking for you there.'

Hannah looked puzzled. 'Me and Toby are

446

going to spend some time at the new site. It's not far away.'

'But Hannah — '

'I'm going, Ella. You told me I should be doing things and this is what I want to do.' Hannah walked to the door.

'Are you going because of today?' Ella's heart was booming so much she was afraid she'd not be able to hear Hannah's reply.

'No. I was thinking of going anyway.' She wrapped her arms around her body, pulling the T-shirt tight across her breasts. 'I'd like to give it a try.'

She is so lovely, Ella thought, *and she doesn't even realize.*

41

'How gorgeous you look,' Sadie said, getting out of the taxi. 'No wonder you've hooked a man, you beautiful creature.'

'Denis isn't hooked.'

Sadie simply looked sceptically over the top of her round sunglasses.

They watched the taxi leave and then walked arm in arm round the side of the house, each carrying one of Sadie's bags. Sadie stopped next to the garden table.

'Dump it here for now, darling. First things first, let's crack open a bottle.'

Ella went to fetch one of the white wines she had cooling in the fridge. She glanced behind her to see Sadie kicking off her sandals and shrugging off her jacket to reveal a white camisole. Scoot was sitting a short distance away staring at her as if he were worshipping a goddess from afar.

'So will I meet him?' Sadie wanted to know as soon as the wine was poured.

'Of course you'll meet him.'

'I don't know what took you so long.'

'I guess the time wasn't right before.'

Sadie reached out a hand and clasped Ella's. 'I might get drunk and say stupid things tonight but I want you to know before I do that I am very happy for you.'

Ella laughed. 'I'm not marrying him, Sadie.'

'We'll see. Hello, who's this?'

Ella turned round. 'That's Kirsten, Henry's girlfriend.'

They watched Kirsten stumble towards them in a full, flowerprint skirt and high-heeled sandals; her face was bright red by the time she reached the table. Ella made the introductions. She knew that behind her sunglasses Sadie was sizing Kirsten up.

'I'd ask you to join us,' Ella said. 'But I know you're here to see Henry.'

'Henry's girlfriend? Really?' Sadie hissed as Kirsten went into the house. 'She's not at all what I imagined.'

'I'm not sure she's what Henry imagined either. He's supposed to be asking her to go to Spain with him but who knows in the end.'

'And where's Tyler, and my lovely Hannah?'

Ella's heart sank. 'Hannah's still away.'

'Still with the gypsy boy?' Sadie said and Ella smiled. Sadie always did have a way of twisting reality enough to make it sound more exciting and glamorous but still plausible. 'You know, it got me thinking after you came to stay with me,' Sadie said. 'Maybe we should go on a trip of our own? Our last hurrah.'

'Not our last, surely? The start of our many lasts.'

'But you've got Denis now.'

'Denis won't mind. He's a very understanding man.'

Sadie took her sunglasses off and looked Ella in the eye. 'What I want to know is whether you've still got that wardrobe stuffed full of your husband's clothes and the shrine to Edward which you call his bedside table?'

Ella dropped her gaze.

'Darling, I'm sorry. I don't mean to be cruel but it must be time to let go.'

'You're right. I haven't dared face it, that's all.' It would soon be five years. Five years that she had been without Edward. 'I thought for a while that Denis was only second-best until I realized that he's actually my second chance.' She felt tears gathering and went to brush them away. Sadie stopped her hand.

'Let them fall,' she said and so Ella did. Sadie cradled her hands in hers as they dropped onto the table between them.

'Will you help me do it?'

'Of course I'll help you.'

'I think I'll have to be drunk.'

'Well, tell me where there's another bottle, darling, and let's see what we can do.'

Kirsten

42

Kirsten decided to surprise Henry by taking the afternoon off and arriving at Spindle House earlier than usual. She stopped off at her flat to pick up some clothes and toiletries. In the communal foyer, she collected the post which had accumulated in her mailbox and looked through it as she walked up the stairs. All this month's magazines had arrived and, as she glanced at the covers, her heart leapt as she noticed one of them was featuring a house in East Anglia. When she opened her front door, she was shocked to see how small and dusty her flat was. She couldn't wait to get away.

★   ★   ★

She saw Hannah and Toby sitting in Toby's car as she drove up Spindle House's drive. Hannah called out of the window to tell her where the back door key was and then Toby spun out of the drive, his wheels kicking up gravel as young men like to do when they're showing off. They both looked shifty to Kirsten; it wouldn't have surprised her to find out they were up to no good.

Henry hadn't mentioned he was going out that day but Kirsten didn't mind. It felt good to be trusted in the house on her own and her first thought was that she should make herself useful but instead she made herself a cup of tea and took it into the living room.

She pushed off her shoes, lifted up her skirt and wriggled out of her tights. She sat on the settee facing the French windows so that she had a good view of the garden. The white flowers in the border sparkled prettily amongst the green foliage as if they had been singled out by the rays of the afternoon sun.

She pulled the leather footstool towards her to put her feet up and placed the magazines that she'd brought with her in a pile on the seat beside her. What could be more perfect, she thought, sipping her tea. The featured house was in a village near Swaffham that she had never heard of. Architecturally, Kirsten didn't think it was anywhere near as impressive as Spindle House although she had to admit that the modernized interior was much more to her taste.

The phone rang. Although she hated to leave a phone unanswered, she hesitated before picking it up.

'Hello?'

A hollow-sounding woman's voice asked, 'Is that Hannah?'

'No, it's Kirsten. Hannah's not here. Can I tell her who rang?'

'No, no, it's not Hannah I want. It's Henry.'

For a moment she considered ringing off and walking away but she forced herself to reply. 'Henry's not here, either. Who can I say called?' she asked, even though she knew who it was.

'Sophia,' the woman said and gave an

454

exasperated sigh. 'Ask him to call me. At home. This afternoon. Usual time.' Her words stabbed into Kirsten's ear like a string of military orders. Sophia paused for a moment. 'Who did you say you were?'

'Does he have your number?'

The woman laughed. 'I should hope so. Who — '

Kirsten put the phone down. She returned to the settee and sipped at her tea which seemed too cool, and tasteless. She felt the echo of Sophia's laughter sitting high up in her stomach, making her feel sick.

As soon as she heard Tyler's motorbike, she ran into the hallway and looked through the glass panel to the right of the front door. The thick, amber glass distorted her view but she could make out the shapes of Tyler and Henry as they dismounted from the motorbike. She heard them laughing and, although she knew it couldn't be her they were laughing at, she felt her heart twinge with humiliation.

She ran back into the living room and sat on the settee, assuming a casual pose and trying to look calm, although her chest was heaving. Seconds later, Henry tapped on the French windows and pressed his face against the glass. She noticed the blur of Tyler passing behind but she didn't break contact with Henry's eyes as she got up to let him in.

He kissed her on the cheek. 'You're early.' He put the helmet on the side table and began to take his jacket off. She watched how he had to shrug off the shoulder of his damaged arm.

455

'Someone rang for you.'

'Oh yes? Who?' His body became still for a brief moment and his eyes flickered towards her face before he dropped his gaze.

'Sophia.'

He straightened up. 'What did she say?'

'If you could ring her. At home. The usual time.' Her face burned as she repeated the words but she held her ground and looked him in the eye. He swore softly under his breath.

'How long have these usual afternoon chats been going on, Henry?'

'It's not what you're thinking.'

'How do you know what I'm thinking?'

'What did you say to her?'

'Don't worry, I didn't blow it for you and tell her I was your other girlfriend.'

Henry shook his head and took a step forward. 'You're making something out of this which it isn't.'

'Really? Because I think it's the other way round. You told me it was over between you and it obviously isn't.'

'We talk, Kirsten, that's all.'

'About what?'

'Sorry?' Her question had evidently thrown him. He peered at her, frowning.

'It's a simple question. What do you talk about?'

'It doesn't matter — '

'Of course it matters,' she cut in. She hated to think of the two of them sharing news, hopes, dreams, laughter. She glared at Henry.

'It's friends' talk. I don't know.' He flapped

456

his arms around. 'It's not really any of your business.'

A long silence drifted across them as they stared at each other. She blinked, then turned and snatched her bag and shoes off the floor.

'Kirsten, wait,' he called after her as she pushed past him. She felt the briefest, lightest touch on her arm before she slid through the open French windows and ran round the side of the house. She glanced behind her as she paused at the edge of the drive to put on her shoes. Henry hadn't followed.

★ ★ ★

Although Kirsten declared she had a headache and tried to keep a low profile at work the next day, Emma soon came sniffing around her desk.

'So how is it going with you and Henry?' she asked.

Kirsten hadn't eaten anything since lunchtime the day before and she felt dizzy looking into the harsh overhead lights. She blinked rapidly to bring Emma's face into focus.

'Is something wrong?' Emma asked and Kirsten felt hot tears in her eyes. She tried to talk but her words came out in sobs and jolts and then she was crying properly, tears flooding down her face as if something had been unleashed inside her over which she had no control.

She felt Emma beside her, rubbing her back, and she heard urgent whispers passing between her and Valerie and then there was a sudden

457

stillness. She raised her eyes to see Mr Matthews standing on the other side of her desk, looking tight-lipped.

'She's a bit upset,' Emma said, while Kirsten frantically scanned her desk for something to wipe her face with.

'I'm sorry,' she muttered, blowing her nose into the tissue that Valerie passed her.

'Perhaps you should go home for the day, Kirsten,' Mr Matthews said curtly, and walked away.

Emma and Valerie returned to their desks while Kirsten hurriedly packed up for the day. She blushed furiously at the thought that Mr Matthews would always think of her as one of those women who couldn't keep their work and personal life separate.

By the time she arrived home, she was feeling much calmer and stronger. She had stopped on the way to buy a chicken sandwich and a bar of chocolate and she ate these straightaway before she got changed.

She spent the afternoon cleaning and tidying the flat. She washed and dried two loads of clothes as well as washing all her delicates which she hung on the heated towel rail in the bathroom.

A little after six, she rang Spindle House. Henry answered.

'Are you coming over?' he asked. He sounded subdued and hesitant. 'I'd like to talk to you.'

Kirsten inhaled. 'I think I need a few days to myself,' she said. She was half-hoping he would insist that he needed to see her but instead he said, 'OK,' and then asked, 'Shall I ring you?'

'No,' she said, not knowing where this sudden certainty had come from. 'I'll call you.'

★ ★ ★

The Sunday visit to her parents' loomed large in Kirsten's head. She almost considered phoning to say that she couldn't make it, but steeled herself to go and actually began to look forward to seeing them as she drove over.

As she parked outside the house, she thought she caught sight of her mother at the window as if she had been looking out for her. She opened the door to see Joy standing at the far end of the hall, in the weak light coming from the kitchen.

'To what do we owe the pleasure?' she asked, and turned abruptly, leaving Kirsten at a loss until she remembered that she had stayed at Spindle House the previous Sunday.

When she entered the kitchen, Joy said, 'I'll have to do more vegetables now,' and began to dash from one corner of the kitchen to the next as if she had forgotten where she kept anything.

'I can go away again if you like,' Kirsten said.

'Don't be rude to your mother.' Her father had come into the room without her knowing. 'Why don't you give her a hand instead?'

'I don't need her help,' Joy said. 'Just leave me in peace.'

Kirsten followed Clive into the living room and sat on the sofa as she always did while her father sat in his armchair. Without looking down, he reached for the newspaper which was slotted into the newspaper rack beside him. Kirsten jumped forward and grabbed it.

He looked at her with astonishment as she held the paper on her knee. 'How are you, Dad?'

'Same as usual, love,' he said.

And how is that? she wanted to ask as his gaze lowered and fixed on the paper. The silence was so deep she could hear the ticking of her wristwatch.

She stood up and dropped the paper in his lap before going over to the window.

'Do you like gardening?' she asked over her shoulder.

'I've never really thought about it,' Clive replied after a moment.

Kirsten watched a small, brown bird fly around the garden, its wings fluttering as it looked for somewhere to land. Suddenly it rose steeply until it had cleared the fence and flew away.

'Lucky escape,' she whispered.

'What's that?'

'Nothing, Dad.'

'Sit down, love. You don't look like you're stopping.'

* * *

At the moment when her mother refused her help with the washing up, Kirsten decided to call Henry. As soon as she was out of the village, she rang Spindle House.

'Henry? It's Kirsten.'

'Are you coming over?' he said immediately

and she didn't even have to think before she said yes.

★ ★ ★

Was everyone connected to the Rulands glamorous and beautiful? Kirsten wondered as she headed into the house away from Ella and her friend Sadie. Sadie looked like one of those women in the social pages of *Harpers*. She seemed friendly enough but she was wearing a large pair of sunglasses and you could never tell what anyone was really thinking behind dark glasses.

'Henry?'

'Hi, Kirst.' Henry waved at her from the settee but he didn't get up; he had his laptop balanced across his legs. 'Won't be too long. I've got the bloody thing connected at long last, it would be a shame to waste it.'

Kirsten walked to the French windows. It wasn't that she was expecting a fanfare or anything but she wasn't sure anyone had even noticed that she hadn't been there for days. She looked at Ella and Sadie, laughing, sharing a bottle of wine, holding hands. If Kirsten walked back out of the house, right now, this very minute, how long would it take before Ella noticed she was missing? She pictured years passing and then Ella suddenly saying, Whatever happened to that rather plump girl Henry had a thing with one summer? You know, lots of brown hair, local girl. Karen? Christine? Kirsten. Whatever happened to her?

461

'Do you want a cup of tea?' Kirsten asked Henry.

'Yeah, great,' he replied, barely looking up.

She tidied the kitchen surfaces while the kettle boiled and the tea brewed. It was such a beautiful house; Kirsten could do wonders with it.

'If you were mine,' she said softly, 'I would look after you.'

She returned to the living room as Henry was sliding his laptop under the occasional table.

'Sorry about that.' He watched her put the hot mugs onto the coasters on the coffee table and then held out his hand.

'How have you been?' He drew her towards the settee and she let herself fall backwards, landing close without touching.

'I really missed you,' he said and when she saw the concern in his face, she realized that he meant it. He leaned over her and kissed her. It was a light kiss, a gentle brushing of his lips against hers which made her long for more when he stopped. She could hear his breath quicken, felt his hand moving, searching for a way into her skirt. He dipped his mouth onto hers again, pressing harder this time. He pulled away suddenly, urgently.

'Let's go upstairs and I'll show you how much.'

She nodded, unable to speak. Her whole body wanted him so much that she would have taken him inside her, right there, in broad daylight, with Ella and Sadie only a few metres away. She followed him up the stairs, keeping her eyes lowered, focusing on the slants of light hitting the stairs so as not to break the spell.

A sudden clatter from above shocked her. She looked up to see Tyler leaning on the balustrade, watching them go up. She blushed so hard she could feel the heat coming off her face, as if they'd actually been caught naked together.

'Hey, Kirsten,' Tyler said. 'I haven't seen you for a while. How are you?'

When Kirsten tried to speak, her voice croaked and then came out too loud. 'Fine thank you, Tyler. And you?'

'Great, thanks.'

She knew that some look or sign had been exchanged between the brothers because she could sense a tension filling the silence. At the top of the stairs, she passed in front of Henry and slipped by Tyler and into Henry's bedroom without looking at either of them.

She stood close to the door and tried to get her breath back. When Henry came in a few seconds later, she knew that their moment to make love was lost and that they would now have to talk.

Henry slid onto the bed and sat with his back against the wall. 'You're right, I haven't been honest with you,' he said.

If she moved at that moment she would crumble like sand into a pile on the floor, so she remained motionless, her eyes fixed to the left of his face.

'I have been talking to Sophia but it's not because I want to be with her.'

'Why then?' She walked over to the armchair

by the window and sat down awkwardly on top of the cushions.

Henry shrugged. 'Perhaps because of what we've been through. I found it hard to let it go, especially as I've been stuck here without anything to do but think about it. And,' he said after a short pause, 'I was talking to her about a job in Spain I could get for a few months through a mutual friend of ours.'

'I thought you wanted to stay here.'

'I'm not sure I can, Kirsten. I don't know. Maybe I'm not made to stay in one place, maybe I'm more like Edward than I thought.'

'So you've decided — '

'No, no.' He scrambled off the bed and squatted down in front of her; he put his hands behind her knees to steady himself. 'That's why I'm asking you. I want you to come with me.'

'To Spain? For a few months?'

'Yes.'

'And then what?'

He shrugged. 'Whatever happens next.'

'And what if I say no?'

'Then I won't go either.'

'You wouldn't go?'

He shook his head, stood up and pulled her to her feet.

She heard the engine of Tyler's motorbike start and then peter away. A great burst of laughter from Ella and her friend reached them.

'They're pissed,' Henry murmured, and began to unbutton her blouse.

★ ★ ★

Late in the night, Kirsten heard more laughter and shouting and the sound of footsteps running up and down the stairs; later still, there was a strange bumping noise which seemed to roll through the house like thunder.

She woke in a panic in the early light, thinking, 'I can't go. My parents are getting old. They need me. There's no one else.'

She turned over and her heart jumped when she saw that Henry was awake and was looking at her. 'And you'll stay here if I don't want to go?'

'Yes. I'll do whatever you decide,' he said and she fell straight back to sleep.

43

'What's this, Henry?'

He tried to grab the travel documents out of her hand but she moved too quickly, so quickly that the tickets fell out and slid across the floor.

'Leave them,' she said, and Henry retreated to the other side of the room while she bent down to pick them up. Her pulse was racing but she took her time studying each one. One was a single flight from Stansted to Almeria and the other was the credit card confirmation.

'When were you planning on telling me?'

'Look, I only bought it in case. It doesn't make any difference to what I said the other night.'

'Except you said you wouldn't go if I didn't want to.'

'That's right.'

'So tear it up.'

'What?'

'Tear up the ticket. We're not going. I don't want to.' She held it out to him and he took it. 'Go on, then. Or shall I do it for you?' She made as if to take it back and he snatched it away.

'I thought not,' she said and let the credit card docket drop to the floor.

'Kirsten.'

'Save your breath.'

It felt different this time. Although she knew her body would soon start trembling as it succumbed to the aftershock, her mind felt perfectly calm and clear. She walked down the hall and out of the front door, closing it carefully behind her. She looked at the rose growing up the wall, she glanced at the outbuildings to her right and then scanned across the drive to the fields behind it.

It was a shame, she thought. She could have made it nice enough to be in a magazine. If only they'd let her.

She drove out of the lane and was at the first turning towards Ely when the shaking became so violent she had to pull onto the verge. Dry sobs heaved in her chest but she didn't cry.

Tyler pulled up alongside her on his motorbike, making her jump. He tapped on the window and mouthed something at her. She lowered the window.

'Are you OK?' he shouted before cutting the engine.

'I don't know.'

'Do you want company?' He took off his helmet and his hair frizzed with static. He studied her with kind, worried eyes.

'We can't stop here.'

'We could go into Ely, if you like?'

'OK.' She didn't feel she had it in her to say no.

'Hang on a minute. I'll come with you.'

He rode a couple of metres up the road and then turned down a bridle path, parking the bike close behind the hedge.

'Will it be safe?'

'Hardly anyone comes this way, in case you haven't noticed.' He grinned at her and suddenly she was pleased to have him with her, grateful for his easy-going manner. 'So?' he said, getting into the passenger seat. 'You don't have to tell me, but it might help.'

'Henry offered me the choice of either going to Spain together or staying here, together.'

'What did you say?'

'No. But I found he'd bought himself a ticket to go anyway.'

'Perhaps he thought you'd definitely say yes to Spain.'

'Then why didn't he buy two?'

'Ah, well, you know Henry. He says a lot of things he doesn't mean.'

'I didn't know that,' Kirsten said, feeling a little stupid. 'It would have been better if I did.'

'He's a selfish bastard,' Tyler said unexpectedly, which shocked her. 'A charming, nice guy but a selfish bastard. Like my dad.'

★   ★   ★

Tyler looked surprised when she parked in her space outside her flat. 'I've always liked this building.'

'Do you want to come up?'

'If that's OK.'

As she was opening the door, she realized that the only other guest she'd ever had in her home was Paul. She flushed at the thought and felt uncomfortable leading Tyler inside. But Tyler wasn't anything like Paul: he scanned the room enthusiastically and declared, 'I like it.'

She noticed he was heavy on his feet as he

marched over to the window and she thought of her parents calling her flat-footed and clumsy and shouting up the stairs for her to be quiet.

'Great view of the cathedral,' he said.

He followed her into the kitchen and leaned against the work-surface while she made tea. She lifted a tin down from the top shelf. 'If you tell anyone about this tin,' she said, 'I will have to kill you.'

His eyes opened wide like a child's when she took the lid off and revealed her collection of chocolate bars and biscuits.

'You know my weakness,' he said, rummaging through the contents and settling on a KitKat. 'So what do you do with yourself in the evenings?' he asked.

Kirsten had to think hard to remember what she used to do in her life before Henry.

'I help out on Thursdays at the church Kids' Club in Ely,' she said, although she hadn't been there for several weeks.

'That sounds like fun,' Tyler said. 'Except for the church bit.'

'It's not preachy,' she told him. 'It gives the kids somewhere to go and something to do.'

They dropped into silence for a few moments while they finished their biscuits and leaned on their elbows over their mugs of tea like builders on a site.

'Can I ask why you don't want to go to Spain?'

She thought about it for a moment. 'It doesn't seem like it would be a real life. Not the life I want.'

'What do you want?'

'The same as most people. A husband, kids, oh yes, and Spindle House please.'

'That's because you've only seen it at its best. It's freezing in the winter and the roof leaks when it rains.'

'Well, I suppose it doesn't really matter now.'

'You don't have to stop coming over because you and Henry . . . ' Tyler paused and she looked at him quickly.

'It would be awkward.'

'He'll be gone soon. You'd be my guest,' Tyler said and her heart fluttered at his sweet expression as hope briefly flared and then fizzled.

'I'll drive you back.'

He stood up and walked towards the door. 'Don't worry. I'll give my mate Colin a ring.'

'If you're sure.' She was torn between wanting to be on her own and feeling guilty that he'd come all the way over to Ely.

'He'll probably be up for a drink; he usually is.'

'That's OK then,' she said, relieved. 'I'll feel much better if you haven't wasted your time.'

She stood in the doorway and watched him walk towards the stairs. As she was about to close the door, he called out her name.

'Yes?'

'It wasn't a waste of time. Not for me, anyway,' he said. Before she could respond, he was thumping down the stairs and out of the building.

Hannah

44

Hannah woke to the rack-rack call of a corncrake close to the tent. She sat up to reach her watch which she'd left on the strip of bare groundsheet to her left. Behind her, Toby rolled over and slumped across the patch of roll mat she'd just vacated, leaving her no choice but to crawl forward and get out.

The grass was damp with dew under her bare feet. She squatted in front of the tent, pushed her head back inside, wrinkling her nose up at the pungent air. She pulled her bag towards her by the strap and grabbed her blue skirt and yellow, long-sleeved T-shirt from the corner where she'd left them in a folded pile.

As she put on her clothes, she was annoyed to find them creased and stained. Nothing stayed nice, living in a tent. It had been a muggy night and she felt sticky and desperate for a wash. She unpegged the towel she'd left to dry on the makeshift washing line and walked away from the main camp to the back of the field where a stile gave onto a pathway down to the dyke.

The water in the dyke was low and she didn't like the look of the brown foam which had collected around a pipe. She headed left and found a spot where the water appeared clean. She laid out her towel, stripped quickly and jumped in. The cold water sent shockwaves across her skin. The water was too shallow to

473

swim in; she had to hunch very low in order to keep her shoulders under. She dipped her head to soak her hair and splashed water onto her face several times before getting out.

She dressed in knickers and T-shirt, put sun cream on her legs and lay on her stomach on the towel. She took out her reading glasses and notebook from her bag. She'd written very little since they'd been at the camp. The creeping urgency, the desire to write didn't seem to come to her here. She opened the book cautiously and began to read through the last pages she'd written. A flush of panic and horror ran through her when she saw each clumsy word, each rambling, sluggish sentence. She snapped the notebook shut and turned over. She stared for several seconds directly into the sun, making her eyes water.

She returned to the camp by the main gate. Pam had parked her van close to the camp-fire area; she was preparing the communal meal for lunchtime. Hannah offered to help.

'I can't pay you, love,' she said, but Hannah told her she didn't mind.

Pam took her inside her van. It was as clean as a whistle although it smelt of fat and spices. Pam shook out a heap of washed carrots into a colander and gave Hannah a knife and chopping board. She sat on the ground next to Pam's chair outside and looked around before she started. It was a good spot. She had a view of almost every vehicle and tent.

There were two kinds of people at the site, Hannah decided. There were those for whom it slotted into their everyday life. A lot of these people worked and so only came to the camp at the weekend; others, like Frank, who was an Open University tutor, used WIFI to teach and Bridget commuted to Cambridge most days to work, but Hannah wasn't sure what her job was.

Then there were others, like her and Toby, who had nothing to do except the occasional run into Ely for shopping and errands, and to keep the camp tidy.

Pam told Hannah that she'd been on the road for ten years but she stopped when she got married and had kids. For the next twenty-five years, she worked as a dinner lady in her kids' school. 'Then I got divorced, my kids left home and I thought, hang on, what do I do now?' She scraped the pile of onions into the biggest saucepan Hannah had ever seen and shook out five long, red chillis from a plastic bag. 'So I bought my van and started working the festivals and that was that.'

'What do your kids think about it?'

Pam laughed. She was a small woman with a big laugh and she was strong, too; she lifted up the sack of rice as if it weighed nothing.

'They hate it,' she said. 'They think I should be babysitting their kids. I told my daughter, they're your kids, you look after them. This is my time now.'

'Do you ever get bored?'

'Do I look like I have time to get bored?' Pam laughed. 'And besides, there's always someone to have a good chinwag with.'

Hannah finished chopping the last carrot and

laid down her knife. She found Pam was watching her.

'It's because you don't really want to be here, love,' Pam said, before taking the chopping board from her and scraping the pile of carrots into the pan.

The smell of the chilli gradually brought everyone out to sit around the remains of the previous evening's fire; Toby finally made an appearance. Hannah waved and then went to sit with him when Pam said there was nothing more for her to do.

'How long are we going to stay here?' she asked him.

He shrugged.

'I mean, what are we doing here, really?'

He turned towards her and their eyes connected for a brief second before Toby's cigarette smoke blew across their faces. 'Hanging out, I suppose. Waiting.'

'Waiting for what?'

'New Circles, maybe. Something to happen.'

Hannah sighed. 'I don't think anything's ever going to happen.'

★ ★ ★

It grew dark stealthily. One moment it seemed possible that daylight would stay forever and then suddenly Hannah found she was no longer able to see the people around her clearly. She tilted her head and concentrated on focusing on her hands to try and settle her vision.

It was a cooler night so she went to fetch her

sweatshirt from the tent. When she returned, Toby pulled her to sit down next to him. The smell of wood smoke, cigarettes and the cloying scent of grass was seductive but the smoke stung her eyes.

She put on her sunglasses which she'd hooked inside her top to keep them safe. She immediately felt cocooned by the dark; only the firelight flickered in the corner of one eye. Even the conversation around her seemed to have been reduced to a muffled hum. Words rushed in to fill the space; they danced across her mind as if she were seeing them already written on the page; they whispered in her ears so it became impossible to listen to them and to what Toby was saying at the same time.

She felt the vibrations of someone running towards them before she recognized the sound. Everyone moved at the same time, grabbing at whatever came to hand. Someone pulled a stick out of the fire and it glowed as red as molten metal.

'Quiet,' a voice called and they all froze.

'It's only Leon,' Trevor shouted out.

'For fuck's sake, Leon,' Frank said as Leon arrived at the fire.

'Fucking hell,' he wheezed. 'I was having a wazz and came eyeball to eyeball with this giant fucking stripy animal. It scared the shit out of me.' He spat into the fire which hissed back.

'It was a coypu,' someone said.

'They killed the last of them in 1989. It was a badger,' Hannah said. 'And it would be more frightened of you.'

477

'I didn't stop to find out how frightened it was.'

'Maybe it was Black Shuck,' Toby said and Piper asked, 'Who's Black Shuck?'

'The question you should ask,' Toby said dramatically, 'is, *what* is Black Shuck?'

Piper laughed. 'OK. What the hell is Black Shuck?'

'Hannah,' Toby whispered. 'You'll have to tell the story. I can't remember it.'

'Black Shuck,' she said, and she felt her body tingle and her voice deepen as if Magnus was inhabiting her, 'is a black demon dog who has haunted this part of the country for hundreds of years, taking the lives of innocent people wherever he goes. What you must remember, if ever he crosses your path, is that you should never — ever — look him in the eye, no matter how much he draws you in. Because anyone who looks him in the eye will be dead within a year.'

'Oh my God, Leon. Did you look him in the eye?'

'Fuck me. I did,' Leon said. 'Just my fucking luck.'

'It was definitely a badger,' Hannah said. 'Black Shuck isn't stripy.'

'Hannah should know,' someone said. 'She's like the fucking guru of nature.'

Toby laughed loudly and grabbed for her hand. Hannah felt rigid with embarrassment. She left her hand there for a minute before slipping it away. Toby didn't seem to notice. She passed on the skunk which was going round. She took a mouthful of the drink that was handed to

478

her but it tasted vinegary and she had to force herself to swallow it.

Like most nights, Hannah went back to the tent before Toby. She enjoyed the time alone, stretching out properly while she read by torchlight, the silence punctuated by friendly laughter, by the bark of a fox or the shriek of a barn owl. She often fell asleep before Toby came to bed.

But tonight, less than ten minutes after she had settled, she heard the drag of Toby's footsteps through the grass. She quickly turned off the torch and curled up on her side so that it looked as if she was asleep.

'Hannah, are you awake?' The tent shook and rocked as Toby tried to see his way in the dark; he swore and landed beside her with a thump. He leaned across her, resting heavily on her arm, he burped loudly and the acid smell of alcohol floated over her. *Leave me alone, leave me alone*, she thought over and over again. She was both relieved and upset when Toby pushed himself away and lay down. They hadn't made love for days and the longer it went on, the less she wanted to. From nowhere, a tear formed in the corner of her eye. It tickled as it followed a slow route across her cheek before landing on the back of her hand.

★ ★ ★

The next morning Hannah was sitting on the grass outside the tent when she spotted Ella's car drawing up in front of the field gate. She didn't move until she realized that the person who got out of the driver's side wasn't Ella but Sadie. She ran towards the car, waving. A small, white shape appeared by Sadie's feet and sprinted towards her. Scoot nearly tripped her up as he jumped and twisted in the air around her, barking excitedly.

'You'll have to come over to my side, poppet,' Sadie said. 'I don't think I'm appropriately attired for fence-hopping.'

'I'd hug you but I think I'd ruin your lovely dress,' Hannah said, climbing over. Sadie was wearing a lemon-yellow, raw silk dress and gold leather Roman sandals. Hannah felt grubby in her two-day-old gypsy blouse, complete with chilli stains, and her black cigarette pants which had gone baggy at the knees from being worn for too many days.

'And where's Toby?'

'He's still asleep.'

'Shame, I was looking forward to meeting him.'

'I can't believe how much he sleeps,' Hannah told Sadie. 'Or snores.'

'That's what men do, love,' Sadie said, laughing.

'Really?' Hannah looked over her shoulder at the tent. 'Did Ella send you?' she asked, turning back.

'She knew I was coming.'

'It's not because of Denis that I'm here. If that's what she thinks.' She paused for a moment. 'Have you met Denis?'

Sadie nodded. 'He seems really nice.'

480

'He looked nice,' Hannah agreed, and she felt bad that she had run away that day. It had been the shock, that was all. That stupid idea had exploded in her head: that you couldn't meet someone new without someone old being taken away. Scoot for Edward. Toby for Ella. Kirsten for Henry. Denis for who?

'So why did you come here?'

'I wanted to see what it was like.'

'And what is it like?'

Trevor was striding towards the other end of the field, holding a roll of toilet paper. It was obvious he was going for a poo and Hannah didn't feel quite right about them both watching him. 'It's OK.'

'What do you do all day?'

'Nothing much.'

'Do you get bored?'

'Sometimes.'

'Do you want to come home with me?' Sadie asked. 'I'm happy to wait while you get your things if you do.' She put a hand on Hannah's arm. 'That's me asking you now. Nothing to do with Ella.'

Hannah shook her head immediately as if she didn't have to think twice about it, but inside she was considering how easy it would be to get her bag from the tent without even waking Toby and let Sadie drive her back to Spindle House.

'She asked me to leave Scoot with you, if you want him.'

Hannah bent down and stroked the top of Scoot's head. 'Yes. Yes please.'

Toby didn't wake up until gone one o'clock and by that time Scoot had made cautious friends with several of the other camp dogs although he stayed close to Hannah and didn't run around like the others.

'He's keeping an eye on you,' Toby said and they laughed, although to Hannah that was exactly what it felt like. Ella had entrusted her with Scoot and he had been sent to protect her.

Toby had offered to drive into Ely to run some errands. He wanted Hannah to go with him but she said no.

'Take Imogen,' she told him, before she could stop herself. She could feel his eyes on her face, even after she had looked away, trying to work out if she was serious. It was Leon who went with him in the end.

Bridget had come to sit beside Hannah practically the second that Toby had left. That was the trouble with this place, Hannah thought, you never had a chance to be properly alone.

'Can I plait your hair?' Bridget always wore a bum-bag where she kept her little tin of tobacco and now she drew out of it a plastic bag containing several lengths of brightly coloured thread, the same kind that was entwined in her own hair.

'Which colours would you like?'

Hannah wasn't thrilled by any of the garish colours but she chose the yellow and the green to be polite and Bridget sat behind her, her knees pressing into the small of Hannah's back.

'It's hard to work with,' Bridget said, her hands constantly tugging and smoothing Hannah's hair. 'It's so silky, it keeps slipping.'

'You can leave it if you like.' Hannah had to keep her neck at an angle and it was beginning to ache but Bridget wanted to keep going.

'How long have you and Toby been together?'

'Not long. It's only a summer thing,' Hannah said, surprising herself into silence for a moment. She pushed her fingers into the hard, dry soil and felt a welling up inside her. She didn't recognize the emotion. Not anger, sadness, or loss; but a welling that dissolved and drained away, leaving nothing. Like a rain shower on the parched ground.

'He's a nice guy,' Bridget said.

'Yes, he is,' Hannah agreed and she felt bad for what she'd just said.

'Toby and Leon are back,' Bridget said. 'I think something's going on.' She stood up. 'Come on, Hannah. Everyone's going over there.'

They ran across the field.

'There's another Circle,' Piper said when they reached the others.

'Where?' Hannah asked.

Toby turned to face her. 'Only a couple of miles away.'

'How did you find out?' Trevor asked, joining the group. He was out of breath and looked annoyed.

'We passed some ramblers who had been to look at it.'

'Did you go in?' Trevor asked.

483

Leon shook his head. 'No, mate. We thought we should let you lot know first.'

They took Bridget's and Trevor's vans. Hannah and Imogen went in Trevor's because he said there was only room for two small people. Hannah presumed he meant skinny as she was six inches taller than Imogen. They had to sit with their feet on the bench as the floor space was taken up with a ladder and boxes of equipment.

'Bridget's done your hair,' Imogen said.

'Yes,' Hannah replied.

'Is that your dog?'

'Yes,' Hannah said and that was the extent of their conversation. For the rest of the journey, Imogen stared out of the window and Hannah pretended to keep Scoot occupied so that he didn't jump around.

★ ★ ★

Something didn't feel right even before they entered the field. There were two boys, aged about twelve or so, who shouted something which Hannah assumed was rude as they got out of the vans.

Trevor asked them if they'd seen anything.

'Yeah, lights,' one said.

'And little fucking green men,' the other added. They hopped on their bikes and pedalled off, laughing.

It was a hoax. The oilseed rape had been broken and bashed to the ground, the edges of the Circle were irregular and poorly defined.

There was a smaller intersecting Circle where part of the crop in the middle was still standing.

'Why would anyone want to do that?' Hannah said to Toby, going to stand beside him. She felt close to tears. It seemed such a wasteful, mean thing to do.

'For a laugh,' Toby said.

She looked at him, shocked.

'To stir things up a bit,' he whispered to her. 'Didn't you say you were getting bored?'

'You didn't?' She tilted her head to bring Toby's face into focus but she still couldn't read the expression on his face.

'I'm only kidding, Hannah. Lighten up.'

'It's not funny.'

'OK,' he said, pushing his hands deep into his shorts pockets and turning away. 'Sorry we brought you over here for nothing,' he called out to Trevor.

'We still document it,' Trevor said loudly and firmly. 'For the records.'

★   ★   ★

That night the mood around the camp fire was despondent; talk was slow and sporadic. Hannah had her sunglasses on again in an attempt to recapture the words that had flickered in her head like the dancing flames in front of her, but nothing came. She idly stroked the warm fur on Scoot's back but she flinched when his cold nose touched her hand.

Imogen had moved closer to Toby; every time he spoke, she leaned towards him and placed her hand on his knee.

Hannah stared into the fire and eventually the words began to float back into her head. She repeated each sentence over and over again so that she would remember the words for when she had the chance to write them down.

Everyone, she realized suddenly, seemed fired up.

It took her a few moments to work out that they were discussing a move to Wiltshire. Trevor had everyone hooked in as he talked excitedly about the area being a hub of Crop Circle activity and described some of the formations he'd seen there. It was as if the last few weeks didn't matter any more; this was what they had been waiting for.

She knelt up and leaned against Toby. 'You're not thinking of going, are you?' she whispered.

'Maybe. Yeah, why not. What else is there to do?'

'But what would we do there?' She stood up.

The moon was bright, lighting the way to their tent — she felt drawn towards it. Something was happening inside her. It began as a trickle, like water finding its way through the faults and fissures of earth until suddenly enough pressure had built up to force its way through, flooding her with a desire to leave. The idea of spending another minute at the camp was impossible, the desire to see Spindle House was immense.

She swept the beam of torchlight across the floor of the tent, searching for her bag. She checked that her notebook, purse, sun cream and phone were in it, then she collected any of her clothes she could see and stuffed them inside.

When Toby put his head inside the tent, Hannah shrieked. Scoot gave a single bark and then lay back down on the sleeping bag.

'You frightened the life out of me.'

'What are you doing?'

'I'm leaving. I'm going home.'

'What, now? You can't.'

She pushed past him out of the tent and he helped her to her feet.

'It's OK, you don't have to come with me,' she said. 'I know my way.'

'You don't want me to come?'

She shook her head.

'Why not?'

'Because you want to stay with the group. Don't you?'

'I guess.' He sounded confused.

She spoke softly despite the excitement that was surging through her. 'There always had to be an ending, Toby.'

'I know,' he said after a moment. 'But why now?'

'Why not?' She kissed him on the cheek and settled the strap of her bag onto her shoulder. She spotted a flash of Scoot's white fur over by the tent. She whistled for him and only seconds later he was alongside her as she headed towards the far stile.

'Hannah, wait.' Her heart was beating fast as Toby jogged up to her. 'Are you sure you'll be OK on your own? You know, what with Black Shuck and that Willow Wisp thing?'

'Will o' the Wisp.' She smiled. 'I'll be fine. I've got Scoot to look after me.'

★ ★ ★

It felt good to be moving after so long sitting around. She strode along the top of the bank, picturing her legs like two chopsticks chomping through the miles. At first Scoot kept investigating the bushes and running down to the edge of the dyke but soon he fell into her steady rhythm and their progress became more purposeful.

By following the dyke and using the footpaths and bridleways back to the village instead of the road, she calculated that she could cut the distance to no more than seven miles. She stopped to read her watch and was shocked to find that it was nearly two o'clock. Knowing how late it was seemed to trigger a desperate tiredness in her; Hannah's pace slowed and she found she was checking her watch every five minutes. Cloud cover was obscuring the moon, making it harder to see the ground in front of her. When she stumbled for the third time, she decided to rest for a while. She walked a little further until she spotted a small tree on the dip to her left.

It was a warm night and she found herself slipping into sleep as soon as she sat down. She lay on her side next to Scoot and pushed her face into his fur. She hugged him to her stomach and his flank rose and fell under her hand, his paws twitched in his dreams.

She was woken a couple of hours later by the

cold dawn air. She dusted herself off and ascended the bank to get a view of where she was. On both sides stretched an expanse of beet fields, broken only by the dyke and the road running parallel with it. There was nothing familiar about it or any recognizable landmark. The harder she tried to control her eyesight the more it jumped around. She decided it was better to go down to the road and walk along until she came to a road sign.

The day had started cool and damp but now it was getting hot so she stopped at the top of a farm track to reapply sun cream. The smell of pigs drifted on the still air. Scoot found some green-looking water in a broken water trough which he drank greedily even though she called him away.

They walked on for another half an hour without seeing any road signs. The soles of Hannah's feet were burning and her canvas shoes were rubbing badly. She took them off and found a blister on the heel of her right foot and one on the side of the small toe on the left; she pinched them between her nails until they burst. When she put her shoes back on, the pain was worse.

She could no longer ignore how thirsty she was and so had to detour off the road back over to the dyke. As she reached the top of the bank, she caught sight of a farmhouse she thought she recognized and turning round slowly she began to get her bearings. She was a mile or so along from the pillbox. Once she reached there, she knew a short cut which would take her to the north side of the village where she could pick up the path along the dyke back to Spindle House.

Scoot put his front legs into the water to drink, Hannah bent low and scooped up handful after handful. She licked her wet lips — they felt silky and cold.

★   ★   ★

The back door of Spindle House was open but no one appeared when she shouted out. She went into the living room and sank onto the nearest settee. She was going to take her shoes off but she simply couldn't manage it. She dropped sideways and tucked her legs up.

She woke to see Ella's and Tyler's faces looking down at her.

'Hello, squirt,' Tyler said.

'Darling Hannah. How lovely to see you,' Ella said and Hannah thought that she saw a tear glistening in the corner of her eye but she fell back to sleep before she saw it fall.

45

It was Ghost Society night and Hannah walked into the village to catch a bus to Ely. While she waited, she scanned the postcards in the window of the village shop. A notice written in beautiful copperplate handwriting caught her eye. It read: 'WANTED. A CLEANER AND COMPANION CARER FOR TWO ELDERLY GENTLEMEN.'

It asked anyone who was interested to ring George at Lavender Cottage and gave the telephone number. Hannah tapped the number into her mobile and pressed dial.

'George speaking.'

'It's Hannah. From Spindle House.'

'Hannah, how nice to hear from you.'

'I wondered if you thought I'd be suitable to apply for your job? I've cleaned houses before but I don't know what is required for the carer part.'

'You want to apply for the job?' he asked, sounding surprised and excited.

'Yes,' Hannah said. She could hear George whispering to someone else. 'I've been working for Silver Maids but . . . '

She heard someone, presumably Ray, say, 'Get her to call round.'

'Could you call round?' George boomed down the phone.

'I'm on my way to Ely now but I could come tomorrow morning, if that's OK?'

'That would be wonderful. Come tomorrow. Shall we say about ten?'

★   ★   ★

'Hello, Hannah,' Maggie said, clipping down the corridor towards her. 'We missed you last month.'

'I was away,' Hannah told her.

'Anywhere nice?' Maggie unlocked the door and the familiar woody smell greeted them.

'Yes. But I'm glad to be home.'

They drew the curtains and set out the chairs together while Maggie filled her in on everything she could remember from the previous month. All Hannah could think about was the notebook in her bag. She had been working on her story ever since she got back and she believed it was as ready as it was ever going to be.

Both Kimberley and Sue greeted Hannah as if she'd been away for a year. Magnus sat on his chair like a judge while Maggie tried, ineffectually at first, to calm everyone down. Finally, she clapped her hands and went pink when the room went quiet. 'So,' she said, 'has anyone got anything for us?'

With a deep breath and a quick glance around, Hannah said, 'Yes.' She pulled her bag onto her knee and took out her notebook and glasses. 'It's called *Paper Monsters*.'

It was hard to catch enough light on the pages in the dim, dusty room and her nerves made the words jump around like fleas but she didn't need to read them anyway, she knew the story by heart.

For hundreds of years now, every summer, every year, all over the world, thousands of beautiful dragonflies take to the skies, leaving behind a paper case of the monstrous bodies in which they used to live. Every year, when the wind blows across the marshes, the paper monsters sigh as they grip onto the reeds and watch their beautiful creatures leaving them behind.

One year, on one day, in one pond, the most beautiful dragonfly that ever existed discarded its ugly old body and flew to the top of the reed where the sun sparkled on its delicate wings and made its jewelled body gleam.

Far below, as the old body began to dry and thin to the breadth of paper, it called up to the beautiful creature, 'I wish that I could come too.'

'You?' said the dragonfly as it rose into the sky. 'Why, you are merely a paper monster.'

At that moment, a gust of wind blew down amongst the reeds and the paper monster's wish was caught up into the air and then a second gust of wind blew across the marshes and it whisked the paper monster up, spinning it higher and higher until it dropped onto the back of a rat who happened to be running by.

The rat twitched its tail and nibbled with its teeth but the paper monster was tangled in its fur and it couldn't shake it free. For a day and a night, the paper monster rode around on the rat's back, into the ground and above again, and it was happy to see all the creatures that lived in the soil and that crawled in the grass. Hour after

493

hour, as the paper monster's grey, paper body became a little rosier and plumper, the rat moved slower and slower until it suddenly lay down on the ground and died.

The paper monster felt sad that its journey was over but a moment later a breath of wind blew it up in the air and onto the fold of the wing of a crow which was sitting on the branch of a tree. The crow began to dance around, pecking and flapping its wings, and the paper monster wriggled to get itself free but the more it wriggled and the more the crow tried to shake it off, the harder the paper monster stuck.

For two days and two nights, the paper monster was happy roosting amongst the leafy trees and soaring across the sky. But with every hour that passed, the rosier and plumper the paper monster became, the slower and slower grew the crow's wings until they stopped altogether and the crow fell out of the sky like a stone.

The paper monster was sad that it would never fly across the sky again but just as its rosy hue was beginning to fade and its body to thin to the breadth of a leaf, a gust of wind blew it into the air and onto the top of a fox's head.

Hannah didn't dare look up. The words seemed to be flowing out of her with a life of their own.

The fox scratched at the paper monster with its claws and it flicked at it with its tail, but the more it tried to dislodge the paper monster, the harder it stuck.

For two days and two nights, the paper

monster was happy as the fox jumped across ditches and ran through woods and across fields. On the third day, the paper monster saw that its body had become as plump as a bee and as pink as a rose but the fox had grown thinner. Its run began to slow to a trot, the trot to a walk, the walk to a crawl and then the fox sank down in the long grass and died.

The paper monster was sad that it would never be able to run across fields again but it felt even sadder that its wish had caused the rat, the crow and the fox to die.

As its body faded to a grey as pale as dust and shrivelled to the breadth of a leaf, and the paper monster was preparing for its end, it was plucked from the dark and held out in the sun.

'What are you doing here?' the man said. 'You're a long way from home.'

He took a tiny glass bottle out of his bag and slid the paper monster inside, sealing in its final breath forever with a cork stopper. He put the bottle in his coat pocket and, for three days and three nights, the paper monster was carried around and all it could see was soft, woolly darkness.

Then, on the fourth day, a hand lifted it out of the darkness and placed the bottle on a shelf from which the paper monster could see, through the glass of the bottle and the glass of a window, grass, hedges, a field, trees and the sky.

The paper monster was happy to see the sun rise and fall, clouds gather and drift off and the seasons come and go. And it was happy when it looked down to see the grey hue of its body had

495

a dusting of pink and that it was almost as thin as the breadth of a leaf.

★ ★ ★

There was a silence when she had finished and then they all started clapping.

Marcus said, 'That was worth the wait.' He stood up and shook Hannah's hand and Maggie gave her a hug. She knew they were being kind, too kind, really. As she had been reading the story, she could hear where it needed to be changed, where it didn't quite work, but it also felt as real and shiny as a precious stone in her hand.

The rest of the evening flew by without her taking much in. Words and phrases from *Paper Monsters* kept returning to her, haunting her with their hunger to be worked to a finer, purer state.

★ ★ ★

Hannah was sitting on the car park wall behind the Old Court House waiting for Ella to pick her up when she looked down at the canal path a few metres below her and saw Tyler. She was about to call out to him when she noticed he was talking to a woman walking beside him. It was a few seconds before the woman came into Hannah's clear view and when Hannah saw that it was Kirsten she drew back and waited for them to pass.

She watched them from above and, although

they never once touched, there was something about their ease with each other which set her wondering.

Ella beeped.

'Come on, daydreamer.'

Hannah got in the car.

'How was Ghost Soc?'

'I read out *Paper Monsters*,' Hannah said.

'How did it go down?'

'OK, I think. Ella, I've just seen Tyler and Kirsten walking together along the canal.'

Ella looked surprised, then Hannah saw something pass across her face.

'Did you know?'

Ella shook her head. 'Not until you told me. Well, well.' She spun the car round to the exit. 'I think this might be a classic case of the tortoise and the hare.'

'Do you think Henry will mind?'

'Not once he's gone. I think he'll forget all about Kirsten after a few weeks in Spain.'

'He won't forget, surely?' Even though she didn't imagine she'd ever see or speak to Toby again, she was sure she'd always remember their time together.

'No. You're right. He won't forget but it won't be important any more. Poor Kirsten.'

'Not poor Kirsten. Not if she's got Tyler instead.'

'We shouldn't jump to conclusions,' Ella said. 'We'd better wait and see what happens.'

'Will *you* mind if Kirsten comes back?' Hannah asked.

Ella appeared to think about this at length.

'No, I don't think so. Not if she makes Tyler happy.'

'As long as she doesn't cut all your flowers for the house.'

Ella smiled. 'As long as she doesn't do that.'

46

The front garden of Lavender Cottage was bursting with colour: fuchsias, begonias, asters, sweet peas, dianthus, phlox, astilbes, lavenders. Most of the plants would never have made it into Ella's borders but they looked right here.

'Welcome, welcome.' George stood on the doorstep and beamed at Hannah. 'I see you spotted the white lavender,' he said, although Hannah hadn't and still couldn't see it. 'That was a cutting from your mother's one. It's quite beautiful, isn't it?'

George ushered Hannah into the house and, although she hadn't been inside it since she was a child, she remembered it instantly. The polished, dark wood on the floors and the panelling on the walls reminded her of a boat. It looked well-kept but there was a slight mustiness in the air, like the smell of an unheated room in winter.

'Here she is,' George announced in his big, boomy voice as he led her into the living room. It was a large room with a piano dominating one end and a dining table, with rather grand, dark red chairs, the other. Hannah didn't see Ray at first; he was partly obscured by the wings of the leather chair which had been turned to face the window. He was dressed in a pair of brown cords and a light blue linen shirt; he wore leather slippers but no socks and Hannah could see a

499

slice of thin, white ankle. He pushed himself upright and stepped forward. It was only then that Hannah saw he was attached to a cylinder behind him. 'My portable air,' he explained when he noticed her surprise. 'We've been looking forward to you coming.' Each word was punctuated by a little gasp or wheeze. 'It's all we talked about yesterday evening and this morning.'

'How lovely it would be to have you about the place,' George added.

'But you haven't interviewed me yet,' Hannah said, looking from one to the other.

'No, we must do that.' Ray had a cheeky, mischievous look which Hannah liked. She remembered he was an artist and wondered if any of the paintings on the wall were his. 'Sit down then and let's get serious.'

'I can't drive, so I wouldn't be able to do the shopping, I'm afraid,' Hannah said, frowning. 'Unless it's a few bits and bobs from the village.'

'Oh that's OK,' George said. 'I like doing that. It's nice to get out and about.'

'He likes to get away from me,' Ray chipped in.

'I'm good at cleaning and I can cook a little and help out in the garden.'

'That sounds marvellous.'

'Ray needs a bit of help getting outside some days and it'll be lovely for him to have some company if I'm busy working or if I go out.'

'I'm strong,' Hannah said, thinking of the cylinder contraption which looked a weighty thing to lift out of the house. 'I get that from

500

Ella; I can lift pretty heavy things.'

'I don't think we expect you to carry Ray,' George said and he and Ray burst out laughing.

'Oh, no, I didn't mean — '

'We're teasing, darling. You'll get used to us after a while.' George produced a handkerchief from his shirt pocket and dabbed at his eyes.

'We can't believe how lucky we are,' Ray said. 'To have someone we know.'

'Does that mean I've got the job?' If so, this had been the easiest interview in the world. Hannah smiled broadly.

'You had it the moment you phoned up, Hannah. We were thrilled that our prayers had been answered in such a marvellous way.'

'What about hours and um, um . . . ?' She suddenly thought that they might not intend to pay her, it seemed almost too nice a job to warrant it.

'Shall we say three or four hours a day, except for Sunday, and I think ten pounds an hour is about the going rate, isn't it?'

'Oh, no. That's too much — '

'You're bargaining the wrong way, love,' Ray said. 'You're supposed to ask for more.'

'It's what we want to pay,' George said. 'We think it's a fair amount.'

'You'll soon think it's nowhere near enough, once you get to know us.'

'Oh, I really don't think so,' Hannah said and Ray winked at her.

'Now the formalities are out of the way, how about we have a cup of tea to celebrate?' George said.

Hannah jumped up. 'I'll do it if you wouldn't mind showing me where everything is.'

The kitchen had Wedgwood-blue cupboards with a cream trim. The floor was stone which was pale as sand. It looked like it would feel nice under bare feet. There was a row of willow plates on a dresser and a large, polished wood coffee-grinder. The tea, coffee and sugar were in blue ceramic canisters with cream lids. The tea was loose-leaf not bags and George showed her how many spoonfuls to put in the pot.

'You have some lovely things,' Hannah said. She could see that their possessions were well cared for and loved. It seemed to her that this was also true of George and Ray themselves. As if George were reading her thoughts, he said, 'Ray has looked after me so well over the years, I feel that I'm letting him down now it's come to my turn.'

Once you saw past the jollity of George's round, burnished face, you noticed his exhaustion.

'I am very happy to help you look after him,' Hannah assured him.

'You're such a sweet girl,' George told her. 'Ray,' he bellowed from behind Hannah as she was carrying the tea tray into the living room. 'I was just saying what a lovely girl Hannah is, but it's only to be expected coming from such a nice couple as her parents.'

'Your father used to bring us back the local moonshine from his travels, you know,' Ray said. 'We had more than a drunken night or two with him.'

'We were so pleased for him when he met Ella. We worried about him when he was on his own up there. We used to worry about Ella, too, when you were all so little and he was away. But she's a strong woman.'

'She is.'

'You are the image of her, you know.'

One of them had told her that before but she didn't think she'd ever tire of hearing it.

George saw her out. He gave her a key so that she didn't have to knock when she went over and she found this trust in her touching.

'Ray sleeps for quite long periods but he is desperate for company when he's awake. He gets bored and he hates TV.'

'Maybe I could read to him?' Hannah suggested.

'He'd love that.'

Instead of going back to the house the way she'd come, Hannah took the short-cut down the track where Toby used to leave his car, through the wooden gate and round the edge of the carr.

There was a circle of flattened and yellow grass where Toby's tent had been and a black circle from the fire. The ground was scattered with leaves; the parched trees had begun to shed their foliage early. The rain would be coming soon and the grass and moss would have grown back before winter. Next year it would be hard to find any evidence that Toby had ever been there.

★　★　★

When she got home, Ella was waiting for her in the kitchen.

'How did it go?'

'I got the job,' Hannah said. 'I start tomorrow.'

'They're lovely people,' Ella said. 'They've always been very kind to me. They used to come along with gin and bitters when Edward went away, to cheer me up.' She gave Hannah a quick hug and began to water the plants on the window sill. 'Oh, I forgot,' she said over her shoulder. 'There's a letter for you on the table.'

Hannah slid the envelope towards her. It had a Cambridge postmark and Hannah's stomach dropped. What could the Silver Maids be writing to her about? She unfolded two sheets of paper slowly, not comprehending at first that it wasn't from Silver Maids at all, it was from Moonlight and Magic Publishing.

Her hands trembled; the words slipped all over the place. 'Read it for me, Ella.'

Ella wiped her hands dry on a tea towel. 'Dear Ms Ruland, Thank you for letting us see *The Silver Eel*. We were impressed with the style and standard of your story and we feel that your writing shows great promise. We are planning a series of ghost stories for children and we would like to ask you to submit two stories for us to consider. Please see the guidelines, etc, etc, etc.' She handed the letter back to Hannah. 'Darling, that's wonderful. Edward would be so proud of you.'

Hannah turned the letter over in her hands.

She thought of her first notebook. Edward had brought it back from India and its thick, creamy pages smelt of mildew and roses.

He had come into her bedroom one day and found her in tears, a harsh black line scoured down the length of the page because her eyes had been playing up and she couldn't get the words onto it.

He sat on the bed and pulled her onto his knee.

'It's not a race,' he said. 'What you have is a passion to savour.'

And she wondered how he had known. How he had seen that, for her, writing was the best feeling in the world? How had he known that giving her that notebook was the best present she would ever have?

47

Hannah was waiting for the storm. Distant thunder rumbled, grey clouds swirled and rolled as if someone was stirring them up, but the sticky heat continued to build. She felt as if all her energy was being drawn out slowly, leaving behind a boneless, brainless shell. Scoot had taken refuge in the cool hall; he lay flat on his stomach, his legs splayed out as if he'd been dropped from above onto the stone floor. A dog would probably know better how to survive such things, Hannah decided, so she lay down too. The cold stone pinched painfully but luxuriously where it came into contact with her bare skin. She closed her eyes and imagined a cold wind blowing across her skin, she pictured icy rain stinging her bare skin like needles.

She woke up when a draught blew across her body, leaving her skin bumpy, the hairs on her arms erect. There was a loud bang, then silence. Scoot stood up.

Bang, bang, bang, bang. A window was being knocked about by the wind. She ran upstairs, threw open the door to the bathroom, then Ella's room, then her own, where she found a window swinging free, the one she'd left on the latch that morning.

The first drops of rain fell, fat as bugs. The sky outside was so dark it felt as if night had impatiently pushed forward. A deep roll of thunder vibrated through the house and down her body. A shot of lightning ran across the low skyline, followed by a crack of thunder so loud it made Hannah flinch. The sky broke open and the rain streamed down so forcefully it bounced back up when it hit the ground. She leaned out of the window and caught sight of Ella trying to close the hothouse vents.

The rain felt like stones pelting her body as she ran outside. Ella slid the door open and she slipped inside.

'Help me with the ones at the back,' Ella shouted above the drumming of the rain on the glass. The hinges were stiff from lack of use and they had to break off the stems of some of the climbers which had grown out of the top.

When all the vents were secured, they took a look outside.

'I don't think it's going to stop any time soon,' Ella said. 'We'll have to make a run for it.'

Hannah squealed as she charged head-down across the lawn. Water sloshed into her face and soaked her clothes instantly as if someone had thrown a bucket of water over her. She slipped on the grass and cried out as she landed hard. Ella pulled her up. Her hair was stuck to her face, her clothes were clinging to her body.

Scoot stood at the back door barking as they held their faces and arms up to the skies and spun around laughing and laughing, letting the rain flow over them.

They stripped off in the kitchen; a rivulet made its way down the slope of the floor towards the stove. Ella went to fetch towels and came back with a pile still warm from the airing cupboard, and their bathrobes. Hannah hugged her towel around her. It felt deliciously soft on her skin.

Ella made mugs of hot chocolate and they took them with a plate of ginger biscuits into the living room. The ceiling light flickered and buzzed. The thunder and lightning were overhead, coming one after the other without any gaps.

'Did you know that thunder is the noise that lightning makes?'

'Is that true?'

'Yes.'

'I hope the roof holds up.' The old roof had been holding on by the skin of its teeth since Hannah could remember and it was Ella's constant worry that one day one of the violent Fen winds would bring the chimneys crashing down through it.

The French windows had become opaque with steam so that it was impossible to see anything outside.

'We could put the TV on,' Hannah suggested.

'Not with lightning around.'

'I hope George and Ray are all right,' Hannah said.

'I'm so glad you're helping George and Ray out,' Ella told her.

They sat facing each other, their legs drawn up, their toes meeting in the middle of the settee.

'Ray's got cancer. He's dying,' Hannah said.

'Yes, I know, love.' Ella touched her hand. Her fingertips were still cold. 'But George will make

508

sure he enjoys the rest of his days.'

'That's what I want,' Hannah said, seriously. 'A love like that.'

'That's what most people want.' Ella pulled the throw off the back of the settee and tucked it round their legs.

'Do you?' Hannah asked, feeling that she could ask Ella anything at that moment and Ella would answer her truthfully. 'Is that what you have with Denis?'

It seemed a long time before Ella spoke. 'I don't know,' she said. 'But I think it might be.'

* * *

The next morning, the air was cool and damp and the colours in the garden were deeper, as if they'd been soaking in dye all night. Hannah walked across the lawn, the grass squeaking underfoot. A weak sun was out; mist hung above the frog pond. Water dripped on her from the bushes as she brushed through the gap in the hedge. The ground around the carr was sodden and she had to avoid a patch of mud which had appeared overnight.

When she came out of the gate onto the driveway, she saw Toby's car. She approached it cautiously, not sure whether to believe it was real, and then felt embarrassed when she saw that Toby was inside and had been watching her all along. He wound down the window.

'What are you doing here? I thought you were going to Wiltshire.'

'I did for a while.'

509

'Any crop formations?'

He shook his head. 'Hannah, can I ask you something?'

'OK.'

He gave a sheepish smile before delivering his question. 'What did I do wrong?'

'Nothing,' she said quickly. 'Except for Imogen, of course.'

'You knew about that? It was only the once.' He blushed. So she was right to have had suspicions about them at least, she thought, with a slow turn of her stomach.

'But it wasn't that which mattered.' She concentrated hard on keeping his face in focus; his skin was as smooth as hazel bark, a glint of green showed under his busy eyebrows; his hair fell forward, even longer than before. 'It just stopped being what it was.'

He pulled on his lip piercing with his teeth and Hannah found herself running her tongue across the cold metal of her own lip ring. 'Yes,' he said, finally. 'I suppose it did.'

'And you and Imogen?'

He shook his head. 'Anyway, I'm going back to university soon.'

'To do mappy things.'

He laughed. 'Yes. To do mappy things. What about you?'

'I'm working for George and Ray as their cleaner and Ray's companion.'

'Not much of a commute,' Toby said. He looked down the driveway at the house. 'They're nice fellas. And at least *they* won't make any unwelcome advances.'

'Not funny.' She prodded him gently on the arm. 'I'd better go. I don't want to be late for work.'

'You don't think . . . ' he said and then stopped. 'I've blown it with you, haven't I?'

'I like you, Toby . . . '

'But?'

Hannah backed away from the car. 'Maybe I can come visit you sometime,' she called to him and began to walk towards the cottage.

'I'd like that.' Toby started the engine and reversed slowly so that the car kept level with Hannah. 'Thanks for showing me around and everything. I hadn't imagined it would be so beautiful.'

Hannah turned suddenly and took a step towards the car. Toby stopped and Hannah leaned into the open window. She planted a kiss on his lips and passed an arm around his neck. She could feel his breath on her collar bone. 'It was a good summer,' she whispered into his ear. 'One of the best.'

We do hope that you have enjoyed reading this large print book.

Did you know that all of our titles are available for purchase?

We publish a wide range of high quality large print books including:
Romances, Mysteries, Classics
General Fiction
Non Fiction and Westerns

Special interest titles available in large print are:
The Little Oxford Dictionary
Music Book
Song Book
Hymn Book
Service Book

Also available from us courtesy of Oxford University Press:
Young Readers' Dictionary
(large print edition)
Young Readers' Thesaurus
(large print edition)

For further information or a free brochure, please contact us at:
Ulverscroft Large Print Books Ltd.,
The Green, Bradgate Road, Anstey,
Leicester, LE7 7FU, England.
Tel: (00 44) 0116 236 4325
Fax: (00 44) 0116 234 0205